WYOMING!

is the third unforgettable book
in the WAGONS WEST series—

INDEPENDENCE!

In 1837 a dauntless band of pioneering men and
women set out from Long Island and headed
west to Independence, Missouri—among them:
Claudia Humphries, the fiery young widow and
Sam Brentwood, the bold wagon master. Traveling
under secret orders from President Andrew Jackson, Brentwood's task was to win a desperate race
against England and Russia, and to bring the
great Promised Land of the Pacific Northwest
under the American flag.

NEBRASKA!

The legendary caravan drives onward—to forge a
new link in the wilderness trek from Independence,
Missouri, to the Promised Land beyond the
Rockies. This is the story of fearless devotion to
a hard-won ideal, of betrayal from within and of
sabotage from British and Russian agents. Above
all, it is the story of Whip Holt, the ruggedly
quiet leader of this leg of the perilous migration;
and of Cathy van Ayl, who leaves her family
behind in Missouri to continue on with Whip
Holt's train—perhaps, to win his heart.

✷✷✷✷✷✷✷✷✷✷✷✷✷✷✷✷✷✷✷

WAGONS WEST

WYOMING

THE CONTINUING SAGA OF THE COURAGEOUS MEN AND WOMEN BLAZING THE FIRST WAGON TRAIL ACROSS THE BREADTH OF AMERICA . . .

LA-ENA,
the black haired, hauntingly beautiful
Indian woman whose presence on the wagon
train throws lives into turmoil—until
she makes the ultimate sacrifice for love.

MICHAEL "WHIP" HOLT,
the taciturn mountain man whose
frontier skills are no help when he
must choose between two women.

CATHY VAN AYL,
the young widow, newly disappointed
in love, who must find a new
man to assuage her loneliness.

LEE BLAKE,
Lieutenant Colonel in the U.S. Army,
assigned to protect the wagon
train against sabotage, he comes to
share in its joys and sorrows.

✷✷✷✷✷✷✷✷✷✷✷✷✷✷✷✷✷✷✷

✶✶✶✶✶✶✶✶✶✶✶✶✶✶✶✶✶✶✶✶

EULALIA WOODLING,
a former South Carolina belle, she
learns about life from her own
horrifying experience in the wilderness.

CINDY,
the former prostitute from
Louisville, determined to start life
over. She thought she could never
truly love a man—until now.

TED WOODS,
a giant of a man, whose towering rages
endanger those whom he holds most dear.

CLAIBORNE WOODLING,
a Southern gentleman who loses his
heart to the West—and to a woman.

DOLORES,
the half white, half Indian woman
whose unique and startling visions are
the salvation of the wagon train.

PAUL THOMAN,
Harvard-educated show-off, who
learns the hard truths of being a
man on the road to Oregon.

SALLY MacNEILL,
pretty and unassuming,
she can put a man in his place
with her straight talk.

GINNY DOBBS,
a lonely woman tossed around
by life, she is looking for an
easy way through life and
someone to take care of her.

✶✶✶✶✶✶✶✶✶✶✶✶✶✶✶✶✶✶✶✶

WAGONS WEST ★ VOLUME 3
WYOMING!
DANA FULLER ROSS

BANTAM BOOKS
TORONTO · NEW YORK · LONDON

WYOMING!

A Bantam Book | December 1979

2nd printing	.. December 1979	8th printing	.... January 1980
3rd printing	.. December 1979	9th printing	.... February 1980
4th printing	.. December 1979	10th printing	.... March 1980
5th printing	.. December 1979	11th printing	.... April 1980
6th printing	...... January 1980	12th printing	.... April 1980
7th printing	...... January 1980	13th printing	.. December 1980

14th printing .... April 1981

Produced by Book Creations, Inc.
Executive Producer: Lyle Kenyon Engel

ISBN 0–553–14849–4

Published simultaneously in the United States and Canada

Bantam Books are published by Bantam Books, Inc. Its trademark, consisting of the words "Bantam Books" and the portrayal of a bantam, is Registered in U.S. Patent and Trademark Office, and in other countries. Marca Registrada. Bantam Books, Inc., 666 Fifth Avenue, New York, New York 10103.

PRINTED IN THE UNITED STATES OF AMERICA

22 21 20 19 18 17 16 15

WYOMING!

**THE EPIC TALE
OF THE MEN AND WOMEN
OF WAGONS WEST
AS THEY BLAZE THROUGH
THE ROCKY MOUNTAINS**

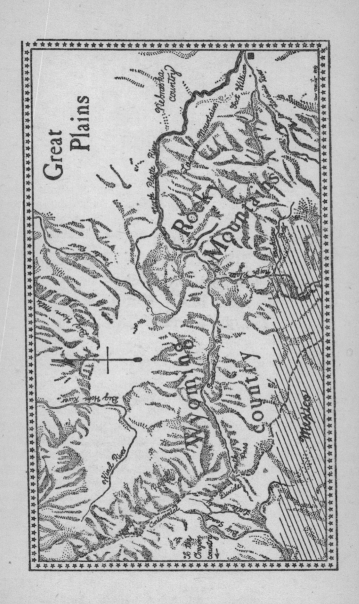

Prologue

The first wagon train to the Oregon country moved slowly across the Great Plains, reaching the foothills of the Rocky Mountains in the early autumn of 1838. Its five hundred travel-weary members considered themselves fortunate if they coaxed ten miles a day out of their teams of workhorses and oxen. At night, however, as they gathered around their campfire, a new spirit seemed to invigorate them. This was the time of day when friends gathered, romances flourished, and pioneers from twenty states ate and relaxed together.

Tonight, however, Cathy van Ayl was in a trance-like state. She was scarcely aware of her surroundings as she supervised the work of the large group of women preparing the evening meal. The stew of buffalo meat, wild onions, beets, and Indian corn bubbled in huge pots. It was fortunate that she had little to occupy her, for she was seething. At this moment, she hated the world and loathed herself. She wasn't a fit companion for anyone.

A wooden spoon clutched in one hand, Cathy wandered away from the fire and tried to take stock of her situation. Never had she been so devastated, so stripped of her pride.

I am twenty-four years old and a widow, she thought. I have two thousand dollars in gold that I inherited from my husband, who never expected me to benefit from his lifelong miserliness. I'm in sound health, with a better-than-average figure, and I know that men are attracted to my blond hair and blue eyes. Most of all, I've always thought myself to be reasonably intelligent, capable of thinking clearly—until tonight. Now it seems I've been a stupid, romantic idiot, as naive and moon-struck as a girl in her mid-teens.

For months I've fooled myself into believing that Whip Holt has been falling in love with me. Oh, I know he's shy and that words don't come easily to him. But from the way he looked at me, from little gestures and remarks, I convinced myself that he was seriously interested in me—as seriously interested as his senior partner, Sam Brentwood, was in my sister, Claudia. When Claudia and Sam married and settled down in Independence, Missouri, to run the supply depot, I allowed myself to dream that after Whip had led this wagon train to Oregon, he and I might fall into the same pattern. How I wish he were like Sam, who raced back to Claudia in Independence, to be there when she has her baby. I disgraced myself by letting Whip think I might be receptive to him.

There he stands now, beside the fire, with the Indian girl, La-ena, whose very existence was concealed from everyone on the train. The only one who knew about her was our scout Stalking Horse, her half-brother. All I know is that she's part Arapaho and part Cherokee, that she's very beautiful, and she's in love with Whip. He must be in love with her, too, after living with her for several winters in the Rockies.

I can't even bear to look at them, their shoulders touching. He's certainly not shy now!

"Cathy!"

The young woman turned and saw a tall man approaching, Lieutenant Colonel Leland Blake. All she knew about him was that he had come from Washington City, that he seemed to know President Martin Van Buren well and—above all—that he had been attentive to her from the day he had arrived.

Lee Blake smiled as he approached Cathy, but when he spoke, there was a note of concern in his voice. "I hope you aren't ill."

Cathy's back straightened. She didn't want anyone, least of all Lee, to know she was upset, much less the reason why. "I'm fine, thanks," she replied. "Supper is cooking itself tonight."

Lee was the army's leading counterintelligence expert. He had been sent on this expedition to ward off possible attacks or acts of sabotage by the British or the Russians. His identity as an army officer had been kept secret when he first joined the wagon train, but by now his real status had become known. Noting Cathy's rigid self-control, Lee knew instantly that something was very much amiss. He could guess the reason for her distress, and perhaps he could help. Not that he wanted to smooth her relations with Whip—he wasn't keen on helping that relationship along. Besides, Whip would have his hands full, now that his Indian mistress had joined the train. No, Lee was acting strictly for Cathy's sake—and, he knew, for his own. A confirmed bachelor in his mid-thirties, who had always said that his profession would make it impossible for him to marry, he had entertained second thoughts in recent weeks—since meeting Cathy van Ayl.

However, his first task was to restore Cathy's wounded dignity. The train had a long way to travel, and he would take his time advancing his own suit, letting it develop naturally now that his competition was out of the running. He could feel sorry for Whip, knowing the guide's interest in the young widow was genuine.

"May I speak freely? I know how you feel."

She became even more tense. "You do? How?"

Lee shrugged. "I've come to know Whip well, and he's a fine man," he said. "I'm sure he regards this new development as very unfortunate."

"I prefer not to talk about him," she said coldly.

"Just for a moment, if you don't mind." He was firm, feeling he had to clear the air on Whip's behalf before revealing his own deepening interest for her. "Mountain men are a strange breed, working alone for months, always by themselves when they're hunting and trapping. At best it's a lonely life, which is why many of them drink too much. La-ena is a pretty girl, and you can't blame Whip for giving in to temptation."

"She appears to be very attractive," Cathy said, "but Whip's personal life is strictly his own business and has nothing to do with me."

"Quite so." Enough of being fair to Whip; now Lee was on his own. He paused, then cleared his throat. "Your new buckskin outfit is very pretty. Did you make it yourself?"

She nodded. "Tonie Mell—Tonie Martin, that is, now that she's married—helped me cure the skins. We weren't taught things like that in New Haven and on Long Island. But I did all of my own sewing."

"You're clever with a needle."

A more sophisticated woman might have smiled at the clumsiness of his praise, but Cathy had had little experience with men. Married at sixteen to a contemporary of her father's who had bedded her only on their wedding night and, until his death last year, had treated her like a daughter, she failed to recognize Lee's remark as a signal of his interest in her.

All the same, she was aware of that interest through a more obvious sign—the admiration that she saw in Lee's eyes—and she warned herself to be careful. Her older sister, Claudia, who had reared her after the premature death of their mother, had told her frequently that it was dangerous to plunge into a new romance too soon after being disappointed in love. One's judgment was apt to be clouded. But the warmth Lee was expressing was precisely the balm Cathy needed.

Lee was forthright and honest, always a gentleman, and exceptionally handsome. What was more, he had to be very bright to have risen to such a high rank at his age. It was flattering to be singled out by such a man, and Cathy's quick smile was as brilliant as it was natural.

"If you need any sewing done, just let me know," she said. "It must be hard for a man traveling alone to attend to such chores."

"That's kind of you," he answered, "but I wouldn't want to burden you. After all, you're taking care of your own wagon and team, and you're in charge of fixing meals for all of us. So you have your hands full."

She spoke slowly and deliberately, and if there was a trace of coquetry in her attitude, she didn't realize it. "I always have time for my friends."

In the distance they heard someone banging on a pie plate, signaling that supper was ready. The notice was given by Cindy, a former prostitute from Louisville who was hoping to create a new life for herself in Oregon.

Cathy promptly felt a twinge of guilt. Cindy was not only her first assistant, but also her confidante, and tonight she was bearing the full responsibility for the meal while Cathy indulged her own feelings. "Oh, dear, I'm neglecting my duties," she said.

Lee strolled beside her as they made their way to the fire, where families with children were being served first. "You're too conscientious for your own good," he said.

"Am I? I didn't think that was possible."

"You said that the meal was cooking itself tonight. The next time we call a halt for a rest day, I suggest you come berrying with me. I understand there are delicious wild blueberries in these hills, and they should be ripening just about now."

"I accept the invitation," Cathy said, "with great pleasure." She was about to add something to her remark, but stopped short when they suddenly came face to face with Whip Holt and the Indian girl.

La-ena was beautiful. She was tall and slender, and her snug-fitting doeskin dress did justice to her trim but feminine figure. Her hair, blue-black and straight, cascaded down her back.

Cathy spoke impulsively, breaking the brief but awkward silence. "Welcome to the wagon train," she said.

La-ena inclined her head. "Thank you," she replied, with only a trace of an Indian accent.

"How wonderful—you speak English!" Realizing that Whip was uncomfortable, Cathy was prolonging the conversation.

The Indian girl was conscious of his tension, too. "One winter when the snows were very heavy," she said, pausing occasionally to search for the right word, "Whip taught La-ena the tongue of his people."

"I wish he had told us you were coming. We could have prepared a real welcome for you," Cathy told her, superficially cheerful.

Under the best of circumstances Whip was ill at ease in the presence of women. Now, conscious of Cathy's deviltry, he froze.

Lee was seeing an unexpected side of Cathy's nature. She was a fighter. He admired her and made no attempt to intervene.

"Let me know if there's anything you need," Cathy said. "Not that we enjoy many comforts on this train. But—if you need a place to ride, for instance—there's plenty of room in my wagon." There. That gesture would squelch any gossip that she was jealous or believed herself humiliated.

La-ena glanced at Whip, but he, ordinarily sure of himself, was too stunned to say anything. La-ena was forced to rely on herself, and her natural dignity came to the fore. Aware of complicating forces she couldn't yet define, she could not ignore a gesture of hospitality. "La-ena will do what Whip wishes. But it is my hope he will let La-ena ride with you."

Lee felt obliged to end Whip's misery. "We'd better get our food," he said, "before the youngsters get back in line for seconds."

Whip looked at him for an instant over the heads of the two young women, and his eyes expressed his gratitude.

I

Major General Winfield Scott attracted attention, no matter what he did, and today was no exception. Every passer-by on Washington City's rutted Pennsylvania Avenue stared at him as he rode with an aide-de-camp from the War Department to the White House. His dazzling uniform of gold-trimmed blue, which he had designed himself, and his erect bearing were partly responsible for the attention he received, as was his prancing white stallion, which he rode as if he were on parade.

Many people who recognized him exchanged greetings with him, including members of the Senate and the House of Representatives. They knew there was a man of substance behind the glittering façade. "Old Fuss and Feathers" might be a demon for military protocol and show, but he had fought with distinction in two wars, currently served as Deputy Commander of the United States Army and had already been tapped for the top spot in three more years. In the event war developed with Mexico over the acquisition of Texas, or the dispute with Great Britain over the ownership of the Oregon country erupted into armed conflict, he

1

was sure to lead the American forces in the field. Certainly, no one was better qualified. He had spent years in Europe studying the strategies and tactics employed by every major power, and it was true, as he himself claimed, that he was his nation's first professional soldier.

Arriving at the main entrance of the White House, General Scott dismounted with an ease that belied his fifty-two years. Leaving his aide to attend to the horses, he announced in a parade-ground voice, "The President has sent for me and wishes to be told of my arrival at once!"

A waiting secretary immediately conducted him to the cramped, simply furnished office at the rear of the building that had been made into a room at the request of former President Andrew Jackson by knocking down a wall between two wardrobe closets. Martin Van Buren's awe of his predecessor was so great that he didn't quite dare transfer his private quarters elsewhere, even though he would have preferred a larger working space.

Circumstances had not dealt kindly with the eighth President of the United States. The native New Yorker had proved himself a capable politician and a superb diplomat, but the financial crisis that had plunged the United States into a state of economic depression, the worst in the country's history, was beyond his ability to control. He was vilified by the press. Cartoonists delighted in picturing his bald head and sagging paunch. It seemed that, in all probability, he would be a one-term president.

In spite of his many concerns, however, he was smiling when his visitor was ushered into his office. General Scott stood at rigid attention, his spurs clanking, and saluted his commander in chief.

2

The cosmopolitan Van Buren, a widower who lived quietly, hated pomp. "We're alone, General," he said, "so there's no need for flourishes. Please sit down."

Winfield Scott carefully placed his sword on the chair beside him. "I await your pleasure, Mr. President," he declared.

"I take precious little pleasure in the latest news," the President said, sighing. "Sam Houston is holding the Mexicans at bay for the present, but the moment we annex Texas, they're sure to go to war with us."

Scott's manner changed, and he spoke with quiet confidence. "That's one war we'll win, sir."

"Perhaps. But I prefer to see us engaged in no war. However, that may be a goal we can't attain. Frankly, Scott, I'm worried about the Oregon situation, which is what I want to discuss with you."

"As you know, sir, one of my best officers, Lieutenant Colonel Leland Blake, is currently traveling to the Oregon country with our first wagon train. He's a man of great talent as well as discretion, and I have complete faith in him."

"I share that faith, General," Van Buren said. "But the efforts of one man may not be enough. A report from an American sea captain who visited the Oregon country has now been corroborated—informally—by our legation in London. Lord Palmerston, the British Foreign Secretary, has tacitly admitted that the British garrison at Fort Vancouver on the Columbia River is going to be strongly reinforced."

Scott whistled under his breath, then brightened. "If you want my opinion, Mr. President, London is bluffing. I'll grant you it would be a horrendous undertaking for us to send men and supplies all the way to Oregon. But the British would have the same problem in Canada, where the winters are even longer. I hardly need remind you, sir, that we beat the British in the War of Independence and the War of 1812. They certainly don't want a third war with us, not when we're expanding year by year and our population is booming, thanks to the immigrants who have been pouring in since the uprisings all over Europe eight years ago. The reinforcement of the Fort Vancouver garrison is a bluff intended to frighten us, sir. The Hudson's Bay Company operates that fort as a trading post, and I guarantee you their stockholders want peace."

"Lord Palmerston is an ambitious man who is determined to increase the boundaries of Queen Victoria's empire. I know Palmerston well, thanks to my years as head of our London legation." The President picked up a quill pen from his desk and twirled it absently. "I have what I consider conclusive proof that far more than a bluff is responsible for the augmentation of that outpost."

General Scott ran a hand through his gray hair and waited.

"The State Department has just received a secret memorandum from one of our—ah—unacknowledged operatives in London. He not only confirms what we've already learned—that a British agent named Henry St. Clair has tried to halt and destroy our wagon train —but he's certain a major effort will be made before winter."

"There's little we can do, Mr. President, other than let the situation develop and hope Lee Blake has the strength and ingenuity to cope with it."

"It appears obvious to me," the President said, "that if the British succeed in halting our wagon train and preventing American settlers from laying claim to the

4

Oregon country, they are afraid we'll retaliate by sending an expedition to raze Fort Vancouver."

Winfield Scott couldn't help striking a pose. "If our wagon train is stopped, Mr. President, give me four warships, eight troop transports, and a force of two thousand men. I'll command the expedition myself, and I give you my word that Fort Vancouver will be reduced to rubble."

Van Buren sighed. "I don't doubt your abilities, Scott, but I want to avert war, not wage it. Our banks are failing, factories are closing, and farms are being foreclosed. Our citizens are hungry and dispossessed. In all, we have a quarter of a million unemployed out of a total population of sixteen million. It's no wonder people are moving West and settling in the wilderness. We need the Oregon country, but we can't afford a war."

Scott reacted as though he had been slapped. "Yes, sir," he said.

"Our greatest living military leader, President Jackson, once made a very astute observation. He swore the best generals are those who win campaigns without fighting battles."

"Are you suggesting that I send out more officers to support Colonel Blake?"

"That would be premature, I believe. We've made what we regard as adequate preparations. I suggest we don't become panicky. Let's see whether the wagon train can withstand whatever move the British make, and then, if need be, we'll counter it."

Scott had to admire the President's cool nerve. He knew now why Martin Van Buren had won a reputation as a chess player.

"Palmerston is hoping we'll do something foolish

that will give him an excuse to send the Royal Navy to the mouth of the Columbia River. I'm relying on the people of the wagon train to disappoint him."

The General's face creased as he flashed his famous grin. "No two ways about it, Mr. President, those settlers are our best bet. Without them, even Lee Blake can't do much."

"So much for the British, at least for the present. Now I'd like to talk about a matter that is even more complex—that of Russia's interest in Oregon."

"Her traders were there first, no question about that," Scott said. "And they established several villages that are still scattered throughout the Oregon country. But the Russians know they live too far from Oregon to compete with us and with the British, unless they send a major expedition by way of their Alaska territory. And that would be too enormous an effort, even for a great power. That's why the Czar abandoned his claims."

"Not really, Scott. As I see it, that was a tactical maneuver, nothing more. I'm sure you remember the report on the subject that Colonel Blake sent to the War Department—the report he sent back via Sam Brentwood."

"Yes, sir, I know the whole story. A courageous young woman, Antoinette Mell, now Antoinette Martin, is Russian-born and traveling with the wagon train. Her uncle, Arnold Mell, is one of the company's scouts. The Russians have tried repeatedly to force her to commit acts of sabotage against the train. When she consistently refused, they made several crude attempts to murder her. Their acts are despicable and typical of the Czar's approach, but I don't regard their efforts as a serious threat to the security of our wagon train."

"You're wrong, General, but you're a soldier, not a

diplomat. The danger posed by St. Petersburg is a hazard even greater than the British threat."

"Forgive my bluntness, Mr. President, but I'm damned if I can see how that's possible."

"Remember your own visit to St. Petersburg and your talks with Russian generals. Remember they sometimes move sideways and even appear to retreat in order to take a half-step forward."

General Scott nodded thoughtfully.

"Now think in other terms," the President continued. "Alaska is sparsely settled, and they can't really use it as a base of continuing operations. It would be valuable to the Russians only in an emergency."

Scott's smile became grim. "Oregon is a hell of a long way from Siberia, sir!"

"Precisely. The Russians abandoned their claims simply because they knew they couldn't send as many settlers to Oregon as we can, or as the British can by way of Canada. So the Czar himself has gone through the motions of giving up Oregon. That's noble, but it's unconvincing. Now let's examine a couple of details of Colonel Blake's report that provide us with clues to the overall Russian plan. Blake mentioned a couple of Russian agents. Do you recall their names?"

The General frowned slightly. "One was called Munson. He's the one who was killed."

"Munson. An Anglo-Saxon name. Go on."

"The other is one André Sebastian."

Van Buren laughed grimly. "Sebastian. A Spanish name. Poor Spain has lost all of her continental territories here. Even California and New Mexico were lost when Mexico became independent. Do you begin to see what I mean?"

Scott pondered briefly. "Neither Munson nor Sebastian are Russian names."

"That's my point," the President declared. "The name of Sebastian has been used to throw us off the track. The name of Munson is far more sinister because it gives away the Czar's ultimate intentions. He and his advisers want to nudge us into a dogfight with the British. When we and London have exhausted ourselves, either through war or a prolonged diplomatic dispute that ends in a stalemate, the Russians will sneak into Oregon and reassert their claims."

The General grimaced. "Of course! Right now it suits them to be cooperating with the British, or so Colonel Blake reports. When they find it convenient, they'll side with us. They'll do anything to pit the United States and Great Britain against each other so that they can step in when the time is ripe."

"Correct, Scott." The normally mild-mannered Martin Van Buren brought the palm of his hand down onto the top of his desk with such force that his ink jar teetered precariously. "Now you know why it is imperative that our wagon train reach Oregon. If we can actually settle that country, the great powers may connive all they please. But they won't be able to take one inch of soil away from us!"

" '*Hoc sustinete, majus ne veniat malum.* Endure this evil, lest a greater come upon you.' " The gaunt young man, clad only in an Indian loincloth of leather, rode bareback on the great rust stallion. He spoke aloud, even though he was alone in the vast emptiness of the wilderness. "Phaedrus was right. But I never learned at Harvard that one must know adversity if one is to understand it. I'll have to discuss that with my philosophy professor if I ever get back to Cambridge—improbable in the extreme."

The sun was shining in a cloudless sky, but a chilly

wind blew down from the great mountains in the western portion of the Wyoming-Colorado country. In spite of his exertions, Paul Thoman shivered. For the past week he had been enduring a nightmare worse than any he could have imagined, but he had to keep going. The odds against his survival were overwhelming, yet he could not allow himself to stop. Not only had he escaped the Blackfoot, the most vicious of the western Indian nations, but he had stolen one of their horses, and he was well aware of the fate in store for him if he was recaptured. He would die slowly, suffering tortures that no man could endure.

Even though he had eaten nothing since his escape from the town of the Blackfoot three days earlier, he knew he couldn't stop until he located the Oregon-bound wagon train—or until he and the horse died in the attempt.

The past flashed through his mind. He recalled the expressions on his parents' faces when, standing in their prim Boston parlor, he had announced, "I'm not going back to Harvard until a year from this autumn. I'm taking a year's sabbatical."

His father, a distinguished, forbidding man, had locked his hands behind his back and frowned when he heard his son's unexpected announcement. "Perhaps you'll be kind enough to tell us how you plan to spend the next fifteen months."

"Certainly, sir. I—I'm going to spend time hunting and trapping in the Rockies, while it's still possible to do so. The era of the mountain men in the Rockies is coming to an end. They are the victims of encroaching civilization. Even men like Jim Bridger and Kit Carson will have to turn to other enterprises."

Mrs. Thoman was a tiny, proper woman, but she was even more formidable than her husband. "Who are these persons, Bridger and Carson? I've never heard of either family."

"Never mind, Mother. After my year in the Rockies, I'll come home, earn my degree *summa cum laude,* in the family tradition, and settle down in the family business."

How Paul wished now that they had dissuaded him. But, on second thought, nothing they could have said would have prevented him from coming West. The months he had spent in the mountains had been even more exhilarating and exciting than he had dreamed. Not until he had started the long journey back to Boston had anything really gone wrong. Then the very worst thing possible had happened—the Blackfoot had captured him.

God, he was hungry! If he survived, he would be lucky to get home by Thanksgiving. The very thought of the holiday made him flinch. He leaned forward to pat his tired mount's neck. There would be a huge fire blazing in the parlor hearth and another in his father's library. The great feast would begin with smoked oysters taken from the beach at the family's summer house on Cape Cod, followed by his mother's only concession to "foreign" dishes, a thick Dutch pea soup with onions and bits of sausage floating in it. Those would whet the appetite for the roast turkey with sage dressing, boiled and sweetened Plymouth cranberries, candied Indian yams, mashed turnips, boiled potatoes, brussels sprouts, and green beans. Then there would be pumpkin pie, hot mince pie, and a pie of tart Massachusetts Bay berries. It didn't matter what kind of berries. He could easily consume double his share of each pie.

Paul groaned aloud. "Cicero," he said to the stallion, "you're more fortunate than I am. You have your splendid coat. The damned Blackfoot took my weapons, my clothes, and my furs. You eat grass whenever we stop for a rest. I eat nothing. You drink water. So do I, because there's a notable absence of the French château wines to which my palate became accustomed before I ever conceived the harebrained notion of playing at being a mountain man for a year."

The horse, moving at a steady, slow canter, whinnied.

"I heed your opinion, Cicero, and I give you my solemn pledge that you shall be rewarded in full if you'll just lead us to that confounded wagon train. You shall have oats, barley, and hay thrice daily, a mare of your choice for dalliance, and the very best stall in Father's stable. I'll give you horseshoes of silver and, if I can teach you to wear a saddle, the finest that can be imported from Spain. But you must find that train! Or the slaughter of the innocents will pale in comparison to what will happen to those poor, unsuspecting people!" Responding to the pressure of the young man's bare knees, the stallion increased his pace.

Paul became grim. "Not only do we have a score to settle with the Blackfoot, Cicero, but the people of the wagon train are depending on us—although they don't know it. But we have a debt to them and to the United States. I'll reach my majority and become a full-fledged citizen in two weeks—provided I live that long. My ancestors gave me the stamina to ride forever through this Godforsaken wilderness, starving and almost naked, and we owe something to them, too. Yes, and to Harvard, for depriving me of my native ability to reason logically. Only a confounded cretin would not know he was searching for the proverbial needle in the proverbial haystack. If I had any brains, I'd turn you loose, give up, and die. But we Thomans are a stubborn breed. So continue, noble friend, and may your instincts be better than mine!"

The wizened, Russian-born Arnold Mell left the wagon train at dawn, as he did every morning. For a time he would ride with the tall, dignified Cherokee, Stalking Horse. Then they would go their separate ways for the day's scouting. Arnold would head north, and the Indian would ride west.

Long accustomed to each other and to the silence of the endless terrain, the pair felt no need for talk. The wind told them that frigid weather soon would be at hand, so before long they would need to find a place to camp for the winter. Whip and Baron Ernst von Thalman, a wealthy Austrian and a former cavalry commander who had been elected president of the company, wanted to reach the mountains of the Wyoming country before they settled in. Arnold was inclined to agree with them, provided they could find the right place—an area where there was game in the forests, plenty of wood for housing and fires, and rivers and lakes nearby for fishing. If they could not find such a place, they could not survive a winter in the Rockies.

Suddenly Stalking Horse raised a hand in warning.

Arnold squinted in the direction in which the Cherokee was looking, and a moment later he saw something, too. The dot on the horizon grew larger, and he made out a magnificent rust-colored stallion coming toward them. There was a long-haired rider hunched forward on the horse, a man with a bare torso. Arnold took it for granted he was an Indian.

But he was wrong. As the horse and rider drew nearer, Arnold saw it was a white man. He was either wounded or sick, and he appeared to be unconscious, his tightly clenched hands gripping the horse's mane.

Stalking Horse moved instantly to block the advance of the beast, while Arnold circled around and halted the stallion.

"Man not dead," Stalking Horse said.

Arnold nodded and went to work. He looped a length of rope around the stallion's neck, then attached the rope to his horse's saddle, while Stalking Horse lowered the unconscious man to the ground, then hoisted him onto the back of his own mount. They remounted, then turned back toward the wagon train.

Riding hard, they reached the train in a quarter of an hour, just as breakfast was being served. Whip Holt and Ernie von Thalman came forward to meet them, as did the other two scouts, Mack Dougall, a pot-bellied mountain man in his fifties, and Hosea, the escaped slave who was only five feet tall but who had proved to be a courageous warrior, as well as a valuable blacksmith. A few moments later Dr. Robert Martin joined them. The physician took charge immediately.

"His heart and pulse are in good shape," Bob Martin said, "and after examining the man, I see he's not suffering a fever. He isn't wounded, either. From the looks of him, he's half-starved, and I haven't any idea why he's wearing a loincloth in chilly weather like this."

"His horse is tired," Whip said, "but he's in good shape. He's a magnificent animal—I wish I owned him."

Dr. Martin looked around at the crowd that had gathered. "Somebody fetch a couple of blankets and bring a bowl of porridge. And while you're at it, please ask my wife to bring my medical bag."

Two young women hastened to do his bidding. Cindy, the exceptionally attractive former prostitute from Louisville, was joined by Eulalia Woodling, who was her constant companion these days. The equally pretty Eulalia was a former belle and heiress from South Carolina whose family, like so many, had fallen on

13

hard times. Haughty and remote when she had first joined the wagon train, she had suffered an excruciating experience when she had been captured, enslaved, and forced into prostitution by Indians. Since that time, her whole manner had changed. Although she kept her thoughts to herself, it was no accident that she had drawn closer to Cindy, whose wagon she was sharing since her father died.

Cindy and Eulalia quickly brought blankets from their wagon, then stopped at the fire for a bowl of steaming cereal. By the time they returned to the men, Tonie Martin had joined her husband, bringing with her his bag of instruments and medicines. Working quickly, Cindy and Eulalia covered the unconscious man with the blankets.

Edging closer as she watched the ministrations was a freckle-faced strawberry blonde. She and her parents, now deceased, had joined the wagon train in Harrisburg, Pennsylvania. She wore a plain linsey-woolsey dress that in no way concealed her blossoming, seventeen-year-old figure. Sally MacNeill stared hard at the still figure on the ground, then murmured, "Can I help?"

Bob Martin glanced at her and smiled. Only the other day his wife had remarked to him that little Sally was growing up, and as usual Tonie had been right. "Sure," he said. "Sit down there and hold his head. No, Sally, really hold it. He won't eat you alive."

"Folks," Whip said to the people crowding around the unconscious man, "go on about your business. We'll let you know if we need any of you." The scouts, von Thalman, Cindy, and Eulalia remained.

The physician held a vial of smelling salts under his patient's nose, and the man stirred. "Hold his head harder," Bob said. Opening the man's mouth, he poured a small quantity of brandywine down his throat. The patient coughed and opened his eyes.

"Cindy, give Sally the porridge now, so she can feed him."

Paul Thoman gazed up at Sally, who dipped a spoon into the porridge. Then he looked up at Cindy and Eulalia. "I am surrounded by nymphs of unsurpassed pulchritude," he said. "Obviously I have died and ascended to Paradise. Which is astonishing, because I've always insisted that no such place exists."

"Hold still and stop talking," Sally told him, "so you can eat this while it's still hot."

"Yes, angel who probably exists only in my imagination," he said, grinning, then let her feed him.

Whip waited until the man had swallowed several mouthfuls before asking his identity. Paul told them his name, then looked around. "Wagons! By some miracle, is this the Oregon train?"

"It is," Ernie assured him.

"Thank God I've reached you in time!" Paul began to speak so rapidly that he spluttered unintelligibly.

"Eulalia," Whip said, "please ask Lee Blake to come here quickly. Something seems to be brewing!"

By the time Lee joined the little group, Sally had fed Paul the last of the porridge. The young man struggled to a sitting position on the ground. Briefly he explained how he had spent the past year, and then he launched into his recital. "The Blackfoot captured me," he said. "I was their prisoner for three days, until I escaped with one of their horses. I'm a trifle hazy about the passage of time, but it had to be less than a week ago, so you have a little time to prepare. They're intending to launch a full-scale attack on this train, in the immediate future."

Whip remained imperturbable. "How do you know?"

"Because there were two white men with them in the tent next to the one in which I was imprisoned. I overheard them talking. One of them had procured firearms for the Blackfoot from Fort Vancouver. As Seneca so wisely observed, '*Aerugo animi, robigo ingenii*.' For you who have been spared the rigors of Latin, I'll translate freely. 'A mind not used is a mind abused.' "

Lee Blake smiled slightly, but his mind was racing. So two whites, possibly foreign, were inciting the vicious Blackfoot, hoping to destroy the wagon train. This could be serious. "How many warriors are the Blackfoot sending against us?"

"How many trees are there in a pine forest?" Paul Thoman replied. "Hundreds!"

Whip was patient with him. "Can you give us some notion of how many hundreds?"

"White Eagle, the son of the sachem—as nasty a man as I've encountered since I bade farewell to my professor of comparative philosophy—boasted to me that he and his father can put a thousand or more warriors in the field."

Lee and Whip exchanged glances. This confirmed earlier reports. Not only was the pending attack inspired by outside agents, but the Blackfoot could send a major force against them. Neither wanted to reveal his apprehension in front of the others.

Ernie von Thalman understood the situation at once. So did Mack Dougall, Stalking Horse, and Hosea.

"White Eagle is son of Gray Antelope," Stalking Horse murmured to Hosea.

Whip heard him and turned to him quickly. "Are you sure of that?"

"Stalking Horse very sure," the Cherokee replied.

Again Whip looked at Lee Blake. Gray Antelope was the most ruthless and feared chieftain in an area that extended from the high Rockies and across the plains that lay to the east. As skilled in war as he was cruel, he had subdued many lesser tribes and showed no mercy to his enemies.

Whip turned to his scouts. Not only would he send Arnold, Stalking Horse, and Mack Dougall out at once to locate a campsite that could be defended, but he would go on a similar mission himself. Leaving Ernie and Lee in charge, he told them to be prepared for an assault before he returned.

The men of the company were alerted, and after loading their muskets, rifles, and pistols, they took up positions around the circle of wagons. Paul Thoman watched the preparations and could keep silent only for a limited time. "Sir," he called to Lee, who was direct-ing the emplacement of the sharpshooters, "if some-one will be good enough to lend me some attire more suitable than these blankets and permit me to use some weapon more modern than an ancient blunder-buss, I'd like to volunteer my services. I am not alto-gether lacking in knowledge of the fine art of handling firearms."

Dr. Martin intervened. "Young man," he said, "you're lucky to be alive. You need more food and rest before you'll be in any condition for strenuous activity."

Sally MacNeill backed up Dr. Martin's statement. "Mr. Thoman," she said briskly, "you're coming to my wagon, and I aim to look after you until you regain your strength."

Cindy and Eulalia realized that Sally was attracted to Paul, but it was apparent to both of them that the seventeen-year-old orphan wasn't aware of the complications that might arise if she took a male, even one who was temporarily incapacitated, into her cramped wagon.

"You need a chaperone," Eulalia said, "so I elect myself. I'll move in with you, too."

Paul resented having his immediate future settled for him by two young women. Struggling to his feet, he wrapped himself in the borrowed blankets. "Ladies," he said, "overwhelmed as I am by your hospitality, I nevertheless insist on participating in the defense of our questionable civilization, which the population of this train represents." He tried to walk a few steps, but staggered.

Sally caught hold of his arm and held it firmly. "Lean on me," she directed. "You'll get strong faster if you stop talking so much. Eulalia, ask Cathy for more porridge, some biscuits, and a few chunks of bacon, and we'll meet at my wagon. I'll feed him again before I put him to sleep."

Never had Paul encountered such a domineering girl. If she weren't so pretty and if he weren't so weak, he would have told her in no uncertain terms that he refused to be bullied. However, the idea of eating more food and then going to sleep appealed to him. "I trust someone will be good enough to look after my horse," was all he could mutter.

"Don't worry," Sally replied as she led him away. "Most of us hereabouts are farmers who appreciate the sight of solid horseflesh. Other people will take care of your animal while I see to it that you put a little flesh on your bones!"

No woman had ever taken such complete charge of Paul. "Yes, ma'am," he replied meekly as, thanks to his weakened condition, he leaned on her.

Cindy couldn't suppress a laugh as she watched the young couple. Neither knew it, she thought, but if Paul Thoman remained with the train for any length of time, their relationship could well become complicated.

A giant of a man approached, a brace of pistols in his belt and a musket under his arm. He hesitated for a moment as he made his way to an opening between two of the wagons. As she saw him, Cindy's smile vanished. Ted Woods, the blacksmith from Indiana, who had proved himself a tower of strength to the whole company, had made it obvious that he was interested in her. But she was more than a little afraid of him. Ted had spent ten years in prison for killing his wife and his brother after finding them in bed together. The murders were justified, perhaps—Cindy wasn't one to stand in judgment of other people. All the same, Ted had a terrible temper and was violently jealous. Several times he had come close to throttling Claiborne Woodling, Eulalia's brother, who recently had been showing an interest in Cindy.

Ted was essentially a good person, she knew. She had watched his protective attitude toward Danny, the former bound boy who now shared his wagon. Like so many children in their early teens, Danny could be a hellion, but Ted always demonstrated extraordinary patience and kindness toward the boy. His friendship with Hosea showed his better qualities, too.

Even though she recognized his good qualities, however, Cindy became apprehensive whenever she was near him. She didn't like his brooding intensity or the unvarying steadiness of his gaze when he looked at her. Her instincts told her to keep him at a distance, and she always believed in following her hunches.

Pretending to be unaware of Ted's presence, she hurried off to help extinguish the cooking fires, then assist in moving the horses and oxen to the center of the circle of wagons. If a fight with Indian attackers should develop, the animals must be kept from stampeding.

Whip returned early in the afternoon and reported that he had found a site where it would be easier to ward off an Indian assault. Even though it was late in the day to start a journey, the order was given to move on. Horses and oxen were yoked, and the caravan moved in a triple column up the bank of the North Platte River. Progress was slow because the train had to move steadily uphill to a cliff that stood high above the river. The members of the wagon train needed no other reminder that, after so many months of travel on flatlands, they had left the Great Plains behind.

They reached their destination at dusk, and the wagons were moved into their customary circle again. The scouts arrived. Tired after their long day, they nevertheless joined the other men in cutting down pines from the woods that stood near the cliff.

"We want an open space between us and any attacker," Lee Blake explained. "We'll have our backs to the cliff, and if we're surrounded by open land, not even the Blackfoot can creep up and surprise us. What's more, we'll trim these trees and use them to build a palisade of sorts."

While the women prepared supper and the teen-age boys gathered tall grass to be used as fodder for the horses and oxen, the men cut down trees and built a fence outside the circle of wagons. There was little conversation. Everyone worked steadily, aware of the threat they faced.

Ted Woods and Pierre le Rouge, a redheaded Canadian fur trapper who, it was rumored, was lingering with the train because of his interest in Eulalia Woodling, cut far more trees than any other team, leaving

20

the task of trimming them to others. Ernie von Thalman directed the building of the fence. By mid-evening, the task was completed, and the men ate a late supper.

Afterwards, Whip instructed all of the boys to remain inside the compound. The men formed a bucket brigade and passed up enough water from the North Platte to enable the company to withstand a siege of several days. In the meantime, Hosea led a contingent into the woods again to cut more fodder for the animals.

It was long after midnight when Whip, Lee, and Ernie, who constituted an informal high command, inspected the entire perimeter and announced they were satisfied. The pioneers were as ready as they could be for whatever might transpire.

A special guard of eight men was posted at the supply wagon, which was the lifeblood of the train. Here were stored spare weapons, ammunition and gunpowder, barrels of flour and pickled meats, spare blankets, kettles, and medicines, as well as wagon parts to repair the inevitable damage that would occur on such a long and arduous journey. These guards, under the leadership of a short, stocky farmer named Nat Drummond, would be entrusted with the difficult task of extinguishing any fires that might be started in the vicinity of the supply wagon. The company's veterans, some of whom had already traveled two thousand miles, knew they could not survive if that wagon were destroyed.

Lee gave each man a specific combat post, Whip assigned a double sentry detail that would be changed every two hours, and the men were urged to sleep for a few hours. They would know soon enough whether an attack would develop. Whip tried to set an example by stretching out on the ground near the supply wagon.

La-ena soon joined him there, and without inhibitions, she went to sleep beside him.

Others continued to prepare for the crisis. Perhaps the busiest were Bob and Tonie Martin. Tonie, who had been wearing dresses since her marriage, had now changed into the buckskin trousers and shirt she had worn during the early stages of the journey. She wrapped her husband's surgical instruments in individual cloths, over which she poured generous quantities of brandywine to cleanse them and ready them for immediate use. Meanwhile, Bob Martin carefully measured out doses of laudanum. When water was added to it, the opiate would ease the pain of the wounded and the last moments of the dying. Together the couple set up an emergency operating table near the entrance to their crowded wagon. They would need help during a battle, and it was arranged that Cathy and Eulalia would assist them.

Some of the men were too tense to sleep and gathered at one side of the banked cooking fire, their weapons close at hand.

"What's your assignment?" Ted Woods asked the man beside him as both watched Hosea dipping darts for his blowgun into snake venom.

Tilman Wade, a widower in his early thirties whose baldness and gaunt appearance made him look older than his age, grinned as he rubbed his calloused hands together. "Lee assigned me to the sharpshooter detail that will move around and go into action wherever we're needed most. I was surprised."

"Blamed if I know why you should be," Ted replied gruffly. "You may not be as good a marksman as Lee or Ernie, and nobody is as good as Whip. But you're a heap better than young Woodling, and he'll be working with you, too."

Tilman Wade laughed modestly. "I don't know about that. Last week, when we went hunting together, Claiborne brought down a bull buffalo and a calf. I came back to the train with an empty ammunition pouch and nothing much else, except a beat-up sense of pride."

"You take my word for it," Ted said in a grating voice. "You're better than he is."

"Well, I'm not competing with him or anyone else. All that matters is that we stop the Blackfoot from causing too much damage." As always, the mild-mannered Tilman spoke softly. "Some of the ladies are badly upset already, and I sure can't blame them. Just a few minutes ago I saw Widow Harris sitting outside her wagon, crying her eyes out."

Ted nodded somberly, making no reply. There was nothing he could say. Emily Harris had lost two of her four sons on the long trek, one of them in an Indian attack, so her fears were not exaggerated. It was only natural that she should be overwhelmed by fear.

Others in the company were aware of her mental state, too, and no one was more concerned than Ernie von Thalman. The Baron had taken a special interest in the Harris boys. Gradually, through his association with them, he had drawn closer to their mother.

Now he sauntered toward the Harris wagon, making it appear that his approach was accidental. Emily, a rawboned, maternal-looking woman with a strong face, saw him coming and hastily wiped her eyes. She hated weakness in herself even more than she disliked it in others, and she didn't want Ernie, whom she admired, to see her giving in to her fears.

He paused beside her, his manner casual as he took no notice of her red-rimmed eyes. "Bobby is asleep, no doubt," he said, gesturing toward the interior of the wagon.

Emily nodded.

Ernie was deliberately giving her time to recover her poise. "Boys don't know the meaning of fear. Bobby will sleep like an angel until morning. Only when he's Chet's age will he cause problems."

"I hope Chet isn't in trouble again," she said, sighing.

The Baron's smile was reassuring. "On the contrary, he and Danny are already working out a system for reloading the sharpshooters' rifles."

"I must be honest with you," Emily declared. "Chet is so impulsive that I worry about him."

"Let me be equally frank," Ernie replied. "Nobody will be completely safe if a large party of Blackfoot attacks us, even though we're far better prepared this time than we've ever been in the past. But I'm going to command the sharpshooters myself, and Chet will always be within a few feet of me. I won't allow him or his friend Danny, to do anything foolish."

"You're kind, especially when you have matters more important than my son on your mind."

"Not at all. I'm very fond of Chet." Ernie usually thought out every move before he acted, but now he gave in to a sudden impulse and placed a hand on Emily's shoulder. His touch unexpectedly electrified Emily, but she made no attempt to draw away from him. Instead, she found herself looking up at him. She was grateful, but she also felt something else, something more, that she couldn't quite define.

Ernie von Thalman was startled by the intensity of his own reaction. For years he had associated with some of Europe's most beautiful women. A glamorous Hungarian countess had been his mistress once. So he was shocked by his serious interest in this plain American woman who had spent her whole life on farms and was totally lacking in sophistication.

On second thought, however, he recognized the qualities that were drawing them together. Both were middle-aged, beyond the need for surface glitter. He had learned the value of character, and in Emily he saw someone who was warm and dependable, a woman who was fiercely loyal and had an unlimited capacity for love. His grip on her shoulder tightened. For a moment Emily's worries vanished, and in that instant she looked radiant. Then common sense transcended romance, and Ernie withdrew his hand. "See to it that you keep a close eye on Bobby if trouble comes tomorrow," he said gruffly. "The men will be busy fighting, so mothers will have to watch out for their young."

"He won't leave my side, I promise you," Emily said.

He nodded. "And don't worry about Chet any more than you can help. He has great courage, and he's developing a sense of balance to go with it."

"I hope so."

He touched her shoulder again, then moved off. Emily's cheeks were burning, and she marveled at her emotional reaction. Too flustered to think clearly, she jumped to her feet and disappeared into the wagon, where she would remain, wide awake, on her pallet.

Gradually the camp grew quiet. The cooking fire burned lower, and the men who sat around it drifted off to their wagons to doze while they awaited the summons to duty. The sentries, stationed beyond the makeshift palisade, remained in the shadows of the fence as they peered off into the night, alert to any sound or any sign of movement that might herald an attack.

No one slept more peacefully than Paul Thoman. On the far side of a partition created by hanging a blanket from the wagon ceiling, Sally MacNeill shivered as she listened to him snore. She had been brash, forward beyond belief in taking charge of this strange young man. But she wasn't sorry. At seventeen Sally had become a woman, at least in her own mind, and as a woman she knew what she wanted. At first glance she had decided she wanted Paul Thoman, and she hoped the Indian attack would fail so she could persuade him to accompany the wagon train to Oregon.

II

Henry St. Clair was pleased as he rode with the main body of the Blackfoot. London was depending on him to destroy or turn back the American wagon train bound for the Oregon country, but for a year he had suffered one failure after another. Now, at last, he was certain his mission would succeed.

There were more than a thousand seasoned warriors in the band, and their raw courage and reckless sense of pride more than made up for what they lacked in discipline. All of them were mounted, a magnificent achievement that had been accomplished by denuding the Blackfoot towns of their horses. Some six hundred were armed with the most modern British rifles, recently delivered from the arsenal at Fort Vancouver. It didn't matter that few of them could fire their weapons accurately. Their massed power would be overwhelming, particularly when they fired at the standing wagons, and they could always fall back on using their bows and arrows, which they also carried.

In spite of his optimism, St. Clair did not lose sight of the possibility that problems might arise. Certainly the Blackfoot leadership was not what he would have selected for the enterprise. Gray Antelope, who led the warriors, was an arrogant barbarian whose head had been turned by a series of victories over lesser tribes. He insisted upon conducting the assault as he saw fit, refusing the counsel of Henry, who had spent many years studying military strategy and tactics.

The chief's two principal lieutenants were even more ignorant, but at least White Eagle, Gray Antelope's son, held no responsible post. Thanks to White Eagle's stupidity, Paul Thoman, who should have been executed without delay, had been allowed to escape. It was unlikely, to be sure, that Thoman could have located the wagon train and warned its leaders of the impending attack. But Henry St. Clair didn't believe in taking unnecessary chances. Only when the element of risk had been eliminated was any venture certain to succeed.

Oh, well, St. Clair thought, there was still no real cause for concern. The odds in favor of the assault were reassuring. Within hours he would be on his way to Fort Vancouver, his first stop on his journey back to London. After he took a well-deserved holiday, he would settle into a desk job and spend his evenings drinking champagne with the young ladies of Madame Eliza's elite establishment. Anticipating the pleasures he had been denied for so long, Henry St. Clair sighed quietly.

The invaders rode three abreast in the direction of the North Platte River, where, precisely as St. Clair had predicted, the Blackfoot scouts had found the American caravan. At least he had persuaded Gray Antelope to attack while the settlers were at breakfast, when the confusion would be even greater than at daybreak, which the Blackfoot traditionally preferred.

The element of surprise was always of paramount importance.

On the Englishman's right rode the dark, sallow-faced Russian hireling who called himself André Sebastian. He was a dour, secretive man, and St. Clair would be relieved to be rid of him. Henry St. Clair fully intended to go on alone to Fort Vancouver. Sebastian could fend for himself.

On St. Clair's left rode White Eagle, and the Englishman's nose protested his proximity. The hulking warrior, a giant in his mid-twenties, hadn't bathed or changed his buckskins in weeks, and he smelled like a sewer. The man was a cruel beast who despised most members of the Blackfoot hierarchy because they hadn't yet elected him to serve as his father's heir. St. Clair privately applauded their judgment. White Eagle was cunning and might be a handy ally in a tavern brawl, but he was unsuited for leadership of his people.

About an hour before dawn, one of the Blackfoot scouts returned to the column with word that the enemy encampment lay directly ahead. Gray Antelope halted his warriors, then rode forward, accompanied by the two white men.

Henry St. Clair's heart sank when he saw the crude fence that surrounded the circle of wagons, then noted that the land beyond the circle had been cleared for a distance of more than one hundred feet. The Americans had been warned and were anticipating the attack.

The Englishman turned away abruptly and rode ahead of White Eagle and Sebastian to the head of the line. "They know we are coming," he said at last, speaking in the language of the Kiowa, which most of the Indian nations of the West understood.

"It does not matter," Gray Antelope replied. "We will take many scalps and much booty."

"But it does matter." St. Clair found it difficult to speak calmly. "They have men who can shoot, and many of your braves will die."

Gray Antelope shrugged. "A true warrior is not afraid of death. We will kill more of them than they will kill of us, and we will win."

"I suggest we wait a few days," St. Clair said. "They can't stay forever on that cliff. If we pull back far enough so their scouts don't find us, they'll resume their journey when we don't attack. In a few days they'll grow careless. One night, they'll stop at a campsite that is more difficult to defend. It will be far easier to beat them, and we'll not only take more booty, but you'll capture more of their women and children. And you'll lose fewer braves."

Gray Antelope was unable to accept the white man's logic. He could think only that his courage was being questioned. "We will fight this day," he said, "and we will kill all of our foes."

"I agree," André Sebastian said. "We've taken a large force into the field, so any delay is dangerous. The more time we give the Americans, the stronger their defenses will become."

St. Clair was disgusted. Russians were little better than savages. It was no wonder they suffered shocking losses in combat. "Do what you please," he said.

It was still possible that the wagon train company would be defeated. All the same, he would change his own plans. Under no circumstances would he accompany the first wave of men who would ride and open the assault. He would select a vantage point from which he could watch the fight develop, and there he would stay, safely out of the way. He had done his best for Queen Victoria and his country, and if this effort should fail, he would be forced to return home. What mattered to him most was that, whatever happened, he was going back to England. He had suffered enough hardship in the American wilderness. No one could claim he hadn't tried. Let England find some other way to deny the claim of the United States to the Oregon country.

The weary sentries detected no sign of life as they gazed toward the forest that stood beyond the open space they had cleared the previous night. The women began to prepare a breakfast of wheat cakes, biscuits, and buffalo stew left over from supper. But the men carried their firearms with them to breakfast, and the sentries were served at their posts. Vigilance was not relaxed. Whip, Ernie, Lee, and the scouts held an informal discussion as they ate.

"I realize that we must find a place to stay for the winter," Lee Blake said, "but I think we have no real choice but to stay here for at least three or four days."

Whip rubbed his chin thoughtfully. "We won't find a better spot to defend, that's certain," he said. "But I hate to lose time with winter approaching so quickly, and it is. La-ena says she can smell snow in the air, and her nose is reliable. All the same, we're relatively safe right here, even though it would be suicide to spend the whole winter in the foothills."

"What worries me," Ernie von Thalman said, "is that the Blackfoot might attack while our wagons are strung out on the trail. Then they could carve our line to shreds."

"I say we stay," Stalking Horse declared.

Mack Dougall spat at a small stick that lay on the ground a few feet away. "I hate like the devil to let a pack of savages think they can scare us."

Pierre le Rouge tugged at his beard. "No Indian can scare Pierre!" he said in his booming voice.

"Me, neither," Mack added.

"If this company was made up entirely of men," Arnold Mell said quietly, "I'd be tempted to take the risk. But the lives of women and little children are at stake, too."

Lee Blake became impatient. "Somebody fetch that young fellow who brought us word of the attack."

Whip went off at once, and a few moments later he returned with Paul Thoman, who was wearing a borrowed buckskin shirt, baggy linsey-woolsey trousers, and a pair of boots that appeared to fit him reasonably well.

As he walked he repeatedly dipped a spoon into a huge bowl of buffalo stew, which he ate with relish. Aside from the deep hollows beneath his eyes, he looked none the worse for the experience he had suffered.

"Are you quite positive you were the captive of the Blackfoot and overheard them talking to two white men?" Lee Blake demanded. "You were wandering around in the wilderness for what may have been a long time. Maybe you were dreaming."

"Oh, I spent at least two days hallucinating," Paul replied cheerfully. "Some day—very soon, before I forget the details—I intend to make notes I can use in a treatise for my senior philosophy class. But what happened to me in the town of the Blackfoot was no dream, even though it was a nightmare."

The faces of the men who surrounded Paul indicated their skepticism.

"Hold this for a minute, but don't eat it," he said, thrusting his bowl at the surprised Pierre. Then he tugged up the sleeves of his borrowed shirt. "For three days and nights I was trussed with rawhide bonds," he said.

One look at his chafed wrists satisfied them. What he had told them about the Blackfoot had to be true.

"I'll gladly show you my ankles, too. The rawhide caused an infection on one of them that's just beginning to heal."

"We'll take your word," Lee said. "We had to be certain that you didn't dream the whole thing."

"I wish I had. I was carrying furs worth at least five thousand dollars in New York."

"There are plenty more furs available in the Rockies," Whip said, grinning, then waved him back to where Sally MacNeill stood, a distance away, keeping watch for him.

"As far as I'm concerned, that settles it," Lee said when the leaders were alone again.

Whip sipped his mug of steaming coffee. "We can't leave. A little later, maybe, Stalking Horse and I will take a look around and see if we can pick up any clues. The Blackfoot may be strong and nasty, but they've never been very clever."

Just then Nat Drummond, on sentry duty at the rear of the special wagon, called out a warning. "I think I see something out there, but I can't tell for sure what it is."

Whip joined him, closed his eyes for an instant, and then peered intently at the screen of trees. Stalking Horse stared at the forest from another vantage point, and La-ena joined him.

It was the girl who broke the tense silence. "Men there," she said. "Bad Indians."

Whip nodded in confirmation.

Ernie and Arnold alerted the men, who quietly went to their combat posts, while some of the women and boys herded the horses and oxen into the center of the circle. Older people and small children were moved toward the cliff, as far away as possible from the area of attack.

There was no panic. Everyone, even the little children, knew what was expected of them, and no one shouted or cried out. As Jacob Levine, a former fur cutter from New York who was one of the company's newest members, remarked to several companions, "These people have been through Indian attacks. They know what to do."

Only the Reverend Oscar Cavendish, who had joined the wagon train at the same time as Jacob Levine, failed to distinguish himself. Saying nothing to anyone, he went off to the wagon he had acquired after the death of a member of the company, and helped himself to several large swallows from a jug of whiskey. But even he made no fuss.

It appeared to the invaders in the forest that the company was continuing with its normal routines, unaware that a crisis was at hand.

Lee Blake, crouching beside an opening between wagons, facing the forest, summoned Chet Harris and Danny. "Boys," he said, "I want you to make the rounds. No one is to open fire until Whip and I start shooting. After that, they can let loose. And tell them to make their bullets count!" Chet and Danny separated and began to move around the circle in opposite directions.

Lee continued to stare out at the woods. He was interrupted by Paul Thoman. "Sir," the young man said, "it's my impression that you and the rather formidable

34

mountain man are in joint command, so to speak, of this illustrious regiment. Red blood is flowing through my veins again, and I beg you to permit me to take part in the sport."

Lee started to object.

"Sir," Paul declared, "I choose to disobey the orders of your distinguished physician. A matter far more important than my health is at stake. I assure you I'll be completely restored if I'm given the opportunity to get even with the bastards who were intending to torture me to death!"

Without turning, Lee made a decision. "Don't tell Dr. Martin I gave my permission," he said, grinning. "But if you'll go over to the supply wagon, Nat Drummond—the short fellow—will give you a gun and ammunition. Can you shoot?"

"I survived in the mountains, dear sir, only because I learned to excel at marksmanship."

"Good hunting," Lee told him.

The young man loped off, and a few moments later was equipped with a rifle, a bag of ammunition, and a pouch of gunpowder. Sally MacNeill watched him from a distance but was afraid to protest. The lives of everyone in the company depended on the skill and valor of the men.

Tension mounted, and no one in the waiting circle spoke. Tilman Wade coughed, and several men nervously shifted their positions. Jacob Levine cocked his musket, and the clicking sound seemed to echo across the encampment. A horse whinnied, and then all was quiet again.

Suddenly a group of horsemen moved at a gallop out of the forest and started across the open space toward the circle. Warpaint of alternating black and yellow stripes streaked their faces and bare torsos, and

Whip identified the marauders instantly. "Blackfoot!" he shouted. Taking aim, he fired. Others in the company quickly responded to the challenge, and a volley rang out.

Whip felled one rider, and Lee killed another. Three more Indians were wounded, and two of their horses were struck. The pioneers had gained the initial advantage. Their foes, instead of firing as they charged into the open, employed the traditional challenge of Plains Indians of first making their identity known. As a result, the Blackfoot suffered casualties that might have been averted had they opened fire instantly.

In spite of the disadvantage they faced, however, they rallied quickly. Even as the dead warriors tumbled to the ground and the wounded horses screamed in pain and terror, a second group of attackers rode into the opening and began to fire instantly. It seemed to Lee that the Blackfoot were shooting wildly. Perhaps there was a chance that the wagon train company could hold its own.

As the attackers approached the crude palisade, several of them were shot down in a hail of well-aimed bullets. The survivors wheeled and rode at top speed back to the forest through the ranks of yet another oncoming wave. The size of their force gave the Indians a natural advantage, and some of their shots penetrated the circle, forcing the defenders to remain at least partly concealed behind the wagons they were using as shields.

The first casualty the pioneers suffered was a former bookkeeper from Cincinnati, Edwin Cooper. He died instantly when a bullet entered his heart.

At Lee's direction the sharpshooters flanked Whip, in the center of the line. Claiborne Woodling and Tilman Wade distinguished themselves, causing severe losses in the Blackfoot ranks. Chet, Danny, and two other boys were kept frantically busy reloading spare rifles. Their effort made it possible for the marksmen to keep up a steady fire.

The pioneers' defense was so effective that the assault tapered off after about half an hour. The Blackfoot withdrew into the forest, apparently to regroup for a fresh assault.

"Next time they'll try something different," Whip commented when the lull made conversation possible again. "Stay on your toes. When they strike, they won't give us much chance to change our tactics."

The wait seemed interminable. Paul Thoman became restless. He had, so far, contributed little to the defense. He edged closer to the sharpshooters, who accepted him conditionally, although they didn't spell out their attitude. If he failed to prove himself, he would be responsible for his own undoing; they would be too busy to pay much attention to him.

Cathy van Ayl moved toward the line facing the forest. The lull puzzled her, and she wanted to learn what was happening. Lee smiled at her but firmly waved her back. She retreated reluctantly.

"They're moving again," Whip called in a low voice.

Suddenly two mounted figures appeared at the edge of the woods. It looked as if they intended to direct the next phase of the assault. One was a tall Indian wearing a feathered bonnet, and the other was a white man.

"Gray Antelope," Paul Thoman said. "And the other is Sebastian." He raised his rifle, took quick but careful aim, and squeezed the trigger. André Sebastian slumped forward in his saddle, a bullet between his eyes.

Whip, Arnold, and Pierre fired almost simultaneously at Gray Antelope. He rose in the air, then slid to the ground.

The loss of Gray Antelope jarred his braves, but the deputy chiefs stepped into the breach and revised their tactics. They discarded their rifles, in which they had no faith, and instead sent a hail of burning arrows over the palisade into the circle.

Some arrows became imbedded in the canvas tops of the wagons and burned fiercely. The people who climbed up onto the wagons to extinguish the flames exposed themselves to the enemy, and several were wounded by arrows. A teen-age boy who made a gallant attempt to pluck a burning arrow from the roof of his family's wagon took an arrow in his throat and died before he could be carried to the medical wagon.

Other arrows soared over the wagons and landed inside the circle. Some of the horses and oxen became panicky, and Grace Drummond's strident voice rose above the hubbub. "Take the animals toward the back!" she shouted. "The cliff side. Keep them there!" She herself drove three horses toward the rear.

An arrow landed in the canvas of Cindy's wagon, and reacting instantly, the girl pulled it out and stamped on it. Not until the flames were extinguished did she realize she had suffered a severe burn on the palm of her right hand. Eulalia led her to the medical wagon, where she had to wait her turn as Dr. Martin treated one patient after another. Cindy writhed in silent agony until Tonie Martin gave her a dose of laudanum that made her so groggy she had to be eased to the ground. But her pain was bearable now, and she waited in a semistupor until the physician could attend to her.

The Blackfoot remained partially concealed behind the trees at the edge of the clearing, making it more difficult for the men to counter the barrage of arrows. Following Whip's example, however, some of them fired at the first sign of any movement inside the screen. An occasional shout or scream told them that this tactic was effective.

Jacob Levine raced for his place in the line, into the circle. When wagons were struck by the burning arrows, he ran to them and removed the fiery brands. His hands, hardened by many years of work as a fur cutter, were as leathery as thick gloves, and he suffered no pain.

Two middle-aged farmers followed his example, and the trio managed to hold the damage caused by the flames to a minimum.

Emily Harris could not remain sedentary when so many others were busy protecting the train. Keeping little Bobby close beside her, she soothed the horses and spoke softly to the oxen. Something in her manner pacified the animals.

Claiborne Woodling was hit in the shoulder by a Blackfoot arrow, but his annoyance overcame his pain. "Pull it out for me," he told the man beside him. "I'll be damned if I'm going to stop fighting!"

Tilman Wade hesitated for an instant, then grasped the shaft and tugged. As the arrow came free, Claiborne winced. Then he jammed a handkerchief under his shirt. "A little blood won't spoil my aim," he said. He proved his point by firing a shot at a shadowy figure behind the branches of a pine. The Blackfoot collapsed.

"I'm feeling better already," Claiborne said. He had no idea he was gritting his teeth.

Lee saw that Claiborne's shirt was soaked with blood, however, and intervened. "Go to Dr. Martin, Woodling," he ordered. The commanding ring in his voice could not be denied. "We're holding our own here, and you'll be in worse shape if you don't get your shoulder patched."

Reluctantly Claiborne went off to the medical wagon. As he approached it, he saw Cindy sitting on the ground, her injured hand resting in her lap, her eyes vacant as the laudanum took effect. His own injury promptly became insignificant.

"Come into the wagon," Cathy said. "Dr. Martin is attending to fighting men first."

"Look after Cindy," he replied. "She has a nasty burn, and my shoulder can wait." With his good arm, he helped Cindy to her feet and half-carried her to the operating table.

The battle raged for another half-hour. Casualties on both sides mounted. The Blackfoot were getting the worst of the bargain, but neither side could gain a clear advantage. The Indians were unaccustomed to a prolonged battle, however. It was their custom to overwhelm their foes in the first minutes of combat. In the absence of Gray Antelope's leadership, the warriors became discouraged. Those who held positions on the periphery of the forest began to move deeper into it.

No one was more keenly aware of their change of heart than Henry St. Clair. The braves were bungling the attack, and he felt a growing certainty that they could not now obtain a clear-cut victory.

Consequently, his own danger was greater. With Sebastian dead, St. Clair was the only white man whom the Indians could use as a scapegoat for their failure. Twice he had caught glimpses of White Eagle, and the wild rage he had seen in the face of the young warrior had made the Englishman shudder.

St. Clair slowly edged away from the warriors who were closest to him. To his relief, they seemed to be paying no attention to him. They were absorbed in the fight, but they were obviously reconciling themselves to the prospect of a draw. To them that meant defeat.

St. Clair moved five yards, ten yards, then another ten. Now! He headed toward the northwest, keeping his horse to a steady but unspectacular walk for the better part of a mile. At last he was clear. He let the horse break into a canter. He wouldn't be completely safe until at least the next day, but he would ride through the day and night, if need be, to put as much distance as possible between himself and the Blackfoot.

Henry St. Clair decided that, as soon as he reached Fort Vancouver, he would write to London, urging that means other than sabotage be used to prevent the Americans from settling in Oregon. It was too much to ask any agent to combat the resilience and courage of these pioneers. They were tougher and more determined than he had anticipated.

Neither the Indians nor their foes were aware of St. Clair's hurried departure. It seemed that all at once the warriors lost their will to fight. Their withdrawal was abrupt. One minute they were still sending showers of arrows over the palisades, and the next minute they were gone.

The men crouching behind the wagons remained vigilant, awaiting another assault. But Whip shook his head. "I reckon we've seen the last of the Blackfoot," he said.

"You may be right," Lee Blake said, "but I don't want anybody going into the woods to investigate. For all we know, the Indians might be laying an ambush for us."

An hour passed. Bob and Tonie Martin attended to the last of the injured.

Hosea went looking for Reverend Cavendish and discovered him in the wagon. The minister had consumed so much liquor he had lost consciousness. Hosea quietly fetched a bucket of water and slowly poured it over the clergyman's head. The cold bath had no effect, so he took some dried herbs, crumbled them, and held them under the minister's nose. Oscar Cavendish groaned and opened his eyes. Again Hosea forced him to inhale the herbs.

Gradually the clergyman's eyes cleared, and recognition dawned. Soon he would be needed to bury those who had died in the attack. Hosea's intention was obvious. When Cavendish was needed, he would be ready.

The pine forest became silent again. One Blackfoot remained behind. White Eagle felt disgraced, his humiliation compounded by the knowledge that his peers would not grant him authority to plan a retaliatory attack against these white men who had murdered Gray Antelope. White Eagle decided that he would not return to the main town of the Blackfoot. Instead, he would remain close to the wagon train, waiting patiently until he could wreak havoc. He would remain hidden, awaiting his chance. White Eagle swore to the spirits of the sky and the earth, the sun and the rivers that he would not rest or return home until his father's death had been avenged.

Most of the company was busy or preoccupied when Lee Blake motioned to Whip and Ernie. The trio walked beyond the circle of wagons to the ground the Indians had occupied.

"What's the problem?" Whip asked.

"The time has come for me to earn my pay as a military intelligence officer," Lee replied, smiling sardonically. "I keep wondering why a band of savages —men who know what to do with a bow and arrow but who are obviously unaccustomed to handling firearms—were given such a full supply of muskets."

"An interesting question," Ernie said.

They walked only a short distance before Lee found a weapon that had been discarded by one of the warriors. Stooping, he picked it up, then examined it carefully. The others waited, their impatience growing, but they did not interrupt him.

"It's as I thought," Lee said at last. "These aren't old-fashioned muskets. They're rifles—British rifles. Look at this small mark, just above the trigger. It's a tiny, three-pronged crown—the trademark of the gunsmith in Sheffield, England, who manufactures rifles for the Royal Infantry." Whip's eyes glittered, and Ernie frowned as they, too, scrutinized the weapon.

"These aren't just ordinary English rifles, they're the newest make," Lee said. "They use an elongated bullet instead of the customary round pellet."

Ernie von Thalman looked puzzled. "But how did the Blackfoot get them? I spent many years in the Imperial Austrian Army, and I know that new weapons aren't distributed to outsiders—especially barbarians who don't know how to use them."

"That's the whole point," Lee replied. "All the pieces of the puzzle fit together perfectly. As you undoubtedly realize, Ernie, most generals—regardless of their nationality—are elderly men, conservatives who dislike change. According to information the War Department received from our military attaché in London, the Sheffield foundry has turned out thousands of these rifles, but the Royal Army has been slow to accept them. A regimental commander has the prerogative of selecting his own weapons, and only a few have accepted them. That means other departments of the British government can easily obtain any number of them for other purposes."

Whip had picked up another of the rifles. How well he remembered the problems Henry St. Clair had caused. "I'll bet a pewter dollar to a penny that St. Clair had a hand in all this."

"Whoever may have been directly responsible for it," Lee said, "there can be no doubt of the British government's complicity. New rifles like these can't be purchased in a shop. They're available only to government and military sources."

"You're saying the British government supplied the Indians with these weapons, then?" Ernie asked.

"Definitely! There is no doubt about that." Lee spoke emphatically. "President Van Buren and the War Department will want this information! It proves that the British are even more determined than we realized to make sure this wagon train doesn't reach Oregon and to claim it for themselves. I'll write a full report today."

"Before winter sets in," Whip said, "we're sure to run into some mountain men who are heading East. We'll give your report to the first one who's reliable, so we'll be sure it reaches Washington City." Suddenly he chuckled.

The others looked at him blankly, finding nothing amusing in the situation.

"I've got a job for our boys," he said. "From the

looks of it, the Indians left at least fifty rifles behind. Some of our folks are using muskets that date back to the War of Independence and even earlier. They'll appreciate having modern, accurate weapons."

Lee grinned, too. "It should be easy enough for Ted Woods to make a mold for an elongated bullet."

Ernie nodded approvingly. "From now on," he said, "we'll be better armed than we've ever been, thanks to the British."

In the early afternoon, a party of heavily armed settlers ventured into the forest to cut more trees, then carried the wood back to the circle. Boards were shaped, and several carpenters, aided by Ted Woods and Hosea, built coffins for the five members of the company who had died.

By late afternoon the Reverend Cavendish was sufficiently recovered to conduct a simple funeral service. "We must go on," he said in a brief sermon. "We must prove to ourselves that our dead have not died in vain. No matter what misfortunes Providence may design to test us, we must push on to Oregon."

Graves were dug near the edge of the cliff, overlooking the rushing waters of the North Platte River below, and the dead were buried.

Dr. Martin refused to allow most of the fourteen wounded to attend the funeral, but he seemed confident that all would recover, provided they had a day or two of complete rest. So Whip was forced to postpone the train's departure from the site.

"We'll have to move faster when we take to the trail again," Whip told the group that surrounded him after the funeral. "We'll have to make up for lost time before the snows come. But if Dr. Martin says we've got to stay put for now, we won't budge."

45

La-ena, who stood nearby, saw Cathy van Ayl heading toward the cooking fire. She passed within a few feet of Whip. It was curious, the Indian girl thought, that this beautiful young woman with the pale hair always pretended Whip was invisible, even though it was plain that she was aware of his presence at all times. It was odd, too, that Whip, always direct and blunt in his dealings with everyone, should avert his gaze when the girl with pale hair was near.

La-ena wanted to learn more, but she knew better than to question Whip. A squaw did not badger her man by asking what he might have good reason not to reveal. So she would be patient, as she had been taught by her mother. Ultimately the mystery would solve itself.

In the meantime, she could help Whip and these people, most of whom had willingly accepted her. Waiting until the crowd dispersed, she went to Whip and walked beside him. "Do you remember the Hidden Valley, in the Wind River Range?" she asked in her own tongue.

He frowned. "Not by that name."

"It is the place where you shot a bear four years ago and made me a necklace of the claws."

"Ah, that valley. It's a snug place. What about it?"

"These white people would be safe there in the cold," she said. "There are many trees for houses and fires. There are fish in the lake, and unless the snows are very bad, there is much game."

Whip halted and slapped his leg. He had been irritated when La-ena had shown up and joined the train. He had thought they had parted permanently almost two years earlier. Her presence created serious problems, particularly in relation to Cathy. But right now she was more than proving her worth.

"Hidden Valley is the perfect spot!" he exclaimed. "I just hope we can reach it in time. We'll have to travel fast and pray that the heavy snows don't come too soon."

Claiborne Woodling, his left arm in a sling, was sitting on the rear stoop of Cindy's wagon keeping her company as she rested on her pallet just inside the wagon entrance. He raised his right hand in greeting to the passing Whip and La-ena, but did not engage them in conversation. Instead, he continued to concentrate on Cindy, who was gradually becoming more alert as the effects of the laudanum she had taken began to wear off.

"The doctor says you're not to move your arm," he said, pointing to her bandaged hand.

"You and I make a fine team," she replied, laughing drily. "Between us we have one sound pair of hands and arms."

"I'll be well in a day or two," Claiborne said. "Well enough to drive your wagon for you."

"There's no need to put yourself out," Cindy said. "Eulalia can drive for me."

"First of all," Claiborne said, with a trace of his former arrogance, "I would not be putting myself out. I consider it a privilege to drive your wagon. And second, Eulalia will be too busy looking after you."

"I don't need a nursemaid!"

"You're wrong," he said. "I saw your hand before Dr. Martin bandaged it, and you have a nasty burn. It will take forever to heal if you use your hand too much. So I've already told Eulalia she's going to feed, wash, and dress you."

"Nobody has ever made a fuss over me," Cindy said, somewhat embarrassed.

"Well, there's always a first time," Claiborne told

47

her. "You'd be surprised how many people want to help, now that you're a genuine heroine."

"I'm hardly that!"

Claiborne leaned closer to her, and his admiration was evident in his voice and eyes. "Back in South Carolina," he said, "most ladies were pretty useless creatures who spent the majority of their time primping. You're prettier than any of them, and you not only work hard, you risked your life when you grabbed that burning arrow!"

Cindy's laugh was harsh. "In case you've forgotten, I'm no lady."

"You're worth a dozen of them," he replied. "You're a woman who stands on her own feet and isn't afraid of anything."

Her embarrassment increased, and she tried to make light of it by teasing him in return. "I thought gentlemen from South Carolina preferred helpless women." In spite of the throbbing in her hand, she couldn't help flirting with him.

"No one has called me a gentleman in a long time," Claiborne said, laughing mirthlessly. "All I own in the world are a couple of changes of clothes, a dilapidated wagon, some odds and ends worth a few dollars at a junk sale—and my gun."

Cindy became serious, too. "What I like best about this train is that nearly all of us are in the same boat. Oh, Cathy is well off, I guess, and Ernie is rich, but the rest of us are living on our hopes for the future. Sometimes I think we'll never make it to Oregon. But we must."

"We will," Claiborne said. There was a ring of certainty in his voice. "I came on this trip because my father, may his soul rest in peace, saw no other way out for us. But his vision was greater than mine." He hauled himself to his feet, involuntarily touching his injured shoulder. "It looks like supper is just about ready. I'll get Eulalia to bring you something to eat."

As he made his way toward the fire, he failed to see someone draw back into the shadows. Ted Woods had been eavesdropping on the entire conversation. As he moved into the opening between Cindy's wagon and the one that stood adjacent to it, Ted frowned, his dark eyes smouldering. He knew that he had no right to expect Cindy to be loyal to him. She was free to do as she pleased.

All the same, he had been taking it for granted that, when Cindy was ready and able to put her past behind her, their friendship would develop into a romantic relationship. The fact that Claiborne was courting her infuriated him. Ted well knew that his jealous rages could cause him as much trouble in the future as they had in the past. But when he was in the grip of blind fury, he couldn't control himself.

His knuckles whitened as his grasp on the hammer he held in his hand grew tighter. He wasn't even aware that he was carrying it. The day had been long and difficult, but he had no appetite for food. He retreated slowly to his wagon, sat on the back stoop, and stared up at the black clouds that filled the sky and matched his mood. He was unfit company for anyone right now. He forced himself to sit quietly until his anger passed and his ability to think clearly returned. Paul Thoman and Sally MacNeill walked past him on their way to supper, but they were so absorbed in their conversation they didn't even notice him.

"My year in the mountains has given me recuperative powers that have astounded your Dr. Martin,"

Paul said. "The cuisine offered by your chefs, combined with today's invigorating exercise, has rejuvenated me."

"I can tell you're feeling better," Sally said. "You're talking even more."

"You'll be delighted to learn I'm no longer dependent on your hospitality. Mr. Tilman Wade has been kind enough to offer me sleeping space in his wagon, and I've accepted."

"You don't need to move until you're strong again."

"Ah, but that's the point. 'No profit grows where is no pleasure taken,' as friend Shakespeare observed when he tamed his shrew."

The girl looked at him blankly and shook her head, convinced that he was out of his mind.

"I am a male," he said, "and you are a raving beauty of a female. Do I make myself clear?"

"No," she said, but her face colored.

"I've regained enough of my strength that I cannot tempt the fates by spending another night under your roof. Proximity and propinquity are dangerous bedfellows."

Sally saw his point, even though she found it difficult to cut through the maze of words. "Will you be staying long with Tilman?"

"That is a matter I wish to discuss with Mr. Holt and Colonel Blake. So, while you procure our supper, I'll excuse myself and have a word with them. I hardly need remind you that I'm ravenous tonight."

She nodded. "You're always hungry—I know that much," she said as she headed toward the fire with their bowls.

"May I interrupt, gentlemen?" Paul asked as he approached Whip and Lee. "I want to ask you about the admission requirements to this illustrious company."

Lee smiled. "You've already paid your entrance fee."

Whip looked at the young man. "Are you thinking of joining us?"

"The thought has flitted through my mind since the battle that I have two distinct choices. I can go back to Cambridge and reenter Harvard, but the excitement of the fight today convinces me that I might find the academic life too tame now. I've spent one winter alone in the Rockies, and I don't care to repeat that experiment. So my only other alternative is to become a member of your band. I've heard tales of Oregon's glories, and hard as it may be to believe them, I'd like to see the country for myself. I might even be tempted to settle there."

"I hope you've thought enough about this to decide if you're prepared to live your life as a farmer," Lee said.

"A farmer?" Paul laughed. "I wouldn't know one end of a plow from the other. But seeing all the children in this train has given me some ideas." He became earnest. "You'll need a school for the youngsters, and I believe I'm well qualified for such work. In fact, I hope to make arrangements with my professors at Harvard to take my final examinations by mail in Oregon so I can earn my degree. I'm intrigued by the notion of establishing a school. In fact, I've had a chat with a couple of your teen-age boys—Danny and Chet. They're both urgently in need of further education, and so are the younger children."

Whip smiled. "I can think of nothing that would give the parents in this train more pleasure than knowing their children will be able to get a good education in Oregon."

Paul cleared his throat. "If this isn't presumptuous,

it has occurred to me that I could start holding classes when you set up your winter quarters. I'll do my share of hunting and other chores, of course, since I'm familiar with the mountains, but I'd rather teach than eat. Well, almost."

"Welcome to the wagon train," Whip said. He extended his hand.

Lee turned to tell the good news to Emily Harris and Ernie von Thalman, who were moving past them, carrying dishes laden with food. "My prayers have been answered!" Emily exclaimed.

Paul Thoman suddenly became shy and inarticulate. Mumbling something unintelligible, he bolted, breaking into a trot as he headed toward the fire in search of Sally MacNeill.

Ernie guided Emily to a flat boulder where they could sit and eat. "You're in a far better frame of mind now," he said.

She nodded. "Bobby is safe, and Chet did well today. He came through the battle without a scratch. So I think that maybe my luck has finally turned."

"I'd like to help you make sure of that," Ernie said, looking at her.

She froze, her spoon poised partway between her bowl and her mouth.

"This will come as no surprise to you, Emily," he said. "You and I get along wonderfully together. We seek each other out all the time."

"I hope I haven't been too forward."

"You? Hardly." He paused. In spite of his sophistication, he almost stumbled over his words. "Neither of us is growing any younger, you know, and it seems to me we'd be wise to take advantage of the present— especially when there's no way of predicting what the future may hold in store for us."

Emily Harris was not one to dissemble or pretend a coyness she didn't feel. "Speak it plain," she said.

He cleared his throat. "I'd be honored if you would consent to become my wife."

"Oh, Ernie. Look at me! Do I look like any baroness you ever saw?"

"I'm plain Ernie von Thalman. Before we left Fort Madison, I sent an application to Washington City for United States citizenship. I've put my title behind me, along with the Old World. First I fell in love with America, Emily, and then I fell in love with you."

She averted her face so he wouldn't see her tears. Their meal was growing cold, but neither of them cared. After a moment Ernie reached out to touch Emily's work-hardened hand.

"I have children," Emily said in a choked voice.

"No one knows it better than I do. I've spent a great deal of time with Chet, guiding him, advising him, trying to help and keep him under control. He's too old to be spanked, I'm sometimes sorry to say, and he needs a man to clamp down the lid on the pot firmly when it threatens to boil over. As for Bobby," he continued, motioning toward the boy who was playing a game of tag with several other children, "he shouldn't go through life without a father, especially since whatever lies ahead for all of us will undoubtedly not be easy. You're a wonderful mother, Emily, but Bobby needs two parents if he's to become a self-reliant man in the Oregon wilderness."

"You're—willing to accept responsibility for—for my children?" Emily's throat was so parched she found it difficult to speak.

"I accept it gladly," Ernie said. "I'm almost fifty years old, and I've done many things in my life. Now, before it's too late, I want a family of my own. Chet

53

and Bobby will be my sons and heirs, not my stepsons. Even if you refuse to marry me, I claim the privilege of keeping watch over them." His generosity left Emily speechless.

Ernie misunderstood her silence. "When people reach our age," he said gently, "the flames of love may not burn so brightly any more, but they still provide warmth for aging bones."

Emily turned to face him, and as she brushed away her tears, she was transformed. A light that matched that of the campfire glowed in her eyes. "Land sakes alive, Mr. Ernest von Thalman," she said. "The way you talk, a body would think we're both half-dead. I do believe you're in for a surprise! You'll be amazed at how big and bright a fire two middle-aged sticks of wood can make."

Only La-ena saw them rise from the boulder, their food forgotten, and walk hand in hand to the shadows beside Ernie's luxurious wagon, where they embraced.

White people were strange, La-ena reflected. She couldn't understand them. Lacking the natural dignity of Indians, they were sometimes remote and at other times as emotional as children.

Whip was no exception, La-ena thought. She wondered if she had been wrong to join him. After their long separation, she had thought he would be delighted to see her, but instead he seemed withdrawn, almost resentful of her presence.

Stalking Horse had warned her that Whip would never become her husband and spend the rest of his days with the Cherokee "He is our friend," her half-brother had explained. "He is more like us than any other man of his color. He knows our ways, and when he wishes, he becomes one of us. But his heart is still that of a white man. He would not be happy spending endless moons living in a tent of skins, hunting and fishing with our warriors. He does not pray to our spirits."

La-ena had rejected Stalking Horse's words. Even now she could not accept them. For two years she and Whip had slept together. She had been his woman, he had been her man. But now, in the company of his own people, he was changed. It disturbed La-ena when she saw him look at Cathy with veiled eyes. It bothered her even more when she read the hidden pain in Cathy's face.

What there might have been between them did not matter to La-ena. The thought that they might have been lovers did not disturb her. She had a prior claim on Whip, and she was determined to exercise it. She knew that his responsibilities were greater now than they had been when she lived with him in the mountains. Eventually she would reawaken his desire for her, and they would live as they had in years past. The gods of the sun and moon and stars would help her to reclaim him as her own. No matter how sorry she might feel for Cathy, Whip belonged to her and to no other woman.

III

Andrew Jackson sat in the warm, early autumn sun-light on the terrace of the Hermitage, his plantation outside Nashville, and looked out across the rolling Tennessee hills. He squinted slighty, but he knew every acre of his property so well that he didn't bother to wear his spectacles.

"Sam," he said to his guest, "I can give you some of our own home-distilled whiskey, a dram of New England rum, or a glass of brandywine that the minister of the French legation sent me. Name your poison."

His protégé, Sam Houston, a giant with a ravaged face, was renowned for his agressiveness. Yet he was neither brash nor assertive in the presence of his mentor. He spoke quietly. "They're all poison," he said. "I'll join you in a cup of tea."

Old Hickory laughed, thinking Sam Houston was joking. "The only reason I drink tea at this hour is because the doctors are limiting me to one glass of whiskey a day, before supper. And that damned niece of mine keeps the liquor cabinet locked until sundown. But that's no reason you can't have a real drink. She'll open the cabinet for you."

Sam Houston shook his head. "I mean it, General. Liquor has caused me enough grief over the years, and I haven't touched a drop in more than twelve months."

Secretly pleased, Jackson pulled a bell rope, then ordered tea from the servant who answered the summons.

Sam Houston, presently serving as the President of Texas, brushed the dust of the road from his boots. As always, after a visit to Washington City, he had come on a pilgrimage to the Hermitage, and he couldn't wait to discuss with America's most distinguished citizen the matters uppermost in his mind. "General," he asked eagerly, "how soon do you reckon the climate will be right for Texas's admission to the Union as a state?"

"Sam, you're still too impatient for your own good. Never dig a knife into a melon that isn't ripe. Immigrants are still pouring into the country—whole shiploads of them from the British Isles and Germany and the Austro-Hungarian empire. They're even starting to come from the Italian regions and Spain. Most of them are heading west, like so many of our own citizens, thanks to the Panic that poor old Van can't bring under control. After a spell, there will be so many Americans in Texas that admission to the Union will be a natural marriage. But don't rush it."

Houston, who had terrorized the armies of Mexico and forced his own Congress to jump when he cracked his whip, swallowed hard. "Yes, sir," he said meekly.

The servant arrived with a pot of tea, and Andrew Jackson insisted on pouring it himself, although his hand shook slightly.

"The United States and Texas," he said after the servant left the terrace, "take to each other as naturally as beef and gravy. Your people are already Americans, and in a few more years the clamor for a union will be so great on both sides that it will become irresistible. Santa Anna will be fit to be tied, of course, and I more or less expect we'll have a war with Mexico, but that can't be helped."

"I've already whipped the daylights out of Santa Anna once, at San Jacinto. I'll be glad to do it again," Houston said.

"That doesn't worry me. I'm just telling you not to be in too much of a rush, Sam. Not only must nature be allowed to run her course, but there's something that takes precedence over Texas."

Sam Houston was amazed. "There is?"

"Oregon," Andrew Jackson declared. "We're in a three-sided race with Great Britain and Russia for the Oregon country, and don't ever forget it. The British have set up a strong military garrison at the main Hudson's Bay Company trading post at Fort Vancouver, and they have several smaller posts as well. One of them is at Walla Walla, up north, from what Van has written me. And even though the Czar's claims are weaker, there are still a number of Russian villages and hamlets scattered around Oregon. So we've got to make up for lost time."

"Not at the expense of union with Texas, I hope."

"Nothing can stop the acquisition of Texas," Old Hickory said. "You couldn't stem that tide, and neither could I. It's Oregon that worries me."

"I thought our immigration plans for the Oregon country were pretty well set."

"They are, theoretically. John Jacob Astor, several other fur men, and a group of bankers have put up money—lots of it—to finance the sending of one wagon train after another out there. Before I left the White House, I signed a bill giving every Oregon settler a tract of six hundred acres of land, free of charge. Our first train is well on its way, and the last I heard, it's almost across the Great Plains and is about to head into the mountains in the Wyoming country. The prospects look good—on paper."

"Then what are your worries, General?"

"When you've been in government as long as you and I have, Sam, we're inclined to forget that people —groups of people—aren't carved figures we push around on chess boards. They're human beings. That wagon train of ours has run into plenty of trouble, and it's not out of it yet. The weather, Indians who don't like whites invading their hunting grounds, the British—even the Russians might start something."

"You're worrying needlessly, General. Whip Holt is a competent man, and he knows what he's doing."

"Yes, Whip is first-rate, and so is Colonel Lee Blake, who was my aide-de-camp for a year. If any men can lead that expedition safely to Oregon, those two can do it."

"They'll manage, General."

Andrew Jackson sighed. "It's hell to grow old. When somebody has lived as long and seen as much as I have, imagination runs wild. I keep thinking of all the things that could go wrong, and not only wreck our wagon train, but destroy our hopes of making the Oregon country part of the United States. Hell and damnation, Sam, if I'd been this pessimistic when I was younger, I wouldn't have accomplished anything? Pay no attention to my rambling. Everything will work out fine. It must!"

The wagon train traveled quickly when the journey was resumed. Instead of the ten miles each day, which up until now had been their average, Whip coaxed fifteen miles out of the company. Still following the North Platte River, the caravan moved steadily onto higher ground. The sight of majestic, white-capped mountains in the distance told the travelers they would soon be moving across "the top of the world," as the verbose Paul Thoman described the Rockies.

Now the night air had a chill to it. Early risers could see their breath in the air. The scent of the pines was clean and sweet, and the pioneers were startled by abrupt changes in the landscape. One day they rode through forests rich in cedars and junipers, pines and hickories. The next they made their way across bolder-strewn plateaus on which nothing grew except a few wildflowers.

The rapid approach of winter added a sense of urgency to the journey. The so-called nooning, a midday period when a halt was called so the horses and oxen could rest and graze, was shortened. The company's hunters traveled ahead of the main party, there being no time for hunting after a halt was called late in the day.

At Whip's suggestion, the hunters brought down more elk, deer, and moose than the company could eat. The extra meat was either pickled or dried, and volunteers carried barrels of it in their already-crowded wagons. Food would become even more precious after the snows came.

Because time was so important, Ernie von Thalman insisted that his marriage to Emily Harris take place after the regular overnight halt was made. "We are on the move seven days a week now, not even resting on Sundays," he said. "So the marriage of two people cannot be allowed to jeopardize the safety of all. Emily and I are not children, and we require no extravagant ceremony."

Nevertheless, the wedding aroused considerable excitement. Cathy van Ayl used enough precious flour to bake a large cake, and decorated it with wild berries that some of the children found. "I want no fuss," Emily told the women, but they paid no attention to her protests. Some of her friends made a gown for her from a bolt of silk that Cathy contributed from her own store of goods.

Jacob Levine and Arnold Mell saw to it that Reverend Cavendish remained sober on the day of the wedding. During the nooning, one or the other accompanied him wherever he went.

That evening the usual precautions were observed. The wagons were drawn into a circle while the wood and water were gathered. Buffalo quarters were roasted over a fire, with some of the men helping Cathy and her crew turn them from time to time, and the regular sentry outposts were established.

The weather cooperated. The Wyoming sky was filled with stars, some of them seeming almost close enough to touch. Many people dressed in their best clothes for the occasion. Some of the men even slicked down their hair, and a number of women used cosmetics.

Everyone, with the exception of the sentries, gathered near the main cooking fire. Reverend Cavendish solemnly took his place near the leaping flames, a Bible in one hand. Then Tilman Wade played a tune on his fiddle. No one cared that it was a popular song extolling the virtues of the Oregon country.

Ernie von Thalman resplendent in a broadcloth suit, a shirt with a white collar, and a string necktie, made his way through the crowd, which parted when he appeared. Walking beside him was his best man, Chet Harris, soon to be his stepson. As always, Ernie was smiling and cheerful, but Chet was overwhelmed by the solemnity of the occasion and looked very somber.

Sally MacNeill's happy sigh heralded the approach of the bride. Emily looked lovely in a dress of blue silk with white polka dots. In her hair she wore a sprig of wild white blossoms picked that evening, and she carried a bouquet of wildflowers that Danny had gathered for her. For the first time since anyone in the company had known her, she was wearing jewelry—silver hoop earrings that Hosea had forged from a coin.

Giving the bride away was her younger son, Bobby, whose arm she held. The boy acted as though he were the center of attention, beaming at everyone. He waved to his friends, and would have conversed with them had Ernie not caught his eye and discouraged him with a glance.

Emily halted when she reached the clergyman, and Ernie took his place beside her.

Between them, Cathy thought, they represented all that was good and solid in this expedition. With all her heart, she wished them a lifetime of happiness. Then she shifted her position slightly so she wouldn't see Whip and La-ena at the far side of the makeshift aisle.

"Dearly beloved," the Reverend Cavendish intoned, "we are gathered together here in the sight of God and in the face of this company, to join together this man and this woman in holy matrimony . . ."

Grace Drummond, the tallest and huskiest of the women, stifled a sob. As the ceremony proceeded, the only sound other than the clergyman's deep voice was the sighing of the wind through the mountain pines. At the appropriate moment Ernie placed his only ring, which bore his family seal and which he had worn on his little finger, on his bride's hand.

Some of the children began to cheer when the bridegroom kissed his bride, and Chet relaxed and grinned broadly. Everyone crowded around the couple to offer congratulations. Jacob Levine, with the help of Paul Thoman, opened two barrels of cider. There was just enough for each adult to have a small cup. It was just as well, since the drink was potent.

"May Emily and Ernie enjoy long, happy, and prosperous lives together," Lee Blake called out as he raised his cup. The cheers of the couple's friends echoed across a nearby canyon.

Then the cooks began to serve the evening meal. In addition to roasted buffalo meat, wild corn, and wild beets boiled with onions, the settlers were given their choice—since there wasn't enough of any one dish to serve everyone—of duck soup, trout taken from the river, or berries served with sugar. Emily insisted that everyone have a tiny taste of the wedding cake.

The children grew sleepy, and Eulalia Woodling took Bobby Harris off to his mother's old wagon to tuck him into bed. It was the last night he would spend there. The following day he and Chet would move into Ernie's far more magnificent wagon.

While the celebration was at its height, Emily and Ernie slipped away. They knew that the journey would be resumed on schedule the following morning. Winter weather would not wait for honeymooners. The steady climb to higher ground as the party penetrated into the heart of the Rocky Mountains would be difficult, a task that would strain animals and humans to the limits of their endurance.

Cathy sipped her coffee as she chatted with various people and pretended to a gaiety she was far from feeling. The wedding depressed her, and she was irritated by her reaction. She was still reacting like an adolescent to her disappointment over Whip. She supposed that, in the deeper recesses of her mind and heart, she had imagined herself going through an identical marriage ceremony with him.

Now she knew better, but her already tangled emotions were further complicated by her genuine liking for La-ena. The Indian girl was not only attractive, but was passionately loyal to Whip. She was simple and direct, and remarkably lacking in deviousness.

Occasionally Cathy had wondered whether she should fight for Whip, or at the very least ask him to explain the situation. While it was true that her pride stood in the way of making any gesture, she refrained from going to him for another, equally important reason. She had proved to herself that she was resilient, capable of overcoming the problems that widowhood had thrust on her. She knew that she could make her way in the world alone. Granted that she had wanted a life with Whip, but she didn't really need him or any other man. The journey across the face of North America had taught her self-reliance, and she felt confident in her ability to cope with almost any situation she might face.

But that was not true of La-ena, Cathy thought, even though the Indian girl was accustomed to the wilderness and probably could eke out an existence, even in these inhospitable mountains. La-ena was strong physically, but when she looked at Whip, her eyes never straying from him, she revealed her dependence on him. Whip constituted the core of La-ena's existence. Her need for him was overwhelming, and Cathy realized that, without him, La-ena would lose her reason for being. Even if she could take Whip away from the Indian girl, Cathy knew that her own sense of principle made such an idea unthinkable.

Someone was speaking to her. She forced herself out of her reverie and to the present. Lee was smiling at her. For the first time since he had joined the wagon train, he was wearing his army uniform of gold-trimmed blue, in honor of the bride and groom. He looked quite dashing.

"You're very pensive," he said.

"A wedding sometimes affects a woman that way," she replied. "At least that's what it does to me."

"Weddings bored me when I was younger," he said. "That was before I began to wonder about the advantages of marriage. I've never understood—until recently—why anyone would willingly give up freedom for a life of shared responsibility with another person."

"It's quite a wrench," Cathy said. "I was so young when I married that I was incapable of independent thought. I was just obeying my father. And now that I've learned enough to know that most people aren't what they seem, I'd hesitate for a very long time before making a commitment that would bind me for the rest of my life."

"My experience is even more limited," he replied. "From what I've read and observed, it's love that impels two people to get together. I'm beginning to see that one could well crave an active life of sharing experiences with someone else."

Was he speaking in the abstract or hinting that he had fallen in love? Cathy wondered. He was always friendly and pleasant, but he didn't often show his feelings, much less confide in outsiders. Perhaps he was interested in a girl back in the East. He was solid, dependable, and personable. A girl would be fortunate to get him as a husband.

"What counts most," he said, his eyes suddenly becoming opaque, "is that both partners feel the same way. One-sided love would be miserable."

"Oh, I couldn't stand that kind of marriage," Cathy said. "I'd prefer to stay single for the rest of my days."

"I can't imagine you remaining a widow," Lee said. "You have too much character, too much to offer. Mark my words, one of these days the right man will come along."

Perhaps that was true, but right now she didn't want to think about such things. She bid him good night, and she started toward her wagon. She saw Cindy and Eulalia sitting on the rear stoop of their wagon and slowed her pace, thinking she might join them for a few minutes of idle talk. But from their expressions she saw that they were engaged in an intense discussion, so she continued on her way.

Eulalia was overwrought. "You'll probably find this hard to believe, Cindy," she said, "but a lady who grows up on a plantation back home is reared for just one purpose—marriage. She learns how to charm a man, how to talk to him, how to prepare meals he's sure to like. She's taught to run a home, to supervise servants, and to dress in a manner that's pleasing and alluring."

"You learn how to keep your rosebud lips shut at the right time, too, I suppose, and never express an opinion that contradicts the lord and master," Cindy replied, grinning.

"Naturally!" Eulalia said earnestly. "I also learned to play the piano, recite little romantic verses in French, and do needlepoint. I practiced flirting with my father and Claiborne before I could walk, but everything stops with a flirtation. A young lady is expected to be a virgin when she marries. If she isn't, she's returned to her family in disgrace, and that's the end of her. She hides in back rooms of her family's mansion for the rest of her life."

"I certainly wouldn't qualify as a bride down your way," Cindy remarked dryly.

"Neither would I. Laugh at me if you like, but I was able to live with myself until the wedding tonight. Now, all at once, I feel just awful."

"I wouldn't laugh at you, honey," Cindy told her. But you have no cause to be upset."

"But you know that for all the time that I was a captive, before Whip rescued me from the Indians—you know those savages used me as a—a whore." Eulalia's fists were clenched. Her voice trembled as she continued. "Really a whore," she said, her face working. "It was the only way I could eat. I was given food only when I went to bed with those disgusting creatures."

"That's the usual reason a girl becomes a whore. Your situation wasn't as usual as you seem to think."

"But these men were savages!"

Cindy laughed harshly. "Most men become savages when they're paying a girl for her favors."

"But—but when you worked in the bordello, you did it because you wanted to. I had no choice!" Eulalia bit her lower lip.

"You're wrong, honey. I did it because it was better than starving. I didn't know then that I might be suited for any other kind of life. It was that simple."

Eulalia's lavender eyes widened, and for a moment she was silent.

"I refuse to be shocked. No matter how many men took you to bed, I knew more, lots more," Cindy added.

"Remembering it doesn't drive you out of your mind?"

"I don't think about it," Cindy said. "The whore that I was got left behind in Louisville. A new person came on this trip."

Eulalia sighed. "I wish I could feel that way."

"You can. And you should." Cindy spoke forcefully, without raising her voice. "You're not pregnant or diseased?"

"No, thank God!"

"Then your body is none the worse for what you went through. I can see from here that you have all the normal parts in all the usual places. And you still have your figure. It's better than mine."

"I'll dispute that."

Cindy shrugged. "Not that it matters. I'm just trying to make you realize that you haven't been disfigured or injured physically in any way."

Eulalia said, thoughtfully, "I guess that I haven't."

"You didn't go mad, either, which might have happened to you. In all the time that we've been friends, I've found you to be quite sane."

"Well, yes." Eulalia's admission was grudging.

Cindy deliberately antagonized her. "Not one of those men owns your mind or your soul?"

"I should hope not!" Eulalia became indignant. "I'm no man's mistress! I'm my own!"

Cindy smiled broadly. "That's the point I'm trying to make. The only real harm you've suffered is in your mind, but that damage doesn't have to be permanent. Look on the bright side. You must understand men better than you did."

"It wasn't so long ago," Eulalia said, "that getting a man to pay court to me was the most important thing in my life. Now I can't stand the idea. Oh, I don't mind talking with people like Lee Blake or Tilman

Wade—they're gentlemen. But I wouldn't trust either of them alone with me in this wagon."

"You're not a South Carolina belle any more," Cindy told her. "You're a woman, a woman with a better understanding of herself, I hope."

"I do know myself better, and to tell you the truth, I'm not overly fond of me. I'm mean and selfish, and although I'm trying to change, I don't think I'm doing very well."

"You've learned you've got to rely on yourself to get along in the world, that's all. You've discovered that batting your eyelashes at some stupid man isn't the answer. He'll help and protect you only so far, for his own interests. And seeing that you brought up the subject, I'll tell you what I think, Eulalia Woodling. Your experience may have been a horrid nightmare, but it's made you into a real person and a grand woman."

"You're just trying to make me feel better."

"No," Cindy said. "Cathy likes you now, and so does Tonie Martin."

"I wouldn't blame her for hating me. I really made a fool of myself, before she got married, flirting with Bob Martin."

"Only because you didn't know any better. You've become one of the most popular people on this wagon train. Ask any woman—or any man, for that matter."

"Not the men, thank you very much!" Eulalia exclaimed. "I'll keep my distance from them."

"Amen to that," Cindy said.

Virginia Dobbs stood outside the guest cabin on the grounds of the old Spanish monastery located high in the Sierra Nevada Mountains of northern California. Shading her eyes from the glare of the sun, she gazed steadily toward the east. Somehow she had to get back to the United States, to Americans who spoke her own language. She was desperate. She saw the magnificent scenery only in terms of obstacles.

She and her companion, who called himself Garcia, had already traveled through the valleys to the west, where the towering giant sequoia trees, many of them hundreds of years old, formed a forest that was unique in all the world. Ginny didn't appreciate trees any more than she did the glistening, snow-capped peaks that formed a wall before her. Those mountains stood between her and the world she had so foolishly abandoned. Now she had to depend on Garcia to take her north of the Nevada desert, across the Rocky Mountains and the Great Plains and, ultimately, home.

Ginny shivered and rubbed her arms, thinking she should have donned two rather than just one of the men's shirts she had bought in the little town of Yerba Buena. Ginny wore only men's clothes these days, and she had cut her brown hair short. An attractive woman was asking for trouble around here, and Ginny already had enough problems. It didn't help her state of mind to know she had brought them all on herself.

The scent of cedar and pine was strong, and the early autumn air was crisp and clear, but Ginny wasn't impressed. She wouldn't have been, even if she could have guessed how this wild, remote region would be transformed in another decade. It was enough for her to know that Mexico had gained jurisdiction over California from the Spaniards sixteen years earlier. She loathed Spaniards and Mexicans alike and blamed them for her predicament.

She had come a long way from the orphanage in Trenton, New Jersey, where she had spent the first eighteen and a half years of her life. To think she had believed her existence there had been rough! She had eaten three meals each day, earned a reasonable sum as a seamstress, and had slept in a cubicle of her own, where she had been warm and safe. She couldn't possibly have imagined her present situation.

In a sense, she brooded, it was all the fault of Mrs. Macomber, the director of the orphanage. The old hen had insisted that "her girls" acquire a full, rounded education. She had insisted that Ginny learn Spanish, which had led her to respond to a magazine advertisement when she had been fifteen. She began corresponding with a ranch owner who had lived near Yerba Buena. After three years of writing letters, Ginny had happily accepted his invitation to come to California and marry him. It was an escape. Taking all the money she had saved from her sewing, she had booked a cabin on a packet ship on which she spent months, traveling down and around South America, and up to the California port of town of Yerba Buena, which, in ten years, would be known as San Francisco.

Then her world had been shattered. The old rancher had died, and his son and daughter-in-law, who had inherited his property, had wanted nothing to do with her. She had been forced to shift for herself.

Spitting into the pine needles at her feet, Ginny refused to dwell on her more recent past. She had been forced to earn a living in Yerba Buena. Even the hard life she had known at the orphanage hadn't prepared her for the clawing and fighting in that rowdy port, now crowded with American, British, and Russian trading ships and whalers. The only thing that mattered was that she had survived. Regardless of what she might face, she would live. Even Garcia couldn't lessen her determination.

What a bastard he was! Half American and half Spanish, he had been a sailor, a carpenter, a bartender in a San Diego tavern, and a cardsharp. He had always lived by his wits, and Ginny had discovered recently that he was a professional criminal. But he still was her only hope of salvation.

Soon after they had met on the Yerba Buena waterfront, Ginny had struck a bargain with Garcia. Despairing of obtaining passage back to the United States by ship because her funds were exhausted—and ships made that long voyage all too infrequently—she had brightened immediately when Garcia explained that he intended to make an overland journey into America, traveling by way of the Wyoming country and the Great Plains. Without hesitation she had offered to accompany him and agreed to sleep with him in return. He was handsome and could be charming when he wished, and she hadn't known then that he was a vicious animal. Not that she was afraid of him, of course. Not in the least!

Ginny Dobbs weighed only one hundred and ten pounds and resembled a boy in her man's attire, but she could take care of herself and was afraid of no one. Garcia had already learned to watch his step with her.

Ginny watched the swarthy, solidly built man as he made his way quickly up the hill toward her, from the main buildings of the monastery. They had spent two days as guests of the monks, posing as husband and wife. Ginny Dobbs loathed Garcia. She tolerated him only because he was a means to an end. His lovemaking made her flesh crawl. However, he knew the wilderness and was able to make his way across rugged, almost impassable country, so she accepted him temporarily.

She was deeply ashamed when she recalled how Garcia had abused the hospitality of their most recent hosts, a Spanish rancher and his family. Like everyone else in California, these kind and generous people lived an isolated existence. Their nearest neighbors were almost thirty miles away, and they had to depend on themselves to provide shelter, food, and clothing.

Garcia had been well aware of this. Nevertheless, he raided their larder before continuing on his way, taking meat, flour, and dried fruits. His theft was unnecessary, which made it even harder for Ginny to take. The rancher, following the usual California custom, gladly would have given the visitors any supplies they had needed. Then, as a crowning blow, Garcia had stolen several handfuls of old Spanish doubloons.

Ginny had wanted to leave Garcia then and there, but if she had done so, she would have had to go back to Yerba Buena, return to the waterfront, and sink even lower into the slime of a frontier-port existence, with virtually no hope of saving enough money to buy her passage back to the United States. Thus, she was forced to continue her travels with a man who had no ethics, no morals, and no sympathy for anyone.

When she had left the orphanage in Trenton, she had sworn she would never return. But it was the only home she had ever known, and now she found herself longing for it. That was absurd. In a few weeks she would be twenty-one, far too old for the orphanage. Regardless of where she ended up, she would have to make her own way in the world.

She had told herself, too, that never again would she work as a seamstress. Oh, she was clever enough with a needle, but sewing had been dull, and she had grown sick of it. Now she could almost see herself doing such work again. It was a pity that nowhere in California, not even in Yerba Buena or San Diego, the two principal towns, was the population large enough to allow a seamstress to earn a decent living.

First she had to get back to America, Ginny reminded herself, a feat that would require courage, stamina, and herculean effort. Then she would worry about earning a living.

Garcia was hurrying as he climbed the hill. As he approached, he called to her, "Why haven't you packed our belongings? The mules should be ready to move out right now."

"I thought I'd wait until after breakfast," Ginny replied. "We're not in that much of a rush."

"The hell you say. We're not staying for breakfast. We're getting out of here right now!"

There had to be a reason for the unexpected hurry, and Ginny looked at him carefully. Over his shoulder he carried a leather bag she had never before seen, and from the way he clutched it, she knew it contained something of value.

"What's in there?" she asked, and pointed.

"Mind your own damned business," he said roughly.

Ginny held her ground. "I want to know."

Garcia opened the drawstring and allowed Ginny to peer inside.

A magnificent gold chalice gleamed in the early morning light, and Ginny caught her breath. "You've stolen that cup from the monks' chapel!"

"Never mind how I got it. We're getting out of here right now."

Garcia tried to brush past her to pick up their saddlebags and other belongings, which sat on the ground just outside the guest cabin, but Ginny blocked his path. "It was bad enough when you stole all those things from that rancher. Not only have the monks been kind to us, but this cup must be worth a fortune."

"All the more reason for it to change hands." Again he tried to pass her.

"But this is no ordinary cup. They use it for communion wine. You can't take something that's sacred to them."

"I don't have to argue with you!"

"You can't take it, and that's final," Ginny said. "You've gone too far!"

Garcia caught hold of her wrist and started to twist it. Without thinking, Ginny quickly pulled out the knife that she carried in her belt and pressed the point against Garcia's chest. "Take your hand off me right now," Ginny said in a low voice that was filled with menace, "or I'll carve out your insides."

Garcia hesitated. The blade pressed harder. He knew this she-wolf wasn't bluffing. He might be unscrupulous, but she was even tougher, and when she was threatened, she could fight like a wild beast. Garcia released his hold on her wrist.

"You know better than to get rough with me," she said.

He remembered what had happened to a Russian sea captain in San Francisco who had tried to maul her. The Mexican authorities there had exonerated her, and, if the sea captain lived, they were intending to arrest him.

"Put away that knife," he said.

"You'll return that gold cup to the monks' chapel," Ginny told him. "Do it now."

"What if one of them sees me?"

"Oh, you'll find an excuse. You always do. By the

time you get back, I'll have the mules packed, and we'll leave."

"What about breakfast?"

"After this," Ginny said, "I couldn't face the monks at the breakfast table. We'll eat what's left of the meat pie they cooked for us last night. Get moving, Garcia, and none of your tricks, or I swear I'll tell the monks to lock you up until the next Mexican cavalry patrol passes through here, and then you'll be hanged!"

Garcia started down the hill again, hating her and vowing to even the score.

La-ena's position in the wagon train was difficult, and no one realized it more than she did. She was accepted to a limited extent by many people in the company, thanks in large part to the unfailing kindness of Cathy van Ayl. Each day La-ena rode with Cathy, then joined Whip at night, whenever his duties permitted. She was different from the other people in the train, however. Her knowledge of English was limited, and her acceptance was tempered by reservations.

It never occurred to her that there were some who objected to her on moral grounds. When she lived with Whip in the past, it had been natural and normal to both of them. She had no idea that there were people who avoided her simply because she and Whip were not married. All she knew was that there were women who were cool to her and men who were uneasy in her presence.

Whip was her lifeline. She traveled with the caravan only because he led these people. Had he not been there, she would have gone off to rejoin the Arapaho in one of their remote mountain strongholds. She and Stalking Horse understood each other, but there was little communication between them, even though they were related. It was not the custom for an Indian warrior and a woman to exchange confidences.

All La-ena knew was that she wanted to draw closer to these people. She was spending all of her time with them and would remain with the train until Whip led it safely to Oregon. But it was hard for her. Conversations halted in her presence, and talk became stilted. Few people ever laughed with her, and she was rarely invited into wagons when people relaxed together in the evening.

Yet, she felt sorry for these men and women from an alien world who struggled so hard to make themselves at home in an environment she knew and loved. There were food, shelter, and clothing here for those who knew how to adapt, and she thought it odd that few of them seemed to enjoy the mountains, her mountains. Their faces were lined and pinched, and at night they huddled around their fires and then withdrew into their wagons, where they burrowed deep into blankets. They didn't seem to share the exhilaration she felt when she looked out at the snow-capped peaks in the distance.

Perhaps these strangers would like her better if she proved to them that their welfare was of concern to her. Perhaps they were more like her own people than she realized.

One evening La-ena waited for Whip while a dozen people came to him with various problems and complaints. She stood in the shadows until, finally, he had satisfied the last of them. Then she beckoned. Usually she made herself subservient to Whip, so he was surprised by her gesture, but he went to her at once.

She walked out of the circle of wagons into the open. He followed, realizing she had something on her mind. There were matters she would not discuss within earshot of these people, even though she spoke to him in her own tongue, which only Stalking Horse and the scouts understood.

"It is the plan of Whip," she said, "to take these carts to the Wind River Mountains and make a camp there for the winter."

He nodded, and when he replied, his voice was troubled. "You know the valley there, La-ena. It's a safe place, with good hunting. But I'm not sure we can go that far before winter sets in. I'm afraid we might have to stop this side of the South Pass."

"You must stop," La-ena replied. "The carts crawl only a short distance each day. You saw the coat on the lynx that Mack Dougall shot yesterday. It was a full coat of heavy fur. You saw the hide of the elk that you shot two evenings ago. It is a tough hide. The elk was ready for the winter."

He sighed. "I know. When I see the frost on the ground in the mornings, I know that snow can start at any time. But I don't know of any snug place that's closer."

"There is such a place, but Whip has forgotten it," La-ena said, tempering her words with a smile. "Four summers ago Whip caught a large fish in the waters of a lake, and La-ena baked it over the coals of our fire."

He stared hard at her for a moment, then snapped his fingers. "You're right! Little Valley, the place that Kit Carson discovered about ten years ago!"

"That is the place."

Whip thought for a time. "We'll be crowded, trying to squeeze that many people into the valley. But it does have everything we need—plenty of wood, water, fish—fair enough hunting, provided game stay in the area. And there's just enough space—maybe—to build cabins and shelters for the animals."

"There will be enough game," La-ena said. "The spirits will know the place is right, so they will see that mouths are filled."

It was her nature to be optimistic, Whip thought, but he knew better. Hunting parties would have to go out as soon as camp was made, and only if they enjoyed exceptionally good fortune would food supplies last through the winter. Little Valley was too narrow and cramped an area for elk, deer, and moose to stay in the vicinity when snow was thick on the ground, particularly when people were living there.

All at once Whip sensed someone lurking nearby. He quickly grasped his left ear lobe, a signal he and La-ena long had used to warn of possible danger. The girl froze, standing still as she, too, peered off into the gloom.

Whip cocked his rifle, but not wanting to give the intruder any warning, he refrained from raising the weapon.

He caught a glimpse of a lone Indian warrior in a feathered headdress silently heading toward the woods, but he couldn't determine the color of the brave's war-paint.

It was wiser, Whip decided, to let the man escape. It was inevitable that the wagon train would draw the attention of curious warriors, most of whom meant no harm. If he shot the man, he might invite reprisals from the brave's tribe. It was better not to harm him. On the other hand, if he was a scout for a party bent on making mischief, Whip had been alerted. The sentries assigned to night duty would be doubled.

As soon as the brave vanished, Whip and La-ena returned to the circle. Ernie and Lee were notified, and extra men were assigned to keep watch through the night, a practice that would be followed for at least a week or two.

Whip would have felt less complacent had he known that the warrior he had seen was White Eagle, the son of the late sachem of the Blackfoot. White Eagle had followed the train doggedly, ever since his father had been killed. Unable to understand the white men's language, he felt certain that the spirits of his ancestors were guiding him. The leader of the wagon and the girl had been talking in the tongue of the Arapaho, which he knew fairly well. He had learned where they planned to spend the winter.

Now he would no longer be obliged to follow their tracks for day after weary day. Instead, he would go directly to Little Valley, where he would find himself a winter lair in one of the many caves in the nearby mountains. He would do his own hunting and store his food supplies before they arrived, and then he would remain in hiding, awaiting the right moment to take his vengeance. When White Eagle returned to the Blackfoot, his belt heavy with the scalps of his foes, the elders would change their minds and elect him to the post he deserved, that of his father's successor.

Whip completed the preparations for increasing the sentry detail, then stretched out on the ground not far from the banked fire. La-ena silently joined him, as she did every night, and snuggled close to him for warmth. Holding her but not speaking, Whip was tense. He envied the deep, even breathing that told him she had dropped off to sleep.

This, he knew, would be another of the many nights that he had remained awake since she had joined him unexpectedly on the trail. Now the situation was becoming even more complex. He could understand how his dilemma had come about, but he had no idea how to solve it.

Whip had been in Tennessee and had worked as a scout for Andrew Jackson while still in his teens. Then, when the frontier moved westward, he had become a mountain man, and for ten years he had known no other occupation.

For the first part of that time, women had not played an important role in his life. On his trips to the East with his furs, he had followed the example of his older colleagues and had visited the bordellos in St. Louis and other towns. But all that had changed—when he had met La-ena. She had fallen in love with him and had become his woman, living with him during the winters, then rejoining her own people during the hunting and trapping seasons.

They had enjoyed a natural, trusting relationship, with neither demanding more than the other freely gave. Not until he had bid her what he had assumed to be a final farewell and had joined Sam Brentwood in leading this wagon train had he realized that he had finally outgrown La-ena. He had assumed that she felt the same way.

Well, he had been wrong. He could face a mountain lion without flinching or stand up to a horde of Indians who wanted his scalp. But he had been too stunned to do anything when La-ena had shown up and taken a place beside him on the wagon train.

Once he would have welcomed her, he supposed, and wouldn't have minded having her accompany him. But that was before Cathy van Ayl had come into his life. His heart had pounded, and his blood had raced the very first time he set eyes on Cathy, in her Long Island farmhouse, the night before the wagon train had gotten under way. But she had been a married woman then.

During the first few weeks on the trail, Whip had tried not to think about Cathy. He had been relieved when he could leave the leadership of the train to Sam, and before rejoining the group at the end of last summer, he had convinced himself that Cathy meant nothing to him.

As soon as he had seen her again, however, he had known he was mistaken. Then, when he found out that she was a widow, he had assumed that, before the long trek to the Oregon country ended, they would get together. Unable to make fancy speeches, uneasy in the presence of women, he had preferred to let nature take its course.

La-ena's sudden reappearance had destroyed his hopes. He wanted to cringe every time he saw the scorn and contempt with which Cathy now regarded him. He would never be able to regain her respect, much less win her love.

A dozen times he had been on the verge of dismissing La-ena, but on each occasion he had hesitated, not wanting to hurt her or insult Stalking Horse, who was his trusted blood brother. Whip could be as tough and hard as any mountain man when a situation demanded it, but his own standards of honor and decency were too high to permit him to repay loyalty with cruelty. So, not knowing what else to do, he had allowed La-ena to accompany him.

He realized that some people were upset because he wasn't married to La-ena, but that didn't bother him. What really upset him was the knowledge that La-ena was concerned for the wagon train's welfare. Her suggestion of Little Valley as the best of all nearby places to spend the coming winter was a contribution of great importance. His sense of fairness required that everyone learn they were in her debt.

Now there was no way he could dismiss her and send her back to her people. La-ena had earned a place in the caravan and was welcome to stay as long as she pleased.

Knowing now that he loved Cathy, Whip also realized that he had lost her.

What lay ahead for him? The era of the mountain man was drawing to a close. In the back of his mind, there had lurked the half-formed notion of settling in the Oregon country—with Cathy as his wife. But he couldn't imagine spending the rest of his life with La-ena. She was a good companion and a useful helper in the wilderness, which she knew and loved. But she would be lost and miserable in civilization, and she would make him miserable, too. It would be difficult enough to acclimate himself to the demands of a society of farmers, ranchers, and fruit growers. It would be impossible, at the same time, to help a wife become accustomed to a society alien to her.

Whip couldn't allow himself to peer too hard into the future. At breakfast he would announce that, thanks to La-ena, the train would move immediately into winter quarters in the nearby Wyoming Rockies. He would have enough problems to keep him occupied through the winter, and when spring came, the train would be on the move again, with only one more chain of mountains to cross before reaching Oregon.

He would let the future work itself out. He didn't see any other choice.

IV

The Reverend Jason Lee was a persistent man. The founder of a tiny mission in Oregon, this determined Methodist missionary had traveled overland all the way to Washington, and in conferences with President Van Buren and other Administration officials, he had presented his case for the formal recognition of the area as a territory under the jurisdiction of the United States.

Now he was seeking the additional support of the Whig Party, and for that purpose was spending an evening visiting the leader of the Whigs, Senator Henry Clay of Kentucky, at his modest suite in a small Washington City inn. In his early sixties, Clay looked far younger than his visitor, who was his junior by a decade.

In fact, Henry Clay had been best described by his colleague and current political ally, John C. Calhoun of South Carolina, as "a phenomenon unlike any other in the history of our Republic." Aside from his white hair, Clay looked like a man in his thirties. He carried no fat on his lean body, and he was remarkably vigorous.

Few people could match Clay's distinguished record of public service. Twice he had been a candidate for the Presidency and was presently regarded as the man most able to defeat Van Buren in 1840. He had long represented Kentucky in the House, where he had become Speaker. He had been an efficient Secretary of State under President John Quincy Adams, and it was said that his constituents would keep him in the Senate as long as he wanted to stay there.

Nibbling on a square of sailor's hardtack, which he ate to keep slender, Clay seemed amused as he watched his visitor warm himself in front of the sitting room hearth, where a fire of oak logs was burning. Hickory was more plentiful, but Henry Clay wanted no reminders of his greatest political foe, Andrew Jackson.

"Reverend," he said, "for a man who made a voyage past two continents to reach Oregon and who then crossed the North America continent by land, you seem strangely susceptible to the vagaries of our Washington City weather."

"I've never known any like it," Jason Lee replied, rubbing his hands briskly. "One day I suffocate here, and the next I freeze. The air feels like lead. Especially," he added, never losing sight of his purpose, "after living in the glorious climate of Oregon."

Clay chuckled but made no comment.

"Senator," the clergyman said, "I know you're opposed to giving free land to immigrants, but I still want your support for the recognition of Oregon as an American territory."

"My position has been badly misunderstood," Clay told him. "The government is in desperate need of funds, and the treasury is almost empty. We're importing fewer goods, thanks to Van Buren's financial panic, and our import duties have declined, so I see the sale of public lands as a splendid device to raise money."

Not many people dared to debate Henry Clay, but Jason Lee was fearless. "I can't and won't argue the merits of the subject in such places as Missouri—even Texas, if it should be granted statehood in the near future. I know too little about those parts of the country. But folks have to travel three thousand miles from the East to Oregon, and they need a strong incentive to draw them that far. Clearly, six hundred acres of free land is a very powerful incentive. And what a magnificent land it is—the rivers and seas teem with fish, the soil is so fertile that anything will grow there, and sheep and cattle thrive on the pasture lands. It has the most beautiful forests on earth, with enough timber to support the entire United States. And there's ample water power, not to mention that only the Almighty in his wisdom knows what valuable minerals are to be found in the mountains!" He paused for breath.

"Reverend," Clay said, his amusement now plain in his eyes, "your rhetoric is superior to that of most senators—I congratulate you. As to the merits of free land for Oregon settlers, I'm of two minds."

"The alternative is simple and could be catastrophic. Either we settle Oregon, giving people enough reason to go there by ship or by wagon train, or the British will take possession of it. I met the people who are traveling out there on our first wagon train, Senator. Our paths crossed in the wilderness. And if I hadn't been zealous already in a cause second to none, those people would have inspired me. They're enduring terrible hardships, but they're determined to reach the Oregon country, settle there, and claim the whole area for the United States!"

"What makes you think the British will take such

decisive action?" The amusement faded from Clay's eyes.

"My mission is located fairly near Fort Vancouver, on the Columbia River. I've watched the whole character of the fort change. It used to be just a trading post for the Hudson's Bay Company. Now troops—British regulars at that—are coming down from Canada and being landed from transports. There were several hundred when I left, and the officers talked about increasing the garrison until it can dominate the entire Pacific coastal country, north of Mexican California and east of the mountain areas that the United States is claiming in Wyoming!"

"I had dealt frequently with the British when I was Secretary of State," Clay said, "and I found them to be eminently reasonable gentlemen."

Jason Lee was becoming incensed. "Gentlemen? Indeed they are, Senator. Reasonable? To be sure, as long as they get what they want. And I tell you they want Oregon. I know. I've lived there for years, and I've watched them moving very slowly and carefully, never stopping. Unless we exert our own jurisdiction, nothing will stop them from taking possession of the entire Oregon country. And we'll be obliged to fight another war with them in order to dislodge them."

Clay's political foes said he had a closed mind on most subjects, but that was an exaggeration. He was difficult to convince, particularly when he had a strong opinion, but he was a shrewd bargainer and a patriot. "I don't dispute what you've seen, Reverend. And I must admit that I don't completely trust Lord Palmerston, the British Foreign Secretary. He's very ambitious. Have you reported your findings to Winfield Scott?"

"Indeed I have, Senator! And General Scott would send several divisions of troops to Oregon at this very moment if he had the means to transport and supply them. That's why settlers are our best hope—our only hope!"

Henry Clay sighed. "I dislike visiting the White House, but it appears I'll have to have a chat with Van. I'm not doubting the veracity of anything you've said to me, Reverend, but the President has sources of information unavailable to other people, and I want to learn the full situation from Van Buren."

"You won't regret it, Senator." Jason Lee hadn't dared to hope for this much of a concession.

"If the White House corroborates what you've told me, and if the British threat to Oregon is as great as you've indicated, then we're compelled to pour settlers into the area—by wagon train and by ship. In that event, Reverend Lee, I give you my word that I shall change my position. What's more, I'm sure that not only will most of my colleagues shift with me and actively support a policy of free land for Oregon settlers, but they also will join with the present Democratic Administration in advocating the establishment of a formal Oregon Territory."

The wagon train moved steadily onto higher ground. Then, after filling every available container with water, the party left the North Platte River that they had been following and traveled into the foothills of the Rockies that lay just east of the river valley.

Most of the pioneers were comforted by the knowledge that they weren't quite as cut off from all civilization as they had thought. Fort William had been established as a trading post four years earlier, and could be reached in an emergency after several days of hard riding. Whip explained to only a few of his companions that he was reluctant to make their winter headquarters at the fort, partly because it was not an easy place to defend, and more important, because he was afraid some of the less respectable elements that gathered there might cause trouble.

He conducted the train across a trackless plateau, and for two days, before they came to an unnamed river, the members of the company and their animals had to subsist on the water they were carrying. Wood was scarce, too, and the nights were becoming colder. Still below the timberline, the pioneers were surprised to see vast fields of slate, strewn with boulders, where nothing grew.

With difficulty, they rode through a narrow, seven-mile-long pass, a task that took from daybreak to sundown, even without a pause. Off to the right stood a snow-covered mountain, its peak hidden in clouds, the lower slopes covered with timber. The unmarked trail twisted and turned, causing many people to lose their sense of direction.

They moved to still higher ground, then began to descend again. All at once, the now-familiar mountain on their right was joined by towering twin peaks, one directly ahead and another slightly to the left, all covered with snow. Canyon walls of stone seemed to surround the immediate area, and the members of the caravan were astonished to find themselves in a small valley crowded with pines and cedar, with open areas of waist-high prairie grass. At the heart of the valley was a lake of pure blue.

This was Little Valley, Whip said, and announced that it had been named by La-ena. None of the three mountains that towered over the valley and dominated it had ever been given names. The wagons were parked around the lake. Whip explained that the security precautions that had been in effect for months were not applicable here. Any large body of attackers could approach only from the direction from which the train itself had come, although it was possible for a few people to make their way down from the heights that stood to the north, south, and west.

The entire valley, Whip said, was about two and a half miles long and perhaps half as wide. There was game in the far reaches, but more was to be found higher in the mountains to the west, where he intended to lead a group of hunters the following day. The lake was filled with fish, and there were berries and edible roots still growing in the woods.

That night everyone ate emergency rations, consuming a similar meal before dawn. At daybreak, all went to work. While Whip led twenty of the best marksmen into the mountains on an urgently needed hunting expedition, most of the men stayed behind to chop and trim trees, fashioning them into logs that would be used to build cabins and barns.

The stronger women followed the men into the forest and, using makeshift sleds, worked in teams to drag the logs to the lake. It was back-breaking work, but they persevered, spurred by the knowledge they would be in serious trouble if winter snows arrived before the new village was completed. Meanwhile, the older boys went into the open fields and cut down high grass that would be stored and used as fodder for the animals. The older girls fished in the lake, using lines and poles fashioned for them by Stalking Horse before he went off for the day with the other hunters. Even the younger children were kept busy gathering berries; impressed with the importance of their task, they showed a remarkable sense of responsibility.

Jacob Levine brought down the first trophy of the hunt, a cow moose. But he barely had time to reload when a bull moose, upon seeing his mate killed, went berserk and charged. Levine fired at point-blank range but merely stunned the moose. Quickly he reloaded again. His second shot penetrated the bull moose's head as he was charging, but the animal's momentum was so great that it carried him forward until he collapsed at Levine's feet.

Other hunters brought down an elk, several deer, and a number of antelope. The carcasses were butchered, then piled on the crude sleds, or travoises, that Stalking Horse showed them how to make. The men led their mounts, hitched to the travoises, back to the lake. A fire already had been built there, and Cathy and her team of cooks immediately went to work slicing and smoking the meat, setting aside the better portion of it for future use. The hunters, Whip explained, would be required to go out every day in order for the wagon train to accumulate enough meat to provide the company with its basic food supply for the entire winter.

The initial efforts were encouraging, but Whip was far from satisfied. Everyone was given the same chores the next day and the next, and by the end of the third day, the people could see they had made substantial progress. More than twenty buildings were taking shape, among them a community house where they would cook and eat their meals, barns for the animals, and storage sheds for the fodder, meat, and fish. Ernie von Thalman decided that it would be unnecessary to construct a building suitable for the extra supplies; they would remain locked in the special wagon.

Individuals were left to make their own living arrangements with their friends. Far more work needed to be done before the cabins would be ready for occupancy, and the woodcutters, led by Ted Woods, continued to fell trees from dawn until sundown. They would continue to cut logs for many weeks, since there would be a continuing need for firewood after the cabins were completed.

Tilman Wade, with some of the older boys, climbed the nearest slope, and they spent several days rolling boulders and stones down to the base of the valley. There they broke up the larger rocks with sledgehammers and then began to build fireplaces for each of the cabins. As roofs were completed, they were covered with boiled pine tar in order to keep out snow.

Each day the hunters returned with more game. Ernie brought down a black bear that weighed more than three hundred pounds, Hosea killed a wild boar with his blowgun, and other hunters brought in deer and antelope. Meat was beginning to pile up in the storage sheds, but Whip was not satisfied and drove the hunters ceaselessly, demanding that they continue to exert maximum efforts.

La-ena led a large group of women into the forests and showed them how to find edible roots. She set an example for them, digging endlessly and filling entire sacks with roots. At one end of the valley, she enjoyed exceptional good luck, discovering a field laden with wild onions. With the help of several women, she carefully took all of them from the ground.

"Nobody works harder than the Indian girl," Emily von Thalman remarked one evening. "Ernie says her people don't live too far from here, so she could tell us all to go to blazes and just disappear for the winter. But she's more conscientious than any of us."

Cathy van Ayl was forced to agree with the assessment. She admired La-ena's perseverance and devotion to a company of strangers who meant nothing to her, but that didn't mean she liked the girl. This attitude was strictly unfair, and Cathy knew it. She could hardly blame La-ena for loving Whip, much less for her loyalty to him over the years. It was a weakness in her character, she decided, that would not allow her to put Whip out of her mind.

At the end of the train's first week at Little Valley, a light dusting of snow fell before dawn. Even though it vanished after the sun rose, it was a strong hint of what lay ahead. Everyone returned to work with even more energy. The hunters had to range farther afield, scaling the heights and crossing into the next, even smaller, valley in their search for game.

By the end of the second week, many of the cabins were almost completed. Crude fireplaces had been built, also, but the one in the community house was constructed with greater care. All available fodder had been gathered and stored, and the older boys and girls spent most of each day fishing. Cathy and her companions smoked the fish and meat. The storage sheds, it was discovered, were not large enough, and still more had to be built.

On the first two Sundays, the Reverend Cavendish held services in the partially completed community house. Everyone who wished to attend was excused from his duties. Several men explained to the clergyman that now was not the time for lengthy sermons; there would be ample time during the winter for the longer orations that he preferred.

The first building finished was the cabin that Bob and Tonie Martin would occupy. Since it would also serve as an infirmary, it was larger than any of the others. Partitions were built to set off a tiny reception room, a combination consulting and operating room, and a crude but serviceable hospital ward where slab-like bunks lined the walls.

The tempo of the work began to create problems.

People labored for twelve to sixteen hours each day, never resting, never taking a day off, and, as a result, became irritable. Grace Drummond and Lena Malcolm engaged in a shouting match. Their dispute made no sense, especially since Lena was usually one of the meeker and more gentle members of the group. Both of them apologized after they were separated by others.

Ted Woods and Claiborne Woodling were the next to erupt into a violent argument. Ted returned to the camp one evening after spending the entire day cutting trees. Still holding his ax, he exploded in anger when he saw Cindy and Claiborne sitting on a boulder, eating together.

Glowering, he stalked toward them, and addressed Cindy. "I don't like the way you flirt with this fellow every time my back is turned."

Claiborne immediately jumped to his feet, but Cindy placed a restraining hand on his arm. "I'll handle this," she said, and turned to the blacksmith. "Ted, you have no right to tell me what to do. It so happens I wasn't flirting, but if I have a mind to, I'll flirt with anybody I please."

Claiborne refused to be silenced. "Woods, if you know what's good for you, you'll mind your own damned business!"

Ted's eyes gleamed, and scarcely realizing what he was doing, he started to raise his ax. Claiborne saw the gesture and reached for the pistol he carried in his belt.

Tilman Wade was the first to reach the pair. Stepping quietly between them, he caught hold of Ted's wrist with one hand and pushed the muzzle of Claiborne's pistol aside with the other. "Here, now," he said, his tone almost conversational, "we have no need for private feuds."

Lee Blake came up behind Ted and quickly wrenched his ax from him. Ted looked sheepish, and the red-faced Claiborne stuck his pistol back into his belt and muttered under his breath.

Ernie von Thalman and Whip arrived, and Ernie said, "I know you've both been working hard, but so has everyone else. So there's no excuse for such conduct, and I won't tolerate it. Under the bylaws of this wagon train, I'm empowered, as president, to take any steps necessary to keep the peace, and that's what I intend to do. The next time there's trouble between you two, I'm going to confine you away from the company for a few weeks. And if that doesn't work, I'll throw you out and let you fend for yourselves."

Cindy was still indignant. "It was Ted's fault. He had no right to—"

"Enough." Usually Ernie was genial, but his voice had a rapierlike edge. "I forbid anyone to discuss this matter again. We're thousands of miles from civilization, settling into a Godforsaken wilderness for the winter, surrounded by Indian tribes that may be hostile to us. We have no hope of getting help from anyone except a few mountain men of dubious virtue. The lives of five hundred people are at stake, and I'll allow no one to upset the balance of this community."

Ted Woods was calm now. "It was my fault," he said. Retrieving his ax from Lee, he walked off to his wagon without a backward glance. Cindy rubbed her arms and shivered.

"I guess I could have been a little more tactful," Claiborne said. "Next time I'll know better."

Ernie was unyielding. "See to it that there is no next time."

Whip nodded. "If we start fighting among ourselves, that's the end of us," he said as the group dispersed.

Claiborne sat down and began to eat again. Eulalia, who had watched the incident in silence, took a clean bowl, filled it, picked up a slab of hot bread, then turned away.

"Where are you going?" Cindy asked her.

"Ted has worked too hard to go hungry, and you know he feels too ashamed of himself to come back to the fire," Eulalia replied. She walked into the shadows and made her way to the blacksmith's dilapidated wagon. Ted was sitting on the back stoop, his head in his hands, and didn't look up as the girl approached.

"Eat this before it gets cold," she said, her manner friendly but firm. He glanced at her, then looked away.

She placed the food on the stoop beside him, then folded her arms. "You know what we've been telling the children. We don't have enough food to waste any. The day may come before the winter ends when we'll be sorry we didn't eat every last bite."

"Why do you bother with me?" Ted muttered.

She picked up the bowl and bread, thrust them at him, and seated herself beside him, smoothing her buckskin skirt. "Eat your supper, and I'll tell you," she said.

The odors of the venison stew and fresh bread reminded him that he was ravenous, and he began to eat.

"Claiborne is my brother, so I know his temper. And Cindy is my friend. You were wrong to strike out at her, but you're a person, too, so I want to have a little talk with you."

"I know what you're going to say," Ted replied between mouthfuls, "but it won't do any good. Something comes over me, and I can't control myself any more. I don't know what it is."

Eulalia was surprised at herself. Not very long ago, nothing could have made her acknowledge the existence of a common blacksmith, much less a convicted murderer. But she felt sorry for him and wanted to help him.

"You're in love with Cindy—or think you are—so it amounts to the same thing." He shook his head. "Don't deny it, Ted, not to me. I've seen you looking at her."

"For all the good it does me, Miss Eulalia."

"Just Eulalia. Never mind the formality. Cindy isn't ready for love, Ted. Not your love or anybody else's. I won't even try to predict how long it will be before she's receptive to the idea of love, but you're making dead sure she won't fall in love with you."

"I am?"

"Of course. You're trying to grab hold of her this way." Eulalia's delicate hand formed a fist. "But you're going to get her only one way. This way." She opened her hand and extended her fingers. "Do you see what I mean?"

The blacksmith shook his head.

"Suppose you tried to kiss me right now—"

"But I wouldn't!"

"Just suppose. Say that you caught hold of me and tried to haul me toward you. What do you think I'd do?"

He pondered the question. "Slap me in the face, maybe, or kick me where it would do the most good."

"Exactly. But suppose you treated me nicely, the way a lady should be treated. Suppose you were kind and thoughtful and considerate. If you behaved that way, you wouldn't have to grab hold of me, would you? I'd come to you of my own accord, and you can bet I'd find a way to let you know that I wanted to be kissed."

Ted finished his meal and wiped his mouth on the back of his sleeve. "What you're trying to tell me, Miss

—I mean, Eulalia—is that I'm going about things all wrong with Cindy. By being so damn jealous of every move she makes, I'm just driving her away from me instead of getting her to move closer to me."

"That's what you're doing, Ted," she replied solemnly, pleased that he finally grasped the point. "I don't know whether my brother is becoming your rival—I don't discuss such things with him. But he knows how to flatter and please a girl, I can tell you that much. And if you don't want to lose Cindy, you'll mend your manners in a hurry!"

"Do you think I'd have a chance with her?"

"As good as any. You're a big, fine-looking man. Everybody knows, from the way you've protected Danny and looked after him, that you're a kind person. Nobody works harder than you or gets more done. And people depend on you when a horse loses a shoe or a wheel rim breaks. You're valuable to all of us."

"I was feeling like dirt, but you've really made me feel better. Much obliged to you, ma'am." Ted turned slowly and for the first time looked hard at Eulalia. "Why are you being so nice to me?"

"Why shouldn't I?" His sincerity embarrassed Eulalia. "Either we'll all reach Oregon or we'll all die together along the way. I'll grant you I didn't want to join this train in the first place—my father gave me no choice—but I'm here now, and I want to go the rest of the way. We don't have any alternative, any of us, so we've got to band together!"

An even greater uproar occurred the next night. Just as people were lining up for their supper, a party of four Indians, all mounted, rode up to the lake. Three were warriors whose paint identified them as Jicarilla

Apache, one of the most widespread and powerful nations of the West, but it was the fourth Indian who was the center of attention.

Mounted on a spirited mare and riding bareback was a young woman who appeared to be in her late teens. Her dark skin, coal-black hair, and beaded doeskin dress identified her as an Indian, but her features were strangely Caucasian. She was less than five feet tall and weighed no more than one hundred pounds, but her manner was remarkably self-assured.

Glancing at the people who crowded around her and her companions, she quickly identified Whip as the leader of the party and spoke directly to him. To everyone's astonishment, she spoke British-accented English. "I hope we are welcome. We saw the smoke of your fires, and they led my cousins and me to you. I knew you would be in this valley."

Even Whip was taken aback. "Of course you're welcome. Join us for supper and stay as long as you please."

"I am Dolores," she said, dismounting gracefully. "I have waited a long time for all of you."

No one stared harder at her than Hosea, who was no more than two inches taller than Dolores. She seemed unaware of his existence and continued to direct her attention toward Whip and Ernie von Thalman, who came up beside the guide. "My story is long," she said. "If you will listen, I will tell it to you."

Hosea, springing into action, brought her a bowl of food, and La-ena saw to it that the silent warriors also were served. People clustered around Dolores, and even those who couldn't come close nevertheless could hear her high voice.

"My father, like my cousins," Dolores said, "was a warrior of the Jicarilla Apache. My mother was Spanish. They met and were married at a mission in California, where he went to sell furs. The next year—I don't know how it came about—the British offered him work at Fort Vancouver in the Oregon country, where you are going. My mother was carrying me, and they didn't want to be separated, so she went with him. She died the day after I was born."

Some of the things she said raised questions in many minds, but no one spoke.

"For twelve years I stayed at Fort Vancouver during the winters. That is where I learned your language. Every spring my father came for me and took me to the land of the Jicarilla Apache. Every autumn he returned me to Fort Vancouver. Then, when I was twelve, he came no more. He died of the smallpox plague."

Whip remembered the plague, which had struck five years earlier. La-ena recalled it vividly, too, and nodded.

"For two years I lived all of the time at Fort Vancouver, but I was not happy there. So I came alone through the mountains and joined the Apache. Last year I realized their ways were not my ways, either. I knew my place was with you."

There was a stir, but no one spoke.

Ernie broke the silence. "A year ago," he said, "the wagon train stopped at Fort Madison, on the eastern end of the Great Plains. A number of Indians visited there. Are you telling us that one of them brought word to the land of the Apache that we were on our way to Oregon?"

Dolores shook her head, and there was a gleam of humor in her eyes. "I met no one who spoke to me of this expedition," she said.

Cathy van Ayl could keep quiet no longer. "Then how did you know about us?"

Dolores looked at her, hesitated, and then turned to La-ena. She spoke to her in an Indian tongue. Rarely had anyone seen La-ena lose her poise, but now she gasped and became uneasy. "Dolores," she said, "is medicine woman."

It was obvious that the explanation satisfied no one. Again Dolores spoke to La-ena.

Whip, however, seemed convinced she told the truth. "She has second sight," he declared.

Some people laughed, and most were skeptical. Many shared Lee Blake's opinion that the half-breed was joking. Someone must have brought word to the Apache that an American wagon train was crossing the continent en route to Oregon.

"I have visions only when it helps others," Dolores said. "The spirits told me this expedition was traveling to the land I love but had to leave because I do not like the English. Always they made me feel I was a stranger to them. But my visions said I would find my true home with you because I can help you. If you will allow me to stay with you, my cousins will go back to their village in the mountains tomorrow."

Regardless of whether or not she was telling the truth, Whip realized that they needed time to discuss and explore her offer further. Accordingly, he announced, "Supper will be burned to a crisp if you don't get your food, folks. We have all evening to talk."

The crowd reluctantly dispersed.

Hosea snatched Dolores's untouched bowl, took it back to the fire, and brought her another. She noticed him for the first time and smiled. The former slave stood transfixed until Whip and Ernie led Dolores to a table built of wooden planks. Then he stood nearby, silently eating his own meal while he continued to watch her.

Emily von Thalman joined her husband. "You've

spent all your life in Oregon," she said to Dolores. "Is it as wonderful there as we've heard it is?"

"I know only the Oregon country and the mountains of Wyoming, so it is not easy for me to say," Dolores replied. "The mountains are as high, perhaps higher than in Wyoming, but there are fewer of them. Only in the high mountains are there snow and ice, never in the valleys. The Snake River is the little brother of the Columbia, which is much larger and has many more fish. There is no taste that compares with that of the salmon from those waters—or the tuna in the Pacific."

"Is it true that any kind of crop will grow there?" Emily persisted.

The girl nodded. "Drop seeds into the ground, and soon they come to life. Even the English soldiers keep gardens of vegetables and fruit trees. No one is ever hungry in Oregon."

Ernie cleared his throat slightly; there was much more he wanted to learn. "You said you didn't like the English."

Dolores became bitter. "I am half-Indian, so they looked down their noses at me. The English send only men to Oregon. There are no women among them. They use Indian women. When I was no longer a little girl and became a woman, they wished to make me a concubine. I would not do this, so I left them. The people here are different, and there are many women. The English send only soldiers, but you will make your homes in Oregon. That is why I was sent to join you."

A few others joined the group around Dolores, and she willingly answered their questions. Distances in Oregon were vast, and most of the land was unoccupied. Most of the Indian tribes were small and almost without exception kept the peace, largely because they

103

enjoyed bountiful supplies of food and ample living accommodations. They had no need to fight for territory—there was more than enough space for everyone. The only Americans in Oregon lived at a small mission established by the Reverend Jason Lee. The British seldom ventured far from Fort Vancouver or Fort Walla Walla, where hunters, trappers, and other traders brought them furs. There were a few tiny villages on the coast that had been established by Russians, who appeared to have been abandoned by their country. But living conditions were so pleasant that none of them wanted to return to Russia, although several warships had sailed down the coast from Alaska to pick up any colonists who wanted to leave.

Suddenly Dolores broke off in the middle of her recital. Her pretty face became contorted, and she shuddered violently, then became rigid.

Emily was alarmed. "What's wrong—are you ill?"

At a signal from Whip, Ernie caught hold of his wife's hand and silenced her. Dolores continued to shake. She closed her eyes for a moment, and when she opened them again, they were glazed and staring. Sally hastened to fetch Dr. Martin.

Gradually Dolores stopped moving. For a moment she sat, immobile. Then she opened her mouth and spoke in a deep, rasping voice that in no way resembled her own. Her words were those of an Indian tongue.

"She says," Whip interpreted, "that in two days and two nights from the present, heavy snow will fall on Little Valley. Her visions are warning us of what is to come."

All at once Dolores pitched forward and collapsed onto the table. Dr. Martin had arrived in time to see her crumple. He took her pulse, his expression indicating that he regarded it as normal, and then reached into his medicine bag for a flask of brandywine. Someone handed him a cup, and he poured a small quantity into it.

Dolores stirred. The physician held the cup to her lips, and she took a small sip, then sat upright and smiled. "I hope I didn't frighten anyone," she said in her normal voice. "Sometimes my visions take me out of myself."

Although she didn't explain her remark, no one dared to question her. Sally volunteered to take the newcomer into her wagon, and the offer was promptly accepted.

A short time later the leaders of the train gathered informally in the community house, which was now almost completed. Lee Blake, always a pragmatist, spoke first. "Speaking strictly for myself, I think that girl put on a great act. I don't believe she sees visions or can prophesy the future. And I can't help wondering whether she's a party to some kind of a hoax that's intended to gull us."

"I must agree," Ernie said. "Except that I think she's harmless. She may even be convinced in her own mind that she communicates with spirits."

Whip shook his head. "Don't be too quick to judge Dolores. Indian ways aren't our ways."

Lee grinned. "What does that mean?"

"Indians are much closer to nature than we are. And from the time they're babies, they're taught to watch for all kinds of signs from their gods, from their ancestors, and from all kinds of spirits. I've known medicine men of several different nations. Some of them have powers that nobody has ever been able to explain. I felt the way both of you do, until I came to the mountains. But some of the things I've seen medicine men do have made a believer of me. And don't forget that Dolores is a medicine woman. She told us that right off."

The entire group turned to Bob Martin for an opinion. The physician looked into the fire. "I've seen people recover from supposedly incurable illnesses, and I can't tell you why they got better," he said. "Personally, I neither believe nor disbelieve in second sight. I can't demonstrate scientifically that there is such a phenomenon, but I'm willing to accept a demonstration of it, even if science can't figure out the principles. Our young lady put herself out on a limb tonight. We'll have a better idea of her powers if it starts to snow in forty-eight hours. By the way, I checked the time and, according to Dolores's prediction, the snow should start about seven o'clock. So we'll see."

"In the meantime," Whip said, "we've got to decide whether we want to admit her to the company. She's invited herself, and we've got to give her an answer."

"The warriors who came with her will be leaving tomorrow," Lee said, "and although I think she spouts nonsense, I don't see what harm she could do us."

"The Jicarilla Apache won't bother us here," Whip said. "They know that whites carry firearms stronger than their bows and arrows, and they have too much sense to attack a fortified place. They might take a swipe at us on the trail, of course, just to see if they can't separate us from some of our belongings, but that's another matter."

"I vote to allow Dolores to stay with us," Ernie said. "If she turns out to be a troublemaker, we can always ask her to leave."

"If I'm any judge of Indians," Whip said, "she'll be an asset, not a liability. I cast my vote with Ernie."

"Under the circumstances, so do I," Lee said.

Bob Martin laughed. "I can hardly wait for the next forty-eight hours to pass!"

Even the most skeptical members of the company went to work with renewed vigor the following morning. Dolores might well be a charlatan, they reasoned, but if winter was really at hand, there was much that still had to be done to make the camp ready for the harshest and cruelest of mountain seasons. Ever since the caravan had set out from Long Island, more than a year and a half ago, the travelers had been dreading the winter they would be obliged to spend in the Rocky Mountains. That time was now at hand, and their mettle would be tested.

Many people labored without pause all day, taking cold meat with them for a small meal at noon. The barns were finished, but some of the dwellings weren't quite ready for occupancy. After they were completed, belongings would have to be moved from the wagons into the cabins, and then the wagons would be stripped of their canvas and ribs so they could better withstand the rigors of the months ahead.

Dolores acted as if her acceptance were permanent. She suggested that she visit the heights south of the valley to search for various herbs that she said would prove useful if people became ill. Dr. Martin strongly approved, knowing that many native remedies were superior to those developed by science. But Hosea objected. "You not go up to mountains alone," he said.

Dolores raised an eyebrow. "I can't imagine why not," she said. "I've crossed two mountain chains by myself, and I've spent weeks at a time alone on the heights."

"Mountain lions and lynx begin to get very hungry now," Hosea replied. "Rattlesnakes getting last days of sun on rocks before snow makes cold and wet. Maybe bad men up there, too, waiting to kill people of wagon train."

"Well," she said, "I'm not afraid. I do need more herbs, several kinds of them, and nothing is going to stop me from gathering them."

"Not try to stop you," he replied, smiling, "Hosea go with you."

Dolores was flattered, and accepted his offer of protection. But she had to laugh when she saw the small wooden clubs he carried as weapons, as well as his blowgun and quiver of tiny darts. In one hand he held an enormous shield made of several layers of rawhide. It was so large, in fact, that Dolores would have been completely hidden if she had stood behind it.

Hosea allowed the girl to precede him as she walked briskly. Obviously at home in the wilderness, she made her way through the woods to the south, then started up the steep slope. After an hour or so, they came to a field of shale and loose stones, but Dolores's footing was as firm as Hosea's, and she continued to climb steadily, neither pausing nor losing her footing.

When he had first seen her, Hosea had been struck by Dolores's beauty. Now he admired her for her abilities, too. Had he been at home in his African jungles, he might well have been given a woman such as Dolores as a wife. However, here he would have to prove to her that he would be a worthy mate.

There was one thing of which Hosea was sure. Ultimately Dolores would be his. From the moment she had appeared, he had known that the earth, sun, and water gods to whom he prayed had taken pity on him. Not until then had he realized how lonely he had been, since being abducted by Arab traders and sent across the sea on a slave ship to the slave pens of a

Georgia plantation. The overseer there had whipped him, and the bigger slaves had mocked him because of his size. He had escaped and made his way north. After smuggling himself, with the help of Danny and Chet, into the wagon train, he had won the respect and admiration of the entire company. No one ever mocked him now. He was free, able to live his life as he pleased.

Certainly he had many friends in the caravan. He and Stalking Horse enjoyed many adventures together, and Ted Woods was his good friend, as were Cathy van Ayl and Cindy, who sometimes saved tidbits for him like eyes from the killed animals that no one else would eat. People didn't look down on him because his skin was a different color, any more than they looked down on Stalking Horse or La-ena. But Hosea himself had remained conscious of the difference and had felt that it set him apart. Now there was another, a woman who was set apart. Dolores wasn't black, but her skin was dark, she was small, and Hosea already felt drawn to her. Perhaps that was why her laughter rankled.

Hosea realized that Dolores was no ordinary mortal. One of his uncles was a witch doctor, a man endowed with strange and terrible powers. Even Hosea's father, the chief of the tribe, had paid homage to him. No one in his right mind ever incurred the wrath of a witch doctor. Hosea had gleaned from Stalking Horse that the medicine men of American Indian nations were in similar accord with the forces of nature. And Dolores was a medicine woman. He would have to be careful not to annoy or anger her. Hosea knew that Dolores's powers were real, and he respected them more than anyone or anything on earth.

Yet, in spite of her strengths, Dolores was a woman.

If the gods had intended to make her one of them, she would live with them, but instead, she inhabited the earth. So, as Hosea saw it, the gods willed that a mortal man would become her mate. He intended to be that man. But before he could even hope to win her, he had to teach her to respect him. The process might be long and difficult, but he had to begin at once. The sound of her laughter still echoed in his ears, infuriating him, spurring him, giving him courage.

They moved still higher until they were near the timberline, where the vegetation was increasingly sparse. A chilly wind blew down from the snow-capped peak that loomed ahead, but Dolores seemed impervious to the cold, unaware of the elements, so Hosea refused to shiver. At moments such as this, he wished he were back in the heat of Africa. But Dolores was here, so this was where he wanted to be.

Abruptly Dolores halted, then darted toward a crevice and plucked several small plants. Hosea moved closer, intending to join her. But Dolores, concentrating on what she was doing, waved him away. He was even more offended. He had merely wanted to help her, but if she was refusing his assistance, so be it; he would not offer again.

For the next hour or more, inching gradually up toward the timberline through a field of boulders and stones where plants grew only close to rocks, Dolores continued to pick her herbs. Apparently she knew what she sought, and she became oblivious to her surroundings and, it seemed, to the man who was keeping watch over her.

About ten yards away, in the opening between two rocks, Hosea sensed rather than saw a faint movement. A mature rattlesnake, its skin blending with the color of the rocks, was sleeping in the unexpectedly strong sunshine. It was at least five feet long, and as thick around as a man's wrist. Though it caused no immediate threat, it provided an opportunity for Hosea that he could not let go by. He approached Dolores, tapped her on the shoulder, and silently pointed.

Dolores recoiled instinctively when she saw the snake. Hosea averted his face so she wouldn't see his smile of grim satisfaction. She might be a medicine woman, but she was mortal. In his experience most women, in America as in his own land, were afraid of snakes.

Dolores looked ill. Not wanting to prolong her agony, Hosea drew one of his little clubs and quickly threw it with all of his might. It spun dizzily as it flew toward its target. Ordinarily Hosea would have stunned the rattler and then killed it with his knife, but he was showing off, so he threw it with all of his strength. The little club decapitated the snake, and its headless body writhed convulsively. Hosea ran forward and to his satisfaction found that the snake's poison sac was still intact. He detached it from the smashed head, then milked it, letting the poison dribble into a small container which he carried. Later he would dip more of his darts into the substance.

Picking up the body of the rattler, he returned to Dolores. "Tonight," he said, "Hosea make skin into belt for you."

She murmured her thanks, then hastily moved on to another part of the field of rocks. Hosea followed. Continuing to keep watch over her, he felt a sense of accomplishment. He had seen respect for him in her eyes and knew that never again would she laugh at him or his unusual weapons.

By the time they returned to the valley at sundown, others were ending their day's hard labors, too. Most people were so tired that there was relatively little talk at supper, but people were uneasy. They had not forgotten Dolores's prophecy, and believers and skeptics alike were anxious to get on with their work the next day.

No one needed urging the following morning. People continued to work at a whirlwind pace, and the hunters seemed to feel the need to make every shot count. Tilman Wade, who had joined the hunting party, brought down a huge buck elk. A number of antelope were found in an open field located in the adjoining valley. "It won't surprise me any if snow comes tonight, just like that girl said it would," Whip remarked to Ernie. "I can't smell it in the air, but wild animals seem to know, and those antelope were busy filling their bellies before the field gets covered."

At supper that night, tension was thick in the air. Some people laughed loudly and talked too much, while others brooded.

Soon after the last of the food was served, a few snowflakes began to fall. The clouds overhead became thicker, blackening the night sky, and within a short time heavy swirls of snow were falling, whipped by a strong wind.

The fortunate few whose cabins were completed went off to them without delay, while the rest retreated to their wagons. Dolores showed neither surprise nor pleasure as she accompanied Sally MacNeill to the younger girl's wagon. Obviously she had expected to be right.

The snow continued to fall all night. By morning more than six inches lay on the ground. There was a layer on the wagon tops, too, which had to be removed so water wouldn't drip through the canvas into the warmer interiors. Breakfast was prepared in the community hall, and Whip made an announcement. "Take your time eating this morning, folks. The storm is over, the sun is coming out, and we'll have warmer weather today—warm enough to melt the snow, which will make it easier for the tree cutters and the hunters."

He was right. By mid-morning the snow had vanished, and the ground dried quickly in the clear, warm air. The work parties went off as usual, several hours late, delighted the snow was gone. They had won a respite from the winter, for however long it might last, and before winter returned to stay, there was a chance they would finish their work on the camp. At the very least they had been warned that the most difficult of seasons was fast approaching.

Many people thanked Dolores for her prophecy, and she accepted their praise calmly. "I did nothing myself," she told them. "It was my visions that brought you word of what was to come."

Even the doubters looked at her with new eyes. They could not dispute the proof she had given them that she was indeed endowed with second sight.

Quietly, as though nothing out of the ordinary had happened, Dolores elected to accompany La-ena's party of women in their search for edible roots. Lee Blake, who was supervising the remaining work on the winter dwellings, watched Dolores as she departed. He was still stunned by what had happened, and his face mirrored his feelings. A smiling Bob Martin joined him. "I don't suppose you happened to notice the time the snow started to come down last night?"

Lee shook his head.

"I made a point of noting it. Dolores said it would

come in forty-eight hours, which would have made the time seven o'clock. If my watch is right, the fall actually began at seven-twenty. Regardless of what you or I might believe, that's a pretty accurate accident!"

V

Fort Vancouver, located at the head of deep-water navigation on the Columbia River, boasted the largest English-speaking population of any community west of the Continental Divide. About one hundred miles inland from the Pacific coast, it was, in fact, the only English-speaking center, except for the smaller Fort Walla Walla.

Its heart was the fort itself, a sprawling collection of buildings constructed of cedar logs and surrounded by a high picket fence. More than one thousand British troops were currently stationed there. Beyond the palisades, however, a town of several hundred had grown up since the fort had been established in 1825. No one knew the precise number of people living there—the population shifted constantly, due to the absence of Englishwomen.

The factors, or managers, of the Hudson's Bay Company—which had founded Fort Vancouver as a trading post—long had intended to allow wives to accompany their husbands to this distant outpost, but the influx of large numbers of the military had made it necessary to postpone the plan. In the meantime, a number of employees had taken Indian wives.

Most of the transients were mountain men, trappers, and fur traders. Some were Spaniards and Mexicans who had drifted north from California, a number were Americans, and they were joined by French Canadians and adventurous Englishmen. There were still a few Russians, too, men who had lingered since the time when the Czar had tried to lay claim to the area.

Thanks to the factors, who put business ahead of all else, there was a permanent cadre in the little town that had grown up outside the palisades of the fort itself. The community boasted a sawmill, a gristmill, and a brickyard. The tiny school, which Dolores had attended, was the only institution of learning in the entire Pacific Northwest.

The scenery was magnificent. Most of the region was covered with rolling hills, low but steep, and off to the east, rising out of still higher ground, was a handsome snow-covered peak that dominated its surroundings. Other peaks, also capped with snow, stood to the north.

The Hudson's Bay Company, had been wise, as always, in its choice of a site. Ocean-going merchant ships rode at anchor, flying the flags of Great Britain, the United States, Sweden, and Mexico. The first American steamboat to enter the Pacific, the USS *Beaver,* built in England, had visited the post four years earlier in 1834. She had arrived under sail; her engines and paddle wheels, which had been carried on deck, had been installed at Fort Vancouver.

John McLoughlin, the resident factor-in-charge, often remarked that ships were the lifeblood of the community. He was a crusty, opinionated, and hard-working Scotsman whose proudest boast, which happened to be true, was that he had never cheated a man in his life. He had deliberately located his offices on a hill overlooking the swift-flowing Columbia River. From this vantage point, he could indulge his greatest pleasure, counting the number of ships in port.

At the moment, McLoughlin was in a terrible mood —which was not unusual—and the clerk who had brought him a written message waited for the inevitable explosion. McLoughlin paced the length of his sparsely furnished office. With his perpetual suntan and his buckskins, he resembled a mountain man. An intermittent column of smoke belched from the foul-smelling pipe that he clenched habitually between his teeth. At last he halted, and the clerk braced himself.

"So," the factor said, picking up a sheet of paper from his desk and waving it vigorously, "Colonel Morrison wishes a meeting with me. Very well, let him come to see me. Phillips Morrison may command the troops here, but I still outrank him, as he bloody well knows! I haven't set foot inside that palisade in more than eighteen months, and I don't intend to go there now. Take back a message to Morrison for me Tell him that if he wants to see me he knows where to find me. And he'd better hurry because I want to check the cargo going aboard that clipper ship from Baltimore."

"Yes, sir." Glad to escape, the clerk sprinted back toward the fort.

McLoughlin began to pace again, muttering that the Royal Army was a bloody nuisance. Of course he charged the garrison a stiff rental for its quarters, and they paid him for everything from food to firewood. They therefore provided Hudson's Bay with a handsome annual profit. Nevertheless, the army thought it owned the place. It was McLoughlin's, and it was high time the thick-headed buggers knew it.

Another clerk came to the door. "Colonel Morrison is here, Mr. McLoughlin."

The factor glanced at his gold pocket watch, fishing it from a waistcoat pocket, and grinned sourly. That had been quick. The army must want something again.

Colonel Phillips Morrison came into the room and bowed slightly. He and McLoughlin saw each other daily, often meeting for dinner at night, but the officer, who was the son of a viscount, felt a deep-rooted contempt for this member of the merchant class, no matter how competent he might be.

McLoughlin returned the bow with a certain irony. He had no use for the dim-witted bluebloods London assigned as garrison commanders.

The formalities over, Morrison sank onto a chair, the spurs attached to his highly polished boots clinking. "Henry St. Clair arrived last night," he said, without preamble. "Naturally he reported directly to me."

McLoughlin's expression did not change. He relit his pipe, taking his time doing so. "Who the devil is Henry St. Clair?"

The Colonel sighed. "A secret agent working for the Foreign Office. He's probably the most brilliant agent in all of Her Majesty's realm. You and I have discussed him from time to time. Surely you remember, John."

McLoughlin's expression indicated that he thought even less of secret agents than he did of high-born officers. "What about him?"

"The poor chap has had a horrible time. He's made several superbly planned attempts to sabotage the American wagon train that's heading this way, but each time he's failed. The farmers and all the other clods in the train seem to be leading a charmed life."

McLoughlin's face was hidden for a moment behind a cloud of smoke.

"I'm sending St. Clair back to England for the rest he deserves. He'll sail on the sloop of war that leaves here in a few days, and I'm writing a letter to his superiors, which he will carry, heartily praising him for his efforts."

"Kind of you, I'm sure," McLoughlin said dryly.

"So that leaves you and me with a problem, John. We've got to prevent that wagon train from reaching this part of North America!"

"I give you the problem. It belongs exclusively to you, Phillips. I want no part of it."

"Every British subject in Oregon has a problem! Frankly, I'm worried. St. Clair had no chance to retrieve the rifles that his Indians threw away when their attack on the wagon train failed."

"I dare say the Crown can afford the loss of a few rifles."

"You don't understand." Morrison sighed deeply. "They were our newest, still packed in grease when they arrived here by frigate. They're British rifles, and the stupid Indians littered the field with them. St. Clair should have known better than to give powerful firearms to savages who have no idea how to use them."

The factor smiled broadly.

"It's no laughing matter. The Americans are certain to have appropriated the rifles, and undoubtedly are using them at this very moment."

"I've long admired the ingenuity of the American people." McLoughlin spoke with irony. "The members of this wagon train demonstrate that quality admirably.

119

They live off the land as they cross an inhospitable continent. They make good use of everything they find. And naturally, that includes new British rifles. If I had a final voice in this matter, I'd give them this country. They seem to want it enough to make sacrifices for it, which is more than our own people are doing!"

"But the Foreign Office is demanding that Great Britain claim jurisdiction over the entire Oregon country. Lord Palmerston feels very strongly that—"

"I'm told what Palmerston feels every time another contingent of your bloody troops lands here," McLoughlin growled. "To be perfectly candid with you, I don't give a hang what Palmerston feels. Thank God I draw my pay from Hudson's Bay, not from him."

"You're still a subject of the Queen, you know."

"I very much doubt if that wee slip of a girl fills her pretty head with thoughts of murdering and maiming a harmless band of Americans who have every right to settle in Oregon!"

The Colonel became tight-lipped. "You must be able to comprehend the obvious. They'll support the stand of that—that visionary vicar, Jason Lee. There are hundreds of them. They'll clamor for formal American recognition of Oregon as a part of the United States. The President will listen to them and so will the Congress."

"It seems to me that that would be a pleasant and peaceful solution—far better than hacking them to death." Morrison made a strangled noise. "Of course," the factor continued, "you could wait until the wagon train arrives here. Then you could order your artillery to bombard the poor people, and your infantry could bayonet the survivors. How does that strike you?"

"It's not a laughing matter, John."

"I'm not laughing," McLoughlin said.

"Once the Americans arrive, it will be too late for us to do anything. If we try to drive them out or intimidate them, Washington will send stiff notes of protest to London. Before you know it, we'll be involved in a new war with the United States, which is precisely what the Foreign Secretary is trying to avoid."

"In that case, Palmerston would be well advised to let nature run her course, just as the Columbia River flows where it pleases."

Morrison rose. Planting his feet wide apart, he scowled as he clasped his hands behind his back. "You shock me, John. You don't care! It doesn't matter to you whether or not the Union Jack flies over Oregon!"

McLoughlin went to his desk and slowly refilled his pipe. "This," he said, his Scottish burr becoming more pronounced, "is a rich, fertile land that's ripe for settlement. If the Americans come here, I'll welcome them, and I hope they'll be followed by more wagon trains than you and your staff can count. You seem to forget that I'm in business here. The farms, industries, orchards, and sheep ranches the Americans will start here will increase our trade enormously. And as long as the cash flows in, I don't care whose flag flies over Oregon. So, if you intend to find some way to halt them before they arrive here, Morrison, you'll have to do it without my help. Yes, I'll welcome them with open arms!"

Every morning Whip Holt studied the sky, and every morning he became gloomier. "The clouds stay thick now, even when the early morning fog clears away," he commented to Lee Blake. "Winter is on its way for sure, and when it hits, we'll need days and days to dig ourselves out. La-ena says it's going to be a cold, wet winter, and I'm afraid she's right."

Lee remained fairly complacent. "The frames of most of the cabins are done, with only some fireplaces still to be installed," he replied. "The animals are already snug in their barns, and most people have finished stripping their wagons. The storage sheds are done, too."

"What goes into them is what worries me most," Whip said. "We've got five hundred people to feed, and at the moment I estimate we've accumulated only enough meat to last us about a month. So we need more, much more."

Lee nodded. "The hunters haven't missed a day in the field, but game is definitely getting scarcer. We may have to start riding farther afield."

"When the passes fill with snow, we won't be riding anywhere," Whip declared.

Lee had come to know Whip well enough to realize he had some sort of scheme in mind that would solve the problem. "What do you suggest?"

"I'm not sure I'm making a suggestion," Whip said. "There are risks involved." He paused for a moment. "Yesterday, when we headed up to the plateau beyond the next valley, I wonder if you noticed anything unusual."

"Not particularly."

"Well, the scouts and I did. There's a fair-sized herd of buffalo grazing on that plateau, maybe as many as three hundred. Since grass is becoming less plentiful this time of year, the herd should still be there today."

Lee grinned. "It sounds good to me."

"Maybe, maybe not," Whip said. "There are steep rises on both sides of that plateau, far too steep for the buffalo to climb. If we cause a stampede, they have two choices. They can go forward and drop off the edge of a cliff—that's the good way. They'll fall about five hundred feet, so we won't have to shoot them. We'll station enough men with pack horses near the base of the canyon to butcher the carcasses and bring them back to camp. In that case, all of our problems will be solved."

"Surely they won't throw themelves off the edge of a cliff," Lee said.

Whip's smile was humorless. "It's plain you don't know buffalo. Their sense of smell is okay, but their eyesight is weak. Once they stampede, they'll go anywhere. I remember one time in the Nebraska country, I saw a herd plunge right smack into a prairie fire that burned some of them to death and saved us the trouble of having to cook the meat. But they kept right on stampeding, and the animals in the back stumbled over the bodies of those that had already been suffocated."

"All right, I'll accept that they might go over the edge of the cliff." The West, Lee thought, was teaching him many things he hadn't learned in the army. "What's the other alternative?"

"The buffalo might turn in the opposite direction and stampede straight at us," Whip said somberly. "Those stone walls on either side of the plateau are too steep for us to climb. So, if the buffalo charge us, every member of that hunting party will be trampled. It means most of us will die, maybe all of us."

"Can't you induce the buffalo to head toward the cliff?"

"We can try, that's all. But there's no guarantee as to what they'll do."

"I see." Lee jammed his hands into his pockets. "But what you're saying is that the risk must be taken?"

"It's either that or possible starvation before the winter ends," Whip said. "I'll get that party started to the base of the cliff right off, so they can be ready if we're lucky enough to move the buffalo in the right direction. It'll take my party a little longer to reach the plateau."

"Count me in on your party," Lee said quietly.

Whip frowned. "I don't need many, and I want men who know how to deal with buffalo—Arnold, Mack, and Stalking Horse, of course, plus Pierre le Rouge and young Paul Thoman, because he spent long enough in the mountains to get acquainted with the beasts. I won't need more than one or two others—Tilman Wade, because he's steady and won't fluster—"

"Neither will I," Lee interrupted. "I'm not the panicky sort."

"The reason I'm holding back, Lee, is because this train will need you more than ever if something happens to me."

"I'm going with you." Suddenly Lee was Lieutenant Colonel Blake, and he was firm. "Ernie can always take over, and there are plenty of others to help him. He might have to send to Fort Bridger for new guides, but I see no choice there, either."

Whip hesitated, then extended his hand. "Welcome to the craziest hunt you've ever seen."

Within a short time a large group left camp heading for the base of the canyon, with Claiborne Woodling in charge. He was warned not to allow anyone to wander near the section directly below the cliff since the bodies of the buffalo, if they stampeded in the right direction, would come hurtling down without warning.

Then Whip's small party started out, riding at a steady pace as they crossed the ridge at the end of the valley. They made their way through a narrow pass and, taking a shortcut, rode past a series of caves toward the plateau.

At the approach to the plateau, Whip halted, dismounted, and studied the ground. "The buffalo are still grazing here," he said.

The men were pleased, but no one spoke.

"Arnold," Whip said, "you, Mack, and Stalking Horse all know what to do. You, too, Pierre. What about you, Thoman?"

Paul grinned. "I saw this kind of hunt in Kansas, although I didn't participate in it. Have no fears; I'll give a good account of myself."

Whip turned to Tilman Wade and Lee. "You two pay close attention and do exactly as I say. Don't use your rifles until I open fire. There are only eight of us, and if hundreds of the beasts start charging, we'll be dead long before we can reload more than once or twice. And I don't care whether we kill any of the animals with our weapons. The purpose of the gunfire today is to scare them enough so that they'll run away from us. So we'll hold off until the last possible second."

"How do we go about frightening them?" Tilman asked.

"It's a special knack," Whip said. "Each of us will sneak up on a buffalo, always making sure we're moving against the wind so they don't smell us. Find yourselves a mature bull or cow, one that looks like a leader."

Lee laughed. "How in the world do you distinguish a leader from a follower?"

Whip was puzzled. "Well, I can't really explain it. You get a feel for it."

"I can give you one pretty good hint," Arnold Mell

said. "In my experience, most of the leaders are the cows, not the bulls. It's the opposite of what you'd expect. And never pick one that has a calf near her. The mothers are protective. Look for the middle-aged cows, the big ones that haven't started to get flabby."

In spite of the dangers ahead, Lee was amused. But he sobered when Whip spoke.

"What we plan to do is something the Great Plains Indians have been doing for hundreds of years. You pick your buffalo and then creep up to him—and don't make a damn sound. If one of us sneezes or coughs, we're all dead. Once you've got a buffalo, smack him on the rump as hard as you can with the butt of your rifle. Or else slash him on the hindquarters with your knife. But, most important, *always make sure the beast is standing with his head in the direction of the cliff.*"

Lee wondered what his West Point classmates would think of such instructions. The entire venture was mad.

"Don't penetrate too far into the herd, either," Whip continued. "The whole idea is to make those at our end start moving toward the ledge. If we do it right—I hope—the whole herd will start crowding in the direction of the ledge, and then the stampede will start. With any luck, they'll keep heading that way. If they turn back on us, we're goners."

"One more word," Arnold added. "We should try to time our initial blows as simultaneously as possible. When you see or hear somebody else in action, don't waste any time."

"When we open fire," Whip added, "the whole idea is to scare the beasts into moving away from us."

"Right." Arnold smiled grimly. "No matter how great the temptation, don't bring down a buffalo that's running toward the cliff. They're the ones that'll cause the stampede. If the buffalo decide they have a clear road in our direction, they'll turn in no time."

The whole maneuver, Lee decided, sounded like a hit-or-miss game, but he had faith in these men, who presumably knew what they were doing. After all, as Whip had said, the Plains tribes had used the same techniques for centuries. There had to be some logic behind them. Nevertheless, he was apprehensive, more nervous than he had ever been when going into battle. He could face men—he understood the human emotions that ran high in any battle—but buffalo were alien to him, and he did not feel comfortable with things he didn't understand.

"Stay away from hoofs, too," Pierre warned. "Buffalo have bad, tough feet."

The men tethered their horses in the pine woods and started forward. The buffalo should be directly ahead, in the open. Whip gestured, and the party spread out. Lee noted that Tilman Wade was on his right and Pierre on his left. Very well, he would follow the French Canadian's example.

The trees thinned, and the party could see the grassy plateau ahead. It looked much as Whip had described it. Towering walls of rock stood on the left and right, cutting off both sides. Only the ends were open, with the entire area extending for about three-quarters of a mile. It was impossible, at this distance, to make out the drop of the cliff at the far end.

The buffalo were there, a large herd of them, spread out over the entire open area. Bulls, cows, and calves were all grazing peacefully. So far, at least, the beasts had no idea they were being stalked.

Whip raised a hand, then began to advance cautiously. The others followed him.

When they emerged from the trees and were completely into the open, Lee saw Pierre crouch low. He did the same. His pulse quickened, and he crept forward very slowly now, making certain his footsteps were silent.

Directly ahead of him was a huge bull buffalo weighing more than a ton. As he munched on the grass, the beast seemed to be looking straight at Lee, who halted. He half-expected the bull to charge him, but, to his surprise, the buffalo placidly continued to munch. Whip had been right when he said that these creatures had poor eyesight. The stench of the herd was almost overpowering. For a moment Lee felt queasy, but he blocked the odor from his consciousness as best he could. His immediate problem was that of not arousing the bull. He made a wide detour around the creature, then paused. He paid no attention to Tilman Wade on one side of him, glancing instead at Pierre le Rouge, who was moving slowly toward a large cow.

Lee finally selected his own target, a cow that was facing toward the cliff. He estimated she weighed about nine hundred pounds, her size indicating her maturity. No calves were grazing near her. He smiled as he came to the conclusion that she was a leader. Slowly he crept toward the buffalo, astonished that neither she nor any of the other beasts had yet realized that men were penetrating their midst.

At that moment he heard the slap of Whip's rifle butt against the hide of a buffalo. There was no time to lose now. Lee sprinted forward, grasping his own rifle by the barrel. Using all of his force, he struck the buffalo across the rump with the butt of his weapon. The startled cow began to run toward the cliff.

The other men were doing the same now, and the thunder of their hoofs made it difficult to hear Whip's voice. "Open fire!" he shouted. The roar of his rifle told his companions what to do.

Lee sent a shot over the buffalo's heads, then instantly reloaded. Common sense told him not to move forward any farther and became enmeshed in the milling herd. Tilman had also halted, but Pierre continued to edge forward and caused another buffalo to bolt before he, too, came to a stop.

A portion of the herd was now gathering momentum, and within moments a stampede was well under way in the direction of the cliff. The pounding of hoofs filled the air. A bull came within inches of knocking Lee to the ground.

It was difficult to see clearly, but it appeared that many of the buffalo were plunging off the cliff and dropping into the canyon far below. Some, however, perhaps even a majority, had not yet moved. They stood with their heads raised, in the midst of the confusion. Perhaps it was instinct that prevented them from participating in the stampede.

Suddenly, a large cow started toward the woods. She was immediately followed by another, a calf beside her. Two bulls lumbered after them, and all at once Lee realized that a counter-stampede was under way in the direction of the woods, with part of the herd still heading toward the cliff while the others moved in the direction from which they had come.

Both stampedes quickly gained momentum, causing clouds of dust to rise in the clear air and making it difficult to see precisely what was happening. Lee could see Whip waving and shouting, but the noise of the thundering buffalo made it impossible to hear a word he was saying. His meaning, however, was obvious—every member of the party had to protect himself as best he could.

Pierre fired at a cow heading toward him, and she swerved before she reached him. Tilman Wade dropped to one knee, raised his rifle to his shoulder, and held it ready.

Lee braced himself, his own rifle raised. He didn't have long to wait. A large bull, his tiny, red eyes crazed, his shaggy head lowered, hurtled across the plateau toward him. The army officer realized he would have only one chance to shoot. The beast would run him down before he could reload and fire again. So he waited, forcing himself to hold back until the last possible moment before he fired.

The bull came closer, and Lee knew this was the most important shot of his life. Holding his rifle steady, he squeezed the trigger. He shot the buffalo between the eyes. But the bull's momentum carried him forward, and his heavy body grazed Lee, knocking the man to the ground before the beast collapsed a few feet away.

A direct collision that would have met death had been averted. Lee, still clutching his rifle, hauled himself to his feet. He was bruised, but he was safe.

By now the double stampede had ended. The carcasses of five buffalo littered the ground, but the rest of the herd had vanished, either over the cliff or into the woods.

Miraculously, none of the hunters had been injured. They hurried to the cliff and peered down at an awesome and bloody sight. The bodies of dead buffalo were piled up at the base of the canyon. Claiborne Woodling and his large group were just edging forward, leading their nervous mounts, as well as pack horses pulling travoises.

"It's my guess," Whip said, "that about a hundred

buffalo went over the cliff. It'll take work parties two or three days to butcher them and bring all that meat back to camp."

The small group on the plateau had more work of its own to do. They butchered the five dead buffalo and loaded the meat onto travoises, pulled by the horses they had ridden to the scene.

It was dusk before the weary hunters arrived back at camp. Ernie was already making up a schedule for the next day's force that would go to the base of the canyon to collect the rest of the buffalo meat. The cooking fires had been built higher so that the meat being brought to camp could be cooked or smoked without delay.

Whip was not content to wait until morning, however. That same night, he led a small party back to the base of the ravine. The carcasses, he explained, would have to be guarded against coyotes, wolves, and vultures.

At daybreak, most of the men and older boys were pressed into service. They labored through the day at the bottom of the cliff, butchering the buffalo. By that night so much meat had been brought into camp that the women worked in relays, smoking and roasting it. The storage sheds were filled to overflowing, so the next day Ted Woods went into the pine forest with a group of men, returning with enough logs to build still more sheds. The atmosphere at the lake site changed. Now that they had ample food supplies, people no longer had to fear starvation, even though the diet might become monotonous by winter's end.

Winter arrived more subtly than anyone had imagined it would. Each day the temperature dropped, and every morning there was a skin of ice on the lake. One night was colder than any that had preceded it, and when dawn came, the members of the water brigade had to chop holes in the ice to draw water. The ground was frozen hard, too.

It began to snow several days later, and it continued to come down steadily for the next seventy-two hours. When it finally stopped, there were two and a half feet of it on the ground. In many places, thanks to the bitterly cold wind, the drifts resembled white boulders. The twin peaks and single mountain visible from the camp now had a covering of snow that extended from their crests to places far below the timberline. Whip said they would not be bare again before spring.

"It's lucky we won't need to hunt," he said, "because this is going to be a nasty winter. If the game have any sense, they've gone off to warmer places. I'm inclined to believe this whole area has been deserted by everyone except the people of this wagon train and a few stray bears who might be hibernating in caves on the heights."

No one left the lake except those who had to cut trees for firewood, a never-ending task that would reduce the better part of the valley forest to stumps by the time the wagon train departed in the spring. Convenience dictated the establishment of new routines. Those who fetched water found it easier to collect pails of snow, which they melted, than to clear an area on the lake, chop a hole, and draw out buckets of water that froze again before they could be taken indoors. Paul Thoman's school, which he set up in one of the cabins, kept the children busy, and he made a point of giving the older girls and boys regular homework. The community hall wasn't large enough to accommodate everyone comfortably at one time, so people ate in two shifts.

La-ena and Dolores showed a number of the men how to cure the buffalo hides, most of which were made into robes that many people used as blankets. Those who wanted additional clothing were free to help themselves to hides, but they soon learned that it took far longer to cure the tough skin of a buffalo than that of a deer or elk.

Sentries kept watch for intruders near the entrance to the valley. Because of the cold, it was hazardous for any man to stay outdoors for more than a couple of hours at a time, and Lee warned the sentinels to keep their faces wrapped and never to stand still for more than a few moments.

Ted Woods turned over the supervision of the woodcutters to Tilman Wade and went to work repairing metal wheel rims and forging tools for those who needed them. Hosea forged tiny knives that many of the women used when they sewed, and he also made a necklace for Dolores out of a small piece of scrap metal. It was a medallion on which there appeared the mystical symbol his uncle had always drawn in the dust before beginning a witch doctor's ceremony. The symbol, which consisted of several interlocking circles, with objects that resembled bamboo poles protruding from them, had no specific meaning to Dolores, but she knew they had a more than ordinary significance. Accepting the gift with great solemnity, she wore the necklace at all times. Hosea was pleased that she liked the gift and hoped it might enhance her powers as a medicine woman, even though she was unfamiliar with the magical chants of African jungle tribes.

Women who were not responsible for preparing

meals spent much of their time sewing, either making new clothes from bolts of cloth they had purchased in Independence or engaging in the endless task of mending.

Each morning, immediately after those on the second shift finished breakfast, Dr. Martin treated anyone who was ill. Bobby Harris came down with the measles and was placed in isolation immediately, in Emily and Ernie's cabin. Chet was sent to live temporarily with Ted Woods and Danny. In spite of Ernie's promptness in following the doctor's orders, however, it was too late. Bobby had attended school regularly, and nine other children caught measles. The patients were given doses of sulfur and molasses three times each day, and without exception loathed the medication. All recovered without incident, but their parents, living with them in exceptionally close quarters, suffered from chronic irritability that lasted until the children were well again.

There were enough chores to be performed to keep everyone busy for at least part of each day. Idleness was discouraged. Too little to do, according to Whip, Paul, and Pierre, might induce in people what mountain men called "cabin fever." People who succumbed to it behaved unpredictably. Sometimes they became listless and other times dangerously violent, without cause. No one was permitted to indulge in lethargy, and the leaders, particularly Ernie, saw to it that those who did not have enough to do were given additional duties.

People existed in even closer proximity to one another than when the wagon train was on the trail, and temper flare-ups were inevitable. One such incident took place when Sally MacNeill, much to her embarrassment, developed a rash on her face that Dr. Martin's medicines could not cure. La-ena offered to make a salve that the Arapaho found effective, and Sally, who was avoiding Paul Thoman until her appearance improved, gladly accepted.

La-ena cut strips of inner bark from a cedar tree, then took them to the community house to boil until they were reduced to a paste. Intent on her labors, she failed to realize that she was in the way of the women who were starting to prepare that night's supper.

Cathy van Ayl reacted with unreasonable and uncharacteristic annoyance. "Can't you dabble some other time?" she demanded. "We're trying to fix a meal for hundreds of people!"

La-ena was surprised by the assault, but showed no emotion. Cathy's anger increased. "I've already told you to take that pot elsewhere!"

The Indian girl stiffened. She was proud as well as stubborn, and had no intention of obeying such orders. "La-ena will go when the paste is done," she said firmly. Then, because she liked Cathy, she added quietly, "Soon be done."

Cathy started to snatch the pot from the metal tripod that suspended it over the fire, but Cindy stopped her. She ran to Cathy, caught hold of her shoulders, and dragged her away, at which point Cathy burst into inexplicable tears.

"Finish what you're doing, La-ena," Cindy said. "Cathy, stop being so foolish. It won't matter in the least if we wait another few minutes to put the meat on the fire."

Cathy straightened, then looked at La-ena, her face wooden. "Forgive me," she said. "I had no right to snap at you like that. Cindy, take charge, please. I've got a terrible headache, and I'm going back to the cabin to rest."

La-ena, behaving as though nothing unusual had taken place, continued to boil the bark until it reached the consistency she wanted. Then she took it to Sally, who applied the paste while it was still hot. That same evening her rash was reduced. Within a few days it had vanished completely, and Sally became La-ena's devoted follower and friend.

The better part of a week passed before Cathy mentioned the incident to Cindy. "I don't know what came over me the other day," she said, as the two of them sat together, chopping herbs to add to a soup of plant roots. "I lashed out at La-ena when she was trying to do Sally MacNeill a favor—a favor that has been highly successful, I gather. I don't know whether to apologize to La-ena again—or what to do."

"My advice, if you want it," Cindy said, "is not to mention it again."

"I do want your advice, but La-ena has been avoiding me, and I can't say that I blame her."

"Oh, she'll forget the whole thing, and so will you. It really wasn't all that important."

Cathy sighed and let the matter drop.

Later, as Cindy and Eulalia were returning to their cabin, Cindy was far more candid. "I wouldn't tell this to Cathy," she said, "because she appears not to know it herself, but the reason for that little temper tantrum she had last week is obvious."

"What you're saying," Eulalia said, "is that Cathy is still in love with Whip and is jealous of La-ena."

"I'm afraid so."

"When will she regain her balance, do you suppose?" Eulalia asked.

Cindy's face was wrapped in a scarf to protect her from the biting wind, and the length of woolen cloth concealed her ironic smile. "One of these days," she said, "Cathy will realize that no man is worth a tear or the loss of a minute's sleep!"

A sudden burst of excitement at breakfast the following morning caused many people to forget their petty quarrels. Dolores was among those who ate at the second sitting, and she was talking with Emily von Thalman and Grace Drummond at a long table of pine planks when she shuddered, suddenly closed her eyes, and became rigid. Hosea quickly went over to her and stood nearby, to prevent anyone from mistakenly trying to help the medicine woman.

People stopped eating, and everyone stared at Dolores. It was apparent to anyone who had watched her when she had undergone a seizure that she was going through a similar experience. She opened her eyes, which were glazed, and stared vacantly into space, her body becoming even more rigid. Hosea's eyes were fixed on her.

A deep voice emanated from Dolores, and she spoke in a tongue that no one in the room understood. Neither La-ena nor Stalking Horse could make out a word, and Whip seemed confused, too.

Dolores went limp, then opened her eyes and smiled. She sipped her tea, which she had learned to like while at Fort Vancouver. Then she rose swiftly and announced in a quiet voice, "I must speak to Whip, Lee Blake, and the Baron."

The trio withdrew with her to a far corner of the community hall. Even the skeptical Lee Blake realized she had something important to tell the leaders of the expedition.

"My visions," Dolores said, "showed me a place high in these mountains. There is a tall mountain that looks like the face of a man who has a long nose. On this side of the mountain there is a pass, a narrow pass."

"I know the mountain you mean," Whip said. "When we move west again in the spring, we'll drive through the pass."

"Tomorrow," Dolores said, "two people will arrive at that pass. But heavy snows are coming, and they will not be able to get through. They will need help."

Perhaps Dolores had been lucky in her previous prophecy, Lee thought, it was certainly hard to take her present vision seriously.

"Why are you telling this only to us?" Ernie wanted to know. "Why couldn't you tell everybody?"

Dolores frowned, and for a moment she looked blank. "I do not quite know myself. I—I have a feeling of evil. So maybe the two people who will come to the pass are not good."

This was absurd, Lee thought. Not only was she predicting that two persons would reach a pass in the mountains the next day and would be unable to proceed further without help, but she was even prophesying the character of those persons.

Whip accepted Dolores's words without questioning their possible accuracy. "Even a couple of no-good mountain men can't be left out there to freeze to death," he said. "It snowed last night, and if there's more snow on the way, we'll have the devil's own time making our way to that pass in less than two days."

Lee found it incredible that Whip was intending to lead a rescue mission based on nothing more than this half-breed girl's second sight.

"I reckon I'll just take Thoman and Pierre with me," Whip said. "They know the mountains at this time of the year better than anybody else."

Lee might think the venture was mad, but he was determined to be included. "I'll come with you, too."

Whip grinned at him. "I guess you can take care of yourself just about anywhere," he said. "Come ahead."

The expedition was organized without delay. Every man wore a double layer of buckskins and a buffalo robe. All carried rifles and pistols, but the supplies they loaded onto two pack horses were even more important than weapons in the dead of winter. They included meat, parched corn, buffalo robes, and blankets.

Whip and his companions greased their faces, hands, arms, legs, and feet with bear fat to make them less vulnerable to the cold. Then they saddled their horses, and leading the pack horses, they rode out of Little Valley, making detours around snowdrifts that were sometimes as high as twenty feet.

Not until they reached the open heights beyond the valley did Lee Blake realize how fortunate they were in their choice of winter quarters. Here, in the open mountain country, the wind was colder and more penetrating, cutting through protective garments like a razor. Lee knew he could have been comfortable and safe back at the campsite, but nothing would have persuaded him to miss this experience. Mountain men were a remarkable breed, Lee thought.

There was no conversation, and Whip, Paul, and Pierre all rode steadily ahead, never pushing their horses too hard, yet never halting or slowing their pace too much. It was of paramount importance that the animals, as well as the men, not become chilled.

Whip permitted only one halt, behind the shelter of a boulder that cut off the icy gusts of wind. Lee discovered that his eyes were running and that the tears were freezing on his face. Just before he left, Cathy had handed him a scarf of thick wool to wear for extra protection. He took it from his saddlebag and wrapped it around his face. In weather like this, one could freeze to death without even being aware of it.

The ride was resumed, and not until an hour before sundown did Whip break the silence. "It won't be long before we're all right for the night," he said.

Paul Thoman nodded complacently, and Pierre seemed to take Whip at his word, too. Only Lee was surprised when they came to a cave opening. Whip led the little party into the cave, where the riding horses were unsaddled and packs removed from the backs of the workhorses.

Pierre and Paul went into the open again and soon returned with a dead tree. Vanishing once more, they returned with another. "I saw these a few minutes ago," Paul said. "Only in weather like this does one truly appreciate the propensities of combustibles."

The four men went to work, immediately chopping the wood, then made a fire at the entrance to the cave, a tall chamber that was about thirty feet long and twenty feet wide. They sat close to the fire, and enough heat entered the cave to make it reasonably comfortable for men and horses alike. They fed the animals, and then, despite the weather conditions, they enjoyed the luxury of eating warm meat, rather than just jerked or smoked. Because of the altitude, a somewhat longer time was needed to bring their container of coffee to a boil. Then they were able to relax, impervious to the elements, as they sipped coffee from tin cups.

"How did you know of this place?" Lee asked Whip.

"When you have lived in the mountains as long as I have," the guide replied, "you remember every shelter you've ever come across. Sometimes it means the difference between life and death. Knowing that if it weren't for this cave and a couple of others like it down the line we'd be spending the night in the open without shelter—that sort of sharpens a man's memory."

Pierre le Rouge nodded. "I can draw a map of fifty shelters in the mountains of Colorado," he added. "Not one would be in the wrong place by more than a mile."

As always when Paul Thoman became serious, his language became simpler. "I've just spent a year in this part of the country," he said, "so I don't know more than a half-dozen hideouts. That's why I spent most of last winter holed up in one place. There are so many stories of mountain men growing careless and freezing to death that you learn a respect for the elements you were never taught in school."

Lee was impressed by the calm that all three displayed. Mountain men, he thought, took hardship for granted and exposed themselves to danger as a matter of course. He had heard both Andrew Jackson and Winfield Scott, who rarely agreed, say that the most courageous soldiers were those who left their imaginations behind when they went into battle. But the hunters and trappers who spent their lives in America's highest and most extensive chain of mountains were different. They seemed to be acutely conscious at all times of the hazards they faced. That awareness enabled them to take the precautions necessary for survival. Lee wondered what would happen if Dolores's vision proved false, but he refrained from asking.

The entire group slept comfortably in the cave, adding wood to the fire before they went on their way again at the first light of dawn. Lee questioned this, and Whip explained that when they retraced their steps on their way back to Little Valley, the cave would be waiting for them, and they could thaw out there.

The early morning cold was numbing. Lee discovered it was painful to breathe and found himself moving his arms and legs constantly to provide circulation. Snow had fallen again during the night, as Dolores had predicted, but now the sun rose in a surprisingly clear sky, and as it climbed above the peaks to the east, it gave off remarkable warmth. Lee was forced to shed his buffalo cape, and although he saw no snow or ice melting, he could actually feel his skin burn.

The horses were friskier, thanks to the warmth of the sun, and Whip led the party at a faster pace. The mountain that Dolores had described lay directly ahead of them, and within a few hours they were making their way up its east face. Turning sharply to the left, they found themselves at the entrance to the pass. The peak loomed above them, and the high walls of the gorge cut off all sunlight. The snow was deep, soft, and treacherous. There were no footsteps, no signs of humans or animals anywhere.

Slowing to a crawl, Whip allowed his stallion to pick his way. The horse's instincts were better than those of a man. From time to time the stallion paused to paw at snow directly ahead and test it before continuing to advance, sometimes making detours as he threaded a path through the gorge.

It seemed inconceivable to Lee that anyone could be alive here. He was astonished when Whip suddenly called, "There's somebody or something up ahead."

The party dismounted and went forward a short distance on foot. There they found a man in his thirties and a young woman huddled in a hollow. Both of them were exhausted. Their cold, miserable horses feebly stamped their hoofs in the snow near them. Dully, the couple looked at their rescuers.

"I reckon you folks can stand some help," Whip said calmly.

"We lost our pack horses about three days ago," the man said hoarsely, speaking slowly and with great difficulty. "We ran out of food, and it's a miracle we haven't frozen to death."

The couple's horses were so weak they could scarcely stand. Whip took in the situation at a glance. "Can you walk a few yards?" he asked.

"I guess so," the man said, struggling to his feet. Whip began to help him to the party's waiting mounts.

The girl rose shakily to her feet, took a single step, and would have fallen if Lee hadn't caught her. Giving her no chance to protest, he picked her up and carried her.

Responding to a signal from Whip, Pierre le Rouge and Paul Thoman stayed behind. Suddenly two shots broke the silence, and the echoes rolled across the vast empty spaces of the mountains. The couple's horses had been put out of their misery.

Before mounting, Whip placed the man on the back of his own stallion. Lee wrapped the girl in his buffalo cape, lifted her into his saddle and, mounting behind her, held her steady. She seemed too tired to speak, and Lee did not question her. For the present, it was enough that Dolores had been right again. The couple had been found almost precisely where she had indicated, and never again would Lee doubt her word.

They reached the cave in mid-afternoon. Although the cave was still warm, Paul Thoman and Pierre fetched more dead wood. Lee chopped it and built up the fire while Whip prepared a meal.

"Eat slowly," Whip cautioned the couple, "or you'll get sick. You've got the rest of the day and all night, and there's plenty more we can fix for you. So just take a bit at a time."

The girl obeyed, taking small bites and resting between swallows. The man, however, ignored the advice and gulped his meal.

At last the couple introduced themselves. The girl said her name was Ginny Dobbs, and the man called himself Garcia. They had been traveling northeast from California, they said, in an attempt to reach the United States.

Color began to appear in Ginny's face as the food and fire gave her strength and warmth, and she became more talkative. "Everything went wrong," she said. "We don't know the Wyoming mountains, and after we came through the South Pass, we got lost twice. We should have shown a little sense and tried to find some protected place to stay through the winter." She glared at her companion.

"It wasn't my fault we lost our pack horses," Garcia said defensively. "One minute they were behind us, and the next they were gone."

The girl did not reply, but continued to regard him contemptuously. Lee couldn't figure out their relationship, but he was sure of one thing: there was no love lost between them. "Your accents tell me you're Americans," he commented.

Ginny's laugh was feeble, but Lee detected a savage undercurrent. "I'm sure a long way from home—Trenton, New Jersey. And only God knows when I'll ever see it again."

Garcia said nothing.

"I reckon you'll be spending the winter with us," Whip said. He went on to explain that the wagon train was camped nearby. "It would be nearly impossible to cross the mountains and the Great Plains at this time of year, even for an experienced mountain man. And with all due respect to you, Mrs. Garcia, I doubt if any woman could do it."

"I'm not Mrs. Garcia," Ginny said, offering no further explanation.

Lee felt uneasy. He had already developed a strong dislike for Garcia, which was absurd, since he hardly knew the man. All the same, he thought it significant that Garcia had offered no word of thanks or appreciation for his rescue. As for the girl, she had a chip on her shoulder, and he made up his mind to keep an eye on her, too. Even if the couple had come from California, the British or the Russians could easily have hired them to sabotage the wagon train.

After feeding the horses, the members of the rescue party ate their own supper. Ginny, better able to walk now, took a blanket to a far corner of the cave, curled up in it, and promptly drifted off to sleep. Garcia stayed awake, however, and asked innumerable questions about the wagon train, the people on it, and its destination.

Lee's instincts were fully alerted. His training as an intelligence officer warned him this was a man who couldn't be trusted. Thanks to Dolores's intuition—or second sight, or whatever one wanted to call it—the lives of a man and a woman had been saved. They had been rescued before either had suffered permanent harm. That much was all to the good. But Lee couldn't help feeling that this couple was bringing trouble with them to Little Valley.

He caught Whip's glance across the fire and knew instantly that the guide shared his doubts. It was little consolation for Lee to realize he was not the only one who felt apprehensive.

VI

Nicholas the First, Czar of all the Russias, was the last monarch with absolute power to sit on a major throne. He was the only one of a small band of heads of state whose wishes were taken as commands, to be obeyed without question. His more enlightened colleagues, like Victoria of Great Britain and Louis Philippe of France, had limited powers and answered for their actions to their ministers and national legislatures. Even the Sultan of the Ottoman Empire reigned rather than ruled, and was responsible to his council of state.

The tremendous power concentrated in the person of one man created a court of sycophants at the Winter Palace in St. Petersburg that was reminiscent of the Middle Ages. The wealthiest nobles, princes, and dukes whose vast armies of serfs were doomed to spend their entire lives in bondage, themselves wore invisible shackles. Gentlemen in glittering, gold-encrusted uniforms and ladies wearing elaborate gowns trimmed with precious jewels stood for hours in the chilly throne room, a huge chamber designed and constructed by Peter the Great. There was only one chair in the hall, the throne itself, which was set on a dais. The mere presence of that symbol was so strong that no one dared to sneak out of the room, however briefly, to sit down. The men's feet ached in their heavy boots, and most of the ladies, who wore high heels in imitation of the current French fashion, had swollen ankles. Yet everyone remained in place, awaiting the pleasure of the Czar.

Nicholas, a liveried servant had reported several hours earlier, was sleeping, but he might appear at any time. No one in his or her right mind wanted to brave the imperial wrath by being absent when he did show up. Nicholas was not the brightest of the Czars, but he had a remarkable memory for faces, and he had been known to banish from his court, on sudden whim, people who dared to be absent without his advance authorization.

This winter the Czar had decided that too much money was being spent on firewood. Accordingly, the three hearths in the throne room were empty, and the hall was bitterly cold. Those who stood, shivering, took small comfort in the fact that St. Petersburg was far less cold than Siberia, to which anyone who complained might be banished.

The elite spoke to each other exclusively in French, long the language of the court; few had ever visited France, but, like their parents and grandparents before them, they had been taught the language by tutors. The nobles were patriots who sought the greater glory of Russia, but they regarded those beneath them with the same contempt that the Czar showed to everyone except the members of his immediate family. Consequently, they used their native tongue only when addressing servants.

A few ministers of state, generals, and admirals discussed various decrees they hoped to persuade

Nicholas to sign, but their advocacy of various causes was cautious. When the Czar became bored with the business of the empire, he left the government in the hands of his subordinates for months at a time, never interfering and not caring what they did. Then, when his mood changed, he gathered the reins into his own hands once more and made all decisions. Since it was impossible for one man to deal with every detail of such a large and complex government, business was often neglected, and many of the decrees that were drawn up by clerks were never to be signed.

The majority of those gathered in the throne room chatted about inconsequential matters. The ladies discussed new additions to their wardrobes, while the gentlemen lied to each other about their recent amatory exploits or successes in hunting. No one really expected to be believed.

At last an aide in a white uniform with over-the-knee boots entered the throne room and, mounting the base of the dais, removed his fur hat, a sign that he intended to make an announcement. The lords and ladies fell silent.

"Prince Orlev," the aide said, "you're wanted in the private sitting room. Ladies and gentlemen, His Majesty is indisposed today and must deprive you of the pleasure of his company."

The nobles dispersed at once, most of them hurrying to their own smaller palaces and manor houses, where they would eat and drink for hours. Prince Orlev, one of the most competent of the ministers, headed for a door behind the throne, then mounted a spiral staircase two steps at a time.

Nicholas sat before a roaring fire in a small, overheated chamber crowded with bric-a-brac. Sprawled in an easy chair, he was wearing an old padded dressing gown, a dilapidated pair of fur-lined bedroom slippers, and a tasseled nightcap. No one looking at him would have known he was one of the wealthiest and most powerful men in the world. He stared moodily into the fire, and from time to time, he spat in the direction of the hearth.

Prince Orlev entered the room and bowed low, almost bending double, then stood erect, waiting to be recognized. A long time passed before the Czar roused himself from his reverie and became aware of his visitor's presence. "You're home, Orlev," he said.

"Yes, Your Majesty."

"I'm told you landed the night before last, at midnight."

"I did, Your Majesty." The Prince was not surprised that he, like everyone else of consequence, was kept under surveillance.

"How did you enjoy America, Orlev?"

"I didn't, Your Majesty. It's a barbaric country ruled by commoners who are no better than their subjects."

Nicholas grimaced, then waved the Prince to a chair. The Prince would have selected a chair farther from the fire, for the heat in the room was suffocating. He resisted the almost overwhelming impulse to open the top buttons of his heavy tunic.

"How did you fare, Orlev?"

"Well, the Americans have agreed to receive the trade mission we want to send there, but I fear the negotiations will be difficult. Even their highest officials count coppers, and it won't be easy to make successful deals with them."

"We must. America is a growing country, and we need the money. So see to it, Orlev."

"Very well, Your Majesty."

"What of our situation in the Oregon country—how do we stand there?"

"There is no situation there, Your Majesty. As you know, the Americans are sending a wagon train to Oregon. Our legation sent two agents to halt their progress and even tried to enlist the services of a young woman whose parents were still in St. Petersburg. But our agents have disappeared, and the young woman refused to cooperate."

"Then dispose of her parents."

"I intended to do just that yesterday, Your Majesty, but I learned they're both dead."

A petulant expression crossed the Czar's face. "It was inconvenient for us to press our claim to Oregon ten years ago, when we first sent settlers there. But it's logical for us to extend our borders south along the Pacific coast from Alaska. If we can extend our domain by that much, not even the British will be able to boast that they control a larger empire. I want Oregon!"

Orlev felt a chill, even though he continued to perspire. "That's easier said than done, Your Majesty. Not only are Americans sending hundreds of settlers there on this first train, but they're organizing a half-dozen other trains. Meanwhile, the British are increasing their garrison at Fort Vancouver."

Nicholas raised a trimmed eyebrow. "And what are we doing?"

"I've taken the liberty," the Prince said, "of setting certain steps in motion. The Americans don't want war with us any more than we want to fight them. With our fleet, such as it is, concentrating on the Turks, we can't afford a war with the British, either. Their fleet would destroy us."

"Stop telling me what we *can't* do!" Nicholas sounded like an angry child. "I want to know about these steps you've set in motion."

"I've learned that several of the villages we established in the Oregon country are still inhabited. I hope to increase the Russian population of those villages to give us a stronger foothold and make our claim—when we renew it—more valid."

"I see no problem in that," the Czar said. "We can transfer prisoners from Siberia to the New World by way of Alaska—as many thousands of them as we need to take possession of Oregon."

"I've had the same thought, Your Majesty, but it won't do. Oregon is a wilderness. If we sent prisoners, we'd need thousands of guards and the means to support them. Not only are our facilities in Alaska too limited for such a venture, but it would be a simple matter for any prisoners we might send there to escape and join the Americans, who have a positive mania for what they regard as freedom. I'm afraid if we followed that course of action, we would be guaranteeing that the United States would be successful in claiming Oregon."

Nicholas controlled his cold rage. "I'm waiting to hear how you propose to accomplish your miracle."

"I am inaugurating a vigorous campaign, urging our citizens to volunteer to settle in Oregon. We will have to be discreet, so that the Americans and British don't learn of it. I intend to offer free transportation and a cash bonus to every family who volunteers."

The Czar's attempt to curb his temper failed. He became livid. "I refuse to allow my treasury to be depleted for such a purpose!" he cried, pounding the arm of his chair. "I won't stand for it!"

Normally Orlev would have been terrified, but he had guessed what the Czar's reaction would be and was prepared for it. "Your Majesty won't have to spend a single kopek of your own funds," he said soothingly.

Nicholas caught his breath. "Oh?"

"I shall ask for contributions—in your name, naturally—from the nobles and from merchants of substantial means. These voluntary sums will be paid through the tax collectors—for the sake of convenience, of course. I have no doubt that every wealthy man in Russia will show his patriotism and give freely. I—ah—intend to make a substantial contribution myself."

Nicholas sat back in his chair, a thin smile on his pockmarked face. "A touch of genius, Orlev. I myself shall compose the proclamation requesting contributions."

Prince Orlev had been relying on him to do just that. The Czar's personal literary style was simple and crude, immediately recognizable, and would guarantee that everyone with the means to contribute would hasten to hand money to the tax collectors.

"Stay to dinner, Orlev. I'll have it served right here, where we can be comfortable."

"I'm honored, Your Majesty." The Prince hoped he wouldn't faint from the heat before the meal ended. His scheme was far from foolproof, and he warned himself to remain alert. The basis for his plan was brilliant, as the Czar had indicated. But corruption was so commonplace on all levels that only a fraction of the money raised for the venture would be available for the immigrants he hoped to send to Oregon. In fact, he had every expectation that his share of the proceeds would be far larger than the contribution he would make.

Hopefully he would be able to nudge the lazy government workers into organizing the idea promptly, thus sending several thousand Russian colonists to the New World. That should provide a counterbalance for the American immigrants, and there would be too many Russians for the British troops to drive out. Right now, Russia might place a poor third in the race for the rich prize, but soon she would take the lead.

Prince Orlev accepted a glass of French brandywine from a manservant and raised his glass in a toast to the Czar. But actually he was toasting himself.

Although one of Ginny Dobbs's feet was frostbitten, Dr. Martin said it was not serious. Garcia survived his ordeal unscathed and was in remarkably sound physical condition. Ginny was given quarters in the cabin that Cathy, Cindy, and Eulalia shared. Tilman Wade took Garcia into his cabin. That night Tilman escorted him to the community hall for supper.

"Where were you headed?" Tilman asked, in an attempt to be friendly.

Garcia was curt. "New York or Baltimore."

"Well, you're a long way from the Atlantic Ocean. You may change your mind by the time the winter is over and decide to come to Oregon with us."

"What's in Oregon?"

"Good land and forests, rivers for fishing, and water power. Everything we need to build a civilization."

"After California," Garcia said vehemently, "I'm sick of wilderness. Give me a city where there's women and decent liquor to drink and a good game of cards for an evening. Only fools get calluses on their hands digging up tree stumps and planting crops. Last year I was tempted to stay in California when I heard a story that there's gold to be found there. But the rumor didn't amount to anything, so I got out. I smell money in the East, and that's where I'm going!"

The man's sentiments were so opposed to everything the wagon train members considered important that Tilman was taken aback. Certainly he didn't agree with the assessment that someone who dug up tree stumps and plowed the land was a fool. There was a viciousness in the newcomer's voice he disliked, but he warned himself not to be hasty in passing judgment. Garcia had gone through a harrowing experience, and no one could blame him if he wanted nothing more to do with the wilderness for the present. Nevertheless, Tilman felt a trifle sorry he had volunteered to give the man a place in his cabin.

Meanwhile, Tonie Martin brought Ginny to her new quarters. The girl's foot was heavily bandaged, and Tonie left her there in the care of Cindy and Eulalia, who tried to make her feel at home.

"Since you lost most of your belongings when the packhorses went off that ledge," Cindy said, "you'll probably need new clothes. We can loan you things until you can get some new skins."

"I've dreamed of wearing buckskins all my life," Ginny replied sarcastically. "What do you want in return?"

Cindy's eyes narrowed, but she curbed her temper. "Not a thing. We have a lot of treated doeskin and buffalo hides available, and Eulalia can give you a hand if you want some help."

"I'll do my own sewing."

"Suit yourself," Eulalia said, shrugging. This girl was positively rude.

Cindy tried again. "I don't mean to pry," she said,

"but I thought about going to California until I heard this wagon train was being formed. What kind of country is it?"

"Big, wild." Obviously Ginny had no desire to discuss California.

But Cindy was still curious. "Where did you spend most of your time?"

"Yerba Buena."

"What kind of a place is it?"

"I'd rather freeze to death in these mountains than go back there," Ginny said vehemently. "The Mexican governor does nothing, and his troops' behavior is worse than that of the people they're supposed to control. You're risking your life if you go near the waterfront."

"Well, you won't freeze here. We've built a snug retreat for winter, and by spring you may even want to come with us to Oregon."

"I've had enough of the wilderness, thanks. Give me a city any time."

Cindy and Eulalia did not attempt to change Ginny's mind. Wagon train life was difficult at best, and it required personal sacrifices for the good of everyone. It was up to each individual to decide whether the ultimate goal—life in Oregon—was worth the hardships and dangers that were so much a part of the life they were living.

The worst part of continuing her journey East in the spring, Ginny thought, was that she would be obliged to travel with Garcia again. But she couldn't face that prospect now, and she had no intention of revealing what she thought of him to these strangers.

"Well, you can't really make any plans before spring, and there's a long winter ahead," Cindy said. "Once you've recovered your strength, you'll be given a job.

They'll pretty much give you your own choice, whether it's fetching water or cooking or whatever."

Ginny, reminded of her life at the orphanage, bristled. "Suppose I don't want to work. What then?"

Eulalia laughed. "That's the way I felt when I first joined the train—but living with all these people gives you a new perspective. Either you volunteer or you're given an assignment."

"I don't allow anybody to tell me what to do!" Ginny declared.

Neither Cindy nor Eulalia challenged her. The way of life that had been developed, of necessity, by the wagon train members forced people to conform.

As the days passed, however, it became evident that neither Ginny nor Garcia fitted into the community. The girl remained abrasive, while the man was withdrawn and surly. Ernie von Thalman discussed work assignments with them, and with great reluctance Ginny finally consented to help with cooking. She did not admit that she had earned her living sewing.

Garcia seemed somewhat more cooperative than Ginny. "I'll do anything you want," he said.

His performance, however, left a great deal to be desired. At first he was assigned to cut wood, but he loafed so much on the job that Tilman Wade asked that the newcomer be transferred elsewhere. Next Garcia became a member of the group that repaired the cabins, which, having been built so hastily, constantly needed caulking. Nat Drummond, who was in charge of the group, soon complained to Ernie and Whip. "All Garcia does when we're caulking is wander around the cabins. He never does a lick of work."

"Well," Ernie said, "eventually we'll find something that will spark his interest."

"And in the meantime," Whip added, "we're stuck

with him. We can't throw him out of camp, not with the kind of weather we've been having."

The following week Reverend Cavendish, greatly agitated, came to the leaders claiming that his pocket watch and chain had vanished from the ledge beside his bunk while he had been asleep. It was difficult to take the charge seriously because the clergyman was intoxicated so much of the time. So, as Lee Blake said, it was likely that he had simply misplaced his watch and chain.

"I can't imagine why anybody would steal them," Lee said. "We're hundreds of miles from any shops that would buy such items. Money has no value in the wilderness."

Only a few days later, however, Tilman Wade went to Lee. "I don't want to make a fuss about this," he said, "but I believe there's a thief in camp. A little gold locket—with miniature paintings of my mother and father in it—has vanished."

"You're quite sure of that, Tilman?"

"I'm positive, Lee. I kept it in a little box, along with the bits for my drills and other small items, and it's gone."

They went to Ernie and Whip, and all four discussed the problem at length, but could reach no conclusion. "All we can do is keep our eyes open," Whip said. "One of these days maybe we can catch the thief. Stealing a locket makes even less sense than taking a watch and chain."

"It could be the result of cabin fever," Lee said. "Some people react strangely to being cooped up for long periods. We may be in for all kinds of trouble before the winter ends."

Cabin fever began to manifest itself in various ways.

No one was more active than Ted Woods, but the blacksmith felt a sense of confinement similar to that he had suffered while in prison. He had put his past behind him, but he brooded restlessly about his future. One evening he reached the breaking point. After supper, when most people had gone to their cabins, he loitered in the community hall while the cooks finished cleaning up. Cindy was conscious of his presence, aware that he was watching every move she made. His behavior toward her had improved since the night of the unpleasant incident with Claiborne at the campfire, but she still felt uneasy. It was obvious Ted was hanging around because he wanted to speak to her.

Despite her uneasiness, she decided she owed him the courtesy of a chat. After Cathy, Eulalia, and the others had departed, Cindy approached the bench on which Ted was sitting. "You've been waiting for me, Ted," she said directly.

He rose abruptly. "I hope you don't mind."

She shook her head and seated herself on the opposite side of the plank table, deliberately keeping a distance between them.

Ted stared into the glowing embers of the fire, then turned to Cindy. "I can bend an iron bar with my bare hands," he said, "but when I try to put my thoughts into words, I get all twisted around."

"I'll try to understand." Ted looked miserable and forlorn, and Cindy felt sorry for him.

"Just so you don't expect me to make fancy speeches. I'm not very good at that." He paused, then plunged on. "You've come to know me better than most people on this train, so I don't have to sing my praises, such as they are. I stay sober, and I work hard. I'll keep to my trade after we reach Oregon—there will always be a need for a blacksmith, and I like the work I do better than I like farming. I'll never be rich, but I'll earn enough money to get along."

So far he had said nothing she didn't already know. Ted took a deep breath, and his thick chest expanded. "I'm not saying you couldn't do better, but you sure could do a heap worse."

Cindy froze. She suddenly realized he was proposing to her. She didn't want to hurt him, but at the same time, she couldn't contemplate a marriage to him.

"It'll be a long time, maybe a year or two, before the next wagon train follows us out to Oregon," Ted said. "So you can either wait and take your chances with the next batch or take your pick of what's at hand. There are only a few of us who are bachelors, but I'm as good as any of them."

"You're assuming," Cindy said, "that my primary goal in life is to find a husband."

"Sure," Ted said. "That's what every woman wants."

"That isn't necessarily true of the single women on this wagon train. I could have gone from Louisville to Cincinnati or Nashville or a dozen other places, and with a little patience, I could have found a husband who'd support and take care of me. Instead, I'm driving my own wagon across the country. I'm spending the winter—my second in the wilderness—working and trying to keep body and soul together. I must be making all these sacrifices for some purpose other than finding a husband."

"I don't see what—"

"Then listen to me." She spoke more sharply than she intended. "I'm not saying I can take care of six hundred acres of property by myself. I might decide to open a little dry goods store. You see, there are all kinds of things I can do in Oregon—without having to lean on a man. What matters most to me is that I'm free to do whatever I please. If I succeed, I can reap the benefits. If I fail, I'll have nobody to blame but myself."

Ted laced and unlaced his oversized fingers. "I'm not good enough for you."

"You, Ted? For me?" A bitter smile touched the corners of Cindy's mouth. "You forget the way I earned my living in Louisville. A lot of men have wanted me and had me—for pay. You're the only one who has asked me to marry him."

"I don't care what you were. I know what you are," he said fiercely.

"And I'm grateful to you for feeling that way, but I won't be a burden to you, to anyone. A man shouldn't be ashamed of his wife."

"I'd be proud," Ted said.

Tears came to her eyes, and she blinked them away. "Thank you, Ted, but it wouldn't work in the long run. You'd get to thinking about my past, and it would come between us."

"Maybe there's somebody else," he said.

"Not right now. There could be, some day, or I might turn to you. I'm like a person who was very sick. I need a long convalescence, with plenty of fresh air and sunshine. When all the cobwebs have been cleared away, there's no telling how I'll feel or what I'll want."

"It won't be me," Ted said gloomily.

He was right, of course, Cindy thought. He was too violent, unable to curb the seething emotions that welled up in him. As his wife, she would live in constant fear of him and would lose the precious, hard-won sense of liberty she prized. "You'll always be my friend, Ted. I've never had reason to trust a man, but I gladly put my trust in you."

He had to be content with the little she offered him. "I won't let you down," he said.

The weather in the valley turned a little warmer, and for several days the children were able to play outdoors. Women hung out their wash instead of drying it in front of the cabin fires, and some of the men went hunting, even though Whip told them that game had vanished from the area. Ice and snow continued to glitter on the heights, however, reminding the company that the Rocky Mountains were still in the deadly grip of winter. People were warned not to venture too far from the campsite.

These precautions did not apply to Dolores, who was at home in the mountains, and no one tried to stop her when she announced one morning that she wanted to explore some of the caves that lined the ledge on the nearer of the twin peaks. Even Lee Blake refrained from asking what she expected to find; by now Dolores made her own rules and was free to do as she pleased.

Hosea offered to accompany her and was pleased when she did not object. They went off together on foot, both bundled in buffalo capes. After crossing Little Valley, they began to climb. Thanks to Dolores's instinct, they avoided deep drifts and clefts in the rocky ground. Dolores displayed the tireless agility of a mountain goat, and Hosea, whose stamina was unmatched by any member of the company, noted that the girl was never short of breath.

Before they reached the timberline, they halted briefly. At Dolores's request, Hosea fashioned torches out of dead pine and spruce branches. They would need these, Dolores explained, when they went into the caves. Hosea did not question her about her reasons for exploring the caves. He knew she would explain at the appropriate time, and meanwhile he was content to keep her company.

The ice underfoot thickened and became treacherous above the timberline. Only Hosea's natural sense of balance enabled him to remain upright. Dolores lacked physical strength, but she possessed a sixth sense that continued to direct her, and not once did she slip or stumble.

As they were crossing a field littered with huge, snow-encrusted boulders, Hosea put a hand on the girl's arm to warn her. She halted instantly and watched as he reached for a dart and inserted it into his blow-gun. Neither moved.

The dazzling sunlight reflecting on the snow hampered their vision. They caught only a glimpse of what appeared to be a grizzly bear that moved into the open for an instant, then vanished again into the shadows beyond a wild jumble of mammoth boulders.

"Bears don't come out into the open in winter," Dolores said, somewhat puzzled. "They hibernate."

"Not bear," Hosea told her. "That was man. Indian."

She shook her head in disbelief. "What would an Indian be doing up here by himself? And only a few miles from the wagon train camp—it doesn't make sense."

"That was man," Hosea insisted. "Wearing skin of bear. Kill bear, use skin for coat. Like buffalo cape."

"Well, if there's an Indian up here who lost his way, he can see the smoke of the fires down in the valley, so I imagine he'll show up there during the day—particularly if he's cold and hungry."

Hosea shrugged. He would report the matter to Whip and Lee, and they would know how to deal with the situation. One thing was certain: the Indian had been aware of the couple's presence and had avoided them.

For an instant Hosea thought of pursuing the man but abandoned the idea—he would not leave Dolores behind. It was his first duty to protect her. They resumed their journey. Even after they reached the heights of the wide ledge, the sun warmed them. The climb was exhilarating.

They had no idea, of course, that White Eagle of the Blackfoot was watching them. Long after they passed the entrance to the cave in which he was living, he kept his vigil. He was waiting patiently for the right moment to obtain vengeance for the death of his father and the humiliation of his nation's warriors.

Dolores came to the entrance to a large cave and stepped inside. As Hosea was about to follow, however, she shook her head and emerged into the open again. During the next half-hour, she repeated the gesture several times, starting into one cave after another and then changing her mind.

Ultimately they came to a cave with an exceptionally narrow opening. Dolores paused, and her eyes brightened. "This is the cave I seek," she said.

Using a flint and his metal knife to strike sparks, Hosea lit one of his torches, then entered first. The girl followed and they stood together looking at a long, narrow chamber with a high ceiling. It was surprisingly dry. At the far end was another passage with a rounded, archlike roof, and Dolores moved toward it.

Again Hosea took the lead. They crouched as the ceiling became lower, then made their way through a winding corridor that led downhill in the interior of the mountain.

In the distance they could hear a gurgling, rushing

noise, a faint sound that gradually grew louder. All at once they emerged into an enormous cave, its uneven ceiling at least twenty feet high. Rocklike icicles grew down from the ceiling here and there, and in places others seemed to sprout from the smooth floor.

There was an underground river that ran through the chamber, appearing through a cleft in the rocks at one side and vanishing again through an opening at the other end. Outside all liquid had frozen, but here, even in winter, the water was moving. It sparkled in the light of the torch. Hosea bent down, scooped up a handful of water, and tasted it. It was clear and cold, with no taste of minerals in it, perfect for drinking.

Dolores walked slowly down the cave, halted about halfway, and pointed. Directly ahead, sprouting out of the hard flooring near the little river, were scores of pasty white mushrooms with flat tops. Some were tiny, no bigger than one of Dolores's fingernails, but here and there were some that were almost an inch in diameter.

Dolores bent down, picked one of the mushrooms, and examined it carefully. She broke it in half, smelled it at length, and then, for no more than an instant, touched one of the pieces to the tip of her tongue.

"Never eat one of these," she solemnly told Hosea. "They are not for you."

He nodded, but awaited an explanation.

"In these plants," Dolores told him, "there is a strange and terrible magic. They should be eaten only by certain people, for special reasons."

Hosea still was not satisfied. "What happen if I eat?" he asked.

Her expression became stern. "You would have awful dreams, dreams you would remember as long as you live, dreams that would haunt you. My father, who was a medicine man before me, taught me about these plants when I was little. Once he gave me a small piece of one to eat. For two nights and two days, I had bad dreams. Then my visions knew I had learned a lesson I would not forget, and they sent the dreams away." She shuddered. "Sometimes I think of those dreams still, and I must beg my visions to send them away again."

"Hosea not eat," he promised.

"Tell no one at the camp what we have seen here. Do not mention to anyone—not even to Whip or Lee —that we have found this place."

He couldn't understand why she wanted to keep the discovery of this remarkable cave a secret.

"My visions," Dolores said simply, "told me to search for this place until I found it. Now I know it is here. I will not come here again until my visions tell me what to do."

Hosea nodded obediently. He would not dispute her magic or take any action contrary to its dictates. Hosea saw Dolores as two persons. One was a potential lifelong mate, someone he would cherish and protect. The other person would always stand apart from him. That woman was the servant of powerful visions, forces that no human being could comprehend. He could not and would not interfere when she did their bidding. She had been chosen to act on behalf of those mysterious forces, and he was fortunate to be allowed to help her. Perhaps his fidelity would win him the support of her visions, and they would allow him to win her. There was nothing he wanted more in all the world.

As they retraced their steps to the cave entrance, Dolores was very much aware of Hosea's presence. He wasn't handsome, certainly, but he was a man of solid virtues. Suddenly a thought occurred to her—this man was interested in her! She had been blinded by her own lack of experience and naiveté, but now that she was aware of his interest, she didn't quite know how to react. Perhaps she would discuss the problem with her friend, Sally MacNeill. Sally also knew very little about such matters, but together they might work out something.

Dolores was terrified of being wooed. No Indian had ever dared to approach a medicine woman, and the Englishmen she had known in earlier years had disgusted her. But this situation was different.

Dolores smiled at Hosea as they started back toward Little Valley. Hosea's heart hammered, and he felt lightheaded. Perhaps the forces that were guiding Dolores's destiny were already at work on his behalf.

During the warm spell, a mountain man, attracted by the smoke of the fires, appeared at the wagon train camp. Heavily laden and traveling with several pack horses, Karl Cramer was on his way East, giving up the life he had known for almost fifteen years. He would have waited until spring to make the trip, but he told Whip, whom he had known previously, that his heart was not in good condition, and he wanted to see his relatives again before he died.

Making a generous gesture that many of the Oregon-bound settlers appreciated, he offered to take with him any letters they wanted to send to people back home. They responded with such enthusiasm that a sack filled with mail was added to the burden of what he was carrying already.

Before he departed, Karl had a private word with Lee Blake. "I'll make sure that your reports to Washington City get there, Colonel. I'll carry them in my pouch—that stays tied to my belt night and day."

After he had gone, a number of people were concerned whether or not Karl could actually cross the mountains and the Great Plains at this season of the year. Whip had no doubts. "Don't worry about old Karl," he said. "His hide is as thick as a buffalo's, and he has the strength of a bear. He'll show up at Independence before the Nebraska snows even start to melt, you can depend on it."

The weather turned colder again, and life settled into the humdrum routines of everyday survival. In years ahead, the pioneers would tell their children and grandchildren about the exciting winter they spent in the Rocky Mountains, but in actuality, there was little sense of adventure in the experience.

Those who went out to cut firewood or draw water had to be careful to avoid frostbite, so they remained in the open only for as long as absolutely necessary. Whip warned the men who went out on short hunting expeditions to be careful of any mountain lions, lynx, or other animals they encountered. "Shoot fast and aim straight," he told them. "Any beasts on the prowl these days are bound to be mighty hungry, and they'll attack in a hurry. Starvation makes them less cautious."

One day while fishing, Danny became frostbitten, much to the distress of Ted Woods, Cathy van Ayl, and others who felt close to him. He was confined in Dr. Martin's cabin for treatment, and thanks to his age, he responded rapidly. Nevertheless, he had to remain in bed for several days.

Cathy visited him one afternoon. Then, instead of going straight to the community hall to supervise the preparation of the evening meal, she decided to stop first at her own cabin to pick up several carving knives that Ted had just sharpened for her.

No candles were burning, and the oiled paper that covered the windows admitted only a feeble light, so the little dwelling was in semidarkness. Cathy heard, rather than saw, someone moving around inside. As she closed the door, she assumed it was either Cindy or Eulalia. But this wasn't one of her friends. She made out the shadowy but distinct outline of a man, bending over a leather clothing box she had brought into the cabin from her wagon. It was obvious he was rummaging through it.

Indignation flooded Cathy. She took a step forward. "Are you looking for something?" she demanded.

The man straightened and turned quickly.

Cathy recognized Garcia, and she felt a twinge of fear. "What are you doing in my belongings? You have no right to be here!"

Garcia realized she had caught him red-handed. For a moment he panicked. It would be useless to brush past the girl and escape. There was nowhere he could go, other than to the cabin in which he was living. He could be in serious trouble. One thing was certain—he could not admit that he had heard about the small fortune in gold she had inherited from her late husband, and that he had been searching for the money. But he had been in worse predicaments, and his wits did not desert him. His best hope was to persuade—or frighten—her into keeping silent about the incident.

First he would try charm. "Don't get excited, lady," he said. "I meant no harm."

Cathy couldn't see his face clearly, but his oily voice sent a shiver up her spine. Not only was Garcia tricky, but she sensed that he could be dangerous. "You

169

still haven't told me what you want here," she said, playing for time.

Garcia edged slowly around the wall, toward the door. After he cut her off from the exit, he knew he would have to become nasty in order to convince Cathy to keep her mouth shut.

Cathy saw him creeping toward the door, and her blood ran cold. She had disliked him from the moment she had met him, and Ginny Dobbs's refusal to discuss him or explain their relationship indicated further that he was an unpleasant person.

"It pays," Garcia said, "for people to mind their own business and keep quiet about what's of no concern to them. You see what I mean?"

"This is my cabin, and you were going through my trunk," Cathy said. As he moved to the door, she inched around the cabin in the opposite direction until she reached her own bunk.

"Lady," he said, "I don't have the patience to argue with you. And if there's anything I hate, it's a woman who talks too much. Just forget you saw me here, and everything will be all right. Start making a fuss, and I'll have to make sure you can't talk. Now you see what I mean?"

There was no way Cathy could bolt or even slide past him to the door. And escape through one of the small windows was impossible. Garcia took a step toward her, paused, and took another step.

In spite of the gloom, Cathy could now see him clearly. His eyes glittered, and the viciousness and hate she saw in them shocked her.

He moved forward, flexing his hands, a lopsided smile making furrows in his unshaven face.

Cathy was frightened, but she refused to be cowed. "Get out," she said, "or you'll really be in trouble."

"I guess I'll just have to teach you a little respect," Garcia replied. He leaped forward and slapped her hard across the face with the back of his hand. Cathy gasped and lights seemed to flash before her eyes. Then Garcia's hands closed around her neck. He was losing control, not thinking clearly. All he knew was that he had to silence this woman, even if it meant choking her to death.

Cathy fought to maintain consciousness. She beat Garcia with her fists and kicked, but she was unable to loosen the grip of the hands that were squeezing the breath from her body.

Suddenly one of her arms struck an object, and it clattered to the hard ground of the floor. She had knocked one of her carving knives from a shelf. Slowly, carefully, she reached toward the shelf and groped there until her fingers closed on the handle of another, somewhat smaller knife. Grasping it firmly, she slashed at the man. The blade cut through Garcia's shirt. He released his hold and backed away.

"Drop that knife!" he commanded. "Drop it now, or it'll go even worse for you!"

Scarcely realizing what she was doing, Cathy screamed at the top of her lungs.

Garcia took a tentative step toward her. She slashed at him again, missing but fending him off a second time. Then she screamed again, and the sound bounced against the log walls of the cabin.

The door opened suddenly. It took only an instant for Whip Holt and Lee Blake to absorb what they saw. Whip reached for the bullwhip that he carried around his middle. Before he could uncoil it, however, Lee sprang into action. He ran for Garcia and punched him in the jaw. His fist landed so hard that Garcia hit the wall, and the whole structure shuddered. Lee struck a second time, then a third, his fists finding their target again and again. There was no need for Whip to intervene, so he stood quietly poised, ready to step into the fray if the situation warranted it.

Garcia fought back with his fists, but he was no match for Lee, who scarcely felt the blows and continued to pound unmercifully at the man. Garcia slumped to the ground and seemed on the verge of losing consciousness. Whip stepped forward and calmly removed the knife and pistol from the man's belt.

Licking blood from a scraped knuckle, Lee turned at last to Cathy. Slowly regaining her poise, she thanked her rescuers, then told them the story of what had happened. She had no idea she was still gripping the carving knife. Whip took it from her and placed it on the shelf. "I guess we know now where we can find that missing gold locket," he said.

Lee shook his head. "I didn't agree with Ernie when he insisted we build a little cabin to use as a jail, but he was right. Do you have the key to the padlock, Whip?"

"Right here in my pocket. We'll take him there right now. And I suppose we'll have to pick up an extra blanket and a buffalo robe for him. Since there's no hearth in that cabin, he's going to get a mite chilly."

Garcia was still unconscious, and Lee picked him up and threw him over his shoulder. Nodding to Whip, he headed toward the door.

"Sure you're all right, Cathy?" Whip asked as he followed Lee outside.

She managed a smile. "I'll be fine, thanks to both of you." Hoping she didn't betray her real feelings by trembling too obviously, she gathered up the carving knifes that she would need in the kitchen.

By the time she left the cabin, she could see Whip

and Lee in the distance, approaching the tiny jail. They unlocked the door and threw Garcia inside. Cathy could find something good in most people, but she had no pity or sympathy for Garcia. If Whip and Lee hadn't rescued her, she might well be dead by now.

Cathy didn't feel like working, but she refused to shirk her duty and went to the community hall. The other women in the kitchen, seeing that she was white-faced and shaken, persuaded her to tell them what had happened. When Cathy reluctantly told her story, her friends insisted that she sit down. La-ena made her a mug of herb tea and brought it to her.

Cathy just wanted to be alone. She shut out the sounds of the women's voices as they continued with their work. The experience she had just undergone brought home to her how far she was from the civilized world in which she had grown up. For the first time in many months, she wished she had remained in Independence with her sister, Claudia, and her brother-in-law, Sam Brentwood. The problems of wilderness living had never seemed so great.

As she sipped her tea, someone loomed above her. "Mind if I join you for a minute?" Whip asked.

Cathy's heart skipped a beat, and she nodded in assent.

"I just wanted to make sure you're all right," he said, seating himself on the bench at the opposite side of the table from Cathy. Avoiding his gaze, she nodded again.

"I have another reason." Whip spoke slowly and with great difficulty. "Seeing you trying to defend yourself against Garcia gave me quite a turn. I—I know how I'd have felt if something had happened to you."

"Please," she murmured, "I'd rather not talk right now."

But now that he had started, nothing could stop Whip. "You and I haven't had a real talk in a long, long time. You've been peeved with me, and you've had a right to feel the way you do. But there's another side to the story. I—I want to tell you about La-ena and me—her showing up on the trail and all."

Cathy stared at him. La-ena was at the far side of the community hall, almost within earshot. She might join them at any moment, as she had a perfect right to do.

"No, Whip!" Cathy spoke softly, but her tone was urgent. "There's nothing you can say that would be of interest to me on that subject."

Whip was miserable. "But you have a right to know."

Cathy leaped to her feet, threw her buffalo cape around her shoulders, and fled, racing down the path through the snow to her own cabin. Whip stood, but didn't follow her.

La-ena watched him from the fire, but she did not come to him. Eulalia Woodling felt no inhibitions, however, and crossed the hall. "Sit down!" she ordered.

Few people ever spoke to Whip in such a commanding tone, and he obeyed humbly. Eulalia faced him, her hands on her hips. "You've upset Cathy!" she accused him.

Still unable to understand why Cathy had departed so abruptly, Whip repeated the brief conversation to Eulalia.

Eulalia's brief laugh expressed her wonderment. "Arnold Mell says that, after Jim Bridger and Kit Carson, you're probably the most accomplished mountain man in the West. My brother tells me he's never seen a marksman as accurate, and I know myself that you're the best guide anywhere But you know absolutely nothing about women."

"I reckon not," he muttered.

Eulalia sat on the bench opposite him and leaned her elbows on the long table. "You were actually going to tell her about you and La-ena—with La-ena right here in the room?"

"There's not that much to tell. That's the point. I—well, I took up with La-ena some years ago. A man who spends most of his time alone in the mountains needs a woman. And she was special—she still is. But I thought we'd said our final goodbyes when I went East to lead the wagon train. I had no idea she'd show up on the trail, like she did."

Eulalia smiled. "For one thing," she said, "you picked the worst of all possible times and the most inappropriate of places to talk to Cathy. Not only was she still shaken after what had just happened to her, but La-ena is right here in the hall."

"If she doesn't mind, I don't see why it should bother Cathy."

"Through no fault of my own, thanks only to my many weeks as an Indian captive, I've come to understand the Indian way of thinking, at least to an extent. I strongly suspect La-ena does mind. She keeps glancing in this direction, and she's wondering what all this earnest talk is about. But she's too polite to ask, because it isn't a squaw's place to question her warrior."

"You could be right."

"As for Cathy, did it ever cross your mind that she was as interested in you as you were in her?"

"Sure," Whip replied, becoming more aggressive. "That's exactly why I wanted to explain to her!"

Eulalia shook her head in exasperation. "I don't pretend to know the extent to which Cathy imagined she was in love with you, Whip, but that really doesn't matter—because anything she may have felt for you is either dead or dying."

He blinked. "But my feelings for her haven't changed."

"Whip," Eulalia explained patiently, "your heart is in the right place, and you're basically a good person, but you're hopeless. You're telling me you love Cathy, is that right?"

"Yes. I think so."

"But your life has been complicated by La-ena. She not only joined you on the trail, but she's living with you. You sleep with her every night, just as you did for years when you were active as a mountain man."

He shifted uncomfortably on the hard bench. "When the weather gets warm, La-ena will go back to her own tribe."

"You hope. Suppose she decides she wants to stay with you permanently."

"She knows I'm thinking of settling in Oregon myself. The time is coming when I've got to settle down."

"With La-ena, if that's what she wants," Eulalia said.

"I can't see that. She doesn't say much, but I know she doesn't care for our world. And she misses her own people."

Eulalia glanced at the Indian girl, then turned back to Whip. "You gave her that elk-tooth necklace she wears, didn't you?"

He nodded, not understanding what she was trying to say.

"If you expect her to give you back the necklace when spring comes and then ride off to join her own tribe, you know nothing about women. La-ena loves you, Whip, and she'll go anywhere with you."

"Not to Oregon. That's not her way. Besides, we

never planned to spend our whole lives together. We're not married!"

"I can see how a man would want one woman as his wife even while he's living with another woman," Eulalia said slowly, "but that takes a rather special understanding. I only understand because of the time I spent with the Indians. Cathy doesn't have that kind of knowledge, and neither does any other woman on this train, except Cindy." She paused and studied him. "Not that it's any of my business, but are you telling me that if Cathy would have you and agree to become your wife, you'd send La-ena away?"

Whip was shocked. "No, of course not! What I'm saying is that when the warm weather comes, La-ena will go off of her own free will, because she wants to go. I'll always have warm thoughts for her, and I'm sure she'll think kindly of me, too. But we'll go our separate ways."

Eulalia sighed. "Anything is possible, so I won't debate the point with you. There's just one thing I want to make very plain. If you have any regard for Cathy, let her feeling for you die."

He started to protest.

"No, hear me out," Eulalia said. "There's no way on earth you can win Cathy now. You had your chance, and you lost it."

"But if you can understand my position, why can't she?"

"Once upon a time," Eulalia said, "I was a lady, but I'm not any more. I've learned things about life—and people—and myself—that I never would have believed. Cathy van Ayl is a lady and will be one as long as she lives. Not only was her pride shattered when La-ena arrived, but she lost her faith in you, and it would take years for her to regain it—more years than either of you could possibly wait."

Whip's pain was evident in his eyes. In spite of his wisdom, courage, and strength, he was as vulnerable as a small boy. Eulalia's heart went out to him. "Be glad you have La-ena," she said. "She's a fine woman. Even if you're right, and I hope you aren't, that she doesn't like the ways of whites and intends to leave us, you'll still manage."

Eulalia made a deliberate attempt to end their talk on a light note. "Of course, you've been a mountain man for so long that you're half-savage yourself by now. But I'm sure there are widows and single girls on this train—and all the trains to follow—who'll have the mistaken notion they can tame you and will want to try." Then she became serious again. "But for Cathy's sake, Whip, leave her alone."

VII

Twice each year the Foreign Office held what it was pleased to call its "Punch Hour," and every diplomat accredited to Whitehall put in an obligatory appearance. The punch had a rum base but was so mild that the French ambassador swore it contained no hard liquor at all. The waiters in impeccable livery offered tray after tray of the concoction, but few took more than a single cup. The little cakes served with the punch invariably were stale, and the sandwiches were tasteless.

But every representative of a foreign government made it his business to be present. There were few opportunities to exchange gossip with all of one's colleagues, and even fewer opportunities to chat informally with the austere Lord Palmerston, who had the annoying habit of holding formal meetings only, and these in his office.

The stone floors of the reception hall were cold, and marble pillars contributed to a sense of chill, but it was possible for the gentlemen of the diplomatic corps to speak off the record with Lord Palmerston, and the opportunity was too good to miss.

Tom Brossard, the chargé d'affaires and second in command of the American Legation, bided his time, drinking punch and eating stale cakes as he spoke with his peers from the Netherlands, Spain, Austria, and the Ottoman Empire. Inasmuch as the Turkish chargé knew very little English, this was no small achievement.

But Tom Brossard, like any accomplished diplomat, was a patient man. He had begun his State Department career during the presidency of John Quincy Adams. After more than a decade in the service, he had developed an exquisite sense of timing.

When Lord Palmerston finally approached Brossard, the American looked relaxed, at peace with himself and the world.

"Ah, Mr. Brossard. Your servant, sir."

"Your servant, milord." Brossard paused delicately. "You look well."

A slight quizzical tone in Brossard's voice caused Palmerston to raise an eyebrow. "Is there a reason I shouldn't?"

Brossard's shrug spoke volumes. "The cares of office sometimes bow a man's shoulders. Be that as it may, I want to offer you—strictly informally, of course—the sincere thanks of President Van Buren and John Jacob Astor."

"Is Astor active in your government now?" Palmerston knew something unusual was forthcoming.

"No, but he's a major investor in the American wagon train currently on its way to Oregon."

"And he's thanking me, he and your President?"

"Indeed, milord." Brossard oozed enthusiastic sincerity. "Our people who are making that journey face many hazards—mountains, deserts, wilderness, wild animals, savage Indians. That's why President Van

Buren and Mr. Astor are so grateful to you. Your gift to them of so many dozens of your latest, most accurate rifles is priceless! I assure you, milord, those weapons are being used daily, replacing old, almost worthless muskets. They'll be used in Oregon, too, to protect the settlements our pioneers will establish there, and none of them will ever forget your kindness."

It was said that the Foreign Secretary was never at a loss for words, but the rumor was inaccurate. He turned pale and was momentarily speechless. Brossard knew beyond a doubt that news of the incident in which the warriors of the Blackfoot had discarded the British rifles they had been given before attacking the wagon train had reached London and had caused serious repercussions in the highest circles. The President and State Department soon would know their belief had been verified. "I'd like to add my personal thanks, milord," Brossard said, still straightfaced. "I'm overwhelmed by your generosity."

"Quite so," Lord Palmerston murmured, then moved on, his back rigid.

Somebody, the delighted Tom Brossard thought, would catch hell for that embarrassing mistake. But there had been no need for the United States to lodge an official complaint.

Reverend Cavendish's pocket watch and chain were found at the bottom of one of Garcia's saddlebags, and so was Tilman Wade's locket. There was no doubt of Garcia's guilt. The pioneers faced a problem unique in the experience of the wagon train, and they voted to leave the matter in the hands of their president, Ernie von Thalman, who decided to give Garcia a civilian version of a court-martial trial.

Two days after Cathy's unpleasant experience, the

community hall was cleared immediately after breakfast. Ernie sat at one of the long tables, flanked by Lee Blake and Whip, whom he asked to join him as members of the court-martial board. The various witnesses remained at the far end of the hall.

Guarded by Paul Thoman and Jacob Levine, Garcia was escorted into the building. After spending more than forty-eight hours in the unheated jail cabin, he was chilled to the bone and was granted permission to warm himself at the fire. He stood with his back to everyone, surly and uncommunicative, as he stared into the flames.

Ernie called the board to order. Reverend Cavendish identified his property, which was then returned to him, and he left the hall at once. Tilman Wade then identified his locket and regained possession of it. He joined the small group still waiting to testify.

Cathy van Ayl was called forward, and she told her story succinctly. Then Lee stepped down from the makeshift bench and explained how he and Whip had intervened in time to save Cathy. Garcia continued to stand with his back to the proceedings.

Virginia Dobbs was called forward. As she took a seat in front of the court, Garcia turned slowly, locked his hands behind his back, and glowered at her. Ernie instantly became aware of Gracia's attempt to intimidate Ginny. "You may sit down now, Garcia," he said.

The man continued to stand. Ernie nodded to Levine, who promptly twisted one of Garcia's arms behind his back and forced him into a chair. The tactics were crude, but wilderness justice was rough.

"Tell us whatever you want about Garcia," Ernie said to Ginny. "Since you know him better than any of us, your information will be a help to us."

Ginny glared at Garcia. "All I can tell you," she

said slowly, "is that I wouldn't have traveled with him if I'd known him as I do now."

"Could you be more specific?" Ernie prompted her gently.

"Somewhere in the snow outside his cabin," she said, "you'll find a bag made of antelope hide. In it are all kinds of things he stole from people before we left California."

Garcia cursed her. The girl regarded him coolly. "He's a thief. Even when he has no reason to steal, he can't leave other people's property alone. I wouldn't trust him near anything that belongs to me, no matter what he said or did."

Lee interrupted to ask a question. "When people are living as close together as circumstances force us to live here, how would you stop him from stealing?"

"There's only one way," Ginny said. Fingering the hilt of the knife she carried in her belt, she slowly drew it. "This is the only language he understands. I made him return a gold chalice he stole from some monks at a monastery in California by promising to sink this into him, to the hilt, and he knew I meant it. For the rest of our weeks on the trail, he didn't dare come near me because he knew what I'd do to him."

"That's a damn lie!" Garcia shouted. "I'm not afraid of any woman!"

Ginny regarded him contemptuously. "That's just talk. Give me five minutes alone with him—and then watch him run."

The scowling man cursed her again. "Keep a civil tongue in your head," Ernie told him. "You're not helping yourself by putting on that kind of an exhibition."

"Hang me and be done with it," Garcia replied. "Stop putting on this mock trial."

Ernie turned back to Ginny. "Is there anything you'd like to add, Miss Dobbs?"

"If it were up to me," Ginny said forcefully, "I'd get rid of him. He can't be trusted, and as long as he's around, there's sure to be trouble."

Lee raised an eyebrow. "You'd send him out into the wilderness in this weather?"

"I don't give a damn what becomes of him," she said emphatically.

She was excused from giving further testimony, and it was apparent that several of those in the hall, principally Cathy and Paul Thoman, were startled by the unforgiving, unyielding stand she had taken. She would condemn Garcia to certain death without the slightest sense of guilt.

The members of the board withdrew to the far end of the hall and conferred in undertones for what seemed like a long time. Finally they returned to their seats, all of them solemn.

"There are two major considerations we've kept in mind," Ernie said. "Our first responsibility is the safety and welfare of the people of this wagon train. There can be no excuse for the assault on Mrs. van Ayl and the attempt to rob her. The theft of property belonging to Oscar Cavendish and Tilman Wade are unfortunate acts that speak for themselves.

"Garcia," he continued, "if this were a different season of the year, we'd send you on your way immediately. But if we send you off now, you'll surely die. You certainly deserve to be punished, but death is an altogether inappropriate sentence for the crimes you have committed. At the same time, we wish to make it clear that you are no longer welcome in our community.

"We can't let you stay indefinitely in the unheated

jail cabin, and we can't keep you in Little Valley, either. So we've had to find another solution. Some of the caves up on the slopes are habitable. We'll take you to one of them and give you enough food and firewood to last you until spring. When the warm weather comes, we'll return your weapons to you, and you'll be able to make your way East—or go wherever you please, by yourself, on foot. What becomes of you and whether you survive won't be our responsibility. Do you have anything to say?"

"God damn all of you!" Garcia's voice throbbed with hatred.

"Return him to the jail cabin for the present," Ernie told the guards. "Several of us will go up to the heights today and find a cave that's suitable. By tomorrow we'll be able to stock it with food and firewood, and then Garcia will be escorted there. Is there anything you want to add to what I've said, gentlemen?"

Lee Blake looked first at Cathy and Ginny, then turned to the prisoner. "Only this," he said. "Garcia, you're being banished permanently from our company. I urge you not to come back here because our sentries will be under orders to shoot you on sight."

"What's more," Whip added in a deceptively quiet tone, "they'll shoot to kill."

Justice had been done, but Cathy felt no satisfaction as she left the hall. Ginny Dobbs had a faint smile on her face as she departed, but as Tilman Wade watched her, he could not guess what she was really thinking. It was difficult to believe her desire for vengeance was so great that she had no pity, no sympathy for the man who, no matter what he had done, had been her companion on the trail for many weeks.

WYOMING!

The house on Boston's Beacon Hill, overlooking the Common, was large and solid, discreetly imposing, and the parlor was furnished in understated good taste. The furniture, comfortable but plain, had been imported from England and was far more expensive than it looked. Portraits of ladies and gentlemen covered the walls, and some had been in place for the better part of a century. As everyone in Boston well knew, there was no more substantial a family in the city, or in all of Massachusetts, than the Thomans.

The tall, distinguished-looking, silver-haired shipbuilder stood in front of the hearth, reading aloud the letter he had just received from his son. His voice was that of a self-assured man who knew his place in the world. His sharp-featured wife, genteel in a gown of dark brown silk, sat with her hands folded in her lap, betraying no emotion as she listened.

When Mr. Thoman finished reading aloud, he extended the letter to her. Mrs. Thoman shook her head. "I'll go through it again later," she said, "after I've had a chance to catch my breath and regain my balance. The shock is almost too much. Here we've been expecting Paul to be returning home at any time, and instead—we get this."

"His behavior is inexcusable, and his attitudes are incomprehensible. I don't understand him."

She sighed gently. "I sometimes find it hard to believe he's our son."

Mr. Thoman filled two small crystal glasses with mild sack, which he poured from a cut-glass decanter, then handed one to his wife. "It was bad enough when he left Harvard to spend a year in the Rocky Mountains, thanks to the romantic rubbish he read about the lives led by the trappers there. But now—this." He tapped the letter, then placed it carefully in an inner pocket.

Again Mrs. Thoman sighed. "At least he's live and healthy. And he does make quite a point of insisting that he'll ask his Harvard professors to send him his final examinations after he reaches Oregon so he can earn his degree. He hasn't lost all sense of the proper values."

"But Oregon!" her husband exploded. "Why would any sane young man, even one who craves adventure, go off to a Godforsaken, uninhabited land three thousand miles from home? It makes no sense!"

"He mentioned a girl named Sally. Perhaps she's responsible."

"It's possible, but I think not. He devotes two pages to the wonders of the Oregon country—which he's never seen. He's anticipating Heaven, based strictly on hearsay evidence."

"I know," Mrs. Thoman said. "It's maddening. And the worst of it is that there's no way we can appeal to what little logic he may have left in him. He's spending the winter somewhere in the wilds of the Rockies with a band of immigrant farmers. We can't even write to him."

Her husband lowered his tall frame into a chair on the opposite side of the hearth. "I can understand Paul's craving for adventure. After all, I accepted a commission in the navy during the War of 1812 and fulfilled my craving for adventure by serving for three years as an officer on the *Constellation*."

"So you did, my dear," she said, smiling. "But you were an officer and a gentleman. You didn't wear animal hides, go weeks at a time without bathing, and subsist on buffalo meat."

"I can recall eating buffalo steak many years ago," he said. "I wouldn't care to repeat the experiment, mind you, but in retrospect the taste was somewhat better than I'd expected."

"You've never forgotten your place in the world. That is what so disappoints me in Paul."

"What I can't understand," he said, "is that he's giving up a place in the shipyard that's been in the family for four generations. I suppose he's reasoned that there's no need for him there, what with an older brother and a brother-in-law already in training to take over."

"But one-third ownership would have been his some day."

"Don't despair," her husband replied. "He's still very young, so we can only hope that eventually he'll tire of teaching the fundamentals of reading, writing, and arithmetic to the children of illiterate farmers and will come to his senses."

She considered the possibility, then shrugged. "Exposure to the lowest common denominator can be coarsening, and forgive me if I sound like a snob."

"Oh, we're snobs," her husband said, and for the first time he laughed. "The family has gloried in it for decades, and I can't say I find it one of our more admirable traits. We pay lip service to the principles of democracy, but Paul is the only one of us who tries to live according to them."

"You denigrate yourself," Mrs. Thoman said. "It's common knowledge you treat your hired help generously."

"Well, what bothers me most is that if Paul wanted a sabbatical to satisfy his craving for adventure, he could have done it sensibly. Certainly he could have sailed with Cousin Charles on his trading ship to Cathay, a voyage that would have lasted a year and a half. And his share, after the sale of the cargo from Canton to Shanghai, would have amounted to a pretty penny."

"What's more," Mrs. Thoman said, "Cousin Charles

would have given him a commission as a third lieutenant."

Her husband hesitated before refilling their glasses but decided the occasion demanded a little more sack. "I shall grieve for him, of course, and there will always be a place for him at the yard if he changes his mind. If he doesn't—well, he's a man now, and if he chooses to make his bed out of wilderness boughs, he'll simply have to lie on it."

Paul Thoman was chilled to the bone after spending two hours on sentry duty. He went straight to the community hall, where the fire was far larger then those in the cabins and shed more warmth. As he had hoped, Sally MacNeill was still in the kitchen, cleaning up after breakfast. Not yet shedding his buffalo cape, he stood shivering in front of the fire.

Sally quickly brought him a mug of steaming herb tea. "We don't have much coffee left," she said, "but this is better for you. Did anything happen out there this morning?"

"Yes—two things," he replied, taking the tea gratefully. "On a mundane level, we're going to have some more visitors. I spotted them coming down from the heights a little while ago, and I notified Lee Blake. A couple of stray Indians, I think. On a higher level, I was privileged to witness one of the most glorious of sights—sunrise in a clear sky over the mountains to the east. I felt rhapsodic!"

She looked at him blankly. "You felt how?"

"Do you have that book I loaned you?"

"I brought it with me and tried to read it at breakfast, but I couldn't make head or tail of it. I saved you some oatmeal."

"Verse and food. What more could a man ask?"

She went off, returning shortly with a huge bowl of oatmeal and a slender volume.

Paul took the book from her as he sat. "These are poems by an Englishman named Percy Bysshe Shelley, who died about sixteen years ago. He isn't well-known, but I had the good fortune to pick this up at a shop in Cambridge a short time before I came to the mountains. Listen, and you'll understand how I felt when I saw the sunrise." He leafed through the book, paused, then read in a sonorous voice:

> "Hail to thee, blithe Spirit!
> Bird thou never wert.
> That from Heaven, or near it,
> Pourest thy full heart
> In profuse strains of unpremeditated art."

He paused, looking across the table in anticipation.

"The thong at the neck of your shirt is broken," Sally said. "You're bound to be chilly if your neck is cold. I'll ask Dolores for another strip of rawhide, and I'll sew it on for you."

"Thank you." The thoroughly deflated Paul concentrated on his oatmeal for a time. "What in that verse didn't you understand?"

She realized he was trying to share his joy with her, so she made an effort. "Well," she said, "I don't see how you can hail a bird that never was."

Her education was going to take even longer than he had thought. "This is an epicurean meal. I've never had better oatmeal."

"There's plenty more." Sally became shy. "I made it."

"Did you?" She was not only pretty, but in her own way she was talented. "In that case I believe I shall have another helping."

She jumped to her feet and took his bowl back to the pot where she refilled it for him. From the quantity of food he was eating, it was obvious that he was not paying her an idle compliment.

"You spoil me," Paul said as she handed him the bowl. "Other people around here have to wait on themselves."

"Oh, I like doing things for you," she said.

"And vice versa," he replied. "Later this morning, after we find out why those two Indians are snooping around, we'll take another whack at Shelley. I prophesy that by the end of the winter, you'll have gained a perfect understanding of his most difficult poem, *Prometheus Unbound*."

Sally nodded assent. She had no interest in poetry, but when Paul played the instructor, he spent hours at a time with her, and she was content.

A number of other people were gathering in the hall now, La-ena and Dolores among them, and soon the leaders of the expedition entered, escorting two bedraggled Indian warriors, both so painfully thin that their bones seemed on the verge of poking through their skin.

Cindy brought them bowls of oatmeal, and they ate so ravenously that La-ena, speaking to them in an Indian dialect, warned them to slow down. When they had finished their meal, Whip spoke to them at length.

At last Whip turned to the settlers. "These braves are members of the Ute nation," he said. "Their town is about thirty miles to the south of us, maybe a little farther. They were hunting and saw the smoke from our fires. Ordinarily, they don't travel this far from their homes, but game is scarce. It's the worst winter they've ever known. Even when they spot game, the animals are skittish, and the warriors can't get close enough to kill them. They say their whole town is starving."

"How many people are in their town?" someone wanted to know.

"Almost fifteen hundred."

"We've got to help them," Lee Blake said. "We can't feed them through the winter without running too low ourselves, but we can send them several days' supply of buffalo meat."

"Yes, and we can help them in other ways," Whip said. "I'll take a party of volunteer hunters with me to deliver the meat, and maybe we'll have better luck with our rifles than they've had with their bows and arrows."

"Shelley will have to wait, I'm afraid," Paul told Sally, and immediately offered his services.

"Why do we have to feed a pack of Indians?" The speaker was a burly young carpenter from Illinois, Walter Cooley.

His tiny wife, Fran, nodded in agreement.

Their narrow-mindedness annoyed Lee. "For one thing," he said, "the Ute are our neighbors. And for another, people in the wilderness help each other whenever they can. The survival of all depends on it."

Virtually all the people who were in the hall smiled and nodded in agreement. Walter and Fran Cooley left hastily, muttering to each other in angry undertones.

A rescue party was organized rapidly. By mid-morning the mounted hunters, each leading a heavily laden pack horse, left Little Valley, accompanied by the two Ute, who were riding borrowed horses. Because of the ice and thick snow underfoot, the journey would take two days. That night the chilled group slept in the open, protected by a shield of boulders, and the journey was resumed at daybreak.

Whip led the party into the Ute town late in the afternoon. The Indians poured into the open to greet their own two warriors and visitors. Many of them had distended bellies, a sign of malnutrition.

Skaw-kaub, the chief of the Ute, invited the visitors into his own house, which, although somewhat larger than the others, was built of the same materials—boulders for the walls, with animal skins for the roof. As they crowded into it, Skaw-kaub apologized for his lack of hospitality. Their food supplies were so depleted, he said, that his people were being rationed, with each individual receiving only a half-gourd of parched corn each day.

Whip and his companions immediately presented him with the gift of buffalo meat. Skaw-kaub told the tribe of the gift, and they rejoiced. Despite their weakness and physical exhaustion, they staged an impromptu dance of thanks around the fires they lighted in open pits. For the first time in weeks, the odors of cooking meat rose on the cold air. Even though the visitors were hungry, they ate lightly in order not to deprive their hosts of the food they so badly needed.

Whip, Pierre le Rouge, and Paul Thoman agreed that the most likely place in the area to find game would be a nearby wooded plateau. Skaw-kaub confirmed that elk, deer, and other game were sometimes seen in the pine forest, but the animals were hungry, too, and were so jittery that they raced beyond the range of the tribe's most accomplished warriors.

There were tears in the sachem's eyes as he watched the men, women, and children devouring buffalo meat.

"We have prayed·to the good spirits of the earth," he said to Whip. "They have heard us and brought you to us."

The following day, Stalking Horse devised a plan to drive the game into the open. The wagon train party divided into teams of two men each. Soon after dawn, the teams stationed themselves at various points on the open portion of the plateau surrounding the thick pine woods. All Ute warriors and older boys who were strong enough to walk steadily encircled the woods, then slowly began to move into the forest. More than three hundred braves took part, each rhythmically beating two sticks together. The hunters waiting in the open heard the sound as the warriors vanished from sight, keeping their circular formation as they made their way through the deep snow. The object of the maneuver was simple. The hunters hoped that any game lurking in the forest feeding on the foliage would be driven into the open.

The scheme soon proved effective when a pair of frightened elk made a wild dash onto the open plateau. Jacob Levine and Tilman Wade made the first kills of the morning. Levine brought down the cow with a single shot, and Tilman wounded the buck, then quickly reloaded and dispatched the wounded animal.

The pace was maintained all through the morning. Even Whip was surprised by the number of animals in the forest. After three hours, when the Ute returned from the woods, eleven mature elk and three calves had been shot, along with thirty-seven deer.

The carcasses were butchered on the spot, then each warrior carried a share on his back, and as the entire group trudged slowly back to the Ute town, the braves chanted in unison until they were hoarse. Even then they did not stop, and when they reached the town, the chant was taken up by the sick, the women, and the children. Starvation had been averted, and although the people of the town would not eat well, they would be able to survive through the rest of the winter.

Stalking Horse suggested one further strategem to Whip, who in turn relayed it to Skaw-kaub. "Dig some deep pits in a circle, and cover each with branches. In the center of the circle, place a piece of deer meat as bait. The wolves are hungry also, and it may be that the lure of the deer meat will cause some to fall into the pits."

His advice was followed promptly, the tired braves taking turns digging the pits a safe distance from the town. At dawn, when the warriors returned, they discovered that the bait had vanished. But nine wolves had been caught in the traps. In other seasons, wolf meat was shunned by everyone in the mountains, Indians and trappers alike, but in winter it would be a welcome addition to their larder.

The hunters, their mission completed, prepared to return to Little Valley. The entire town gathered to see them off, and each hunter was presented with a square of leather on which was burned the Ute symbol of peace. The squares were attached to thongs so they could be worn as necklaces, and Paul Thoman promptly decided he would give his to Sally MacNeill. He suspected she might prefer it to poetry reading.

Before the visitors departed, Skaw-kaub made a farewell speech. "The men with white skin who come from the land beyond the mountains are welcome for all time in the land of the Ute," he said. "The Ute have been told by their cousins, the Comanche and the Arapaho, that men with white skins are bad. They say these men kill warriors and steal women. But the Comanche and the Arapaho lie. The men with white skins are our brothers. All other Ute will learn what our brothers did here, and they also will open their arms and hearts and homes to those we salute as our brothers."

Fifty warriors accompanied the party for a short distance as a gesture of friendship and respect.

"How would you like to spend your whole life up here in the mountains, year after year?" Tilman asked Jacob, who was riding beside him. "Seeing no one except Indians and other hunters, gorging on liquor, women, and food in some town for a couple of weeks each year, losing all your money and then coming back to the mountains."

"It's not for me," Jacob said. "When I was a fur cutter in New York, I dreamed of becoming a trapper, but the way we live on the wagon train is rugged enough."

"The same for me," Tilman said. "All I want is an orchard where I can grow apples and pears, and enough wheat to send back East to keep me in cash."

"I've been thinking lately," Jacob said. "What I'd like to do is build a sawmill on a fast-moving, powerful river. I could be happy there for the rest of my life, especially if I never have to kill another wild animal again."

"I don't enjoy hunting, either," Tilman replied, "but it's lucky for the Ute that both of us are pretty good at it."

The first day's journey was uneventful, but snow, whipped by a strong, chilling wind, fell steadily for several hours the next morning. The group was forced to halt and take shelter—as best they could—in a narrow gorge. The delay slowed their progress, and it was noon of the third day before they descended into Little Valley, cheered by the smoke that rose from the chimneys.

As they reached the lake and headed toward the stables, however, they noticed a commotion in front of the community hall. Forgetting their weariness, they hastened toward the scene.

Walter Cooley stood with his back to the building, a cocked pistol in one hand and a hunting knife in the other. Beside him was his wife, Fran, her eyes wild and glazed as she brandished a kitchen knife. "Make them go away, Walter," she said. "I can't stand the sight of any of them any more."

"You heard my wife!" Cooley shouted, his voice ugly. "Clear out!"

Ernie von Thalman and Dr. Martin stood a short distance away, beyond Cooley's reach, with the crowd clustered behind them.

The members of the hunting party dismounted at once, and Danny and several other boys took the mounts and pack horses to the stables to feed them.

"Cooley," Ernie said, "put down those weapons before somebody gets hurt."

"Leave us alone," Fran screamed. "All we want is to be left alone!"

"Walter, Fran, listen to me," Dr. Martin said in a controlled voice. "You've both been suffering from cabin fever for a long time. Usually it's a mild ailment, but your case appears to be rather severe I've seen the symptoms, as I have in so many of us, but right now you're on the verge of going off the deep end. What you both need is medication and rest. Let me treat you, and you'll soon be feeling relieved."

"Go away!" Fran shouted.

Lee and Whip exchanged swift glances. The Cooleys were dangerous.

"If you don't move along by the time I count to three," Walter Cooley snarled, "I'm going to fire at the doc. One—two—"

Jacob Levine leaped forward, a hand extended to take hold of the carpenter's pistol. Cooley fired but missed, then slashed Jacob's shoulder. Bleeding heavily, Jacob staggered backward. Two men caught him before he fell, picked him up, and carried him to the nearby medical cabin.

"There's nothing I can do with the Cooleys now," Bob Martin said to Ernie as he started to follow his wife to the medical cabin. "They've got to be subdued, but God knows how."

"I can't stand any more!" Fran screamed, and plunged the kitchen knife deep into her body.

As the horrified onlookers watched, she sank to the ground, her blood turning the hard-packed snow crimson, and stared up at the clear winter sky with sightless eyes. Cathy covered her face with her hands. Cindy gasped, and Eulalia, who thought herself to be tough, became sick to her stomach.

Walter Cooley drew another pistol and edged closer to his rifle, which was propped against the wall of the community hall. He laughed maniacally. "Don't anybody come near my wife!" he shouted. "She wanted to be left alone, and that's the way it'll be!" He laughed again.

Obviously he had to be rushed, and Lee suggested that a diversion be created. Whip agreed. But Cooley created his own diversion. He fired his second pistol, the bullet landing in Grace Drummond's leg. She crumpled to the ground, screaming in pain. Even as she fell, the maddened man threw aside his pistol, snatched his rifle, and bolted, racing around the community hall and then running wildly toward the woods.

"We've got to catch him before he hurts anyone else," Ernie said.

Whip drew a deep breath. "He's gone crazy," he said. "I've seen it happen to others. Pretty soon, he'll convince himself we killed his wife, and then he'll start shooting up the whole camp."

"I suggest we organize a search party immediately," Lee said.

Ernie wasted no time. All able-bodied men who could handle firearms were ordered to fetch their weapons immediately. As they returned, they were sent off to the woods in teams of two, advancing more or less in unison on a level line, to flush out the insane carpenter.

"One thing more, before we go," Lee called. "If you can, take him alive. But don't run any unnecessary risks. He'll kill any and all of us, if he can. So, if you must, shoot him."

More than one hundred men joined in the search. Some of the older men who remained behind removed the tiny body of Fran Cooley from the scene of her suicide. A coffin was built, and her body was placed in it. A funeral would be held for her later.

Many of the women and children remained clustered together in front of the community hall, talking in low but excited terms.

Cindy knew it would be wise if they dispersed. "Go back to your own cabins, everybody," she called. "If that poor man comes back here, we make perfect targets for him. Go home and stay there until he's caught."

The women and children obeyed, and soon the area in front of the community hall was deserted.

In the medical cabin Bob Martin was very busy. Applying a tourniquet to Jacob's shoulder to stop the bleeding, he said to his wife, "Tonie, give him laudanum. Two tablespoons in an equal amount of water. I'm not sure he can keep it down, but we've got to try. The next half-hour won't be any fun for him."

Tonie prepared the medicine, raised Jacob's head, and told him to open his mouth. Groggy and still in a state of shock, he obeyed, then fell back onto the operating table.

Tightening the tourniquet, Bob Martin watched his patient's face. Laudanum was a potent drug, and it worked quickly. Within minutes, the pupils of Jacob's eyes began to dilate.

"Is there anybody around who can help?" Bob asked.

"Yes—Nat Drummond. Cooley shot Grace in the leg, and she's stretched out in the reception room."

"If Nat can leave her for a few minutes, ask him to come in here."

In a moment Nat appeared. "Don't you worry about Grace, Doc," he said. "Her leg hurts like blazes, but she ain't going to fall apart. She's as strong as a mule, and she'll stay put while you look after Jake."

"I'll give you some laudanum to ease her pain while she's waiting," Bob said. "But first I need your help. Take hold of Jacob's ankles and hang on for dear life. He's going to kick like a steer being branded. All right, Tonie. Hold his wrists." He bent close to the patient. "Jacob, can you hear me?"

His patient nodded feebly.

"You've had a clean cut," Bob said, "and from its location, I don't believe the bone has been damaged. That means you'll probably recover the complete use of your arm, provided you do exactly what I tell you. If you fail me, you'll be failing yourself, and it could cause permanent damage. Do you understand?"

Again Jacob nodded.

"I've got to clean out your wound before I sew it up, and I can't give you any more medication until I'm done. I'm putting a wooden bit into your mouth. Clamp your teeth down on it. That's it. Now harder."

Jacob did as he was told.

"When I clean out the wound, it will hurt, more than any pain you've ever suffered. But it will only last a short time. I'll need your cooperation, and you'll need every ounce of willpower you possess. Don't start kicking, and above all, don't thrash your arms! People will be helping you to hold still, but the real burden is on you. If the bleeding starts again, it will be much more difficult to stop. All right, brace yourself."

The doctor adjusted the tourniquet, drawing it a little tighter, then nodded to Tonie and Nat. They tightened their grips on the patient's wrists and ankles. Tonie, long accustomed to assisting her husband, was calm, but heavy beads of sweat poured down Nat Drummond's weather-beaten face.

Bob picked up a sponge, soaked it in brandywine, the most commonly used antiseptic, then squeezed the contents of the sponge into the patient's open wound.

A searing pain shot through Jacob's arm and seemed to envelop his entire body. His agony was excruciating, the pain more intense than any torture he could have imagined. Tears filled his eyes, blinding him. Moment by moment the pain became worse. He could not think, and gasped repeatedly for breath. The light in the room seemed to fade. He thought he was dying, but he did not care.

Even in his semiconscious state, however, he remembered Dr. Martin's instructions and clung to them. He was no longer aware of the hands grasping his ankles and wrists, but he did not give in to the almost irresistible urge to flail and kick.

Bob Martin was astonished. Never had he known a patient who showed such self-discipline in response to such torment. Working quickly, the physician picked up the needle that Tonie had threaded for him and began to sew together the lips of the ugly wound.

The pain caused by the brandywine was still so great that Jacob didn't feel the needle thrusting through his flesh. Little by little, his body became somewhat numb and his shoulder began to throb. He didn't even realize that the operation was completed. "Drink this," Tonie told him, holding another dose of laudanum to his lips.

The drug burned as Jacob swallowed it, but in a few moments he began to grow drowsy. Later he couldn't even recall being carried to one of the bunks in the makeshift hospital section of the cabin, and not until he awakened the following day did he realize his shoulder had been bandaged. Mercifully, he found refuge in a deep sleep.

Tonie worked rapidly to clean off the operating chamber table, while Bob accompanied Nat to the reception room, where Grace Drummond reclined on a bench. "I think I'm going to lose my leg," she announced, her wound in no way reducing the normal stridency of her voice.

"I doubt it very much," Bob said, giving her a soothing smile. He and Nat half supported, half carried the tall, heavy woman to the operating room.

Grace was given a preliminary dose of laudanum, too, but she remained belligerent. "What are you going to do to me?" she demanded.

"First," the physician told her as Tonie cut away her heavy woolen stocking, "I've got to examine you."

But Grace writhed, kicked, and squirmed, making it impossible for Bob to come near her. "You'll have to cooperate a bit more," he told her. "I can't even look at your wound if you thrash around that way."

Grace kicked harder.

Nat became annoyed. "Stop acting like a child, Gracie, behave yourself." His words fell on deaf ears. It was too much to ask her to hold still.

"I can't give her any more of the opiate yet, not until I know what needs to be done," Bob said. "Nat, go find some people to help in holding her still."

Nat hurried away, muttering to himself and shaking his head. Soon he returned, accompanied by Sally Mac-Neill and Dolores, the first people he had encountered.

The doctor glanced at them dubiously. Sally was slender and delicately built, and Dolores was tiny. Even working together, he thought it unlikely they had the strength to subdue his strapping patient.

Tonie held one of Grace's arms while Nat grasped the other, and Sally and Dolores attempted to grasp her legs. But the moment Dolores touched the ankle below the leg wound, Grace screamed. She heaved and flailed, throwing Tonie off and causing her husband's grasp to slip.

"Mrs. Drummond needs to be made more quiet," Dolores said. "I think I can help." Not waiting for approval, she raced off.

In a few moments she returned, carrying a small leather pouch from which she produced a dark, greenish-brown powder. "Sprinkle a little of this on her tongue, Doctor," she said, "and Mrs. Drummond will stop fighting you."

"What is it?" Bob asked.

"Dried moss of a kind that grows around the bottom of cedar trees in the Oregon country."

Bob hesitated for a moment, but decided there was nothing to be lost by trying the powder. Most of the stronger men had gone off in search of Walter Cooley, and Bob was reluctant to wait until they returned. The longer Grace's leg remained untreated, the greater the possibility of infection.

"Give her a dose," he said.

"Please open your mouth, Mrs. Drummond." Dolores, as always, was polite.

Grace protested. Awaiting the right moment, Dolores let her talk, then quickly dropped a little of the powder into her mouth. Grace spluttered and tried to spit out the substance, but the particles clung to her tongue. Little by little her efforts subsided, and then, giving a deep sigh, she lay back on the table and smiled. "I'm feeling much better already," she announced. Bob promised himself that before the day ended, he would have a long and serious conversation with Dolores about the various herbs and other products of nature she used as medicines.

Grace was so relaxed now that the physician had no difficulty examining her. The bullet had lodged in the fleshy portion of her calf, about an inch below the surface. As a precaution, he asked the others to hold her wrists and ankles, but Grace, although still talking incessantly, remained remarkably quiet.

Using a small scalpel, he made an incision adjacent to the wound, then removed the bullet with forceps. The wound bled enough to cleanse it, even before the antiseptic was applied. Grace did not move, even when he poured brandywine into the opening. Still talking, she obviously felt no discomfort.

The minor surgery had been successful, but rather than allow Grace to return to her own cabin, Bob had her moved to his "ward" for an overnight stay.

It was apparent from Dolores's calm that she believed nothing out of the ordinary had taken place. But the impressed physician asked her to remain behind after the others had left. Immediately he plunged into a discussion of her herbs and powders. Not since he had first entered medical school had he realized how much he needed to learn.

While Bob Martin had been treating Jacob Levine and Grace Drummond, the search for Walter Cooley had begun in earnest, with Lee in charge of the center sector, Whip in command on his left, and Ernie in charge on his right. The three groups advanced cautiously, knowing that Walter Cooley might appear anywhere, at any moment. Then, too, if the searchers weren't careful, they well might shoot at each other in the dark forest of evergreens.

Of course, Cooley might try to escape to the heights beyond the woods at the far end of the valley, but that was unlikely, and he would be seen immediately if he moved into the open. So the odds were great that he was lurking somewhere in the forest, ready to pounce on anyone who came near him.

Each man had teamed with the first person available, and some unusual partnerships had been formed. None was stranger than the pairing of Claiborne Woodling and Ted Woods, who disliked each other intensely because they regarded themselves as rivals for Cindy's affections.

Now, however, they were compelled to put aside their differences. Making their way into the woods, both knew that Cooley would not hesitate to kill any-one who crossed his path. He was irrational, indifferent to his own fate. Searching for him was even riskier than tracking a mountain lion. Consequently, every man had to depend on his partner for at least partial protection; two pairs of eyes were better than one.

Claiborne had made no secret of his dislike for Ted, and had resolutely ignored him. Now he had to depend on Ted's strength and native cunning, and he hoped Ted was reliable. It would be all too easy to get rid of a rival by allowing Cooley to strike first and step in—a moment too late.

Ted was uneasy, too. Claiborne was by far the bet-ter shot and, in Ted's opinion, therefore was better able to look after himself. He might find it convenient to allow Cooley to shoot first—at Ted—before reacting to a threat.

The pair, walking at arm's length, their rifles cocked and ready, paused every few feet to peer ahead into the thick tangle of pines. Most of the forest was in shad-ows, making it difficult to see through the snow-laden branches. Occasionally Ted glanced surreptitiously at Claiborne, and now and then Claiborne did the same, wishing he had Ted's overpowering physical strength.

On either side they could hear their companions edging forward, too, and they did their best to remain on a level with them. There was no need to repeat the warning that tragic accidents might take place if some of the searchers advanced more rapidly than their com-rades.

Claiborne's flesh crawled. He could not forget the way poor, demented Fran Cooley had plunged the kitchen knife into her body, or the way her blood had turned the snow crimson.

Ted was sweating in spite of the cold. Walter Cooley's insanity reminded him of himself. He had been mad, too, when he had shot and killed his wife and brother when he had found them in bed together. And the murderous rage that had taken hold of him when he had seen Cindy and Claiborne laughing and talking together had been equally violent. Only the intervention of others had prevented him from committing murder again.

And the way he had brooded! The Cooleys had brought catastrophe on themselves because they had hidden their feelings, sulked, and refused the companionship of others. Ted promised himself that he would change. He had no alternative. If he clung to his old ways, giving in to his black rages, the day would come when people would be searching for him, too.

This was not the moment, however, to think of the future. The present was so hazardous that he had to concentrate on it alone. They advanced again, then paused. Ted thought he detected a faint movement almost directly ahead. He looked hard, wanting to be sure before he gave the alarm. Then he saw the faint gleam of a metal blade and was afraid it was too late.

"Duck, Claiborne!" he shouted.

The South Carolinian instantly dropped to one knee in the snow. As he did, a knife whistled through the air only inches above his head and buried itself deep in the trunk of a small pine tree directly behind him.

Ted raised his rifle and fired in the direction of the dark, bulky blur he could barely make out only a few paces ahead. At best he was a mediocre shot, and his haste spoiled his aim, so he missed his target. Walter Cooley's high-pitched, maniacal laugh floated through the forest. Ted took a few steps forward and found himself staring directly into the muzzle of the madman's rifle.

Then a shot sounded. Claiborne fired from his kneeling position and, taking no chances, shot to kill. Cooley continued to laugh insanely as he pitched forward, but the sound ended in a gasp. Ted knelt down and examined him. He was dead.

"Claiborne got him!" Ted shouted as he stood, and the other men began to move toward the scene.

Claiborne and Ted stood together and, in silence, looked down at the still body of the man. There was no need for words. Each of the partners realized that the other had saved his life in the last, intense moments of the crisis. Like it or not, they were bound together now by unbreakable ties. Gravely, still not speaking, they shook hands, and that clasp ended their enmity. Neither could, nor would, ever forget what the other had done for him.

Stalking Horse and Whip built a crude litter of tree branches, and the silent men trudged back to camp with the body. They were greeted with quiet relief by the women, but everyone grieved. Fran and Walter Cooley had not been popular, but they had been respectable, hard-working people. Their inability to tolerate the hardships of a Rocky Mountain winter reminded the pioneers that they were all vulnerable to the vagaries of this cruel, beautiful, and relentless land. The price the settlers had to pay for their journey to Oregon was high.

The recent cold spell had frozen the ground so hard that it was possible to dig only shallow graves that wolves or coyotes might enter, so it was agreed that, following the funeral, a small party would take the remains of the victims to the heights, where the bodies would be left in a cave with the entrance blocked up, making it impossible for predators to get to the bodies.

Lee Blake performed the funeral service, Reverend Oscar Cavendish being too intoxicated to officiate.

VIII

Smokestacks of factories and plants in London's East End and across the Thames in Southwark belched steady streams of yellowish black soot, evidence of the progress of the Industrial Revolution. The soot mixed with the fog that rose from the river, and at dusk all of London was enveloped in a heavy blanket that limited visibility to no more than forty or fifty feet.

All the same, Henry St. Clair was so delighted to be home that he inhaled with deep satisfaction as he alighted from his hansom cab in front of St. James's Church on Piccadilly. Peering through the gloom to make certain he wasn't being followed, he cut through the churchyard to Jermyn Street, then made his way quickly to St. James's Square. Holding his gold-handled sword cane jauntily under one arm, he slowed his pace so he could enjoy his surroundings. The trees in the little park in the center of the square were bare, but the grass remained miraculously green, which sometimes happened when London enjoyed a mild winter. It wouldn't be too long, St. Clair thought, before crocuses and daffodils began to appear.

The houses that lined all four sides of the square, a

211

few of them new and some very old, were made of stone, built to last for centuries. Without exception they were handsome, imposing structures. St. Clair stopped in front of one of the largest. Although the shutters were closed over the windows on the two lower floors, the structure looked like any of the neighboring private homes. It would not occur to a casual passer-by that it might be anything other than what it seemed or that it had been chosen for its location, which was only a few minutes' walk from the government buildings that were the heart of the world's most extensive empire.

Henry St. Clair paused briefly to gaze at the building. Then, smiling to himself, he walked up the stone steps and rang the chimes.

The broad-shouldered servant in livery had a broken nose and an oversized ear, which made him look like a professional thug. Indeed, earlier in his life, he had been just that. He peered hard at the man on the stoop, then grunted in surprise. "Lord love us if it ain't Mr. St. Clair," he said. "I'd heard you was dead."

"Rumors are sometimes exaggerated, Haskell," St. Clair replied cheerfully. "I'm expected, I believe, and I know the way." He went through the entrance hall, mounted the broad marble staircase, and then headed toward what had been the sitting room of the master bedroom suite when the mansion had been a private home.

In an anteroom a clerk in shirt-sleeves, perched on a high stool before an even higher desk, was scribbling in a ledger with a quill pen. He paused in his labors, squinted at the visitor, and neither felt nor showed surprise. In this establishment agents came and went constantly, and their globe-circling endeavors meant no more to the clerk than another entry in his ledgers.

"Good afternoon, Mr. St. Clair," he said calmly.

"Good afternoon, Mr. Browne." Henry St. Clair found it difficult to keep a straight face. He had crossed the entire North American continent, spent many months in the wilderness, and avoided death by an eyelash, yet he was being received as though he had paid a visit to the place the previous day.

"I'll tell Sir Edwin you're here," Browne said ungraciously, climbing down from his stool and disappearing through a double door.

Little in the anteroom was changed, St. Clair noted. The same dusty filing cabinets lined one wall, while maps and geography books filled the shelves on another. Only a copy of a recent portrait of young Queen Victoria, looking girlishly innocent, was new.

"You may go in, Mr. St. Clair," Browne said.

Sir Edwin Knowlton was a husky man, renowned for such exploits in his youth as his escape from the Ottoman Empire by swimming the Dardanelles. Now he was gray-haired and portly, his paunch the inevitable result of executive responsibilities that kept him sitting behind a desk.

"I wasn't expecting you for at least another month," Sir Edwin said as they shook hands. "But when your messenger came round this morning with word that you'd arrived, I assumed you came by clipper ship."

"I did, Sir Edwin, and they're marvelous. They cut the time of sea travel by half."

"Well, I'm glad you're here." The director of the most secret of Her Majesty's bureaus waved his subordinate to an overstuffed chair. "The Foreign Secretary is huffing and puffing again."

"Lord Palmerston always huffs and puffs," St. Clair said. "Knowing nothing about conditions in the field,

213

he nevertheless expects agents to perform one miracle after another."

"Oh, I'll grant you we've spoiled him here," Sir Edwin said. "Which is all the more reason for his anger and disappointment when I was forced to tell him you had failed in your efforts to halt the wagon train."

"I think it's unfair to say I failed." St. Clair spoke with meticulous care. "I enjoyed near-successes. But no agent could stop the Americans, not even with the so-called help of the Russians, who are bumbling idiots."

"Are the Americans endowed with supernatural powers?"

When Sir Edwin became quietly sarcastic, St. Clair knew he was dangerous. It was best to offer a full explanation quickly. "There are hundreds of them, far too many to sabotage. And they're well led by intelligent, courageous men I was grudgingly compelled to admire. They can be turned back only by large bands of determined Indians, and I regret to say that even the most ferocious tribes are ignorant savages who happily accept our gifts of arms and haughtily reject our strategic and tactical advice. As you know, I was responsible for two major raids on the wagon train, and both times the Indians muffed their chances. I was responsible, too, for an attack by U.S. Army deserters, but they were driven off and defeated. In addition, I attempted to arrange some natural catastrophes, but lacking the powers of the Almighty, I was unable to carry them off."

"Lord Palmerston will not be impressed," was the dry response.

St. Clair became heated. "If I had felt there was any chance at all of completing my mission, I'd be in America right now. My record speaks for itself. Dr. John McLoughlin, the Hudson's Bay Company factor at Fort

Vancouver, agrees totally with me. So does Colonel Phillips Morrison, our garrison commander there."

"I've read Morrison's reports and so has the Foreign Secretary, who still insists that the United States be denied the opportunity to establish a solid claim to Oregon."

"Lord Palmerston is being unrealistic," St. Clair said.

"Will you tell him that to his face? I won't, and I've known him since our school days."

St. Clair knew he was fighting for his future. He was determined to let nothing stand in the way of a promotion to a desk job right here at headquarters. Two decades of field service were enough, and he had earned the right to enjoy London's sophisticated pleasures. "I'm not afraid to tell the Foreign Secretary the truth," he said. "I've done far more than anyone else here could have accomplished. Send two or three agents—send a dozen, if you wish—but they won't achieve more than I did. There's nothing we can do to stop the Americans from reaching Oregon, and I've spent the better part of two years on the assignment."

Sir Edwin reached for a humidor, offered it to his visitor, and then selected a cigar for himself, meticulously cutting off the end with a tiny knife. He was aware of the danger, loneliness, and frustration that a man in the field felt, but his own position was secure only if results were achieved.

"For the sake of argument," he said, "suppose I accept your assessment of the situation, the inevitability of the wagon train reaching Oregon. What then?"

"There's only one way to solve the problem," St. Clair said firmly. "The land will sustain immigrants, there's no doubt of that. And the Indian tribes of the

215

Pacific are too small to create more than minor troubles. We've already made one major mistake. If we wanted that country, we should have sent our people there first, by way of Canada. But we didn't."

"Palmerston hates negative approaches," Sir Edwin said coolly, "and I'm not fond of them myself."

"Very well, I'll put it to you as plainly as I can. Station an entire flotilla of the Royal Navy at Fort Vancouver, fully manned and armed and ready for combat. Send at least a division of troops into the Oregon country. There are too few at Fort Vancouver now, and even when the garrison is augmented, there won't be nearly enough."

"We're trying to avoid committing belligerent acts."

Henry St. Clair exploded. "My God, Her Majesty's government is as isolated as a puddle of water in the Kansas plains! Doesn't anyone here read the American newspapers? Doesn't our legation in Washington City know what's happening over there? Wealthy citizens in the United States, men like John Jacob Astor, are working closely with the President and Congress. They're intending to send one wagon train after another to Oregon in the years ahead, a steady stream of them. Even if this first group should be stopped, which I very much doubt, others will get through and will settle there. You speak of positive instead of negative approaches. Well, the Americans are being positive, I can tell you."

"You'd solve the problem by using force to occupy Oregon."

"If necessary, yes. But there may be no need to go that far. Send in the Royal Navy and Army. When the Americans arrive, make it plain to them that they're settling on British soil and that if they stay, they will become subjects of the Queen. It's the only way we can win. Within a few years, Americans will be sending wagons there by the thousands. And I don't blame them, because I've seen the country myself, and it's magnificent!"

"By sending large numbers of troops and warships," Sir Edwin said, "we'd be running the risk of becoming involved in war with the United States, a war we don't want."

"Ah, but they're running the same risk by sending immigrants there," St. Clair said. "Martin Van Buren is no Andrew Jackson, always spoiling for a fight, but he had the courage of his convictions. He doesn't want a war with us, either, but he's taking the chance because the prize is so great."

Sir Edwin exhaled a cloud of smoke. "You'll have the opportunity to present your views to the Foreign Secretary. Stay close to your lodgings for the next few days, particularly in the mornings, until I send word to you. Palmerston likes to conduct his business early in the day."

"Nothing will give me greater pleasure," the agent said.

"Oh, I dare say you'll get greater pleasure out of the month's holiday due you," Sir Edwin said, smiling. "Will you go to the south of France, the German states, or the Baltic?"

"I intend to stay right here in London," St. Clair said. "I've been dreaming of the town for a long time."

"That's probably wise."

A chill crept up Henry St. Clair's spine. Although Sir Edwin was smiling, his eyes were cold. "How so?"

"Because I shall have a new assignment waiting for you after your holiday."

"I've been hoping there would be a place right here, sir, as one of your assistants."

Sir Edwin didn't seem to hear him. "The Boers of South Africa have been very unhappy under our rule there in recent years," he said. "At the present time a mass migration is taking place to nearby lands that have been terrorized by the Zulus—Natal and the Highveld. The Boers are traveling by wagon train, remarkably similar in every way to the wagon train that's en route to Oregon. Your experience in America uniquely qualifies you to join one of those trains, posing as a Boer. You'll keep our authorities in Capetown abreast of developments so that, at the appropriate time, we can extend our jurisdiction to these new territories."

Henry St. Clair groaned. He had seen enough covered wagons to last the rest of his life. He was tired of crawling for mile after endless mile behind workhorses or oxen through land where savages made every day's journey dangerous. He was sick of the bickering, quarrels, and gossip of people forced to live in proximity to each other for months on end. And now he was being condemned to precisely that existence.

"Is there no chance of being given a post here at home, Sir Edwin?" he begged.

"If you succeed in South Africa, I shall be glad to discuss the possibilities with the board," Sir Edwin replied. "One enjoys the rewards of success, just as one must suffer the penalties of failure. And, I regret to say, you *did* fail in your efforts to halt the American wagon train."

There was only one way to deal with the Foreign Secretary, Sir Edwin well understood, having known him since boyhood. Lord Palmerston would not tolerate wavering. Just hit the nail on the head, without hesitation. At the moment, Lord Palmerston's scowl indicated that he was displeased. Positive action was needed.

"I've read the report of your man, St. Clair," Palmerston said. "It tells me little I didn't already know. The Americans, thanks to St. Clair, realize all too well that we supplied weapons to the Indians. They know St. Clair has been in your employ—"

"*Our* employ," Sir Edwin interjected. "Her Majesty's."

"Very well, there's no need to deal in technicalities. Our policy is firm. We want the Oregon country. We hope to deal with Washington through diplomatic means, but the fat is surely in the fire. They know we're trying to stop their wagon train from reaching the Pacific."

"It appears we won't stop the train. I quite agree with St. Clair's assessment."

"Then what do you recommend?" Palmerston's voice dripped sarcasm.

"We may as well be drawn and quartered for a sheep as for a lamb," Sir Edwin replied promptly. "We take every step necessary to protect Oregon for ourselves, short of waging actual war. We do it overtly, in the open, without apology."

"Be more specific, Edwin."

"Very well. We reinforce our garrison heavily at Fort Vancouver. We send cannon, cavalry, whatever may be needed to intimidate the American settlers. We send warships and anchor them at Fort Vancouver. We make plain that Great Britain intends to stay in Oregon!"

Reverend Cavendish's continuing drunkenness outraged scores of people in Little Valley. One morning, an impromptu meeting was held after breakfast. Dozens of angry people were present.

Grace Drummond, recuperating from her leg wound

and using a walking stick, limped to the front. "What any man does is his own business, provided he doesn't hurt others," she said. "But Reverend Cavendish hurt every last one of us when he couldn't even say prayers over poor Fran and Walter Cooley. I swear, that man never draws a sober breath these days."

Jacob Levine, who had been released from the medical cabin the previous evening, drew himself slowly to his feet. Although he was still pale after his ordeal, his voice was vigorous. "I've known Oscar Cavendish longer than any of you," he said. "We traveled West together until we joined this train. He's a good man, and he doesn't mean to be this way."

Paul Thoman leaped up to support Jacob's stand. For once he spoke plainly. "Reverend Cavendish is his own worst enemy," he said. "I'll grant you that several of us have tried talking to him and that up until now he hasn't listened to us, but we've got to give him time. I've known mountain men who were drunks, and they either stopped drinking and cured themselves—or they died. It isn't our place to take any action."

"Right," Jacob said firmly. "We have to mind our own business and give him the chance to straighten out."

"No," a man with a bull voice called from the rear of the hall. "I say we ask him to leave. He's supposed to be the spiritual leader, but all he does is set a bad example for everybody, especially the children."

A roar of approval greeted the comment. There was little doubt where the sentiment of the majority lay.

Hosea was disturbed. "Not right to send Cavendish away," he muttered to Dolores. "Poor man sick and foolish. Die in mountains if sent away."

A delegation demanding the immediate expulsion of the clergyman went to Ernie von Thalman. Rarely had so many people been so incensed. Ernie called an immediate meeting of the council—elected representatives of the entire company—and they gathered in his cabin to discuss the crisis. "You've heard the issue," he said as they sat around the small fire in the hearth. "First, I'd like to hear your opinions. Then, obviously, we must find a solution to this problem."

Tilman Wade was the first to reply, and he spoke emphatically. "We threw Garcia out because he was a criminal and a danger to all of us. We had no choice in his case. But Reverend Cavendish has broken no laws. He's let people down, of course, but he's let himself down even worse. It strikes me he's floundering, making a worse and worse mess for himself. He couldn't survive, alone in the mountains, for even a couple of days. To my way of thinking, we'd be murderers if we forced him to leave."

"We simply can't expel him," Lee Blake agreed. "People are so worked up they won't like our decision, but that can't be helped. A man's life is more important than the feelings of people who aren't thinking straight."

Whip was incensed. "I won't tolerate letting Cavendish starve or freeze to death," he said. "He'd be as helpless as a little child out there. I'd rather leave with him and let folks here look after themselves."

"What do you think, Bob?" Ernie turned to the physician.

Bob carefully chose his words. "The medical profession knows very little about alcohol and why it affects different individuals in different ways," he said. "I'm sure everyone in this cabin remembers the time we found wild honey in combs that bees had just evacuated and brewed ourselves a batch of mead. We had a very pleasant evening, and no one drank too much. But if Oscar Cavendish had spent that evening with us, one cup of mead would have been his undoing. He drinks surprisingly small quantities of that dreadful liquor he's fermented for himself, but it strikes rapidly and hard. I've had several long talks with him, and so has Jacob Levine. I'm convinced Oscar doesn't want to drink but can't help himself. It sounds strange, but he behaves as though some inner force is compelling him to drink to excess. What's more, I've known other people, in my medical practice back in Pennsylvania, who acted in the same way. I can't explain the reasons. Studies were made at Harvard about ten years ago and more recently at Edinburgh, but physicians at both schools have admitted defeat and have acknowledged they have no clue to either the cause of or the cure for the problem."

"I know what Bob means," Whip said. "About five or six years ago, there was a mountain man who was the same way. Poor old Charlie O'Connell was as nice a man as ever you've ever met—when he was sober. Then he'd start drinking, and he'd get so ornery that nobody wanted anything to do with him. I saw him drink himself to death. I swear that he knew he was killing himself, but even that didn't stop him. All we could do was give him a grand funeral and bury a bottle of whiskey with him."

Ernie cut to the heart of the matter. "Bob, are you intimating that nothing can be done to change Oscar's habits?"

The physician was troubled. "I wouldn't go that far— I hate to admit defeat. But at the moment I don't know what I could do that I haven't already done to help Oscar."

There was a tentative tap at the door. Emily von Thalman, who was listening to the discussion but taking no active part in it, answered the knock. Dolores, bundled in her buffalo cape, stood timidly on the threshold. "Is it permitted for me to interrupt?" she asked.

Ernie waved her inside. "Sure," he said. "We need all the help and advice we can get."

Dolores entered and removed her cape, then stood staring into the fire for a moment before she perched delicately on the edge of a bunk. "I do not want to interfere," she said, "but I know the mountains better than those who want to send the poor minister into the cold. And my heart is heavy for him."

"I think everyone here feels the same way," Lee said.

Dolores hesitated. "It might be that I could help him," she said.

The entire group stared at her. The power of her visions had proved so accurate that even Lee was inclined to accept her seemingly preposterous statement at face value.

"I do not really know if what I wish to do will help," she said. "I have spoken to my visions, but they will not tell me. It may be that it will be very good for him, but it may be that it will be bad."

"We're stumped ourselves," Lee said. "So we're willing to consider any suggestions."

Dolores seemed to gain strength as she talked. "Hosea will help me," she said. "I wish to take the minister to a place I know. In the time of three suns, we will see if he is better or worse." She folded her arms over her breasts, Indian fashion, and fell silent.

Tilman Wade did not realize that she intended to offer no fuller explanation. "What do you have in mind?" he wanted to know.

The girl returned his gaze but remained silent. At last she said, "If I speak about things in another world, my visions may become angry. If they do, it will be bad for the minister. Bad for all."

For some moments no one stirred. The members of the council were being asked to accept her offer without knowing any details.

Finally Whip spoke. "It strikes me there might be something to be gained and very little to lose. The folks in the train will be furious if we don't act in some way, and poor Oscar will kill himself for sure if he doesn't taper off on his drinking. So I think we should go along with whatever Dolores wants to do."

"So do I," Tilman said.

Ernie considered for a time, then nodded agreement, too.

The last to concur were Lee Blake and Bob Martin. As they exchanged glances, it was plain that both were apprehensive, but they realized they had little choice. The young medicine woman had proved her worth.

"All right," Bob said. "Take charge, Dolores."

Lee sighed. "I have misgivings," he said, "but go ahead."

Dolores rose and wrapped her cloak around her. "Say nothing to anyone," she said. "Let it be thought that the minister has disappeared."

Before anyone could question her further, she was gone.

A short time later, the few who were outside saw a strange sight. Hosea and Dolores flanked Reverend Cavendish, and all three walked slowly into the forest, the lean clergyman towering above his escorts. The clergyman's face was flushed, and his eyes were bright. Because of his unsteady gait, Hosea and Dolores supported him unobtrusively.

Although it was early in the day, Oscar Cavendish was so intoxicated that even the clear, cold air did not help him. In his hazy state, he knew only that he had been promised he would participate in an adventure of some kind. More important, this couple treated him kindly. So many people had been shunning him lately that he was pleased that Dolores and Hosea had actually sought him out.

When they reached the far end of the woods, they began their ascent to the heights, pausing from time to time so the clergyman could catch his breath. He was perspiring freely, and made the climb with difficulty. This long hike was certainly no pleasure. He wondered if they were tricking him, but Hosea's expression remained bland, and Dolores smiled at him encouragingly again and again.

As they drew nearer to the timberline, Dolores said to Hosea, "Bring dead branches for torches."

The next time they paused, he gathered several, guessing that the cave he and Dolores had discovered together was their destination. Dolores had told him no more than she had the members of the council, but Hosea required no explanation. He, too, felt deep sympathy for Reverend Cavendish, and he had complete faith in Dolores's powers.

After several hours, they reached the entrance to the cave, and Hosea lit a torch. Oscar Cavendish, bending almost double, was gasping for breath as he made his way down the tunnel. The walk had exhausted him, and he could barely keep going. "I want to sleep," he mumbled.

"Soon," Dolores told him. "In a moment you will see the place we are taking you."

They emerged shortly into the large cavern. Oscar Cavendish was not impressed. The place was damp and dark, and the fact that a river ran through the chamber in the dead of winter meant nothing to him. His vision was still so blurred he failed to see the pale white mushrooms that grew out of the floor.

"I need rest," he said, giving a deep, tremulous sigh and slowly lowering himself to the ground.

"There is water," Dolores said pointing. "Drink it when you are thirsty."

He nodded, then smirked. Water was not his favorite beverage. "Have to sleep for a little while."

"That is good," Dolores said, "but first I want you to eat something very special." She studied the flat mushrooms, then picked one. Approaching the clergyman, she extended the mushroom on the palm of her hand. "Eat this," she told him.

He shook his head. "I'm not hungry."

"Eat!" she repeated, her voice becoming strong.

Oscar Cavendish took the mushroom, popped it into his mouth, and chewed it slowly. "Not bad," he said, "but what's so special about it?"

Dolores did not reply, but smiled again as Oscar stretched out on the ground four or five feet away from the little river.

The torch was burning low, so Hosea lit another. Dolores motioned to him, then seated herself cross-legged on the ground. Not knowing what to expect, Hosea followed her example. She had ordered him—in no uncertain terms—never to taste the unsavory-looking mushrooms, yet she had insisted that Cavendish eat a whole one. But Hosea's faith in Dolores was undiminished—a medicine woman, he knew, sometimes behaved in strange and even contradictory ways—and it was not his place to question her.

Dolores sat, unmoving, her gaze fastened on Oscar Cavendish. The clergyman closed his eyes. His breathing was labored. They sat watching him for so long that Hosea had to light a third torch.

Little by little, Oscar Cavendish began to breathe more deeply and evenly. In the light of the torch, he looked deathly pale. The color of his face, Hosea thought, was similar to that of the mushrooms.

At last Dolores was satisfied. "He is sleeping the true sleep now," she said. "We will go."

Hosea was startled. "Leave Cavendish here?"

"In three days we will come back for him," the girl said.

"Maybe die here!"

"He will not die," the young medicine woman said. "Mostly he will sleep. Sometimes he will wake up long enough to crawl to the little river for water, but he will not remember drinking it."

Hosea was disturbed. "We leave him torches and flint for making light?"

Dolores shook her head. "He will need no torches," she said, ending the discussion by starting toward the cavern's entrance.

Hosea hurried after her, pausing for one last look at the sleeping clergyman. He believed in Dolores with all his heart, both as a woman and as one endowed with the ability to perform wonderful feats of magic, but as he took the lead and started down the long tunnel toward the open air, he never expected to see Oscar Cavendish again. This time, Dolores was asking her visons to perform impossible deeds.

Flames were everywhere as the fire burned fiercely, tongues of fiery red and pale yellow leaping high in the air. The odors of the smoke were suffocating, and the fire itself was so hot that it was unbearable. By some miracle, however, Oscar Cavendish was not even scorched, although he stood in the midst of the flames. He panted for breath, seeking escape from the conflagration but finding none. There was no way out.

The heat of the fire made him thirsty, and he heard his hoarse voice begging for a drink. A giant claw appeared out of the flames and thrust a glass at him. In it was sparkling water, clear and so cold that the outside of the glass was frosted.

Oscar reached for it with a trembling hand, but as he snatched it, the glass turned into a chipped mug containing the nauseous brew he had concocted after his supply of whiskey had run out. The stench sickened him, but he was so thirsty he took a swallow, then gagged.

All at once the mug began to move in his hand. To his horror, it had been transformed into a snake with a large head. Its beady eyes were fixed on him, and its fangs were bared as it hissed ominously.

As Oscar stood, petrified with fear and loathing, the snake began to grow. In almost no time it was four feet long, then at least double that length. He tried to fling it from him, but the serpent wrapped itself around him, its warm coils grating against his skin. Slowly the coils tightened. Oscar screamed. The snake was squeezing the breath from his body.

The scene was real to him, frighteningly real. He had no idea that the hallucinogenic mushroom he had eaten was causing him to dream.

The serpent was determined to crush him. Its vile face danced back and forth in front of his eyes as it applied more pressure, then still more. A hollow, booming laugh rose above the roar of the flames, drowning them, and seemed to echo endlessly through all eternity.

WYOMING!

Members of the wagon train were still restless and dissatisfied, their isolation and inactivity causing mass hysteria. All they knew was that Reverend Cavendish had vanished from Little Valley and that the men of the council steadfastly refused to discuss his case. They had no idea whether he had been banished from the camp or had gone elsewhere of his own accord. It was plain that further trouble was brewing.

Some of the women accompanied La-ena to the far end of the valley to dig up any edible roots they might find, an enterprise the leaders encouraged because it kept people occupied for at least a few hours. Sally MacNeill was the first to notice that, on a windswept section of the heights where the snow had been blown away, tiny white flowers were growing between several jagged boulders.

The presence of these flowers seemed to the women to be a miracle, although those familiar with the Rockies knew they could be found in many locations, even at this season. Sally suggested that an expedition be organized to pick the flowers. They would brighten up the drab community hall, she said, and many of the women quickly agreed.

The leaders thought the jaunt could do no harm, so a day-long expedition was organized, with Whip, Paul Thoman, and Pierre le Rouge acting as escorts in order to protect the women from any wild animals that might be in the vicinity. The group waited until the sun was high enough to provide a measure of warmth, then set out across the valley. Everyone was in high spirits.

Pierre, who was in the lead, set a brisk pace that enabled the women to keep warm. Before noon, they reached the area where they had seen the flowers. They were surprised to discover how deceptive distances were in the mountains. From the valley it had seemed that

229

the flowers were clustered together in a small area, but actually the boulders were scattered over hundreds of yards. The women, uncertain as to which of the numerous rocks concealed and protected the flowers, decided to spread out, each conducting her own search.

Coyotes and wolves attacked people in broad daylight only when they were starving and desperate, so the danger seemed slight, but still Pierre anchored himself at the far end of the wide ledge, and Paul stayed behind to do the same at the side closest to the valley, while Whip chose a halfway point.

Eulalia Woodling was pleased that she had joined the group and was sorry Cathy and Cindy hadn't come, too. The view from the ledge, high above the floor of the valley, was breathtaking. She didn't really care how many flowers she picked. There was virtually no wind, the sun was surprisingly warm, and the air was crisp and clear. It was good to be alive and young, to know that Oregon beckoned and that before too long the wagon train would be moving toward its goal again.

Whip perched nearby, sitting on top of a boulder, his rifle resting across his knees as he gazed out across the mountains. He looked self-possessed and tranquil, but Eulalia felt sorry for him. La-ena was a generous and kind girl, and it was a pity that Whip didn't return her love. Unfortunately for Whip, he had lost Cathy. There was no way of guessing whether Cathy truly no longer cared for him, but she was strong-willed enough to have made up her mind to have no more to do with him, and she wouldn't change. That was too bad. No man on the train was more resourceful or courageous than Whip, and certainly no one else was as familiar with the wilderness.

Eulalia wandered on, and as she moved behind a boulder, she lost sight of Whip. Consequently, she didn't see the burly Indian who loomed up behind him. Whip was not aware of the man's presence, either.

White Eagle had suffered during his winter's isolation. He had not shaved around his scalp-lock in months, his clothes were matted and filthy, and he had grown gaunt and hollow-cheeked. And his lonely vigil had affected him mentally, as well as physically.

His eyes glittering with the hatred on which he had fed for months, White Eagle drew a deep breath, raised his tomahawk high, and leaped at the back of his foe. At the last instant Whip's instinct told him he was being attacked, and he twisted around, shifting his weight.

That slight move saved his life. White Eagle landed on top of him, but the tomahawk crashed onto the boulder and shattered. The assault knocked Whip's rifle from his lap, however, and it fell beyond his reach.

White Eagle drew his knife and tried to plunge it into his enemy's body. By now, however, Whip was ready for the fight. He struggled with the Blackfoot, one hand grasping the Indian's wrist, and they tumbled together from the boulder to the floor of the ledge. There they wrestled, Whip trying to loosen his attacker's hold on the knife and White Eagle still determined to kill him with it. Whip's experience with the techniques of Indian hand-to-hand combat, combined with his agility, prevented him from being overcome. But White Eagle's strength was that of insanity. Only cunning would allow Whip to avoid being maimed and murdered. They rolled over and over, each of the opponents seeking the momentary advantage that would lead to victory. The guide knew that his stamina would give way ultimately. He had no idea of White Eagle's identity, but that wasn't important. What mattered was that this Indian was a maddened killer, determined to win the battle by any means.

While the pair struggled silently, Eulalia had found a cluster of flowers and was elated. She bent down and carefully plucked them. Holding them by the stems, she retraced her steps, stopping abruptly when she saw Whip and White Eagle locked in a deadly embrace. At first she could only stare at them, but then her mind began to function. Pierre and Paul were too far from the scene to be of help, and there was nothing that any of the women in the vicinity could do. Curbing an urge to shout because she was afraid the cry might distract Whip, she remained rooted to the spot on which she stood.

Eulalia's sense of horror grew as she realized that Whip was losing the struggle. The Indian was gaining, little by little, forcing Whip closer to the ledge, where there was a drop of fifteen hundred feet to the canyon below. Eulalia shivered. Inch by inch, the Indian was moving his foe nearer to the ledge. Within moments Whip would plunge to his death. She had to help him before it was too late. But how?

She saw his rifle, but was unfamiliar with firearms and was afraid she might shoot him instead of his opponent. Nevertheless, she had to do something—right now. One of Whip's legs was already dangling over the ledge.

Dropping the flowers, Eulalia picked up the rifle. Scarcely conscious of what she was doing, she grasped it by the barrel with both hands, took a deep breath, and brought the butt down on the back of the Indian's head.

The blow was not hard enough to stun or injure White Eagle, but it did startle him. That brief respite was all Whip needed. Summoning his reserve of strength, he forced White Eagle to relinquish his grip. In almost the same movement, Whip shoved him hard in the chest with both hands, simultaneously thrusting a knee into his groin.

The Blackfoot was forced back. Frantically he tried to regain his balance, then toppled off the ledge. His wail of desperation and despair was piercingly loud for an instant, then faded away as he fell to his death at the bottom of the ravine.

Eulalia was trembling violently. She was afraid she might faint. Don't be stupid, she told herself. The worst is over now. Whip won, and I helped. But she tried in vain to control her trembling.

Whip slowly pulled himself to his feet, caught his breath, and took in the scene as he brushed off his buckskins. A faint grin creased his face, then spread rapidly. He stepped forward for the rifle, which Eulalia was still holding. "I'll take that," he said. "I reckon it might be a bit heavy for you."

Eulalia's smile was tremulous.

Suddenly Whip bent down and picked up the cluster of flowers. Holding them gently, he bowed awkwardly. It was plain that he was totally unfamiliar with the gesture. "I think you dropped these," he said.

Eulalia took them from him, and all at once a sense of relief flooded her. She laughed.

Whip laughed, too, the wrinkles at the corners of his eyes and mouth deepening. Then he became serious. "I haven't had much practice at this sort of thing," he said, "so I don't know how to thank you properly for what you just did."

Eulalia realized he was shy, as ill at ease in dealing with a woman as he was at home on the wilderness trail. "There's—no need to thank me," she replied. "I —I didn't even know if I was doing the right thing. I just realized you needed help."

"What you did was perfect," he told her solemnly, extending his hand. "And I won't forget it. It hasn't been often in my life that I've been indebted to a woman, but I owe you more than I can ever repay."

Whip held out his hand, and Eulalia took it. The clumsy, formal gesture would have been ludicrous in less dramatic circumstances, but Eulalia could sense the man's dignity, as well as his controlled inner strength. She could understand why Cathy had been so drawn to him.

The memory of that handshake lingered after the others rejoined them. They learned of Whip's brush with death, and after eating the meal they had brought with them, the group descended again to Little Valley.

Eulalia told herself that her imagination was playing tricks on her when she continued to feel a burning sensation in the palm of her hand.

On Sunday morning, long before dawn, Dolores and Hosea left the camp secretly, carrying with them a bag filled with pickled beef, fish they had cooked themselves, a loaf of fresh bread, and a jar of beet greens, lightly preserved in brine. Hosea knew without asking where they were headed, so he moved at a rapid clip, forcing Dolores to hurry in order to stay close behind him. Neither spoke and neither felt the need for talk, but Hosea was worried. He kept his concern to himself, however.

Dolores felt no qualms. She had supreme confidence in the mysterious forces who used her as an instrument of their will. But she was aware of Hosea's uneasiness, and that knowledge saddened her.

Little by little, Dolores had gained respect for this resourceful African whose ways were so unlike her own but who had proved so dependable and loyal. Sometimes she speculated on what her future might be like if she married him, but she wasn't sure that her visions would permit such a union. They might insist that she remain dedicated to their service alone, and if they did, she would have no choice.

It was too soon to ask their approval, however. First, she had to decide whether she wanted to cast her own permanent lot with these people and go on to Oregon with them. She felt more at home with them than she did with her tribe, but even here she was something of an outsider, accepted yet set apart. Because Hosea was also different, they might find, together, the peace that had eluded both of them. She would have to continue to exercise patience and self-discipline until such time as her visions told her whether they would permit her to follow the guidance of her heart and conscience.

Until then, she saw no reason to hold back in allowing her relationship with Hosea to develop. She was incapable of flirting, as she saw many of the wagon train women doing, but on the other hand she need not hold herself inaccessible. She wanted to act naturally, to overcome her shyness sufficiently to let Hosea know that she welcomed his friendship.

They paused for a few minutes while Hosea gathered dead branches they could use as torches. Dolores brushed loose snow from a rock and sat on it, waiting while he completed the task. Then, as he came toward her, she smiled at him.

Hosea's expression remained unchanged, but his eyes glowed, and his heart hammered. Dolores was no longer holding him at arm's length. The improvement in their relationship was enough to make him content, for the present.

The first streaks of daylight were appearing in the sky over the mountains that lay to the east when they came to the entrance to the now-familiar cave. Lighting a torch and taking the lead as they moved slowly through the long tunnel, Hosea steeled himself, half-expecting to find Reverend Cavendish dead.

The clergyman was stretched out on the ground, and at first glance he did look dead. But he stirred, then sat up, as the couple came into the cave. He was pale, but no longer looked pallid and sickly, and his eyes were clear and steady. Dolores greeted him solemnly, then offered him food. He ate slowly, obviously savoring the first meal he had eaten in three days.

No one spoke, yet there was no sense of tension. Not until he finished his meal did Oscar Cavendish break the silence. "How long have I been here?" he asked, after drinking water from the underground river.

"Three days and three nights," Dolores told him.

"I feel as though I've been here for an eternity," he said. "In these three days I have lived several lifetimes, each more frightful than the one before it."

Dolores pointed to the bed of mushrooms. "You ate of the plant that makes strange dreams," she said.

He nodded, shuddering violently, then straightened. "I am in your debt for the rest of my days. You two have saved my life and my soul."

"We have done nothing ourselves," Dolores said. "I just obeyed the orders of my visions."

"Your visions," the clergyman declared, "must be very close to God." He bowed his head for a moment in silent prayer.

The time had come to return to Little Valley. Lighting a new torch, Hosea beckoned. Oscar walked slowly, but his gait was steady as he followed the couple into the open. He showed no ill effects of his ordeal as they began to make their way down from the heights. But, after about an hour and a half, Dolores called a halt and gave the clergymen the remaining food that she and Hosea had brought him.

He was surprised to discover he was hungry again, and as he ate he could feel strength flowing back into his body. The sun rose slowly over the peaks to the east, and he watched the new day arrive. He, too, was on the verge of starting a new day, and he squared his narrow shoulders, a faint smile creasing his lean face. The Almighty was giving him the opportunity to make a fresh start. Now, at last, he could perform the services for his fellow men that had been his intention when he had taken his vows as a minister. He was eager to begin.

Hosea, sensing the clergyman's impatience, walked at a somewhat faster clip after they resumed their march. When they finally reached Little Valley, they saw no sign of outdoor activity. But, from the direction of the community hall, they could hear many voices raised in the singing of a hymn. Sabbath services were under way.

"I have come in time," Oscar said. He halted for a moment, then walked toward the building.

Dolores and Hosea exchanged glances. The clergyman did not seem to understand the depth of the hostility of many of the pioneers. Dolores and Hosea flanked him protectively, then fell behind by a step as he opened the door.

More than two hundred and fifty men, women, and children were crowded into the community hall. Lee Blake, who had volunteered to read Biblical passages, stood facing the congregation. Still singing, people had to squeeze aside as Oscar Cavendish slowly made his way down the center aisle, between the tables, toward the front. People stopped singing and stared at him, an angry murmur gradually replacing the singing. Most people assumed he was drunk, and a number of men looked as if they wanted to throw him out into the cold.

Lee Blake was worried. If the clergyman began to spout intoxicated rubbish, there was no telling what this aroused crowd might do to him. Within moments the situation could get out of hand. But Oscar Cavendish seemed impervious to the tension in the room. He walked to a place beside Lee, then turned slowly to face the congregation. "As we read in Genesis," he said in a firm voice that filled the community hall, " 'I have seen God, and my life is preserved.' "

People were so astonished they fell silent.

"I have given you cause to feel hatred and contempt for me," the clergyman said. "I ask only that you give me a chance to make up to you for my failures of the past and to join with you in worship of the Almighty. Three days ago I descended into the lowest depths of hell. I have come face to face with death. I don't ask you to take me at my word when I tell you I have repented and intend to lead a new life, walking in the paths where God directs me. Let me demonstrate to you, in the days and months ahead, that I am worthy of your trust, that the renewal of my faith may help you to strengthen your own faith in the Lord."

People continued to stare at him, scarcely able to believe what they heard. It began to dawn on them, however, that he was both sober and sincere.

Oscar took the Bible from Lee. Leafing through it quickly, Oscar found the place he sought. He raised his head higher. "Join me in prayer, if you will," he said, "as I read to you from Psalm 116."

A hush settled over the assemblage. As Oscar began to read, humility and triumph intermingled in his voice.

"I love the Lord, because He hath heard my
    voice and my supplications.
Because He hath inclined His ear unto me,

therefore will I call upon Him as long as I live.

The sorrows of death compassed me, and the pains of hell gat hold upon me: I found trouble and sorrow.

Then called I upon the name of the Lord: O Lord, I beseech Thee, deliver my soul.

Gracious is the Lord, and righteous: yea, Our God is merciful.

The Lord preserveth the simple: I was brought low, and He helped me.

Return unto thy rest, O my soul: for the Lord hath dealt bountifully with thee.

For Thou hast delivered my soul from death, mine eyes from tears, and my feet from falling.

I will walk before the Lord in the land of the living. . . ."

As Oscar read, tears ran unheeded down his cheeks, but his voice remained strong and firm. Many in the congregation began to weep, too, and men who had wanted to deal violently with the clergyman bowed their heads. A new spirit of hope and renewal gripped these people. The miracle of the Reverend Oscar Cavendish's recovery gave them renewed hope and courage to face the trials and hardships they would encounter as they continued toward their ultimate goal.

Dolores's eyes were moist as she stood inconspicuously at the rear of the community hall. Hosea reached out to comfort her, and their hands touched, then joined. As they listened to the clergyman reading from the book that was alien to them, they, too, felt strangely comforted.

IX

Chicago, named by Indians for the wild onions that grew along the banks of the little river that flowed into Lake Michigan, offered positive proof of America's astonishing growth. Fort Dearborn, rebuilt a scant twenty-five years earlier after Indians had burned it to the ground, was already an outmoded relic, its palisades almost lost from sight as homes and factories, churches, warehouses, and offices sprang up on the prairie north and south of the river. So many European immigrants were pouring into the town, most of them from nations where personal liberty was a dream that could not be attained, that no one knew the actual population.

Jobs were plentiful for all who wanted work, even though the country remained in the grip of what newspapers were calling, "Van Buren's Panic." Adventure-seekers were drawn at least temporarily to this new mecca. Those with funds found beds in cheap lodging houses, while the penniless either pitched tents on the prairie or slept in the open. These quarrelsome, brawling toughs were a civic menace, especially to the well-to-do, whose handsome new homes graced the Michigan Avenue lakefront and whose State Street shops were crammed with merchandise of all kinds. Fights erupted, private homes were burglarized, and any citizen who ventured out alone after dark risked being robbed. The city hired new constables by the hundreds, but they were so badly outnumbered by the lawless that it was almost impossible for them to bring down the crime rate.

The presence of so many rootless, able-bodied young men in Chicago attracted the attention of recruiters for newly developing areas. President Sam Houston of Texas, anxious to increase the population of the Lone Star Republic, quietly sent a team of recruiters to the city, and their promises of free land and adventure sent scores to Texas every month.

John Jacob Astor and his allies, eager to organize more wagon trains to the Oregon country, were determined not to be outdone by Houston's success. They, too, sent several representatives to Chicago in the early months of 1838. They rented office space in the busiest part of town, on Lake Street, near the river, and actively competed with the Texans.

Houston offered immigrant tracts of one hundred and sixty acres, while Astor promised a generous six hundred acres. The Texans held out the bait of a free horse and rifle to any man needing transportation and firearms who signed with them. Astor's men placed a covered wagon on display on Lake Street, then advertised that anyone whose signature they obtained would not only be eligible to receive a free wagon, but, if accompanied by dependents, also would be given a cash bonus.

Feelings between these rival groups ran high, and the city authorities braced themselves for trouble. The constables further complicated the situation when they began to side with one or the other faction. In fact, dozens of police officers resigned from the constabulary and themselves signed up with one or the other group.

An explosion was inevitable. An Astor spokesman, colorfully but incongruously attired in a beaver hat and buffalo cape to protect him from the raw, icy wind, stood near the covered wagon, urging passers-by to visit the office. "Folks," he shouted, "don't miss the opportunity of a lifetime. Join the big parade to Oregon. It won't cost you a penny. You'll be given—absolutely free—a huge tract of land even more fertile than Illinois prairie farmlands. And maybe you qualify for a splendid covered wagon like this one—without spending a cent of your own money. Ride in comfort and style to golden Oregon—the land of the future!"

A number of people drifted into the office, where they were encouraged to sign up for the third and fourth trains, the second train already having been fully subscribed. As they did so, six Texans appeared on the scene. Three of them subdued the Astor spokesman, and the remaining three produced hatchets and began to demolish the covered wagon. The man's frustrated, angry shouts brought his colleagues out of the office on the run, and the battle began. Passers-by joined in the melee, and soon twenty or thirty people were fighting with fists, clubs, and hatchet handles.

A distinguished gentleman in a horse-drawn carriage saw the commotion and tried to escape, but his horse was seized, and parts of his carriage were torn off to be used as weapons. He was fortunate to get away without being harmed. Two pedestrians were less lucky, however. Both were knocked off their feet and trampled. Not until they were rescued did they discover that one's watch and the other's wallet were missing.

A dozen constables arrived and, taking in the scene at a glance, saw they could not control the riot by themselves. They sent for reinforcements. Thirty more constables appeared. They managed to restore order by swinging with abandon their long truncheons. No attempt was made to find out who had started the brawl; all who took part were presumed guilty. By the time the crowd melted away, twelve men had been arrested, while the Astor representative and one of the Texans had to be hospitalized. The other Texans managed to slip away and promptly established an armed guard at their own headquarters.

The Oregon recruiters repaired their battered covered wagon and began to plan their revenge against their rivals. The mayor posted a notice, warning that all recruiters would be driven out of town if the peace was disturbed again. Everyone knew, however, that he was indulging in an unenforceable threat. Oregon and Texas fevers were high and were still rising. They wouldn't subside for decades, after pioneers by the tens of thousands had settled in both lands.

Ginny Dobbs was creating problems that the wagon train leaders were finding insoluble. Cathy van Ayl, ordinarily mild-mannered, could no longer tolerate Ginny in the kitchens and insisted that she be assigned another job. Unless the newcomer was given another assignment, Cathy declared, she was prepared to resign from her own post at once, and at least four of her helpers would walk out with her. La-ena, normally amenable to any request made of her, steadfastly refused to include Ginny in the group that fished.

Nat Drummond made it plain that his wood and water gatherers formed a harmonious team and that he had no intention of allowing that unity to be disturbed. Emily Harris von Thalman, who supervised a group that repaired wagon-top canvas and also did other difficult sewing, had no idea that Ginny had been a seamstress. But even if she had known, she would have been reluctant to admit the girl to her circle.

The council met to consider the problem.

"It seems to me," Whip said, "that Garcia's mean and nasty nature rubbed off on Ginny. She's so ornery that no one can stand her."

"I don't know why she carries such a big chip on her shoulder, and I don't much care," Lee Blake said. "All I know is that she's incapable of getting along with anybody. But we can't banish her to a cave, as we did with Garcia. For one thing, she's committed no crime, and for another she'd never be able to survive. None of the women want to live with her, for which I can't blame them, but I think it would be wrong to build her a cabin of her own. It would be like a reward for her bad temper."

"People wouldn't stand for it," Ernie said, "just as they'd raise the roof off if we relieved her of all responsibility and gave her no assignment. You'd think she'd be grateful that we saved her life and gave her shelter with us, but apparently she isn't. Even so, I'm afraid we're stuck with her."

Bob Martin looked perplexed. "As far as I can tell, she's so afraid people will try to hurt her or take advantage of her that she strikes first. Tonie and I have tried talking to her, both separately and together. We've tried to show her that she's making life unpleasant for everybody at a time when nerves and tempers are already raw. But she just shrugged and said that anyone who doesn't like her isn't obliged to speak to her."

Tilman Wade cleared his throat. "I have a suggestion. As you know, I've been in charge of the storehouse provisions all winter, doling out what the cooks need each day, giving buffalo skins to those whose clothes or blankets are wearing out, and keeping track of the shortages, such as our present lack of sassafras, cotton cloth, and salt. The work isn't all that arduous, and there isn't really enough to keep two people busy, even though it is a responsible job. If I had an assistant, however, it would be easier for me to get away now and then when some of you go hunting."

"You'd be taking on quite a load," Lee observed. "Are you sure you can tolerate Ginny's sharp tongue?"

"No, not really," Tillman said, smiling. "But I have a tough hide, and I'm willing to try. We can't afford to have the peace disrupted during this last month or two before we move out again."

The others were grateful for his offer and accepted it. Ernie said he would notify Ginny of her new duties.

Tilman went off to the tiny office he had established in the midst of the storage sheds and bins—a small, cramped cabin warmed by a fire that also prevented various herbs and other perishables that lined the shelves from freezing. He built up the fire, then sat down at a makeshift desk and opened the simple ledger he kept. A tap sounded at the door, and Ginny Dobbs came in, her cheeks flushed by the icy wind. "I've been told I'm your new helper," she said abruptly.

Tilman nodded pleasantly. "Take off your cape and make yourself at home," he said. "The work we do here isn't all that difficult. The one disadvantage is that you'll be spending most of your time by yourself."

"Now I see why I was ordered to come here," Ginny said. "I'm to be kept in isolation."

"Not quite," he replied mildly. "Now. One of our most important duties is to keep the fire going so the food stored in here doesn't freeze. I'll bring in the wood from the pile, but you'll have to check the fire now and then, and throw on another log whenever it starts to die down."

"I don't think that will tax my intelligence," she replied sarcastically.

He ignored her tone. "We also check the doors of the sheds and bins—especially at night, before we turn in—to make certain they're secure. Otherwise, wolves and other animals might sneak into camp."

Ginny's expression indicated her contempt for such a minor task.

"It's also important," Tilman told her, "to keep an accurate account of the food and other goods taken out of the storage area so that we can estimate how much we have for the rest of the winter. We're all right so far, and it doesn't appear that we'll need to ration supplies, but you never can tell. If spring comes late and we have to stay here longer than Whip and Lee anticipate, we might be in serious trouble."

"No one can be hungrier than I was on the trail," Ginny said.

"All the more reason to be careful. Now, Dr. Martin comes for various herbs from time to time, and he's allowed to help himself to whatever he needs. His requirements are modest, but make certain you list everything he takes."

"We have no control over what he takes?"

"He exercises his own controls," Tilman said gently. "The biggest part of the job is checking out the food. Cathy van Ayl shows up here every morning—"

"Oh, that one," Ginny interrupted, sniffing.

"—and decides what she needs for the day. We mark

it down, and then she comes back with some of the boys and women, and they collect the day's provisions."

"While we watch them to make sure they don't go off with more than they're supposed to take."

He was puzzled. "Why would they do that?"

"Garcia isn't the only thief in the world, Mr. Wade. Everyone I knew in California was one, and I met a fair share back in New Jersey, too!"

"Cathy van Ayl and her helpers," Tilman said, controlling his anger, "are some of the most selfless, dedicated ladies I've ever been privileged to know. They work day after day, for all of us. I'd never insult them by checking out the precise amounts they say they'll take each day."

"Then you're stupid!" Ginny retorted. "They could be robbing you left and right!"

He clenched his teeth for a moment, then said mildly, "I can imagine no reason why they would."

"You said yourself that there might have to be food rationing if the winter hangs on. They could be storing the extras in some secret place so they could continue to eat well while everybody else goes hungry."

Tilman sighed. Never had he met anyone more suspicious and belligerent. All the same, he had no intention of getting into an argument with her.

"We have one last duty," he said. "Thanks to a highly successful buffalo hunt last fall, as well as the other game our hunters brought down before the deep freeze set in, we have quite a supply of animal skins. Some people don't have cloth for new clothes and blankets, so they come to us for skins."

"Naturally," Ginny said, "we check to make sure they really need the skins and aren't just trying to get something extra for themselves."

He looked at her in astonishment. He couldn't understand her attitude, particularly when the dress of green wool she was wearing had come from cloth given to her after she had arrived at Little Valley. Her scarf had been a gift, too, and her boots and buffalo cape had been made from skins taken from the common stores. Surely she could not begrudge similar benefits to others who suffered misfortunes.

"You'll see a couple of filled, completed ledgers on the top shelf over there," he said, pointing. "Look them over, and you'll quickly understand the system I've been using. If you have any questions, I'll gladly answer them." He turned back to his open ledger, wondering if he had made a mistake when he had offered to give work to this bitter young woman.

During the next few days, Ginny said very little, merely watching when Cathy came for food or Dr. Martin took small quantities of herbs and seeds. She was careful to maintain the fire in the little supply office, even bringing in additional firewood herself, and took great care to make certain that the doors of the sheds and bins were kept closed.

When she had done all her chores she neither read nor conversed, but spent long periods staring into the fire. Her thoughts were far away, and Tilman took care not to interrupt her reveries. Since she never had a good word to say about anyone, he was grateful for her silence.

Late that week, Tilman accepted an invitation to go hunting with Lee and Stalking Horse. They weren't likely to find any game in the silent, frozen wilderness, but the outing would do him good. He was eager to get away from the camp for a few hours. Easygoing and friendly, he still required periods of solitude—almost impossible to attain at Little Valley—and he knew his inner tensions were building. He was unnecessarily irritated by minor matters, and he knew that his temper was wearing thin. Self-control was important to him, a matter of pride, and he felt that the ride into the heights would give him some breathing space, an opportunity to be alone and at peace.

Ginny had learned the routines and understood what was required of her during his absence. She had controlled her vicious tongue since she had started her new job, and Tilman hoped that that self-control would continue during his absence.

She sat alone at breakfast, conversing with no one, then went straight to the office and stoked the fire before going out again to make sure the doors of the bins and sheds were still closed. When she returned, she found Bob Martin helping himself to several handfuls of a pungent herb. Ginny watched him in silence for a few moments. "You're taking a lot of that stuff today, Doctor," she said.

Bob Martin nodded. "Quite a few people have come down suddenly with a stomach complaint. I don't know the properties of this plant—wish I did—but a single dose seems to work wonders."

Ginny spoke a little more loudly. "You're still taking quite a bit of it. Half the people here must be sick."

"Not that many," he replied, refusing to rise to the bait. "Besides, Dolores has promised me she and Hosea will collect more of the herb if we need it, even though it does become harder to find as the winter wears on."

"I'd think you'd try to leave some in reserve." She sniffed audibly.

"When people are sick, it's my duty to help them as best I can, and plants sitting on a shelf do no one any good." He smiled.

Ginny shook her head, then made a point of counting the number of plants aloud and marking the figures in the ledger. "You're taking about half the supply," she said. "I hope you'll be careful not to waste any."

Her rudeness startled him, but he refused to argue with her. Instead, he wrapped the herbs securely and then departed. Later, perhaps, he would suggest that Tilman try to persuade her to mind her own business.

More than an hour passed before Cathy van Ayl arrived with her list of foodstuffs for the day. "We're using leftovers this noon," she said, "so I'm taking about two hundred pounds of buffalo meat for tonight's supper. I'll also take a couple of sacks of beets and one of onions. Oh, yes, and a side of bear bacon." Wanting to avoid unpleasantness, she indulged in no small talk with Ginny.

"Why bear bacon?" Ginny demanded.

Cathy was accountable to no one for her choice of menus, but she tried to be polite. "As you know, most buffalo meat is too tough to be eaten roasted, so we use it in stews. And the diet becomes monotonous when there's so little change in the taste, night after night. That's why we sometimes cook it with various herbs and dried grasses. Not long ago one of the scouts suggested we cook it with bear bacon, which changes the taste. I'll give you the recipe, if you like."

Ginny ignored the offer. "It seems to me you'll be wasting a whole side of bacon," she said tartly.

Cathy shook her head, but remained patient. "Taste is terribly important when people are cooped up for months, as we are here. They need some variety, or they'll lose their appetites and fall ill. Lee Blake tells me that happens in the army when troops go into the field, and some of the mountain men say the same thing. So we're being as imaginative as we can be, racking our brains for new ways to present the same food."

"I'm not so sure I'll let you take that bacon," Ginny declared. "Food is too valuable to be wasted."

Cathy stared at her. "I'll be back with some of the others a little later," she said. Under no circumstances would she become embroiled in an argument with Ginny, but if necessary, in Tilman's absence, she would go to Ernie von Thalman for help in obtaining the supplies she required for that night's supper.

Shortly before noon, while the leftovers were being heated, she returned to the storage area, accompanied by several women and teen-age boys. She had not mentioned her conversation with Ginny, believing that some of her friends would be less discreet than she was, and come back to argue with Ginny. It was important, when everyone lived together so closely, to avoid quarrels and fights. Arguments solved nothing.

Ginny appeared, watching silently as the bags of onions and beets were taken from the sheds in which they were stored. She remained quiet when the women opened a bin and took out chunks of frozen buffalo meat. They could estimate the amount they needed, which she could not, due to her lack of experience. "Are you quite sure you haven't taken more than two hundred pounds?" she asked.

"Not really," Cindy told her cheerfully. "Since we don't have scales, we can only guess, but we aren't far off, I'm sure of that."

"I'm marking two hundred pounds in the provisions ledger, not a larger amount." Ginny spoke with authority.

Eulalia, who made no secret of her dislike for the girl, couldn't resist commenting. "Don't worry," she said. "Nothing will be wasted. We're experts at that.

Anything that isn't eaten tonight will be used tomorrow, either for breakfast or at noon."

Ginny frowned, but said nothing.

Cathy went to the bin that contained the bear bacon, then beckoned to Chet Harris and Danny. "Take the bacon on the top of the pile, boys," she said.

Ginny reached the bin first and peered inside. "That side of bacon is too big to use for flavoring," she declared.

Everyone stared at her.

"Some nerve," Eulalia muttered.

Cathy had hoped to avoid a showdown, but her pride demanded that she settle the matter herself, instead of asking Ernie for help. "Just take it, boys," she said quietly.

Danny and Chet moved forward, but Ginny Dobbs blocked their path, her arms folded, her feet wide apart. She was defying Cathy, daring her to act. Refusing to be cowed, Cathy pushed past her, reached into the bin, and began to tug at the frozen side of bacon, which was separated from another beneath it by a layer of dried grass. Chet and Danny moved forward, too. The latter, who admired Cathy and considered her his special friend, was so eager to help that he inadvertantly jostled Ginny. The ground underfoot was icy, and Ginny slipped, almost falling.

By that time, Chet and Danny had removed the bacon from the bin. Cathy was careful to lower the lid on the bin so she couldn't be criticized for carelessness.

Ginny's self-assumed authority had been flouted, but there was nothing she could do to regain the standing she believed she had lost. She glared at Danny. "You bumped into me on purpose," she said, "and tried to knock me down."

The startled boy tried to protest, but before he

could speak, Ginny reached out and slapped him hard across the face. He was holding one end of the side of bacon and could protect himself only by dropping it onto the ground.

Eulalia instantly put an arm around his shoulder and stood so that she was nearer to Ginny. Rather than strike again and hit the other girl, Ginny dropped her arm to her side. "Pay no attention to her, Danny," Eulalia said.

The boys moved off, with Eulalia still speaking to Danny in an undertone.

Cathy was furious, but Cindy, herself laden with buffalo meat, had seen many violent scenes at the Louisville bordello and recognized the danger signs. "Come along, Cathy," she said firmly. "The bitch deserves a kick in the teeth, but we have better things to do."

Ginny stormed off, slamming the door of the little provisions office behind her. Cindy accompanied Cathy back to the community hall, still trying to soothe her. Ginny remained in the office at noon.

That afternoon there was yet another incident. Ted Woods and Hosea were in the process of taking several logs from the woodpile and loading them into a small cart when Ginny suddenly appeared behind them. "Just where do you think you're taking that wood?" she demanded.

Hosea would have paid no attention to her and started to push the cart away, but she blocked his way. "You haven't answered me," she said.

Ted bristled. "It ain't any of your business, lady," he said, "but if you must know, we're running low on charcoal for our forges. Does that satisfy you?"

"I just want to make sure no firewood is being

wasted, that's all." She saw the gleam of anger in Ted's eyes, but refused to back off. No man could cow her.

"Lady," Ted said, "I cut most of that firewood myself, and it was hard work. Believe me, I wouldn't waste one log. I'm not aching to go back out into the forest in this weather to cut more." He continued to glower.

Ginny returned silently to the provisions office. At least this pair knew that no one could frighten her.

About an hour before sundown, Tilman Wade and his companions returned from their fruitless hunting trip. Cathy was the first to accost Tilman, with Eulalia adding her own indignant comments. While they were still speaking with him, Bob appeared at the entrance to the medical cabin and beckoned.

"I couldn't help overhearing all that," the physician said, "so you may as well know the rest." He described his own experience, then said, "I'm told Ted Woods is fit to be tied, too. Ginny tried to stop him and Hosea when they went for firewood to make into charcoal."

Tilman sighed, the pleasures of his outing fading rapidly from his mind. "I volunteered to take the girl on as a helper, so I guess I'll have to handle this."

"Good luck," Bob Martin said. "She appears to be even more of a virago than anyone realized."

Tilman looked grim as he walked the short distance to the provisions office. Hundreds of people were struggling to maintain their emotional and mental balance until the long winter ended, and the problems that faced them were enormous. The danger of starvation still loomed large, they had another mountain chain to cross after leaving the Rockies behind them, and aside from the normal hazards of the trail, Whip was afraid that they might have trouble with the Comanche, the most warlike Indian nation in the area. They did not need tension caused by a young woman who seemed determined to fight just about everyone.

Ginny was making a final entry in the ledger when Tilman came into the room. "Everything is in order," she said. "There were some irregularities that I've noted in full, so they're now on the record."

Tilman took the book from her, read her report, and then handed the ledger back to her. "I see no irregularities here," he said.

"But—"

"On the other hand, I'm aware of other irregularities. Cathy van Ayl and the ladies who work with her are outraged, not only because you questioned their right to take what they needed—which was their concern and none of your business—but also because you slapped Danny."

"He tried to knock me down!"

"I very much doubt it." Tilman began to seethe, but outwardly he remained calm. "The way I heard it, you jumped to a conclusion. The wrong conclusion, I believe, because I've known Danny for a long time. He shows respect for his elders, and I've never known a boy who tries harder to cooperate with everyone."

"He wasn't that way with me," she said, clenching her fists.

"The only reason you weren't mobbed and beaten is because the ladies showed more common sense than you displayed."

"I'd liked to have seen them try!"

"That's not all. Then there's the matter of your run-in with Bob Martin. Apparently you have no idea how lucky we are to have a physician traveling with us. He contributes his services without reservation for the good of all. The herbs and seeds he uses were collected specifically for him."

"Just because he's a doctor doesn't make him perfect!" Ginny retorted. "After all, he's a man."

"Then there was your quarrel with Ted and Hosea. Not only did Ted supervise the cutting down of the trees that provided the firewood, but he did more of the job himself than any other three men combined. No restrictions have been placed on the use of firewood, and not once has anybody abused that privilege. You have the bad habit of assuming that the entire human race is made up of thieves and cheats."

"So it is!" Ginny faced him defiantly. "You made my duties clear to me, and the entries I've made in the ledger prove it. I know my responsibilities!"

"They don't include antagonizing honest people." Her shouting grated on him.

"If you don't like what I do, get yourself another helper!" Her voice became still louder.

Tilman's self-control began to slip. "Everyone in this company is assigned to some chore, but no one wants you. Cathy van Ayl got rid of you because you created so many disturbances. Nat Drummond won't have you, and neither will La-ena. And there's no point in asking Emily von Thalman to take you, since you have no experience in sewing."

Ginny almost let slip the fact that she was far more accomplished with a needle than anyone in the sewing group, but that would expose her background at the Trenton orphanage, which she desperately wanted to keep secret. People would look down on her even more than they already did if they learned that she didn't even know who her parents were.

"Paul Thoman," he continued, "could stand some

help at his school, especially with the smaller children, but he has enough trouble trying to control all those youngsters. And their behavior is exemplary, compared to yours."

"You're a bastard!" she cried.

"I had a mare like you once," he said. "She threw everyone who tried to ride her and enjoyed every minute of it. She was the worst-tempered animal I ever saw, until I put a rope on her and taught her a little basic respect for the people who fed her and took care of her and tried to be friendly with her."

Ginny's temper snapped. She flew at Tilman, her hands like claws, trying to tear at his face with her nails. He caught hold of her wrists and forced her arms to her sides. Ginny promptly attempted to kick him in the groin. He avoided the blow, but the last of his self-control was slipping quickly away. The girl wrenched free, drew her knife from her belt, and slashed at him.

The blow nicked Tilman on the back of his hand, scratching him superficially, but drawing blood. His temper finally exploded. "It looks like you need to be roped, just like that young mare," he said.

In a single, swift motion he wrenched the knife from her hand, and it fell to the floor. Then, still gripping her, he sat down on a bench and threw her across his lap, face down.

Ginny struggled violently, kicking and pummeling, in an attempt to free herself. "I've never in my life hit a woman," Tilman said, "but my conscience doesn't bother me a bit."

Holding her firmly with one hand, he raised the other and brought it down with full force on her backside. Ginny was humiliated beyond measure, and what was worse, the blow stung. She redoubled her efforts to free herself. The more she fought, however, the harder Tilman spanked her. He was determined to tame this impossible vixen.

The blows that rained on Ginny's buttocks were unceasing, and soon her entire body ached. She wanted to weep, but somehow she held back the tears. She wouldn't give this brute the satisfaction of seeing her cry.

The enraged Tilman's hand smarted, and his arm felt weary, but still he continued to spank her. Finally it dawned on Ginny that he would not stop while she continued to struggle, so she went limp. Tilman responded by shifting his grip on her and spanking her with his other hand.

She was afraid that if she tried to fight him, he would become even more violent, so she endured the torment and humiliation as best she could.

Only when Tilman noticed that his exertions were causing the scratch on his hand to bleed more freely, did he stop. Ginny still made no move. She was exhausted. Tilman picked her up easily and placed her on her feet, facing him. "Had enough?" he asked, and was somewhat surprised to discover that he was out of breath.

Ginny did not reply, but stared at the floor. Tilman bent down, retrieved her knife, and handed it to her. Silently, still avoiding his gaze, she slid the knife back into her belt.

Tilman was satisfied. A part of him was sorry he had subdued her physically, but he was relieved that she had become much calmer. "From now on," he said, "behave yourself. Treat people decently, the way you'd like them to treat you."

Ginny stared at the tops of his boots and made no reply.

He threw another log on the fire. "It's getting late," he said. "If we don't get over to the community hall, it'll be too late for supper."

The girl remained silent.

He stared at her for a minute, unable to decide what to say or do next. Finally he realized that she wanted no more to do with him. Well, he guessed he couldn't blame her. His unpremeditated cure may have been necessary, but it was drastic, and he had injured her dignity as well as her bottom.

Draping his buffalo cape around him, he left the little office and went straight to the community hall. The second shift was already eating. Lee Blake and the Martins beckoned to him.

"I don't think Miss Dobbs will act up as much any more," he said as he joined them. Although they looked at him questioningly, he did not elaborate.

"Cathy and Eulalia won't have her in their cabin any longer, and Cindy agrees with them," Lee said. "But we appear to have averted a crisis."

"Yes," Bob said. "Sally MacNeill and Dolores have agreed to take her. Dolores has the ability to shut out the whole world, and Sally is so good-natured she gets along with just about anyone. So it may work out."

"I helped move her belongings, such as they were," Tonie said, "so the deed is done."

"She's still at the provisions office," Tilman said, offering no further explanation. "Maybe you'll drop in there for a minute after dinner and tell her, Tonie."

A half-hour passed before Tonie delivered the message to the still-silent Ginny, who merely nodded when she learned the news. About fifteen minutes later, Ginny made her way through the bitterly cold night air to her new shelter.

Dolores was pinning material draped on Sally when

she entered, and both paused. "We noticed you didn't show up for supper, so we brought some food back here to you," Sally said as she picked up a bowl that had been placed close to the little fire that provided both light and warmth. "Welcome to our house."

"Thanks." Ginny took the bowl and moved to the bunk on which her meager belongings had been placed. Dolores and Sally returned to making the dress.

Ginny had to admit, grudgingly, that bear bacon did change the flavor of buffalo stew. As she ate, surprised to discover she was ravenous, she saw that what they were doing was all wrong. Dolores was clumsy, unaccustomed to making clothes of anything other than skins, and Sally was giving her confusing instructions.

"This dress just has to be right," Sally said. "It's my last piece of cloth, and I want Paul to see me in something new."

Ginny put down her unfinished meal. "Let me show you how to do this," she said, going to them and pushing Dolores aside.

Swiftly removing the pins, she draped the material again, pausing briefly from time to time to study her handiwork. "Hold still," she said sharply. "I can't do a thing if you fidget." Sally froze.

Still working quickly, Ginny finished the task, inspected the completed job, and nodded. "All right. I'm going to take out just enough pins so you can wriggle out. Do it carefully and take your time!"

Cowed by her tone, Sally obeyed.

Ginny immediately returned the pins to the precise places from which she had removed them. "Who is going to make this dress?" she demanded.

"I am," Sally said meekly.

"How many have you done?"

"Well, none, really. I've made some skirts and ordinary blouses, but it's important for me to have a real dress, so—"

"I'll do it for you," Ginny interrupted impatiently. "Give me a pair of scissors." Dolores handed her their only pair.

"These will have to do," Ginny muttered, and went to work, the rest of her meal forgotten. She labored in silence, squinting occasionally in the dim light. By concentrating on the task, she was able to put the scene with Tilman Wade out of her mind. She paid no attention, either, to the pair who watched her in awed silence.

Ginny discovered she had lost none of her skill, and she worked so swiftly and diligently that, by the time she began to yawn, she had made remarkable progress. "I'll finish this tomorrow," she said.

Sally stammered her thanks. "I don't know how you can make it so fast," she said.

Ginny threw her only blanket and buffalo robe over her new bunk. "Why not?" she asked, contempt in her voice. "After all, it's only a simple dress."

The following morning Tilman Wade did not see Ginny at breakfast, and learned that she had eaten with the early shift. She was waiting for him when he arrived at the provisions office and had already built up the fire. He tried to greet her casually, as though nothing out of the ordinary had happened. Ginny nodded in return, but her eyes strayed to the back of his hand. Tilman thought she looked relieved that the scratch was already healing, but she made no mention of the incident.

He had wondered whether to apologize to her, but her silence convinced him that she was setting the right example, so he followed suit.

"I've been thinking," Ginny said abruptly, "that you don't really need a helper here."

He could not deny the statement. "Maybe I do, and maybe I don't," he hedged. "But that isn't the problem. The rules say that everybody works, and we don't know where else to put you."

To his surprise she remained unruffled. "I know where I belong," she said, her voice defiant, "and that's where I'm going, right now. I'm joining the sewing women."

He was astonished.

"I'm better than any of them. I earned my living as a seamstress back in New Jersey. And," she added, revealing something she had promised herself she would tell no one, "in Yerba Buena, too. I earned just enough to scrape by, because women there are used for other purposes."

"You never mentioned to anyone that you can sew," he said.

"I had my reasons, and I still have them," Ginny said. "But that's how I'm going to spend the rest of the winter." She put on her cape and left the office quickly, her head high and her stride purposeful.

Paul Thoman was tired after a long day of teaching cranky children. Sitting at a table in the shadows at the far side of the community hall, he did not see Sally MacNeill until she deliberately slowed her pace as she passed his seat. His supper companions had departed, and he was alone.

He took in every aspect of her appearance, then jumped to his feet. "What pulchritude. You're like finding edelweiss growing in a crevice above the timberline. Unfortunately, I've never seen any in the

Rockies, so I'm forced to conclude it's indigenous to the Swiss Alps—which makes you equally rare."

Sally was hurt. "You don't like my dress," she said.

Paul realized he had to begin again. "I've never seen anybody prettier," he said.

She was relieved and, beaming at him, immediately sat on the bench. "Finish your supper," she said.

Still looking at her, he began eating again. "When did you make it? I mean, it is new, isn't it?"

She nodded. "The reason it looks so nice is because Ginny Dobbs made it for me. She's wonderful with a needle."

"The reason it looks so nice," Paul said, "is because you're inside it."

Sally blushed furiously and stared straight ahead. Paul was afraid he had gone too far and had offended her. Finishing his meal, he touched her hand, intending to offer an apology, an explanation, or both.

Sally turned to him when she felt his hand, and before either of them quite realized what they were doing, they were kissing each other hungrily and clinging together. The women who were salvaging leftovers for the next day's meal did not notice them in the semidarkness.

Suddenly they wrenched themselves apart. Sally raced from the community hall, her face flushed and her gait unsteady. She knew that if Paul tried to take her right now, she would give herself to him. The knowledge stunned her. She was no longer a young girl, but had become a woman, and what had started out as an innocent, adolescent flirtation had become something far more serious. She didn't think she was ready for marriage yet—she had not even considered the idea. And, according to everything she had been taught, it was wrong—dead wrong in every way—to have an affair. She needed time to think, to evaluate her situation. She would have to find some way of keeping Paul's interest alive without succumbing to him. She was unnerved by the experience.

Paul continued to sit at the table. He was badly shaken, too. The violence of his reaction when he had touched Sally had surprised him. He didn't even know whether he loved her, and he was unprepared for this confrontation. Certainly, he respected her. But he wanted her desperately.

As Paul sat, miserable and confused, Whip came into the hall for a late supper, after completing sentry duty. Cathy left the building immediately, without so much as a glance in his direction. La-ena left a few moments later, and she, too, ignored Whip. Her expression was inscrutable, her eyes were veiled, and she walked quickly. But Paul was too deeply immersed in his own situation to read any significance into what he saw.

Eulalia served Whip his meal, then sat down to chat with him while he ate. Meanwhile, Cindy finished her night's work, and she, too, donned her buffalo cape and started toward the entrance.

Paul roused himself. He had heard rumors about Cindy's background, so perhaps she could help him straighten out the mess in which he and Sally found themselves. At the very least, he might be able to ease his burden by talking about it. "May I have a word with you?" he called.

Cindy halted, smiling slightly. She had liked Paul from the time he had arrived. "I want to discuss something with you in confidence," he said.

"Sure." She opened her cape and sat on the bench at

the far side of the rough-hewn table. "But if you're looking for advice, I'm not certain you've come to the right person."

"I believe I have," he said, and told her about the incident that had just occurred.

Cindy was not surprised. "You and Sally are healthy," she said, "and both of you have normal urges. Women do have them, too, you know. You've spent a lot of time together, and your feelings were bound to get the better of you. There's no need to feel ashamed of yourselves."

Her matter-of-fact attitude made it easier for him to talk. "What do we do now?" he asked.

She shrugged. "You have several choices. First, you could get married, although I'd urge you to think about it carefully before you did it. Your backgrounds are so different. Would you get along in a year, ten years, even twenty years?"

"I'm afraid of marriage right now," Paul said, "and I don't think Sally is ready for it, either."

"That leaves you two choices, then," Cindy said. "If you go to bed together, it can lead to all kinds of complications. If Sally gets pregnant, for instance—and she might—you'd both feel you had to get married, even if you had decided by then that you really weren't right for each other. Then you'd be stuck for the rest of your lives. So your best bet is to forget what happened tonight and just let your future relationship develop naturally."

"That's the trouble," Paul confessed. "I can't forget it when I still want her so much."

Cindy understood far better than he knew. Her experience had taught her that young men found it almost impossible to deny their need after they became aroused. A woman was stronger willed and better disciplined, and she was far more able to keep her own yearning under control.

What Paul needed, she reflected, was an hour or two with a sympathetic bordello girl. That would calm him, and his relative tranquility would make it easier for Sally to stifle her own desire for him.

Cindy liked both Paul and Sally. For an instant, she considered reverting to her former ways, just this once. She could give Paul the relief his male body craved, yet remain untouched emotionally.

She was stunned by her train of thought. Was it possible that she was fooling herself, that she actually craved a fling with this gangling young man? No, he didn't appeal to her in the least. Claiborne Woodling was far more her type, but as much as she enjoyed his company, she had as yet felt no desire for him. Lee Blake and Whip Holt appealed to her, too, as she was sure they would appeal to almost any woman, but their lives were already complicated enough.

There was no question in her mind that going to bed with Paul Thoman would be totally unexciting to her. The idea was insane! She might be tempted if she were still living in Louisville. But here, in the cramped quarters of the winter camp, it would be impossible to keep her gesture secret. Someone would guess, someone would see them together, and then everyone would know. Not only would her own reputation, that she had been rebuilding with such painstaking care, be ruined, but other men—including Claiborne—would seek her out for just one purpose. Not only that, but Ted Woods might murder Paul, and even if he didn't, Sally would have nothing more to do with him.

As Cindy sat, lost in thought, Paul watched her. In some ways she was even more attractive than Sally. Her figure was ripe and full, and her gestures only half-concealed an explosively passionate nature. He swallowed hard.

Cindy roused herself. "I've been trying to think of other alternatives, but there aren't any," she said, smiling apologetically. "You may not like my advice, but you'd be wise to hold off until you and Sally both know exactly what you want for the future." She stood abruptly and wrapped her cape around her.

"Thanks for listening," Paul said as he rose, too. "And thanks for reminding me that people have to solve their own problems." He hesitated for a moment. "May I walk you back to your cabin?"

She was surprised as well as amused. Paul had sensed what had been going through her mind. She had to let him know her decision at once. "That won't be necessary," she said firmly. "I suggest you apply for volunteer sentry duty tonight, or spend a few hours reading one of those books you always carry around—anything to distract your mind." Giving him no opportunity to speak again, Cindy swept out of the hall.

X

Prince Orlev stood before the fireplace in the library of his palace. Smiling in quiet satisfaction, he rubbed his hands together briskly. His scheme was succeeding. Czar Nicholas would be so pleased with his efforts he would probably be promoted; perhaps he might even become Deputy First Minister. His ambition was to become one day the real ruler of Imperial Russia.

Overcoming all obstacles—and they had been horrendous—he was sending a colony of settlers to the Oregon country. No one else could have accomplished such a feat. And he had done so without suffering any personal loss. After contributing one thousand gold rubles to the campaign, he had quietly siphoned off two thousand from sums contributed by other nobles and public officials. He had doctored the books so cleverly that no one, not even the Director General of the Treasury, would be able to unearth the deception. All that really mattered to his treasury colleagues, of course, was that the entire venture wouldn't cost the Czar a single kopek.

Prince Orlev crossed the thickly carpeted room and

tugged at a bell rope. In answer to the summons, a male secretary, garbed in solid black as befitted his station, came into the room carrying a sheaf of documents. He halted inside the door, then bowed deeply. The Prince allowed him to stand there while he seated himself, poured a generous quantity of fine French brandywine into a glass, and inhaled appreciatively before taking a large swallow. "You have the papers I'm taking to the Czar this afternoon regarding the expedition to Oregon?"

"All of them, Your Highness."

"Good." Orlev extended a manicured hand on which a huge emerald and diamond ring glittered. "First, the documents relating to travel plans."

The secretary approached and handed them to him. The Prince seemed pleased as he leafed through them. "Ah, it all appears in order. Carriages will convey the travelers across Siberia to the Pacific as soon as spring comes. Arrangements have been made at inns and hostels for sleeping and eating accommodations on the journey, and a ship will carry them first to our colony of Alaska, then down the coast to Oregon—very explicit." Even the Czar, he thought, would be able to understand these simple outlines.

The secretary dared to look pleased.

"Now, Grudeny, the list of our patriotic volunteers who will reestablish our claim to Oregon for all time."

The secretary handed him additional papers. Orlev started to look at them, and then his face darkened. "What's this, Grudeny? There are only one hundred and fifty-eight immigrants listed here. Fifty-two names and their biographies are missing! I will not tolerate such sloppiness!"

Grudeny trembled visibly. "I crave Your Highness's pardon, but fifty-two of the travelers have backed out and no longer intend to go to Oregon. Naturally, our agents have recovered the handsome bonuses we paid to them."

"How dare they change their minds when the Czar is depending on them?"

"They—they stressed the voluntary nature of the enterprise, Your Highness. They said the journey was too long, and in spite of all that our agents told them about the marvelous land, they are afraid the Oregon country is too wild."

Orlev took a large swallow of brandy to calm himself, then poured more into his glass.

"There is nothing we can do to force those fifty-two persons to go, Your Highness. Our attorneys are firm on the matter."

The Prince drummed his fingers on his desk and glowered. "Very well. Send special messengers immediately to visit each of the remaining one hundred and fifty-eight volunteers. Remind them that they have accepted a sacred obligation. Make it plain to them that any who try to drop out from now on will be sent into permanent exile in Siberia. I want them frightened, Grudeny, badly frightened."

"I shall see to it." The secretary's eyes gleamed in anticipation.

"Out of millions of subjects, one hundred and fifty-eight is a poor showing. But these persons are vital if we are to lay a solid claim to Oregon. So I forbid further defections, no matter what the reason. These persons, every last one of them, will make the journey, even if I am forced to send a regiment of Cossacks to whip them all the way from St. Petersburg to Oregon!"

The winter lingered on interminably, beyond the time that the first signs of spring normally would appear. Tilman Wade reported that food supplies, apart from those being held for emergencies, would not last more than a month. No one had any idea when spring finally would come, and the threat of starvation hung over the wagon train.

The council met, even though every member knew that game was still scarce and unlikely to return to Little Valley in significant numbers in the weeks immediately ahead.

"As I see it," Whip said, "we have no choice. We'll have to deal with the Shoshone, who live south of here. Their main town is about a four-day trip from Little Valley."

"You seem reluctant to have anything to do with them," Lee observed.

"I am. They don't like whites, and mountain men have always avoided them. They're greedy money-grubbers. They have plenty of grain from the Colorado plains, but they hoard it. They'll charge us outrageous prices."

"In cash?" Ernie wanted to know.

Whip shook his head. "Indians have no use for cash. They'll demand cooking pots and utensils, tools, and a huge collection of beads, mirrors, and the like."

"We carry a large supply of those things with us," Tilman said, "and as I understand it, we brought them precisely so that we could trade with tribes along the way."

Whip sighed. "Well, I was hoping to save as much as possible for the tribes we'll find in Oregon. But I'm afraid the Shoshone will take just about all we have."

"I don't think we have any alternative," Lee said, "even if their prices are exorbitant. Like it or not, we've got to deal with them."

The others agreed, and the next day an expedition of

twenty-five men left on horseback at dawn, for the land of the Shoshone. Each man led two pack horses laden with goods to be used for trading purposes.

The weather remained clear and cold. No fresh snow hindered their progress. The pioneers, like the mountain men before them, had learned that snow was the worst enemy a traveler could face.

They found no game on the trail. The scarcity, Whip remarked, was a good bargaining point for the Shoshone. They were sure to demand high prices.

Shortly after noon on the fourth day of their journey, the men came to the land of the Shoshone, and an hour or two later they reached the main town. Impassive men, women, and children stood in the entrances of round buildings made of stone and animal skins and watched them silently.

But not even this surly tribe would violate the first rule of hospitality in the mountains that demanded all visitors be made welcome, particularly in winter. So the men were given the use of two round houses, as well as several barnlike sheds for their horses. At Whip's suggestion all of the merchandise with which they intended to barter was taken into the dwellings.

"I have a hunch," Lee said, "that they're allowing us to stay here only because of all the goods we brought with us."

Only Whip could speak the language of the tribe. He sat down alone with the Shoshone chief in a meeting that lasted until long after dark, but nothing was decided. The bargaining session resumed early the following morning.

The sun stood high in a sky of cold, pale blue when a weary Whip rejoined his comrades. "They'll give us one hundred sacks of corn—our own sacks, filled to the brim," he said.

Some of the men looked relieved. One hundred sacks of corn, combined with the remaining food supply, surely would supply the pioneers with enough food to last until warm weather arrived and the journey to Oregon was resumed.

"In return," Whip said, "they demand every last pot, tool, and utensil, every bead and mirror we brought with us."

There was silence. Then Lee said, "We expected to pay through the nose, so let's do it—and be glad nobody at Little Valley will starve."

"Fair enough," Whip said. "But the Shoshone have laid down another condition. They've had a boring winter, and they don't much care for the color of our skins. So they'll make the deal only if one of us will fight their champion in a free-for-all."

"A friendly fight?" Tilman asked.

Whip looked grim. "Both fighters will be armed with knives and will be expected to use them. It won't necessarily be a fight to the death, although that's possible. It will go on until one or the other can't fight any more."

"Suppose we kill their champion?" Tilman wanted to know.

Whip shrugged. "That's his tough luck, and the same is true of our man. I volunteered to take on any warrior in the tribe, but they said I'm not eligible. I have a reputation in these parts. But I'm damned if I want anybody else to take the risk, so we can just turn down the whole deal and hope the weather will improve quickly."

"That's a chance we can't afford to take," Lee said. "One man's death or injury can't be allowed to place the entire wagon train in jeopardy."

"I volunteer!" Paul Thoman shouted.

Whip shook his head. "You haven't had enough experience, and you wouldn't stand a chance."

Arnold Mell, Mack Dougall, and Pierre le Rouge all clamored for the right to represent the group, until Lee Blake stood and silenced them. "I'm the logical choice," he said quietly. "I've fought Indians in hand-to-hand combat in several military campaigns, and I'm as handy with a knife as I am with any other kind of a weapon. I'm in good physical condition, and what's more, I can look after myself at close quarters, which is better than most of you can do. So I stand a reasonably good chance of coming out of the fight in one piece. I'm sorry we've got to entertain the Shoshone, but if that's the only way we can get that grain, I'm glad to act as our champion."

No one was happy, but there was general agreement that, if Whip wasn't allowed to represent the group, Lee was the best choice.

First the grain deal was concluded. As sacks were filled with corn and tied, the merchandise was handed out in return. The transaction was conducted in silence, and the atmosphere was heavy. Lee watched the grim-faced, somber warriors and reflected that these were the first Indians he had ever known who had no sense of humor whatsoever. He refused to dwell, however, on the ordeal that loomed immediately ahead for him. He had never regarded combat as a sport, and he had known too much bloodshed to enjoy violence. But the Indians' demands had to be met, so he would do what was necessary. He had been a soldier too long to allow his imgination to linger on what might happen to him.

As soon as the deal was completed, the Shoshone and their visitors gathered on the main street of the town. The men from the wagon train carried loaded rifles; they were prepared for any nasty turn of events.

In spite of the extreme cold, the combatants stripped. They smeared their bodies with heavy bear grease, then donned loincloths, the only attire they would wear.

Lee shivered, then studied his opponent and forgot the chill. The brave was broad-shouldered and husky, about six feet tall, with muscles rippling in his upper arms and thighs as he stretched, twisted, and turned in order to become more limber. Lee guessed he was in his late twenties, an age advantage of seven or eight years. It would be a difficult fight.

Whip handed his friend his own knife. "Nobody said what kind we had to use," he said, "and this is the best I've ever owned."

Lee nodded his thanks, then examined the knife. It had a bone handle, the double edges of the steel blade honed so fine a man could shave with it, and the weapon had perfect balance. Lee couldn't have asked for a better knife.

The Chief, a homely old man in faded buckskins, summoned the two combatants to the center of the open area and retreated quickly. Now they were on their own.

There were no limits as to the area in which the fight would take place. Either man was free to move where he pleased. Presumably, the Shoshone, who crowded each other to watch the spectacle, would move out of the way. On the other hand, they might try to help their warrior in subtle ways. Lee promised himself he wouldn't be lured away from the cleared area.

The Shoshone champion looked at his opponent for the first time, then scowled ferociously. The gesture was so dramatic that Lee wanted to grin at first. But the burning hatred reflected in the man's eyes quickly convinced him that this was no laughing matter. This brave intended to kill his enemy.

The warrior made the first move, leaping across the open space with the speed and grace of an antelope. He held his steel knife above his head. Lee stood, poised, waiting for the man's approach.

Just before the pair came within arm's reach of each other, the warrior aimed a vicious kick at Lee's face. His plan was clear now. If he could knock Lee backward onto the ground, he could easily stab him.

But Lee was ready for just such a stunt. At the last possible moment, he shifted to one side. The kick found no target, and the brave was thrown off balance.

In that instant, Lee rushed him and managed to trip him, sending him crashing to the frozen ground. It was tempting, before the warrior could struggle to his feet again, to hurl his own body at the man. But the Shoshone was younger than Lee, physically stronger, and undoubtedly a more accomplished wrestler. Therefore, Lee decided to avoid direct body contact for the present.

The Indian compressed his lips, and a thin, white line formed around them as he struggled to his feet. The white man was mocking him, showing him up, and the tribe's champion at hand-to-hand combat was infuriated.

All at once the tactics Lee needed to pursue became clear to him. His best weapon was his mind, not the knife he held in his hand. He would play on the Shoshone's pride, drive him into an even greater frenzy. One who lost his temper had no self-control. Once that happened, his mind would not function clearly, and sooner or later he would make a mistake. Lee would conserve his own, relatively inferior, strength. Then, when the warrior made an error in judgment, he would act.

The enraged Shoshone rushed Lee again. This time, there was no attempt to disguise his intention. He waved his knife back and forth menacingly. He was like a bear now, intending to overcome his foe by brute strength. Again Lee waited. He hoped his nerves would not fail him. If his courage faltered, if his timing was off by as much as a fraction of a second, he knew he would die.

The brave came closer. His arm no longer moved, and he held the knife poised for a single, deadly strike. As he began to bring his arm down, Lee spun to one side, then shoved the man hard in the small of the back with his free hand. The warrior pitched forward onto the ground. As he scrambled awkwardly to his feet, the tension was so great that it seemed to gather a momentum of its own.

The warrior went berserk. He shattered the silence with a loud cry that sounded like the wail of a wild animal. He stomped, almost literally dancing up and down as he started toward his enemy for the third time.

The time had come for Lee to change his tactics. The Shoshone was wildly angry. He had become totally unpredictable.

Lee had the professional soldier's aversion to killing for its own sake, but he no longer had a choice. The combat would not end until one of the combatants lost his life.

Bracing himself for the onslaught, Lee held his ground. He gripped his knife, holding it at shoulder height. He knew he had to strike first, and that he could not miss the target.

The warrior lunged. As he did, Lee struck with all of his might and stabbed the warrior in the throat.

The dying Shoshone toppled forward. His momentum was so great that he, too, struck home. His knife cut a deep gash in Lee's side, below the ribs.

Although in shock, Lee knew the Shoshone was dead and that he had won the fight. Whip and Jacob Levine were the first to reach him, and they applied bandages to stem the flow of blood.

Several of his friends dressed Lee in his clothes, and Arnold, aided by Mack, made a hammocklike sling that would hold him safely in his saddle.

"We're leaving right now!" Whip called, noting that his companions were ready to depart. "And if the Shoshone try to stop us, open fire on them!"

The Indians, stone-faced and silent, removed the body of their champion from the street. They made no attempt, however, to impede the hasty departure of their visitors. The fight hadn't ended as they had anticipated, but they were abiding by the rules they themselves had made.

Soon the small caravan was on the trail again, with Whip in the lead, setting a smart pace. Only a few hours of daylight remained, and he wanted to cover as great a distance as possible. He forced his companions to test their endurance as he continued to push toward the north long after night fell.

Paul and Jacob flanked Lee, making certain that his sling did not loosen and send him tumbling to the ground. His blood-soaked bandages had frozen, but as nearly as the two anxious guards could judge, the flow was lessening.

Not until a halt was called did Whip and Jacob examine the wounded officer, who was unconscious. They lifted him off his horse and gently laid him on a buffalo robe on the ground. The gash in his side was deep and nasty, but the blood was only seeping out. His breathing was steady.

"It's just as well he's out cold," Jacob said. "His side is going to hurt like hell when he wakes up."

"We've got to get him back to camp as fast as we can," Whip said. "Meanwhile, I'm going to use some herbs that Dolores gave me on his wound."

"Wait," Jacob said. He took a flask of brandywine from his saddlebag. Based on Bob Martin's treatment when he had been injured, Jacob knew what had to be done first. Steadying himself and holding his breath, he poured a quantity of brandywine into the open cut.

Lee moaned in pain, but did not regain consciousness.

Whip made a poultice, first applying a coating of Dolores's herb powder to the cut and then bandaging the wound again. Nothing further could be done until Dr. Martin took charge.

They made the injured man as comfortable as possible, covering him with two buffalo robes to protect him from the biting cold. Only then did the party eat a hurried meal of jerked meat and parched corn before resting for a few hours.

Long before dawn, the group was on its way again. Whip was more concerned about Lee than he cared to say. He was worried especially because the wounded officer remained unconscious. The rigors of the trail and the cold were further weakening him. Somehow, the journey, which normally took four days, had to be completed in less time in order to get Lee back to camp as soon as possible.

No one complained when halts were restricted to

brief periods. They knew it was necessary. They ate only the cold food they carried with them.

Care was taken to avoid frostbite. Some of the men were leading as many as three pack horses to free Lee's attendants and allow Whip to keep them moving is rapidly as possible.

Lee did not become conscious until late that evening, when a halt was called again for a few hours of sleep. He stirred slightly, groaned, and then opened his eyes. Jacob, who was keeping watch, bent low over him and then hurriedly summoned Whip. Together they peered at the wounded man.

"Where the devil are we?" Lee murmured.

They told him they were on the trail, heading back to Little Valley.

The corn for which they had bartered was his first concern. "Are we carrying the grain?"

"You bet," Whip said, "and we got away from the Shoshone without any more trouble. What's more, they haven't dared to follow us. The rear guard is keeping a sharp watch. Now—how do you feel?"

Lee attempted to smile. "I thought I had died and gone to a very cold hell," he muttered. "How badly am I hurt?"

"You've got a nasty wound," Jacob said. "But we'll get you back to camp, and Doc Martin will patch you up."

Lee nodded. Whip and Jacob persuaded him to drink some water, but he had no interest in food, and they didn't insist. It was enough, for the time being, that he was still alive and holding his own.

The journey was resumed very early in the morning. The pace was grueling. Lee felt every jolt as his horse moved beneath him, and the ride was torture for him.

He kept his jaws clamped shut so he wouldn't cry out, but sometimes he groaned despite his best efforts, as searing pain shot through his side, then spread to his entire body.

His friends kept him wrapped in buffalo skins, afraid he would develop a fever. If that should happen, he would have no resistance to the extreme cold, and the men realized he might well die on the trail.

Mercifully, Lee lost consciousness again that morning. Only his rugged constitution and stubborn refusal to give in were keeping him alive.

By the middle of the third day, the terrain began to look familiar. Soon thereafter, the men caught sight of the pass that led to Little Valley. Shortly before sundown they rode into camp, having completed the four-day journey in only three days.

Lee was taken at once to the medical cabin, where Dr. Martin went to work. Thanks to the treatment Whip and Jacob had administered, his wound had not festered. The physician was able to cleanse it with more brandywine, then sew it shut. He applied the strongest unguents he had before bandaging it again.

Meanwhile, although people rejoiced that the mission had been successful, they were unusually somber. Whip assumed their mood was due to Lee's injury until Ernie von Thalman drew him aside. "There's been another tragedy," he said. "La-ena has disappeared."

Whip was stunned into silence.

"Come with me." Ernie accompanied him to the cabin that Whip shared with the Indian girl, then pointed to her bunk. Neatly laid out in the center was the elk-tooth necklace that Whip had given her years earlier. Each tooth was carefully turned inward, toward the center of the circle.

"According to Dolores," Ernie said, "the arrangement of the necklace means La-ena has gone off into the mountains to die."

Whip nodded, his face pale.

"We're not certain when she left, but it was either last night or sometime around dawn. This morning, when she didn't show up for breakfast, somebody looked in here. Search parties have been scouring the area all day—the caves, the slopes of the twin peaks—as high as we could go in the snow. But we found no footprints, no trace of her anywhere."

"I'll go out myself," Whip said. "Right now." His exhaustion after the long, hard ride was forgotten.

The scouts, although equally tired, insisted on joining in the search. They left at once, spreading out in all directions.

They stayed out the better part of the night. Whip was the last to return, his slumped shoulders indicating defeat. "I'll sleep for a couple of hours and then try again," he said doggedly.

Whip knew that the search would prove fruitless. La-ena had known that people would look for her and had prepared for her flight with care. She had taken no food and no weapons with her. It was unlikely that she could survive for more than a day or two in the icy wasteland.

Stalking Horse was grief-stricken, but nevertheless tried to console Whip. "You are not to blame for this terrible thing," he said, speaking in his own tongue. "When a woman decides she wants to live no longer, there is nothing that man can do."

Whip made no reply. La-ena had given herself to one man—to him. Although she loved him, she knew he did not want to spend the rest of his days with her, probably guessing that he had lost his heart to Cathy van Ayl. So she had solved her problem in a typical

Indian manner. She was either dead or dying, facing the end with stoicism and a fatalistic calm.

Whip's guilt was crushing. He shuddered in despair. It was no consolation to know he had always been kind to La-ena, considerate of her feelings, treating her with the gentleness and courtesy that were second nature to him. Perhaps he should have lied to her, somehow convinced her that he *did* love her, that he wanted to marry her.

No, now he was just fooling himself. La-ena had been too sensitive. She would have seen through his false words. Only by giving himself to her without reservation, as unstintingly as she had given herself to him, could he have preserved her life.

Dropping onto his bunk, his fatigue so great that his body felt as though it were crumbling, Whip buried his face in his hands. He was not a religious man; he had not prayed since he had been a child. But he began to pray now, begging the spirits of the Indian after world to receive La-ena into their realm, to cherish her for all time, to allow her to find the tranquility she had not known on earth.

Lee Blake knew only that he was warm, miraculously warm. He could feel the heat of the fire crackling at the far side of the cabin. His side throbbed, but the pain was dull, and his drowsiness told him that he had been given laudanum. He opened his eyes to find Cathy van Ayl sitting beside his bunk in the medical cabin, watching him.

"You're better," she said, smiling.

Lee grinned feebly. "How long have I been here?"

"Several days." She propped up his head, then gave him water flavored with sugar to drink.

"That long?"

"You ran a fever." She did not tell him he had been out of his mind and that Bob Martin had been uncertain whether he would live or die.

He drank more of the water. "What are you doing here?"

"I—I volunteered to look after you. Bob and Tonie have so many patients they're terribly busy. So Emily von Thalman has taken charge of the kitchen for the present."

"You shouldn't go to all that bother."

"Bother?" Cathy was indignant. "Everyone in the train is grateful to you. If it weren't for you, we'd all be starving to death!" She stood and went to the fire. "I've been keeping some soup hot for you." Ladling the soup from a pot into a bowl, she returned to the bedside and sat down again.

"I'm not hungry."

She filled a spoon and held it toward him. "Bob says you're incredibly strong, but you'll never get better without nourishment, so you have to eat."

Lee swallowed meekly, not protesting again as he allowed her to feed him. Why had Cathy elected to supervise his recovery when other volunteers might have shared the task? He was too weary to think, but he knew he was lucky. He had been transported from hell to paradise.

That was just the beginning. Cathy had transferred her own bunk to another cubicle in the medical cabin so she could be on hand if Lee awakened at night. She continued to give him his meals until he became strong enough to feed himself, and she helped Bob change the dressings on his wound.

She did not permit Lee to receive visitors, even though everyone at the camp was clamoring to see him, and she ate her own meals at his bedside until, one evening, he forced her to take a break and go off to the community hall for her supper.

Cathy ate rapidly, wanting to return to the medical cabin as soon as she could. Lee hadn't yet been told about La-ena's disappearance. She thought about the matter, finally deciding she would have to break the news to him before someone else, dropping in during the days to come, let the information slip.

Eulalia, carrying her own bowl of cornmeal flavored with bits of buffalo meat, sat beside her on the long bench. "Well, stranger," she said, "we've been wondering when we'd see you again. You must be tired."

"Not really," Cathy replied. "Lee sleeps a great deal of the time."

"And what do you do?"

"Oh, I read a lot. Paul Thoman loaned me some of his books. What's important is that I'm right there when Lee needs me."

There was a mischievous gleam in Eulalia's eyes. "What do you talk about when he's awake?"

"Oh, all sorts of things. I've learned more than I ever dreamed I'd know about army life and how an intelligence officer does his job. Of course, Lee tires easily, so I try not to let him talk too much."

"I wonder how much longer you're going to keep the rest of us away from him. Dr. Martin says he's your patient now, and you'll decide when he can receive visitors."

"Soon," Cathy said, but did not elaborate.

Eulalia couldn't resist teasing Cathy. "In the meantime, you have him all to yourself."

Color rose in Cathy's face.

"So that's the way it is," Eulalia said gently.

Cathy couldn't reply. She was living one day at a time and didn't want to analyze what the future might be. She knew she was begging the issue, but for now it was enough that she was becoming deeply involved with Lee and that their relationship was far more complex than she had guessed it might become when she had volunteered to nurse him back to health.

She no longer allowed herself to think about Whip. La-ena's tragic disappearance had forced her to put him totally out of her mind. Occasionally she wondered if she was using Lee as a replacement because she needed emotional balm, but that wasn't fair to him. She had been aware of his interest in her for a long time. While she helped him regain his strength, she wouldn't allow herself to think in terms beyond the immediate future.

The weather turned warm suddenly, and the snow and ice began to melt. Everyone rejoiced, and the camp buzzed with plans to put the wagons in shape once more for the resumption of the journey to Oregon.

But Whip remained cautious. Rousing himself from the silence into which he had retreated after La-ena had left, he urged restraint. "Most years that I've spent out here," he said, "there have been two or three false starts before spring arrives for good. Just when you think the end of winter has come, there's another cold spell. Besides, we'll have plenty of time to get ready. We can't take to the trail until the rivers have flooded and receded again. A river like the Snake can be mighty mean when it comes roaring down the canyons."

The excitement did not subside, however, and one day Paul Thoman created a stir when he returned from sentry duty to report he had seen game on nearby slopes. A hunting expedition was organized immediately.

Almost miraculously, birds had appeared on the

heights near the caves, too, and Hosea decided to bag some. He hoped to bring back enough to flavor the dreary supper of cornmeal that the pioneers were forced to eat every night. He left with the other hunters at dawn, then parted company with them and climbed rapidly. He was right! A flock of gray birds, each the size of a man's fist, had been lulled by the promise of spring and were building nests in boulder creases and crevices that were warmed by a pleasant sun.

Within two hours Hosea had brought down fifteen of the birds with his darts and blowgun. He stored the bird carefully in a sack he had brought along for the purpose. He was not particularly proud of the efforts, but at least his catch would add taste to the cornmeal.

The sun disappeared abruptly. Heavy clouds made the day as dark as dusk, and a stiff, bitterly cold wind sprang up. As Hosea looked up at the sky, he was annoyed with himself. He had been concentrating so hard on his hunting that he had ignored the weather. He should have known better.

Heavy snow began to fall, whipped by the wind, and the African shivered. Whip had been right when he had predicted that winter had not truly departed. Now Hosea was in a dangerous situation. Even in the best of weather, the heights were a two-hour trek from Little Valley, and this snowfall promised to develop into a raging blizzard.

If he tried to return to the camp now, he was afraid he would lose his way. Stalking Horse had told him stories of men born and bred in the mountains who became lost during blizzards, never to be seen again. Although he took pride in his sense of direction, he had seen snow for the first time only last year, and he was painfully aware of his lack of experience. He had too great a respect for nature to mock her powers.

He knew he had to find refuge until the storm ended. He thought of the cave in which Reverend Cavendish had overcome his drinking habit, and he remembered that he had left a quantity of wood inside it. He would not only have water to drink from the stream that flowed through it, but, if need be, he could build a fire and cook the birds he had just caught.

Making his way to the cave was a difficult task. Hosea proceeded slowly along the ledge, knowing that a misstep would send him plunging into the canyon below. He walked when he could, but at times he was forced to crawl cautiously, painfully, on his hands and knees. It took him an hour to reach the cave entrance.

Once inside, he paused for a long time and rested. Meanwhile, his eyes were becoming accustomed to the dark. He remembered every detail of the interior and groped slowly toward the cavern.

Suddenly he heard a sound from one of the smaller chambers of the cave. He was not alone. Reaching for one of the little clubs he carried in his belt, he slowly made his way toward the chamber. Then he paused at the entrance and stared open-mouthed. A small fire was burning, the flames rising from the center of a circle, with individual brands emanating from it like the spokes of a wheel. In its light Hosea saw a very old Indian warrior sitting cross-legged on the ground, his arms folded across his chest.

The man's skin resembled crumpled parchment. There were spots on the backs of his hands. He was dressed in a beaded buckskin shirt and trousers, there were fresh streaks of paint on his cheeks and forehead, and on his brow, held up by a band of rawhide, was an elaborate feather headdress.

"Who are you to disturb the last hours on this earth of one who awaits the call of his ancestors to join them?"

Hosea had learned enough Indian tongues to grasp what was being said and to make himself understood. "I mean you no harm, old one," he replied.

The aged warrior heard the note of respect in his voice, and his own tone softened. "I have come here to die. By the time the snows in the beyond are ended, I will not be here. I will live in another world with my fathers and their fathers. If you wish me well, place stones around me in a circle, as is done with my people. I did not have the strength to set the stones myself, but you who have come here will bow with me to the spirits that rule the people of the Comanche."

So the man was a Comanche. Hosea, hastening to obey him, hunted for stones, which he then placed around the old warrior.

The aged brave spoke again. "The Comanche have lived in these mountains since the beginning of time," he said. "Here we find food to eat, shelter for our bodies. The spirits make us strong so we do not die in the cold of the bad season or the heat of the good season."

Hosea nodded. The old brave was making sense, even though his end was near. He realized that there were strong similarities between his people and these Indians of North America. His people, too, were close to nature and respected her whims. That knowledge made him feel closer to Dolores. They were more alike than he had known.

"The Comanche pray to the spirits who rule the world," the old man declared, his voice gaining strength. "When we are hungry, they send deer, elk, and antelope to us. We trade with the tribes of the low country for grain. In the bad season we make clothes from the skins of the animals and make our houses of them. We want for nothing. The spirits smile on the Comanche."

"They have smiled on you," Hosea agreed.

The aged warrior nodded. "In fifty and ten summers, from the time I became a warrior, I have fought in many battles. I have suffered many wounds. But my faith was strong, and always I recovered. The spirits watch over those who believe in them."

The same was true of African warriors who had faith in their gods, Hosea reflected, no matter to what tribe they belonged. He himself had survived numerous brushes with death in the years before he had been captured. He knew he had lived only because of his unswerving faith. Perhaps the visions guiding Dolores were blond relatives of the gods to whom he prayed and who continued to guide him.

"Many are the scalps that I took," the old man continued. "My eyes have dimmed, but my sons have told me that I took fifty scalps, then another fifty and yet another fifty. No other warrior of my time took such a great number."

Hosea was impressed. The dying man must be a great warrior.

"But the number of scalps I have taken is as nothing," the old man continued. "The spirits smile on me because I was always fair to my enemies. Never did I steal into the town of another nation and kill women and children in the dark of night. Always I fought my enemies in the open. Always I knew they had a chance to kill me, just as I had a chance to kill them. I did not play the tricks on them that were played by lesser nations. My sons, my grandsons, and their sons will sing songs about me for all time. I will hear their voices from the world of the spirits, and I will sing, too, because they have remembered me."

The man was not boasting. On the contrary, in his final hours, he was recounting the story of his life, talking to himself as much as to the man who had stumbled upon him.

"Three squaws lived with me, each in her time, and all are waiting for me in the land I go to inhabit. By them I have brought many sons and daughters into this world. Now my sons have sons of their own, sons who are now warriors and who do as I did before them. They hunt as I taught them to hunt. They fight as I taught them to fight. The weapons I have left for them are fine, true weapons, but even if they were broken, it would not matter. What I have taught to my sons and to their sons after them is what matters. They will be true to my teaching, and for this the spirits of my own fathers will make me welcome in the land that awaits me."

Hosea swallowed hard. His own father had taught him all that he knew about the ways of fighting, hunting, and creating a safe world in a jungle where strength, skill, and cunning were the most important weapons for survival.

The old man spoke again. "For a long time I have known that my stay in this world would be short. This morning I knew this would be my last day on the earth I have loved. My sons brought me here on their horses. I embraced each of them. I did not bid farewell to my daughters because they weep, and I was afraid that I, who have not lost tears since I was a small boy, would also weep. But that sadness is a passing thing. Now I am ready to meet the spirits and to accept the welcome of my fathers."

For the first time Hosea saw pain in the old man's eyes and face. He was suffering but refused to admit it. Perhaps there was some way to make his passing easier. "If you are hungry, old one," he said, "I have a sack filled with birds. I will gladly cook them for you."

"Cook them," the aged man said, "but you alone must eat them. A great feast awaits me in the land beyond, and I must not eat until I arrive there." When he realized that Hosea did not move, he commanded, "Cook!"

Hosea hastened to obey. After plucking the feathers, he skewered the birds on sticks and began to roast them over the little fire. "There is clear water in another part of the cave," he said. "Will you allow me to bring you some to drink?"

"The water that flows in the sky waits for me. I have a burning thirst for it, and will drink nothing else."

Hosea was silent.

"Now I will make ready for my journey," the old man said. "Are the stones placed in a circle around me?"

"They are, old one."

"Then bring more wood and make the fire brighter."

There was no more wood in the chamber. Hosea went out to the large cavern, returning with a number of the branches he had put there to use as torches. He broke one into several pieces, then fed the fire.

"When I am gone," the aged warrior said, "place my hands as they are now, on my chest. Take my bonnet from my head and place it on top of my hands.

Outside this room place five stones in a small circle. Then any Indian who comes to this place will know that the body I used on this earth lies here, and will not disturb it. When you leave, be sure that the fire is burning brightly so my ancestors will find their way here and lead my spirit to my new home."

"I will do as you have ordered."

"Now I have no more to worry me, and I will rest." Slowly the old man stretched out on the ground and fell silent.

Even after the birds had been roasted and Hosea had eaten he continued to maintain his vigil over the dying warrior. He felt at peace within himself, just as the old man was at peace.

The warrior's breathing became shallow. Almost unaware of what he was doing, Hosea began to sing softly a chant of his own people, commending the old man to the gods and asking them to favor him. The old man could not understand the words, but he did not protest. Perhaps he did not hear the chant.

The passage of time meant nothing to Hosea. He continued to chant. Slowly the aged warrior's breathing grew more shallow. Then it stopped. Hosea went on to the end of the chant.

For a moment he stayed silent and still. Then he stepped inside the circle of stones, bent down and closed the dead man's eyes, and made sure his hands were as he had wanted them. He placed the Indian's headress on his hands.

Adding the last of the branches to the fire, which was now burning low, Hosea placed five stones in a circle at the entrance to the chamber. Then he crept out and slowly made his way to the entrance. To his surprise it was morning. The snow had stopped. He could return in safety to Little Valley.

As he walked, it occurred to him that only the gods could have arranged his meeting with the dying Indian. Hosea had traveled halfway around the world to discover that his love for the earth and his reverence for nature were like that of these brown-skinned men whose ancestors had inhabited America as long as his own people had lived in the jungles of Africa.

When he reached camp, he would tell only Dolores of his experience. He felt a great desire to share it with her. He knew in his heart that she would understand, that the bonds bringing them closer together would be tightened and made firm.

XI

In Little Valley, the sun was surprisingly hot, although the nights were still very cold. Gradually the snows began to melt, with bald places appearing on the vast expanses of shale and boulders. The rivers were slowly rising, and it was no longer safe to walk on the ice that covered the small lake. Spring was fast approaching, and the pioneers began preparations for the resumption of their long journey to Oregon. Wagons were repaired. Pine boughs were shaped into support struts for canvas tops, to replace those that had been broken, and Ted Woods and Hosea were kept frantically busy making new metal rims for the wheels.

Lee Blake was the only member of the party who was relieved that the winter had not yet ended. The wound in his side was healing but would require several more weeks to mend entirely. He could not yet ride a horse, and he wanted desperately to be able to resume his full duties when the train broke camp.

Lee felt a deep sense of responsibility, not only to those who were making the trip, but to the government that had sent him as its representative. Out of touch with the outside world for months, he had no idea what steps Great Britain and Russia might be taking to protect their own interests in the Oregon country. But given what was at stake in the vast, rich area on the Pacific, he knew that London and St. Petersburg would not be inactive.

In the meantime, however, he had little to do except recuperate. That meant he followed Dr. Martin's instructions to the letter as he continued to live in the medical cabin. He was allowed to leave his bed twice daily, and he faithfully followed the exercise program prescribed for him. Gradually he was regaining his strength.

He spent long hours thinking, examining his values, remembering the past, and pondering the future. Ever since his early childhood in Connecticut, as the only son of a Hartford merchant, his heart had been set on a career in the army. When he had won an appointment to the military academy at West Point, it was a dream come true. Since then, he had devoted himself exclusively to the advancement of his career.

His parents had died before he was recognized as the army's most talented counterintelligence expert. Dedicating himself to his work, he had allowed no time for personal matters. But now, thanks to the wound he had sustained, there was little else to occupy his mind.

His career, he knew, was solidly based. If the American effort to settle Oregon succeeded, he was certain he would become a full colonel and be given command of Fort Vancouver, which the United States would force the British to evacuate. General Scott had hinted strongly that the post would become his.

For the first time since he had been commissioned, Lee was in a position to live a normal life, to think, like other men, of marriage and a family.

Cathy van Ayl was seldom absent from his thoughts.

Her dedication to him, throughout his convalescence, filled him with wonder. He knew he had been attracted to her almost from the time he joined the wagon train. At first, he had resisted his own feelings. He knew that she was then in love with Whip Holt, so he considered his own cause hopeless. Even when Cathy pulled away from Whip after La-ena's arrival, he hesitated to advance his own cause. But La-ena's disappearance appeared to have put the seal upon Cathy's disapproval of Whip.

She had spent a good deal of time and effort looking after him, helping him in his recovery. She not only volunteered for the task, but also she had been faithful to her trust. It was obvious that she had some measure of regard for him. But could he dare to hope that she actually returned the love he felt for her?

Well, there was only one way to find out. But Lee hesitated and condemned himself as a coward for that hesitation. He had fought in more battles than he cared to recall, but now he was frightened by a slender girl with blue eyes and blonde hair who stood no higher than his shoulder. That was ridiculous.

Finally, after several days of lecturing himself, Lee realized that he could no longer postpone talking to Cathy. One afternoon, instead of returning to his bed after doing his exercises, he shaved, dressed in his uniform—which Tonie Martin obligingly fetched for him from his belongings—and waited for Cathy to appear with his supper.

Cathy was surprised to see him up and dressed, especially in his uniform. "Well, this must be a special occasion," she said as she took the pot of cornmeal-based stew to the hearth to be reheated.

"It could be," Lee said. "Let supper wait for a few minutes, unless you're very hungry."

"I have almost no appetite these days," she said, placing the pot beside the hearth. "I'm grateful we still have enough to eat, but every meal is the same now, and the monotony of the diet has killed my interest in food."

"The only reason I've been eating is because you make such a fuss when I don't," he said, grinning.

"It's important that you eat!" she exclaimed. "Otherwise, you'll never get better."

Her comment bolstered his flagging courage, and he took a deep breath. "Why should it matter to you whether I get well?"

"What a stupid question," she said. "You know how much you're needed on the train, how much all of us rely on you."

"That isn't what I meant." It was cool on his side of the little room, but he began to perspire.

Cathy busied herself at the fire.

"Do me a favor and sit down," he said. "I can't talk to the back of your head."

Obediently, she moved to a chair. Lee had been cooped up for so long, she reflected, that he was becoming restless.

The moment she seated herself, Lee began to pace the length of the cramped room. "I intend to stay in the army for the rest of my life," he began.

Cathy was puzzled. "That doesn't surprise me," she said. "It's plain the War Department places a great deal of confidence in you."

"If our mission to Oregon succeeds, I think it likely I'll be staying there for quite a long time. I'll be given command of our troops there and probably get a promotion. At the very least, I'll be sent back to the War Department, although they know I prefer a field appointment. At my level, we're treated pretty nicely.

Wherever I go, I'll be given a large house, and the army will pay for a couple of servants. I'll be able to buy food and various other items pretty much at cost, too. So there are a lot of advantages to my kind of life."

All at once Cathy realized she had been obtuse. He wasn't just making conversation with her, he was leading up to a proposal. For a moment she froze, unable to think. Then, she forced herself to use logic and common sense. She had admired Lee for a long time and had grown very fond of him during the time she had spent taking care of him. But she didn't know whether she had fallen in love with him. Certainly she had no explosive, romantic yearning for him. Only one man had ever affected her in that way, and never again would she be so foolish. Perhaps she would never completely recover from the wounds that Whip Holt had inflicted on her. But that experience had taught her one lesson. Never again would she allow herself to be so vulnerable.

Had she recovered from her infatuation with Whip? In all honesty she didn't quite know, although she was sure that the ghost of La-ena would stand between them for all time. She no longer pined for Whip, and only in rare, unguarded moments did she find herself thinking wistfully of what might have been. No, Cathy told herself firmly, she no longer had an active interest in Whip. She had excluded him completely from her life.

What, then, of Lee? He was straightforward and admirable, kind and considerate—even courtly in his attitudes toward her. If he wasn't particularly demonstrative, she attributed that to his maturity. After all, he was ten years her senior. She could lead a secure, honorable life with him, protected by the warmth of his affection for her and knowing, too, that he genuinely respected her independence. He would never try to dominate and control her, as Otto had done. On the contrary, he took it for granted that she had her own mind and will. If she married him, she would be a true partner, not a servant disguised as a wife.

Lee was looking at her, one eyebrow raised, waiting for her to speak.

"I'm sorry," she said lamely, "but my mind was just shooting off in all directions."

"It doesn't really matter." Lee sounded subdued. "I just said that I hope my sons will want army careers, too, but I'd never insist they follow in my footsteps. There are other careers that involve fewer risks."

"I've learned one thing on this wagon train," Cathy said. "There are risks in everything people do. There's no such thing as real safety, and the only security is what you feel inside yourself."

He nodded, impressed—as always—by the soundness of her attitudes. For someone of her age, she displayed remarkable maturity and common sense. He took a deep breath and stopped pacing.

"Cathy," he said, "the first time I saw you I felt drawn to you. I never let you know it because you had interests elsewhere. If you still have them, I'll keep my mouth shut. If not, I have something else I want to say to you."

She rose slowly, color burning in her cheeks, and smoothed her skirt as she met his gaze with eyes as steady as his. "Whip is the only guide who could have brought the wagon train this far, and we still need him to take us the rest of the way. Nobody knows the trail and its pitfalls as he does. He's necessary. To all of us. But once we reach Oregon, I don't care if I ever set eyes on him again."

Lee drew in his breath. "I've loved you for months," he said. "You've been so wonderful to me during my convalescence that I've dared to hope I mean something special to you, too. I'll be very proud if you'll do me the honor of becoming my wife, and I promise I'll cherish you for the rest of my days."

Cathy felt tears sting her eyes. He was so gentle, so kind. "I know nothing about army life, but I'm ready to learn, Lee. Yes, I'll gladly marry you."

He took her in his arms and kissed her with such passion, such intense longing that she felt dizzy. As they stood locked in an embrace, it suddenly occurred to Cathy that he was demonstrating astonishing strength for an invalid. "Not only are you squeezing all the breath out of me," she gasped, "but you're going to hurt your side."

Lee laughed aloud as he continued to hold her. "I've never felt better in all my life. When will we be married?"

"As soon as Bob Martin gives his permission," she said firmly. "We're going to do nothing that will slow your recovery."

Lee released her, stood at attention, and saluted. "Yes, ma'am," he said. "I always obey the orders of a superior officer."

The Metropolitan of St. Petersburg, the primate of the Russian Orthodox Church, conducted a special service at Trinity Cathedral that was attended by most of the notables in residence in the city. It had been rumored that the Czar would be present—a story that proved to have no basis in fact—but so many nobles, generals, and admirals crowded into the church that there was no room for the supposed central figures of the occasion, the people who were going to Oregon. At the last moment Prince Orlev remembered them, so they were crowded into the rear pews. Their numbers now reduced to one hundred and fifty-two men, women, and children, they looked out of place in their drab hats and coats of lambs' wool, and they were obviously ill at ease and bewildered in this grand company.

Some were peasants, a few were artisans from St. Petersburg and Moscow, while the remainder—the only members of the group who could read and write —belonged to the tiny middle class. These shopkeepers had been persuaded to emigrate because they were on the verge of bankruptcy, thanks to the refusal of the lords and ladies who patronized their establishments to pay their bills.

The Metropolitan, aware that the top-ranking officials of the secret police were present and wanting no trouble with them, devoted the better part of his sermon to lavish praise of the Czar. He found time, however, to commend the departing travelers for their patriotism and remembered to include them in a final prayer.

Then most of the congregation went to Alexander Nevsky Square, the ladies and gentlemen riding in their elegant coaches, the departing emigrants being transported in open carts. It was explained to the latter that they were riding in the open so the crowds could see them. There were no crowds, however, the Royal Chamberlain having forgotten to issue the orders that would have brought all government employees out into the streets.

At the great square a raw, blustery wind blowing in from the Baltic kept most of the gentry in their coaches and kept farewell ceremonies short. The emigrants were transferred to the wooden-seated carriages that would take them all the way across Siberia on the first leg of their monumental journey to the New World. Their personal belongings, already crated, were lashed to the tops of the carriages.

Prince Orlev was too busy to listen to the farewell speeches as he gave final instructions to the two men responsible for delivering the emigrants to the warship that would await them on the Sea of Japan and take them first to Alaska, then down the coast of North America to Oregon.

Colonel Semyon Brodnets, commander of the Cossack cavalry unit that would escort the emigrants, was contemptuous of all civilians but had to be polite to the Prince. "Rest assured your commands will be obeyed, Your Highness, all of them," he said.

Orlev strongly disliked the military. To him, even the highest-ranking generals were men who carried out, rather than initiated, policies. "Be good enough to repeat your orders so I'm sure you know them," he rasped.

Colonel Brodnets glowered, but when he spoke, his voice was civil. "Fresh horses will be provided at all stops. The emigrants are to be fed, housed, and rested adequately, even at the expense of my troops."

"Above all," Orlev said, "they are not to be beaten or otherwise abused. You, personally, have been granted the authority to discipline any who may change their minds about making the journey."

"They will be treated like members of the court," the Cossack officer said dutifully, "except on those occasions when they may stray or try to escape."

"Even then, no whips." The Prince glanced at the frightened travelers, who were peering out through the windows of their carriages. "And keep your men away from their women. It is His Majesty's personal wish that these persons remain enthusiastic patriots when they reach their new homes on the Pacific."

"You may depend on me in all things, Your Highness," Brodnets said. He raised his gloved hand to his fur hat in salute.

The Prince turned to the other man, one of the most competent young physicians in the realm. "Dr. Wizneuski," he said, "your task is even more difficult. The number of emigrants has been reduced to one hundred and fifty-two, a pitifully small number. See to it that all of them stay alive and healthy. Succeed in your task, and when you return next year, you have my promise that you will become my own household physician."

"I am overwhelmed, Your Highness," Dr. Anton Wizneuski murmured. He bowed low so that the Prince couldn't see the expression in his eyes. Not only did he pay no heed to the worthless promises of high-ranking nobles, but he resented the attitude that they presented. The poor, befuddled souls who were being bribed and coerced into traveling to the New World were human beings, not cattle. While studying medicine in Edinburgh, the physician had learned the meaning of freedom and dignity for the first time. That was why he had volunteered to escort these people to America, making certain that his associates at St. Catherine's Hospital believed he was doing it for the large sum of money he would be paid. If he liked Oregon, he well might stay there, as far as he could get from the cruelties and stifling atmosphere of St. Petersburg.

"With all due respect to the Colonel," he said, "I want to remind him in your presence, Your Highness, that my authority on this journey is greater than his."

The unprecedented situation already had left its mark

306

on Colonel Brodnets. "It is my sincere hope," he said coldly, "that Dr. Wizneuski will not abuse his rare authority."

"Certainly not," the physician replied, "provided it is well understood that I place the welfare of the travelers above all else. If one should become seriously ill, we shall halt until he recovers. And I shall insist on proper shelter and food for them at all times. They must arrive in América in radiant health if they are to bring glory to the name of the Czar."

The man's sincerity was refreshing. He was plainly the right choice for the important task that awaited him. Nevertheless, Prince Orlev was bored. He extended his hand to be kissed, rings glittering over his gloves. "I wish you a pleasant journey, gentlemen," he said, his attitude as casual as though they were going only as far as Moscow. "Make certain your venture succeeds, and perhaps one day your statues will stand behind those of Alexander Nevsky and Peter the Great in this very square." He turned and walked off to his carriage, chuckling at his little joke and looking forward to the comfort of the fur lap robe that his current mistress was keeping warm for him in the coach.

The wedding of Cathy van Ayl and Lieutenant Colonel Leland Blake was a joyous occasion that helped the pioneers forget the rigors of the vicious winter that was coming to an end. By unanimous consent, Emily von Thalman used enough of the precious flour from the reserve supplies to bake a cake for the occasion, and the scouts spent three days in the field, bringing down two bucks, a doe, and a pair of mountain goats to provide fresh meat for the wedding feast.

Reverend Cavendish conducted a solemn ceremony, and several of Cathy's friends wept without shame.

The community hall was so crowded that the doors had to be opened from time to time to let in fresh air. Paul Thoman needed little urging to offer a toast of watered brandywine to the bridal couple, and carried away, he quoted at length from Plato, Juvenal, and Cicero on the meaning and sacred nature of marriage. Few of those present understood much of what he said, but Sally MacNeill confided to Dolores that she loved the sound of his voice.

Everyone agreed that Cathy was a radiant bride. Lee stood proud and erect, obviously recovering quickly from his wound. A number of people had shifted quarters in order to make a cabin available for the bridal couple's exclusive use. During the trek to Oregon, they would live in Cathy's wagon.

People pelted the pair with soft snowballs as they made their way to their temporary quarters, and there were cheers when Lee carried Cathy across the threshold of the cabin. Bob Martin frowned, but his wife squeezed his arm.

"Don't worry about Lee," she murmured. "It looks to me as though your patient is recovered."

"I have a hunch you're right," he replied, grinning. "Cathy is just the medicine he needed."

Only the sentries missed the festivities. It was not accidental that a silent and withdrawn Whip Holt had elected to take sentry duty at the point farthest from the lake during the time the wedding and the party were taking place.

"Do you suppose he still loves Cathy?" Eulalia asked Cindy as they headed back to their own quarters.

Cindy shrugged. "There's no way of telling what goes on inside Whip," she said. "But I can't feel sorry for him. He had his chance with Cathy, and he made a mess of it."

"But what was the poor man to do? When La-ena showed up out of nowhere on the trail, he was trapped."

"Now you're just being soft," Cindy replied. "It never bothers me when a man's sins catch up with him."

The next morning, when the newlyweds appeared at the community hall for breakfast, they were roundly applauded by everyone. Cathy managed a smile, although she blushed furiously, and her husband put an arm around her shoulders. Eulalia noticed that Whip was not present, although he almost always ate breakfast at that hour.

The weather grew steadily warmer, and the lakes and rivers no longer froze at night. Snow vanished rapidly, even above the timberline, and overnight, or so it seemed, the grass in the valley turned green. Within a week, the horses and oxen were turned loose, for the first time in months, to forage for themselves.

Everyone was excited, and no one needed urging to prepare for the next leg of the journey. Wagons were scoured, their canvas tops were put back into place, and faulty yokes and axles were repaired. A river appeared, seemingly out of nowhere, in a small canyon, and the women enjoyed the luxury of not only washing clothes and blankets in the clear, clean water, but hanging them out to dry. The doors of cabins remained open all day, ridding them of their musty stench. Dolores and Hosea ventured to the far end of the valley and returned with word that spring berries were beginning to appear.

Members of the council met in private to decide what to do about Garcia. Occasionally they could see his fire on the heights, so they knew he was still living in a cave there, and it was finally agreed to give him ammunition and gunpowder, along with a several days' supply of food, before they sent him off. Wanting no more to do with him than was necessary, they voted to wait until a day or two before they broke camp to contact him.

"Folks are anxious to get back on the trail," Whip said. "I don't have the heart to tell them we've got to hold off for another two or three weeks."

"That long?" Lee, attending his first council meeting since his recovery and marriage, was surprised.

"We've got to wait until the rivers have subsided," Whip explained. "In the spring, little creeks become roaring torrents, and dry beds suddenly look like the mouth of the Columbia. The rivers on the other side of the Continental Divide can be nasty when they're flooding, so we'd be buying trouble if we left too soon. Besides, game is always pretty scarce for about the better part of a hundred miles the other side of South Pass. The animals are coming back to the valleys in these parts, so I recommend we send out hunting parties to build up our meat supplies while we're waiting for the flooded rivers to stop rampaging. That way we'll be in good shape and reduce our risks on the trail to a minimum."

The others accepted his judgment, as they always did in such matters. The following morning the hunters went out in search of game. Meanwhile, the older girls took charge of fishing in the lake, and the older boys went up to the mountain streams to fish.

The warmer weather brought unexpected visitors to the camp. The first to arrive was a military courier, traveling with a cavalry escort. He brought dispatches from Washington for Lee Blake, telling him that a Russian expedition to Oregon was under way and indicating, even more ominously, that the British were expected to send a large body of additional troops to Fort Vancouver in the immediate future.

General Scott's letter to Lee was succinct. "I can't tell you from a comfortable desk in Washington City how to meet and overcome these threats to our future settlements. But I have been directed by President Van Buren to notify you that the government will support any means you care to utilize, short of armed combat, to protect the American position."

Lee smiled ruefully when he read the communication a second time. He had no idea what "means" might be at his disposal. The Administration and the War Department were placing the full burden of responsibility on his shoulders.

Before sending a reply, he showed the documents to other members of the council. "There's plenty of room in Oregon for Russian immigrants as well as thousands of our own people," he said, "provided the Russians are willing to live as peaceful neighbors—which we won't know until all of us get there. The British are another matter. Their garrison numbers at least a thousand men now, and they have cavalry, infantry, and artillery. Add reinforcements, and I'd need a couple of brigades of our own troops to squeeze them out."

"How do you intend to deal with them?" Tilman Wade asked.

Lee shrugged. "Ordinarily, I believe in making complete contingency plans, but this situation is different. The British won't use force to expel us from Oregon —they don't want war with the United States. So I'll wait until we get there, see what kind of a reception they give us, and then act accordingly. The President and War Department have allowed me to handle the problem as I see fit, so the first thing to do will be to evaluate the situation and see what must be done."

The courier also brought two saddlebags filled with mail for people on the wagon train, most of whom rejoiced when they received word from relatives and friends. Cathy received a long letter from her sister, who said that the Brentwood baby was due at any time. Cathy replied with news of her own marriage, and Lee, who had met the Brentwoods and spent a couple of days with them in Independence on his own way West, added several paragraphs.

Tilman Wade winced when he read a letter from a cousin. "Nancy is a real hellion," he said, "and she tells me she's following us on the second wagon train. I don't have any idea what Oregon is like, but I know it won't be the same after Nancy gets there."

Paul Thoman received a letter from his parents, in which they requested his immediate return to Boston and, as bait, offered him a place as an officer on his cousin's next clipper ship voyage to Cathay.

His reply was firm. "My future lies in Oregon," he wrote. "I intend to teach school while I get my bearings, which is how I occupy myself at present. I also intend to explore the possibility of building ships, however, so don't be too surprised if I form a Pacific branch of the family company."

The courier and his escorts spent several days at the camp, then started out on their return journey East.

The next visitor to arrive was a messenger from the Ute. "I bring a warning," he said. "The Comanche are keeping watch on the white brothers of the Ute. They have greed in their hearts, and they want the women and horses and guns of the white men."

Whip frowned as he translated the brave's words for the other members of the council.

"What does he mean when he says the Comanche are keeping watch on us?" Lee asked sharply.

Ernie was tense, too. "How many men can they send against us?"

"And do the Ute know anything specific about the Comanche war plans?" Tilman asked.

Whip silenced them. "I'll go into all of that with you later," he said.

The messenger was given a hearty meal, as well as gifts, and sent back to his own people with assurances of the pioneers' lasting friendship. Then the council reconvened.

"I know enough about the Comanche for our purposes," Whip said. "First off, it doesn't surprise me any that they've had runners keeping an eye on us."

"Isn't there some way we can stop them?" Lee demanded.

Whip shrugged. "They're like any hostile Indian nation. They can watch us from any one of twenty spots around here. Send out scouts to shoot them or drive them away, and they'll vanish before we get near them. They're one of the most powerful tribes, and if the various branches of the Comanche could get together, they could send a couple of thousand warriors against us."

Ernie whistled under his breath.

"I'm not making light of them, mind you," Whip said, "but the chances of their getting together are small. They quarrel so much among themselves they could never send two thousand braves out on a campaign. Besides, that isn't their way. They'll snipe away at us, probably after we get through the South Pass, and they'll try to wear us down with hit-and-run raids. They'd like nothing better than to detach a wagon from the column, here and there, rather than risk a full-scale confrontation with us."

Lee turned to face him. They had had little to do with one another since Whip had offered brief congratulations to Lee on his marriage to Cathy. There was no way to determine how Whip really felt about losing Cathy, but that was irrelevant now. It was plain that, in the days and weeks ahead, the two men would be forced to work together. They, among all those on the wagon train, best understood the Indian mentality and therefore could make plans to counter a situation that threatened to escalate into an emergency.

"Some animals kill by taking little bites instead of swallowing their victims whole," Lee said. "If that's the Comanche way, it makes them every bit as dangerous as the Blackfoot."

"They can be worse. They're capable of doing a lot of damage—it's harder to anticipate their moves."

"But we've got to find ways of doing it."

Whip smiled slightly. "Between us, Lee," he said, "we'll work out ways to protect the folks who are depending on us."

Ernie von Thalman breathed a sigh of relief. Whip and Lee might find it difficult to work closely with each other, but they intended to try. Neither man would allow Cathy to come between them.

The next visitors to the camp approached Little Valley from the heights. Paul Thoman, on sentry duty, identified them by their warpaint as warriors of the Jicarilla Apache nation. The five braves who made up the party made no attempt to conceal themselves as they rode toward the camp. Whatever their purpose, they were moving in the open.

They arrived as the pioneers were eating a light midday meal, and in accordance with frontier rules of hospitality, the Indians were invited to share the food. Although they were somewhat leery at first, they soon lost their inhibitions and ate heartily. It was plain there was a purpose to their visit, but no mention of their mission was made.

These newcomers were members of Dolores's tribe, and she was well acquainted with all of them. But after greeting them formally, she retreated to the far end of the community hall and stayed there. She seemed to have guessed why they had come and was waiting for them to approach her.

They paid little attention to her until they finished their meal. Then, as the pioneers dispersed, the Indians went over to where Dolores waited. The oldest member of the group acted as their spokesman.

"The winter has been long," he said.

"Very long," Dolores agreed politely.

Whip drifted nearer, as did Paul Thoman and the scouts, who understood the language of the Jicarilla Apache.

Hosea came closer, too. He felt uneasy, even though Dolores did not seem perturbed.

"Life has not been good in the cold time for the Apache," the spokesman said. "Many were sick with the Bad Fever of the mountains."

Dolores nodded. "I know. But now they are well again. The spirits took only a few of the very old with them to the after world."

No one questioned her ability to know what she could have learned from no human being. By now, everyone present accepted her extraordinary talent.

"Now the good season comes," the spokesman declared. "Soon the warriors will shoot much game, and

315

the women will catch many fish. Berries and roots will grow."

"Soon all will be well again," Dolores agreed.

"But now," the warrior said, "there is a need for the daughter of the Jicarilla Apache to return to her people. Our enemies surround us, and the Comanche threaten us."

"The Comanche will not attack the Jicarilla Apache before the next snows come and go and the land turns green again," Dolores predicted without hesitation.

"For many years the father of Dolores was the chief medicine man of our people," the spokesman said solemnly. "He told that which was to come, he brought those who were sick back to health, and he led us in our prayers to the spirits. Then the spirits took him with them, and his place was taken by Dolores, who is his daughter and the daughter of all the people of the Jicarilla Apache. But she did not stay with us in the bad season."

"There are three medicine men in the towns of the Jicarilla Apache," Dolores said. "If there is a need for others, the spirits will select them. The medicine men are wise in the ways of the nation. They know the chants and dances, and they can lead the people in them. They also know what plants heal the sick and what plants are bad for them."

The spokesman inclined his head. "What the daughter of the Jicarilla Apache says is true. But no medicine man of our nation has the power of Dolores to look into the future and tell what will be."

The girl lowered her head modestly.

It was becoming apparent that a subtle tug-of-war was taking place. The spokesman was urging Dolores to return to her tribe, and she was resisting the invitation.

Hosea was alarmed. If Dolores returned to her tribe, he was undecided as to what he should do. He could ask for the right to accompany her, but he felt honor-bound to stay with these people who had befriended him when he had been in need and had saved him from the bounty hunter who had tried to return him to slavery. If faced with the choice, he knew he would feel it his duty to give up the one woman he had ever wanted, the one woman he would ever encounter who would be the right mate for him.

The spokesman raised his voice. "For three days the people of the Jicarilla Apache sang chants and danced, begging the spirits to send the daughter of our people back to us."

Dolores took her stand. "I cannot go," she said. "Here also are my people."

Hosea's relief was so great that he felt weak.

But the warrior was unmoved. "The elders of our people have ruled that if the daughter of the Jicarilla Apache does not return of her own wish, we who have come for her must bind her and take her with us." He turned to look at Whip. "The white men will not try to stop us because they know that Dolores is one of us. If they stand between us and Dolores, they will not finish their journey. Every Indian nation in the mountains will attack them. Their men will be scalped, their carts will be burned, and their women will become prisoners of the Indians."

Whip knew that his threat was real. Every Indian tribe in the Rockies and in the chain to the west would be outraged if a gifted medicine woman was prevented from returning to her own nation. It was unlikely that even those who survived the inevitable, endless assaults would ever reach Oregon.

He pondered his reply, wanting to support Dolores

while at the same time not offending the warriors. But Dolores needed no one to defend her. "I am small," she said, "and I do not have the strength of tall men. So I could not stop you from binding my ankles and wrists and carrying me away with you."

Anger flooded Hosea. He was wondering how many of these warriors he could kill single-handed, if necessary, in order to prevent them from abducting Dolores.

Dolores continued to stand firm, however. "If you carry me to the land of the Jicarilla Apache," she said, "you will be taking an ordinary squaw. My visions will become so angry with you that they will leave me. I will have no way to see into the future. I will have no power to heal those who are sick. When I chant, the spirits will not hear my voice. I will cook, sew skins, and fish, but never again will I be a medicine woman."

Hosea had no idea whether she was telling the truth, but there was no doubt that she had checked the warriors. There would be no violence now on anyone's part.

Whip found it difficult to keep a straight face. Regardless of the accuracy of Dolores's statement, her fellow tribesmen were being forced to accept her decision. Furthermore, they could not resent the members of the wagon train for it.

The spokesman bowed his head for a moment. "Why does the daughter of the Jicarilla Apache stay with these people rather than return to the land of her brothers and sisters?"

Dolores folded her arms and spoke slowly and solemnly. "The troubles of the Jicarilla Apache are small," she said, "but the troubles these people will face are great. My visions have told me to stay with them so I may help them in the terrible trials that lie ahead for them."

The warriors had run out of arguments. They had to accept Dolores's decision. They left quickly, not even showing her the usual Indian courtesy of wishing her well.

Later Whip told the members of the council the gist of the debate, and they shared his worry. What were the problems the wagon train faced that made Dolores feel it necessary to stay with them? Lee and Whip went to her, asking her for information. But she shook her head.

"My visions are clouded, and I cannot see them clearly," she said. "All I know is that, even though the sun is shining, the sky overhead is growing black. Terrible troubles lie in store, but my visions will not show them to me yet. I am one of you because you are my people, but in my heart I am afraid for all of us. The blows that will strike us are worse than any we have known."

The troop ships dropped anchor at Fort Vancouver, taking up all of the available space at the three major docks. Most of the little town's civilians gathered to watch the soldiers disembark, and the entire garrison was mustered, the troops standing at parade rest in their scarlet uniforms as they waited to greet the reinforcements.

Colonel Phillips Morrison, resplendent in his dress uniform, stood alone, the members of his staff gathered behind him. The eight hundred new arrivals increased the size of his command appreciably. It didn't seem too much for him to hope that he might soon receive a promotion to the rank of brigadier. Equally important, he reported directly to the War Office, and was not required to share the credit for his successes with politicians and diplomats. His was an independent command, and his augmented garrison would make him the master of the entire Oregon country.

Colonel Morrison savored the moment. His sense of euphoria vanished, however, when a familiar figure in buckskins shambled forward, smiling sardonically, a vile-smelling pipe in his mouth.

As usual, John McLoughlin, the Hudson's Bay Company factor, didn't bother to lower his voice. The staff members, some of the civilians, and the troops in the front ranks could hear every word he said. "I congratulate you, Morrison." There was a note of irony in his voice. "This is a great day for the Royal Army."

"It is, to be sure." Morrison cursed him silently for spoiling this hour of triumph.

"Oh, I'm delighted to see these strapping young fellows." McLoughlin peered out at the transports, their decks lined with scarlet-uniformed soldiers waiting to come ashore. "This very day I'll present you with the bill for the new barracks that were built to house these lads, and I'll be obliged if you'll make a fifty percent down payment on the provisions we've sold your quartermaster. The company stands to earn a pretty penny from this confounded foolishness."

"I do not regard it as foolishness," the Colonel said loftily, "to make a rich wilderness area secure for the Crown."

"Ah, but is it secure?" McLoughlin was mocking. "Now that spring is at hand, the American wagon train will soon be on the move again. One of these days you'll see settlers by the hundreds pouring into the valleys, and they'll be followed by thousands of others. The Americans have a taste for travel, and you'll keep them out only if you order your toy soldiers to shoot them down before they can get here."

Morrison gave him a superior smile. "I assure you, McLoughlin, I shall welcome all immigrants in Queen Victoria's name and shall place them under my protection the moment they swear allegiance to her."

"Suppose they refuse to take the oath?" The factor's eyes became cold. "What then?"

The Colonel was surprised. "My troops are a guarantee they won't refuse."

McLoughlin's laugh could be heard on board the transports. "How quickly the lessons of history are forgotten," he cried. "For nine long years we tried to force the Americans to do just that, and ended by recognizing the independence they had already won from us. Neither you nor anyone else will force them to accept the Crown's claim to Oregon."

"The Union Jack," Morrison replied stiffly, "flies over the area, and I shall make certain it stays there."

McLoughlin silently watched a pair of nine-pounder cannons being unloaded from one of the decks in order to clear the way for the troops on board to come ashore. When he spoke again, there was genuine pity in his voice. "The Union Jack," he said, speaking as one would to a recalcitrant child, "flies only over Fort Vancouver and nowhere else in thousands upon thousands of square miles. Do you think that one flag will prevent the Americans from building their homes here and clearing the wilderness for their farms, orchards, and ranches?"

"Lord Palmerston makes policy. I follow it."

"Palmerston? You're wrong, Morrison. He's a public servant, a mere instrument of policy, which is created by public opinion. The young Queen knows it, even if you don't." There seemed to be a hidden meaning in what the factor said, and the Colonel frowned.

"Let me give you a warning," McLoughlin declared. "Two months ago, when I learned these new reinforcements were coming here, I wrote to the directors of the Hudson's Bay Company. Not only did I protest this idiocy, but I suggested ways to end the impasse with the Americans."

Morrison stiffened. If he had his way, McLoughlin would be arrested for treason.

"There's enough land here, between Mexican California and Russian Alaska, for all of us. I say we reach a compromise with the United States, just as Hudson's Bay will come to terms with the fur traders. There's no other solution, short of war."

"You think public opinion will support that solution?"

"I'm certain of it. I'll grant that you have the manpower to drive off the people who are coming here in the first wagon train, but you can't do the same to those who come in the second—or the twenty-second."

Morrison loosened his sword in its scabbard so he would be ready to return the salute of the senior officers gathered on the deck of the flagship. As they started toward the gangplank, he took several steps forward, hoping to disassociate himself from this unpleasant man. But he couldn't resist firing a parting shot. "Do you suppose the Queen will accept this crazy scheme of yours?"

"You can depend upon it!" McLoughlin called after him. "You don't seem to know that Prince Rupert, King Charlie's cousin, was one of the company's founders. So the Royal Family are major shareholders to this day, and chief among them is the Queen. Like the rest of us, she needs money to live—and far more than most—so, unless you turn your toy soldiers into butchers, she'll be the first to agree to a compromise!"

The sun shone now for the better part of each day, and people were impatient to resume the journey to Oregon. But Whip was not yet ready to march. "The rivers are cresting," he said. "We'll wait a few more days, until we're sure they're going down."

In the meantime, the hunters ranged farther afield each day, returning with larger and larger catches of game. Some reported to Whip and Lee that they had seen small bands of Indians beyond the confines of Little Valley. It appeared that the Comanche were keeping a close watch, waiting for the journey to resume.

But the council decided there was no need yet to raise an alarm. Lee and Whip had devised tactics they hoped would neutralize the Comanche threat. Heavily armed outriders, organized in squads of eight men, would precede the wagon train, while other squads would follow it and range up and down the line on both sides of the column. Each unit would have sufficient firepower to hold off a Comanche band at least two or three times its own size, and when all of the units converged, they would be able to handle close to one hundred and fifty warriors. Whip was sure that no more than that number of Comanche would attack at any one time.

The defense plans would be announced immediately prior to the train's departure. Meanwhile, as Ernie von Thalman said, the company had earned the right to enjoy a respite from worry after the grueling winter. The sentries moved out to the approaches of the valley, and people were free to wander wherever they pleased, provided they did not leave Little Valley or climb the heights. The grass turned green and grew rapidly, clusters of wildflowers appeared everywhere, and the trees were already "stretching," as Cathy Blake remarked, and sending out new branches.

Everyone spent as much time as possible outdoors. The older boys exercised the horses and oxen, leading them to and from the pastures, and the small children played games of tag after school.

Some people enjoyed meandering aimlessly through the woods, looking at flowers and enjoying the unusual luxury of brief periods of solitude.

Certainly no one enjoyed these outings more than Cindy. She was surprised by her deep need to have time to herself. She was pleased she had been accepted by most people on the train, in spite of her past—and she was delighted by her friendships with Eulalia and Cathy. But, she realized, she had never in her life been alone. Her mother had entertained men day and night, and their tiny home in Louisville always had been crowded and cramped. The school to which she had been sent was an institution where privacy had been nonexistent. Then, when she had entered the Louisville brothel, she realized the other girls regarded the place as something of a social club; there was no time to be alone.

So it was a wonderful feeling to stroll alone through the woods, smell the pine-scented air and pause occasionally to admire a tiny flower. When the shade became too cool, it was easy to move into the sun, and when its rays became too hot, Cindy moved out of the open patches.

When she was alone, she could see herself more clearly, and the problems she had thought overwhelming became less intense. She wasn't fooling herself about her future. She knew nothing about farming and had no desire to learn. But people were already talking about forming a small village in the area in which they settled, a village that would grow as later wagon trains reached Oregon. They might even ask Ginny Dobbs to join them. Ginny had become less obnoxious in recent weeks. Perhaps her separation from Garcia had been responsible, or possibly someone had persuaded her to behave herself. It didn't matter what the reason was. It was enough that Ginny could be tolerated now, at least most of the time.

But this was no day to worry about the future. Strolling wherever her feet led her in the valley, Cindy, for the first time in her life, was truly happy. Here, deep in a mountain wilderness far from civilization, she was at peace, glad simply to be alive and healthy.

Looking around to get her bearings, she realized she had wandered to the far end of the valley and was standing directly below the sharp rise that led to the heights. Claiborne was stationed nearby, on sentry duty, and would be annoyed if he learned she had walked this far from the lake. What was worse, at breakfast Ted Woods had been discussing plans, with members of his crew, to chop down some dead trees in this area. She had no desire to see Ted.

It was best to go back closer to the lake, and she began to head in that direction, not bothering to notice that she was moving into a portion of the forest where the trees stood close together, a tangle of white birches impeding her progress.

As Cindy started to move around the stand of birches, she felt someone watching her. She caught a glimpse of dark, glittering eyes and copper skin, a faded buckskin shirt, and a face smeared with vermilion warpaint. Claiborne had told her that the Comanche identified themselves with vermilion. In one hand the warrior held a bone-handled knife, and he carried a bow and a quiver of arrows over one shoulder. A feeling of total panic engulfed Cindy, but then her instinct for survival asserted itself. If she turned and tried to run, the Comanche would overtake her and kill her. If she called for help, Claiborne might hear her. So might Ted and his woodcutters. But by the time they reached her, she would be dead.

This was a situation she had to face alone. Although still badly frightened, she forced herself to return the warrior's unblinking stare.

He did not move immediately. Then he took a single step forward and halted again, his expression changing. Cindy knew the look in his eyes. She had seen it in more men than she cared to recall, and it sickened her. The brave's eyes were shining with lust. It was obvious that he wanted her.

Cindy knew what had to be done in order to save herself. Trying to conquer her fear, she smiled at him, then stood, her lips parted provocatively.

At first the warrior was so astonished he could only gape at her. Then he began to preen himself, believing he had made a conquest. Cindy's tactics were working. She had been right. All men, civilized or savage, were alike, endowed with insufferable male vanity. Her self-confidence rose.

The Comanche jammed his knife into his belt and swaggered toward her. Cindy noted the exact location of his knife and made no attempt to fight him off as he grasped her, his breath so foul she almost choked.

Suddenly, without warning, he threw her to the ground and landed on top of her with such force that he knocked the breath from her lungs. Cindy knew she had no time to lose. He would take her swiftly, then kill her.

The Comanche began to fumble with her skirt, momentarily confused by her petticoats, garments that were unknown to him. During that brief respite, Cindy's feelings underwent a complete transformation. Her terror vanished and was replaced by an icy rage. In this savage, she saw the embodiment of all the men who had ever used and abused her, taking her body and casting her aside, seeking only their own gratification.

Her anger gave her courage. Allowing the warrior to do as he pleased, she wriggled sensually beneath him, hoping to distract his attention. Her trick was effective. He became even more intent on taking her. Boldly and without hesitation, Cindy drew the dagger from his belt and, using all of her strength, plunged the blade as hard as she could into his body. Her fury was so great that the knife sank to the hilt.

Pushing the Comanche aside, Cindy freed herself and struggled to her feet. The Comanche lay sprawled on the ground, blood spurting from his wound, his glazed eyes staring up at her. She realized she had killed him, and terror once more overcame her. She screamed at the top of her lungs, took a deep breath, and screamed again.

She was still screaming when Claiborne arrived on the scene, his rifle cocked. An instant later Ted appeared, his ax ready for use. Both men took in the scene at a glance. Somehow Cindy managed to stop screaming, even though she shook uncontrollably.

"You did this?" Claiborne asked incredulously. "By yourself, with no help?"

She nodded, her eyes wide.

The men grinned at each other and then turned to Cindy in admiration. "I wouldn't believe this if I wasn't seeing it myself," Ted muttered.

"You're all right?" Claiborne asked her.

Again she nodded. Then she began to weep, a torrent of tears cascading down her face.

"Here, now, no need for that," Claiborne said, and put his arms around her to steady her. Cindy clung to him, soothed by the comfort he offered her, relieved by the knowledge that a protector was close at hand.

Ted Woods looked at the couple. Even though he knew Cindy was reacting to what had just happened and that this was no romantic embrace, a familiar black rage began to steal over him. "No!" he said aloud. His effort to regain self-control was so great that sweat poured from him. He could not vent his wrath on this girl for whom he had pined or this man who had become his friend.

Claiborne was patting Cindy's shoulder, but she seemed to be weeping harder. Ted knew that Claiborne had won their competition. Cindy would learn to love this man in time and would become his wife. They looked natural and right together.

"I'll get the others," Ted said, "and we'll do something about that body. I reckon Whip and Lee will want to look at him before we bury the bastard." He turned away and stumbled off into the forest. He felt a dull ache, but there was no hate in his heart. Apparently he was destined to spend the rest of his days alone. He had become reconciled to his loss.

Slowly he straightened, and his step became firmer. Loss? He had suffered no loss. For the first time since the awful day he had killed his wife and brother, he felt like a whole man. He had gained his self-respect. His life was beginning anew.

XII

"We shall break camp at dawn, the day after to-morrow," Ernie von Thalman announced at breakfast. "Make sure your wagons are ready to roll."

His announcement revitalized the pioneers. Little Valley had been a sanctuary that had enabled them to survive the long, hard winter, but they were sick of the place. Some had spent a year and a half on the journey. Barring crippling and unforeseen accidents, they would reach Oregon sometime that summer, and would be able to claim their land and at least start work on their permanent homes before the weather turned cold. With their goal that close, they were anxious to move on. What excited them most of all, perhaps, was the prospect of good weather during the next winter. From all they had heard, snow rarely fell in the land they intended to inhabit.

Immediately after breakfast, the forty men who would act as outriders to protect the column from Comanche raids were summoned to the community hall for their first meeting. The threat would be explained to them and their duties outlined. They drifted into the buildings in twos and threes, aware that something out of the ordinary was expected of them.

Whip and Lee were ready to call the meeting to order when it was discovered that Terence Malcolm was still absent. Tilman Wade went off to fetch him. He returned, white-faced, a few moments later. "Terence is suffering from a high fever and is out of his mind," Tilman said tersely. "Lena is unconscious from the fever, and so is their baby."

Bob Martin was summoned at once, and the meeting was postponed until later in the day. The physician applied wet packs to the patients to reduce their fever, but his ministrations were unsuccessful. Never having encountered such a disease before, he called in Whip, hoping that he could identify it, and sent for Dolores, in case her herbs could cure the ailment.

"It's what the Indians call the Bad Fever," Whip said somberly. "It hits like lightning. I've never heard of anything that can be done for somebody who comes down with it."

"There is no cure," Dolores said. "The spirits decide who will live and who will be taken to the after world."

"Whatever the outcome, we'll know it soon," Whip added. "I've never known it to last long. Either people die from it within a day or so, or they begin to recover. And even if they do get well, sometimes they're left crippled."

Bob Martin was helpless.

Lena Malcolm and her baby, Lenore, died before noon without regaining consciousness. Terence, violent in his delirium at first and then rapidly becoming more feeble, survived them by only a few hours.

The fever spread through the camp like a brush fire, and by afternoon thirty-four people were stricken. The Martins, aided by Dolores, did what little they could to make the sufferers comfortable. "In all the years I've practiced medicine," Bob said, "I've never seen such a frightful disease. I don't know how to begin to help."

It was obvious to everyone that the departure of the wagon train would have to be postponed until the fever ran its course.

Volunteers dug graves and built coffins. By nightfall, eleven people had died and been buried. Before supper, a meeting was held at the community hall, and Reverend Cavendish led the congregation in prayers for the recovery of the sick and the preservation of the health of those fortunate enough to have escaped.

The plague continued to spread. By midnight fifty-seven people were ill. Jacob Levine was among them, and although he fought with all of his courage and strength, he succumbed before dawn. Oscar Cavendish, who had known him longer than anyone else, broke down and wept at Jacob's funeral, but he recovered sufficiently to read selections from the Old Testament that he had chosen with care.

Early in the morning, Cindy discovered that Eulalia Woodling was striken. Claiborne went at once to his sister's bedside.

"I've got to help with Eulalia, too," Cathy Blake told Lee. "It will take several people to keep fixing fresh wet packs and keep her wrapped in them."

Lee wanted to protest that Cathy would be exposing herself that much more to the disease, but he kept silent. He could not urge her to desert a close friend in desperate need. "Good luck," was all he said. "Do what you can for her." Dread clutched at him as she watched her leave their cabin.

By noon the spread of the fever had halted. A haggard and sleepless Bob Martin revealed that sixty-eight members of the company had become ill. Several more people died during the day, bringing the total number of deaths to twenty-seven. The fever was indiscriminate in its choice of victims, taking strong men and young women, along with several children. Some of the older people, who might have been thought particularly susceptible, escaped unscathed.

Shortly before twilight Eulalia Woodling regained consciousness and asked for a drink of water, saying only that she was very thirsty. Bob Martin soon confirmed that her fever was gone, and her brother and friends rejoiced.

Not until the next morning, when she felt strong enough to leave her bed, did she discover, to her horror, that she could no longer bend her left knee nor move her left ankle. They looked normal, but they were locked, and she could walk only with a decided limp.

Bob Martin examined her again. He could do nothing for her condition. "I'm at a loss," he said. "I'd never heard of this illness until the epidemic struck us. I'm afraid I can suggest nothing that will make it possible for you to bend your knee or move your ankle."

"I guess," Eulalia said dully, "I ought to be glad I'm alive. Isn't there anything I can do for my leg?"

"If there is, I haven't heard of it. Just this morning Dolores told me about a middle-aged Apache warrior she knew, a man who contracted the fever when he was in his twenties. Until then he was a fine hunter, but his left arm became paralyzed, and now, thirty years later, he still can't move it. I don't want to discourage you, Eulalia, but I've got to be realistic. It wouldn't be fair to hold out false hope."

Not until she was alone did Eulalia weep. Tears trickled unheeded down her face. She was only twenty, but she no longer had a future. Her life was destroyed.

Later that day Cathy and Cindy tried to console her, but nothing they could say offered her any comfort. They couldn't blame her for being discouraged.

Whip fashioned a walking stick of hickory for Eulalia to help her when she walked, and he handed it to her without a word. "Thank you," she said. She was grateful to him, but she wanted to break the stick in two. She would be a cripple for the rest of her days, forced to walk with the aid of a cane. She hated the symbol as much as she despised herself.

The shocked company grieved for its dead, sympathized with those who had suffered disabilities, and then resolutely looked forward to the future. The departure of the wagon train was rescheduled. Camp would be broken in two weeks. Some of the fever's victims, Eulalia among them, appeared to be recovering their health quickly, and Dr. Martin estimated that in two weeks it would be safe for even the most delicate to travel.

"My visions," Dolores told Cathy and Lee, "did not warn me the Bad Fever would come. They never explain why they sometimes tell me what will happen and sometimes do not."

"Apparently," Lee said, "the fever was what lay in store when you told us that terrible things would happen."

"It was one of the things," Dolores replied somberly. "But there will be others, and they will be terrible, too. I have begged my visions to show me our future, but they have refused. Perhaps they have turned their backs to me because you are now my people. All I know is that the troubles are not ended."

Eulalia remained inconsolable. "I've always been vain," she told Cindy, "but not until now have I realized how much my looks mean to me." She pointed in disgust to her knee and her ankle. "I'll be a freak for the rest of my life."

"A freak? Oh, no. You're still the same person you were." Cindy didn't know what else to say.

"That's not so. People will pity me. I'll never be like the rest of you." Eulalia was silent for a moment. "I must tell you something I could admit to no one else. You and I have fiercely hated men. But I've always felt, deep down inside me, that some day that feeling would pass. I can read and write, and you and I have talked of opening a dry goods shop when we reach Oregon. But I—I've always wanted fulfillment as a woman, too. Now it's beyond my reach."

"You mean marriage?"

Eulalia nodded. "I've told myself I probably would want it, eventually. Now I know it isn't for me."

"Certainly there must be good, decent men capable of overlooking a slight disability."

Eulalia laughed harshly. "Slight? Why would any man want a cripple for a wife when he could have a healthy woman with two sound legs? I've learned too much about the real world since I've been on this wagon train ever again to believe in fairy tales. I no longer have a future as a woman, and that's a bitter pill to swallow."

Cindy tried to interrupt, but Eulalia wasn't finished. "I'd demand that a husband respect me, but how could any man feel respect for a cripple like me? No, I've got to reconcile myself to spending the rest of my life alone, no matter how much I hate the idea!"

Whip Holt did not accompany the hunters when they went out into the wilds on one of their last forays. His mind was reeling, and he felt the urgent need to be alone, to sort out and clarify his thoughts. Offering no explanation to anyone, he rode alone to the heights above the timberline, where there was still a touch of winter in the spring air.

He breathed deeply and stared out at the snow-capped peaks that surrounded him on every side. This untamed wilderness had been his home for all his adult life. Now he was being forced to abandon it, to begin a new and different existence. A feeling of sadness came over him, but he knew he had no choice. He was growing too old for the life of a mountain man.

Dismounting, Whip sat on a boulder, drinking in the view, reveling in the solitude, and enjoying the whisper of the wind that blew down from the peaks. He had a riddle to solve. Ever since the fever had struck the camp, Eulalia Woodling had intruded again and again into his thoughts. Why?

Oh, he felt sorry for her, but that wasn't the real answer. He had been attracted to her since the day that she, her father, and her brother had joined the wagon train. She was a self-centered bitch in those days, but she was high-spirited and exceptionally pretty.

His train of thought reminded him of La-ena. He knew he would be haunted by her ghost for the rest of his life. She had died up here in the heights, freezing and starving, because of him. Well, there was nothing he could do to bring her back, and if he had learned anything from the forces of nature that ruled wilderness living, it was that, in order to survive, a man had to face the future, not spend his days recalling the past.

Cathy van Ayl was on his conscience, too. But she was Cathy Blake now and had moved beyond his reach, had chosen another man—a solid man of real worth. Whip had to approve of her choice. All the same, he had hurt her, and for that he could not forgive himself.

Was he using Eulalia to ease his guilt? Whip pondered the question at great length. As one who liked to think of himself as a man who put honor above all else, he had to follow the dictates of his conscience.

Whip stood up. For a long time he remained motionless, bidding farewell to the life he had loved for so many years. The precise course on which he would now embark would be determined in the next few hours.

Eulalia Woodling sat alone in the musty cabin. She knew she was wallowing in self-pity, but she didn't care. Her cabin mates had gone off to work in the kitchen, but Cindy, trying to be kind, had refused to let her accompany them. "There's no need for you to stand for hours," she had said. "Stay here and rest. We'll take care of what needs to be done."

Eulalia couldn't explain that she didn't want special consideration and hated to be treated like an invalid. She needed no reminders of the illness that had changed her entire life and expected no praise for doing her fair share of work.

There was a tap at the door.

"Come in," Eulalia called wearily.

Whip stood on the threshold, but he did not enter the cabin. "They told me I'd find you here." A glance told him that she had been brooding in the semidarkness. "I want to have a little chat with you, if you'll come out."

Leaning on her walking stick, Eulalia limped out of the cabin. Whip led her to the far side of the lake, then headed into the forest. He did not stop until they reached a sunlit clearing where a large boulder stood.

Eulalia was breathing hard by the time they reached the clearing, and she sat down on a convenient depression in the boulder. She wondered why Whip had brought her this far from the camp for a talk and resented his failure to help her over rough places in the woods. Then she became aware of her inconsistency. She had wanted to be treated like a normal, healthy person, and that was precisely what Whip was doing. In an uncharacteristic, courtly gesture, he offered her his buckskin coat as a cushion.

"You'll get cold," she protested.

He shook his head. "Not a chance." He hesitated. Then, gathering his courage, he began. "About nine years ago, I met an old squaw in a village of the Ute who had been sick with the Bad Fever when she had been about your age. She was completely cured. Both of her legs had been crippled as your leg is right now, but nobody ever would have known it from the way she moved around. The other Ute thought the Indian spirits had performed a miracle. Well, I asked her about that, and she told me a secret. She did exercises for a long time—I don't know how long—exercises she invented herself. And little by little, her legs got better."

Eulalia stared at him, wide-eyed.

"I thought it might be useful to know those exercises, so she taught them to me. I've hauled them up from the bottom of my mind, and I can teach them to you, if you like."

"Will they help my leg?"

He shrugged. "I don't know, but you can't lose anything by trying. It won't be easy, Eulalia. They're hard exercises, and they're painful. You'll feel like quitting every day."

"If there's a chance, even an outside chance, that I can become normal again," Eulalia said fiercely, "I'll

337

do the exercises, no matter how painful they are."

He grinned at her. "Now you sound like my ma. She hurt her shoulder a few months before I was born, and she worked every day for years to get back the full use of it. And she did, just a year or so before she died."

He had never spoken of his parents, and she was fascinated.

"My ma was like you," he said, "pretty as they come and a real lady. I never knew her family, but she came from down around your way, North Carolina. She taught me my letters and numbers when I was five and made me go to school. Then she died when I was seven, and my pa took me out to Tennessee. He put me in school, too, but I left when he joined Andy Jackson's militia, and I went with him." Whip paused and chuckled. "I was so young I hadn't even started to shave yet. Old Hickory practically had a fit. He made me go to school between campaigns and threatened to whale me if I didn't. He meant it, too, so I went. Then, when I was just about grown up, my pa died, and I came out here to the mountains." He paused, looking uncomfortable.

"Thank you for telling me about your family," Eulalia said. "I've wondered about you, just as everyone else has. And I'm grateful for your offer to show me those exercises."

Whip was embarrassed. "There are some other things I'd like to tell you—if you'd care to hear them."

"Of course."

"First off, about my getting mixed up with La-ena."

He had not mentioned the Indian girl to anyone, and Eulalia was surprised. She wanted to save him unnecessary pain. "I think I already understand," she

338

said. "You were lonely, you needed a woman, and you were drawn to her, just as she was drawn to you. You changed your way of life when you came East to lead the wagon train, and you were too decent to send her away when she showed up on the trail."

"I don't know about being decent. Maybe I was just a coward."

"Not you," she said, smiling. "Never."

He stared at her. "Anyway, you really do understand."

Eulalia nodded. "I tried to explain to Cath—to my friends, but they couldn't see your situation as I did."

He squared his shoulders. "Cathy Blake is a fine woman, but she's married to somebody else, to my friend. I've put her out of my mind forever."

Eulalia wondered if Whip still loved Cathy, but it wasn't her place to ask. Besides, he was firm in his declaration that he no longer kept a place for her in his life.

Whip began to pace up and down the clearing. "In a few months we'll reach Oregon, and then all of us will start a new life, including me."

"You aren't coming back to the mountains?"

He shook his head as he continued to pace. "I'm getting too old for battles with Indians and fights with trappers who are either drunk or crazy. I'm tired of watching profits dwindle in the beaver trade year by year. And I have no more appetite for Rocky Mountain winters."

Eulalia was startled by his candor and at the same time touched by the note of sadness in his voice.

"I plan to lay claim to a tract of land near the Columbia River and build a house there. The bottom will be granite, and the rest will be cedar."

"I can't picture you as a farmer, Whip."

"Neither can I," he said, chuckling. "There's a valley north of the Columbia where wild horses roam. I plan to tame some, bring them back to my land, and breed them. In a few years folks will be coming to Oregon by the thousands, and all of them will need horses —riding horses, workhorses, all kinds. I may not get as rich as Johnny Astor, selling them as fast as I breed them, but I won't be poor. I know horses better than people."

Eulalia inclined her head. "I was brought up with horses, too. A whole stable of them."

"I've watched you with them," Whip said. "It's plain you have a feel for them." Then he changed the subject. "It won't be long before the whole Oregon country is filled with Americans. There will be cities and towns where there's nothing but land now, and I'm aiming to be one of the first citizens when it's made a territory. I want to leave something substantial for my sons."

In spite of losing Cathy, he was still thinking of marriage. Again Eulalia was surprised, and her expression told him what she was thinking. "Oh, I'll need a wife, no two ways about it, somebody who'll polish off my rough edges, a lady who will know how to entertain important horse buyers." He broke off abruptly. "We've talked long enough about me. What are your plans?"

"I don't have many," Eulalia said. "Cindy and I are thinking of opening a dry goods shop, provided we can raise enough money to finance the enterprise."

"I don't know much about such things, but it sounds like it ought to work. What about your personal plans?"

She wondered if he was mocking her. "My knee and my ankle make certain I won't have any," she said bitterly.

340

"Oh, you're wrong," Whip said. "You need a husband—somebody like me."

Surely he was joking! Eulalia was so shocked she was at a loss for words.

Whip was finding it painfully difficult to overcome his shyness, but he had to finish what he had started. "When you showed up at camp with your pa and Claiborne," he said, "I thought you were just about the prettiest young lady I ever saw. I'll have to admit you were about the nastiest, too."

She tried to cover her own embarrassment. Was he seriously proposing to her? "I'll admit I was a spoiled brat," she said.

"Well, you changed, the way all people change when they grow up. Now you have character as well as beauty."

"And a leg that's useless."

"Don't expect pity from me," Whip said, a harsh note creeping into his voice. "By now you've learned that folks earn their way in the world. Maybe you can cure your leg, the way the old Ute squaw did. I'm willing to help you all I can. I'll even stand over you and curse you out every day while you do your exercises, just as I reckon you'll stand over me and curse me until I learn how to act and look like a gentleman."

So he was really proposing! And what made the totally unexpected development miraculous was that he hadn't come to her out of pity.

"You and I," Whip said, "have gotten along fine with each other for a long time. You seem to know without being told why I act like I do, and I think I understand you pretty well, too. We can help each other in lots of ways. You share my feelings about horses. We'd have a good life together."

Eulalia felt herself trembling. She fought for control. Whip was courageous and resourceful, as well as handsome. She was astonished that he should want her as his wife. "Are you quite sure," she demanded, "that you aren't being kind to me because I'm a cripple?"

"To hell with that," he said. "You're a woman."

The fever and her disability had made her vulnerable, and she felt confused. Aware of her hesitation, Whip pressed on. "I'll always be honest with you, and I'll try to be fair," he said. "I sure won't lie to you. And I'll work hard for you, protect you, and look after you."

"But why me?" she asked, still thinking of her crippled leg.

"I don't need to tell you that I never loved La-ena," Whip said.

She nodded.

"Right now, I don't know whether I ever loved—somebody else—and I'm not going to search my soul trying to find out. I'm not going to insult your intelligence by claiming that I've suddenly fallen in love with you, Eulalia, but I do keep thinking about you all the time, and I know the potential for love is there. I can tell it in myself, and I can tell it in the way you look and talk and act when we're together. It's all the little things that made me begin to think we should get together."

She shifted the position of her stiff leg with her hands, then laced her fingers together and forced herself to look at him. After her experiences as an Indian captive, she was no simpering virgin, and she was no longer a Southern belle, either. She was a mature woman, addressing a mature man. "I know we've been attracted to each other," she said. "I've felt it, just as you have. As to love, I can't pretend I'm in love with you, either. You may be right when you say there's a potential for love on both sides, but I just don't know for certain."

"Neither do I," Whip said. "There's only one way for us to find out."

"Suppose we're wrong?" Eulalia demanded.

He scowled and hooked his thumbs in his broad belt. "We can't let ourselves be wrong!" he said fiercely.

"About my leg—"

"Damnation, cut it off and I'll still want you as my wife!" he exclaimed. "Can't you get it into your head how much I respect you?"

Respect! The magic word! Respect was what she had told Cindy she needed, above all else, and now it was being offered to her.

Using her walking stick, Eulalia rose to her feet and stood before Whip. "I do thank you, sir, for your offer, and I accept it." She refrained from adding that she hoped they wouldn't regret it.

Whip bowed awkwardly but did not touch her. "I reckon we'd best get back to camp," he said. He did not set too rapid a pace on their return walk to the camp, but again he refrained from helping her over rough places. He was deliberately enabling Eulalia to salvage her pride by refusing to treat her as an invalid. This was precisely the treatment she had craved, and she told herself it was an encouraging sign for the future. She would do her best to help him, just as she knew he would assist her in every possible way. And as soon as she could, she would start to do the leg exercises. Everything considered, there was a chance this strange, unexpected marriage would be a success.

Even before approaching Reverend Cavendish, Whip went to Lee and Cathy's cabin. They were surprised to see him, but Lee quickly invited him in.

Whip shook his head. "What I have to say and ask won't take long," he said. "Eulalia and I are planning to get married tomorrow, and we'd be obliged if you two would stand up with us." The astonished couple recovered their aplomb sufficiently to accept the honor and to offer their congratulations. Whip went off at once, his mission completed.

It had been Eulalia's suggestion to ask the Blakes to act as matron of honor and best man, and Whip had agreed instantly. The gesture would stifle any gossip that Eulalia had caught him after Cathy had rejected him, or that there was resentment between him and Lee.

The news struck the entire company with the impact of a tornado. Only Cindy was not surprised. "I've seen it coming on in both of you," she told Eulalia. "What I didn't know was that you and Whip would see the signs. I'm glad for you—and for him. You're both strong enough and sensible enough to make this marriage work."

The pioneers elected to give the bridal pair possession of the wagon that had been the home of the late Malcolm family. It was a handsome vehicle with a hard roof and sides, windows, and a floor of polished wood.

"It's so fancy," Whip said, "that I won't know how to act there."

"I'm sure you will," Eulalia told him quietly.

Whip insisted there be no festivities to mark the wedding. "Folks," he announced at supper, "we want all of you there for the ceremony, but we don't have enough meat for a feast or enough spare flour for a cake. Once the train reaches Oregon and we build our house there, we'll invite all of you to join us for a celebration on our first anniversary. But until we get there, let's be careful of our provisions."

Most people agreed that, with the departure scheduled to take place in a few days, any wedding celebration should be muted. But Ginny Dobbs did not agree. In spite of her belligerence, which she was now managing to keep under better control, she had a romantic streak. Whip Holt, she believed, was the single most valuable member of the wagon train, having performed deeds of valor and services that had brought the train this far. Eulalia, whom Ginny had initially despised, had recently gone out of her way to be pleasant, ignoring rebuffs. So a sense of guilt may have been responsible for the way Ginny was feeling. In any event, she was determined that something special be done at supper that night, immediately following the ceremony, to mark the wedding.

The larders were virtually empty, she knew, except for some corn and the recently acquired buffalo meat, which had been smoked in order to preserve it. But perhaps there was a side of bear bacon or some other delicacy that could be served to the bridal couple.

Ever since their fight, she had taken care to avoid Tilman Wade. But immediately after breakfast, she went to the tiny provisions office he would soon vacate. He hadn't yet arrived, so she told herself there was no need for her to wait. She would look through the storage bins herself, being familiar with them, and would see if she could find something for Eulalia and Whip.

Leaving the office, she went out to the sheds and bins. Their open doors indicated that most were already empty. It was dark in the cramped areaway, but Ginny noticed at once that a man was standing in front of a bin, searching through it. He heard her footsteps, withdrew his head from the bin, and faced her.

Garcia!

Ginny was immobilized by sudden, unreasoning fear. The man was desperate as well as disreputable, and she was carrying no arms.

Two days earlier, several men had gone to Garcia's cave, intending to give him food and ammunition to start him off on his journey to the East. But the place had been deserted. All of his belongings were gone, so they had assumed he had already taken off on his lone journey. "Good riddance," Paul Thoman had said, and the others had echoed his sentiments.

The trial of living alone through the better part of the winter had left its mark on Garcia. His hair was unkempt, he had grown a full, ragged beard, and his buckskins were filthy, tattered as well as soiled. His eyes burned with hatred as he looked at the girl.

Ginny recovered enough presence of mind to realize she should strike the first blow and keep him off balance. "Still up to your light-fingered tricks, I see," she said.

He glared harder at her. "Your new friends may think they can starve me," he said, "but they can't. Nothing is going to stop me from going on, all the way to New York. I'm taking all the supplies I need, and horses, too."

It was ironic, she thought, that he would have been given enough to see him on his way if he had not vanished from his cave.

"I can't find a damn thing in these bins," he continued, "but you must know where the supplies are kept. Show them to me."

She merely shrugged. "I have no idea where anything is kept," she lied.

"Then you'll help me find what I need!"

"Why should I?"

"Because you owe it to me!" Garcia declared.

She was disgusted.

A sudden idea occurred to him. "Come with me," he said, "like we planned from the beginning."

"No! Never!" The words shot out.

"We'll do fine together in the East," Garcia said. "We'll make a great team, and it won't take us long to get rich."

"I don't steal," Ginny said. "And I won't have anything to do with a thief."

Garcia's manner changed. "You're coming with me," he said, "and that's that. Now, show me the food, and then we'll help ourselves to some horses and be on our way."

"No!" Ginny repeated firmly.

He drew a long knife from his belt. "If you won't come with me, you're not going anywhere," he said.

She realized that his months of solitude had unhinged him. He was dangerous. Yet she could not and would not give in to his insane demands. "Put that knife away and behave sensibly," she said sharply.

Garcia bared his teeth in a malicious smile. "I've never forgiven you for making me give that gold chalice back to the monks in California. That cup was worth a fortune. Now you do what I say, or you pay for it."

He began to advance very slowly, the knife raised, ready to strike. "Do as I tell you!" she ordered. He crept still closer.

Suddenly a deep male voice sounded behind Ginny. "Garcia, drop that knife!" Tilman Wade commanded.

Paying no attention, acting as though he had not

heard, Garcia continued to move toward the girl. Tilman leaped at him, one hand reaching for the man's wrist, and they crashed to the ground together.

Somehow Garcia managed to keep his grip on the long knife. Although Tilman was a powerful man who ordinarily could overcome such an opponent, Garcia was endowed with the strength of a madman. They wrestled. Garcia tried to free his wrist, but Tilman clung desperately to it, simultaneously trying to gain the upper hand. Garcia's strength astonished him. He knew this was a life or death struggle.

Garcia's eyes were glazed. He didn't care if he committed murder and was indifferent to the consequences. Ginny knew that sooner or later he would kill Tilman and turn on her. It was too late to call for help. By the time her summons was answered, Tilman would be dead, and she might well have suffered the same fate. She could flee, to be sure, but she could not allow Tilman to die after he had intervened for her sake.

Suddenly Ginny thought of his rifle. Tilman carried it with him at all times, as all the men did, and she guessed he had left it in the office. She raced toward the cabin.

Tilman's hold on Garcia's wrist was weakening gradually. With his free hand, he lashed out again and again, his fist crashing into the thief's face, but Garcia was impervious to the blows. He intended to bury his knife in the body of this interfering bastard, and nothing would stop him.

Ginny found the rifle propped against the inner wall of the provisions office. Grabbing it, she ran as fast as she could, back to the bins. Neither man was aware of her presence. Their deadly struggle went on.

Ginny cocked the rifle, raised it to her shoulder, and waited until the men stopped heaving for a moment.

Then, with the muzzle only a foot or two from Garcia's face, she pulled the trigger. The bullet entered his brain, killing him instantly.

Panting for breath, Tilman dragged himself to his feet. As Ginny stared down at Garcia's lifeless body, her only feeling was a sense of great relief. In the distance they could hear shouts as people, attracted by the sound of the rifle shot, hurried toward the scene.

"I'm much obliged to you," Tilman said.

"Well, I didn't have much choice." Ginny's insides felt as though they had turned into jelly, but she refused to let him know it. "And while we're at it, thanks for helping me, too. Living alone up on the heights made Garcia crazy, and I'm sure he would have killed me if you hadn't come along."

Tilman took his rifle from her and studied her. She had been at the point of death, then had shot a man she had known well, but she appeared calm and unshaken. She might be a bad-tempered shrew, but she was an extraordinary woman. He grinned at her and extended his hand.

She shook hands with him solemnly. "I guess the time has come for you and me to call a truce," she said.

While on sentry duty, Paul Thoman spotted and shot a young buck elk, so the carcass was butchered and the meat was roasted over an open fire. Those who had wanted something special to mark Eulalia and Whip's wedding were satisfied.

Everyone attended the ceremony, which was held in the open, even though the evening was cool. Emily von Thalman announced that supper would be eaten outside, too; there was no other way that everyone could participate in the festivities.

People began to gather a half-hour before the ceremony. There was a murmur of approval as Reverend Cavendish took his place, close to the lake. Some of the men grinned as Whip, pale beneath his tan, arrived with Lee beside him. They waited beside the clergyman.

Cindy, the bridesmaid, was wearing one of the dresses she had brought with her from Louisville. No one cared that the neckline was too low and the bodice was too tight. The bright red dress lent real color to the occasion.

Cindy was followed by Cathy Blake, pretty and demure in the same gray dress she had worn for her own wedding. She looked at no one and appeared somewhat strained, but when she, too, halted beside the minister, her eyes met Lee's, and a faint smile touched her lips.

There was a buzz of excitement when Eulalia appeared on her brother's arm. She was wearing one of the beautiful silk gowns she had brought with her from South Carolina. It was pale ivory, with a scooped neckline and eyelet embroidery. Her long hair cascaded loosely down her back.

Thanks to Claiborne's support, she had no need to use her walking stick. She limped slowly toward the waiting clergyman and the man who would become her husband. Her face was expressionless.

Oscar Cavendish thoroughly enjoyed performing marriage ceremonies and ordinarily would have prolonged the occasion. Because of Eulalia's disability, however, he knew it would be uncomfortable for her to stand for more than a limited time, so he kept the service short. The bride and groom stood side by side, their shoulders not quite touching. Not once did they look at each other.

Hosea had fashioned a wedding ring out of a gold watch fob that Claiborne had given him for the purpose. When Whip placed the ring on his bride's finger, his hands were steady.

After the ceremony ended, the bride and groom kissed for the first time, but the gesture was a token, their lips scarcely brushing. Determined not to use her walking stick, Eulalia clutched Whip's arm as he led her to a bench that had been carried out from the community hall. There, as he stood beside her, the entire company came to wish them well and to kiss the bride. A number of the women kissed Whip, too, and Emily von Thalman drew a loud laugh when she announced, "You don't know how long I've been waiting for this chance!"

Some people noticed that Cathy Blake merely shook Whip's hand as she murmured her best wishes. Their eyes did not meet, and she moved off quickly with Lee. But if Eulalia was aware of any tension between the man she had just married and her friend, she gave no sign of it.

The roasted elk was a great success. Emily, defying her husband's strict orders, had baked a small cake just large enough for the bridal party. There was a general mood of exuberance. Only Eulalia and Whip were subdued. This celebration was more than a wedding: in another day the journey to Oregon would be resumed at last. This was an occasion no one would forget.

Night fell, supper was finished, and the sky was filled with stars. Parents took their children off to bed. Soon they were followed by many adults, who realized their final day at Little Valley would be hectic.

Eulalia and Whip lingered at the table. Neither

showed any desire to leave. The night was turning chilly, and the bride, with no cloak over her silk dress, couldn't control a shiver.

Whip was immediately aware of her discomfort. "I guess we ought to get indoors out of the cold," he said. She stood and again took his arm.

The bridal couple reached the handsome wagon that would be their home in the months ahead, and Whip helped her up the steps and opened the door, then stood aside, too shy to lift his bride over the threshold.

Eulalia still didn't have her walking stick, so she took one or two uncertain steps into the room. Whip closed the door and helped her to move to the bed. There were no chairs in the wagon. He used a tinderbox and flint to light a candle, and the yellow flame brought the interior to life.

"I'm glad Paul shot that elk," Eulalia said. "People were so eager to celebrate."

"Well, now," Whip said, his voice dry, "I'm glad Oscar Cavendish had the sense not to deliver a sermon that lasted all night. It was bad enough, his going on and on. I'm grateful to the Almighty that I've had done with it and won't have to go through that ever again."

Eulalia glanced at him and saw he wasn't joking. All at once a thought overwhelmed her. It was true they had been attracted to each other. But they had never enjoyed even the slightest physical contact. Their relationship might prove catastrophic, and she shivered.

"If you're cold," Whip said, "I'll find a shawl or your buffalo cape for you."

"Thanks anyway, but I'm fine," she said.

He continued to stand, teetering uncertainly as he rocked back and forth.

Eulalia wanted to scream. "Why don't you sit down?"

"Oh, I don't mind standing."

She had heard of marriages of convenience, but it had not occurred to her that she might be party to one. They might not love each other, but common sense told her that, with only one narrow bed for both of them, there was no way they could remain apart. But Whip was shy, and Eulalia knew she had to make the first move. Conquering her own timidity as best she could, she reached out and lightly touched his hand.

"I wish you'd sit down," she said.

Whip perched beside her at the bottom of the bed, looking as awkward and uncomfortable as he felt. The silence grew. The tension in the wagon thickened.

Finally, mustering his courage, Whip forced himself to turn to her. Unable to speak and not knowing what to say, he kissed her, but there was no real feeling in it. Eulalia sat still, unmoving and unmoved.

Whip found it slightly easier to kiss her a second time and placed tentative hands on her shoulders. She accepted the gesture passively.

A sense of desperation surged up in him, and he kissed her for a third time, holding her firmly. In spite of her doubts and misgivings, Eulalia came to life. Her lips parted, her hands slid around Whip's neck. Before either quite realized what was happening, they were making love in earnest.

Whip was caring and gentle, and Eulalia felt herself responding to him. He was becoming aroused and was awakening her, too. I'm really married to this man, she told herself.

They lost all consciousness of time, of everything except their increasing, mutual desire. Eulalia was astonished by Whip's tenderness, his consideration, his desire to please her. Then their union became complete, and she felt fulfilled.

As they drifted off to sleep, still not speaking, Eulalia knew Whip might still be yearning for Cathy, wishing that his bride were as passionate as La-ena, or even handling her with special care because of her disability. But she didn't care. She had become his wife, and there was hope for their future together.

Long before daybreak the scouts left the camp and rode out of Little Valley, fanning out as they reached the trail to the west. Fires burned brightly as women prepared the last breakfast in their winter quarters. Teams of oxen and horses were yoked, and last-minute searches were conducted for belongings that might be left behind.

The outriders mounted and took their positions, with Lee at the head of the vanguard. Paul Thoman rode forward from his place at the rear. "Everybody is set and ready to roll," he said.

Whip, in his accustomed place at the head of the main column, raised his arm high and made a sweeping gesture.

The vanguard of outriders was on the move, already keeping watch for Comanche. Soon Cathy Blake, in her usual lead place, set her team in motion. Freshly greased wheels creaked, leather moaned, and the familiar sound of pounding hoofs filled the air. The entire line of wagons began to creep forward.

There were many who looked back as they left the lake and the deserted cabins. They had known pleasure and sorrow here, they had suffered and had found protection from the rigors of a Rocky Mountain winter. Now they were putting Little Valley behind them.

Eulalia Holt drove her new wagon, her disabled leg stretched out stiffly. For better or worse she was beginning a whole new life.

WYOMING!

Somewhere in the line someone began to sing the refrain that had become an anthem on the long trail: "Oregon, we come, no more will we roam. Oh, land of beauty, you'll soon be our home."

Trials awaited the company, and everyone knew it. The Comanche, as well as other hostile Indians tribes, might attack them. The threats of natural catastrophe and illness were ever-present, as was the grim possibility of starvation. But in spite of their tribulations, real and potential, they were buoyed by hope. Oregon, the promised land, lay at the end of the trail, across mountain ranges, ravines, and swift-flowing rivers. Oregon was their future. No power on earth would prevent them from reaching that goal.

INDEPENDENCE! NEBRASKA! WYOMING!
and now . . .

WAGONS WEST ★ FOURTH IN A SERIES

OREGON!

By Dana Fuller Ross

The tumultuous adventures of the hardy band of
pioneers on the first wagon train west continue in this
thrilling novel. The men and women who have struggled
to survive the rigors of their trek through America's
untamed wilderness must now face incredible new
dangers beyond the Rockies. Led by Whip Holt and
Colonel Lee Blake, the settlers boldly claim the spacious
Oregon territory for the United States and begin building their frontier community. Oregon offers opportunity
and prosperity for many. For some, it offers hardship.
But great new challenges, more perilous than those en-
encountered on the journey west, are posed by British
soldiers and treacherous Russian agents whose power
and cunning threaten to drive the Americans from their
new-found homes.

Read OREGON! and all WAGONS WEST books,
available wherever Bantam paperbacks are sold.

★ WAGONS WEST ★

A series of unforgettable books that trace the lives of a dauntless band of pioneering men, women and children as they brave the hazards of an untamed land in their trek across America. This legendary caravan of people forge a new link in the wilderness. They are Americans from the North and the South, alongside immigrants, Blacks and Indians, who wage fierce daily battles for survival on this uncompromising journey—each to their private destinies as they fulfill their greatest dreams.

INDEPENDENCE, BOOK I
The wagon train begins its journey on Long Island. Among the travellers are Whip Holt and Cathy van Ayl whose lives are changed by the unseen forces of the vast frontier.

NEBRASKA, BOOK II
Although some members remain behind, many people in the wagon train brave their way against incredible odds as they continue courageously toward their destination.

WYOMING, BOOK III
Only the stalwart survive the hazardous trek through the Rockies—beset by savage Indian attacks and treachery by secret enemy agents on board the wagon train.

OREGON, BOOK IV
The wagon train members are pawns in the clash between three great national powers, all gambling on the riches that lie in the great northwest.

TEXAS, BOOK V
1843. The fledgling republic fights for its life against the onrush of Mexican soldiers. Some of the original wagon train members join the call to help in this struggle.

CALIFORNIA, BOOK VI
Gold is discovered in 1848 and its lure attracts friend and foe alike...in a mad scramble for new-found riches. But many lives become endangered as lawlessness overtakes the territory.

COLORADO, BOOK VII (August '81)
Now gold is found in Central City, and the frontier town of Denver becomes the magnet for hucksters, hustlers and many of the wagon train friends. Shocking events result from this highly volatile situation.

Read all of these novels in Bantam Books, available wherever paperbacks are sold.

TALES OF BOLD ADVENTURE AND
PASSIONATE ROMANCE FROM THE PRODUCER
OF THE COLONIZATION OF AMERICA

A SAGA OF THE SOUTHWEST
By Leigh Franklin James

The American Southwest in the early 19th century, a turbulent land ravaged by fortune seekers and marked by the legacy of European aristocracy, is the setting for this series of thrilling and memorable novels. You will meet a group of bold, headstrong people who come to carve a lasting place in the untamed wilderness.

THE HAWK AND THE DOVE: Book One

John Cooper Baines, living by his wits and braving the wilderness, is brought to manhood in an Indian village and moves on to New Mexico. There John meets the proud, exiled Spanish nobleman, Don Diego de Escobar, and his beautiful daughter, Catarina. Won by John's courage, she sees in him the strength to conquer a savage land. Together they plant the seeds of an empire that will change the course of history.

WINGS OF THE HAWK: Book Two

John and Catarina, pregnant with her first child, meet the challenge of establishing a prosperous ranch. Then John's discovery of a shocking secret and a fabulous treasure reaches the wrong ears. The family, which now includes their new son, Andrew, is suddenly plunged into danger.

TREASURE OF THE HAWK: Book Three

Coming in December.

Read all of these Bantam Books, available wherever paperbacks are sold.

A THRILLING NEW SAGA OF LOVE AND WAR
IN THE TRADITION OF "BEN-HUR" AND "QUO
VADIS"—FROM THE PRODUCER OF WAGONS
WEST AND THE KENT FAMILY CHRONICLES.

CHILDREN OF THE LION
by Peter Danielson

A magnificent family saga unfolds in this new series of unforgettable historical novels set in the lands and times of the Bible.
Here are the passions and adventures of bold men and women
struggling for freedom and survival in a hostile world. People
swept up in the dramatic events of one of the most exciting
and remarkable periods of our history—led by the brave men
who bore the legendary mark of destiny.

CHILDREN OF THE LION
     The gripping saga begins. It is the story of Abraham, the
iron-willed leader whom many underestimated, but none could
deny in his quest to lead his people to their "promised land."
It is the story of Hagar, the beautiful, dark-eyed slave who
bears Abraham's first son, but is cast out on her own. And it
is the story of Ahuni, enslaved as a child, beaten and abused
by his owners, who grows into a highly skilled weapon-maker
—and who bears the legendary mark of the CHILDREN OF
THE LION.

THE SHEPHERD KINGS
     It is a time of civil strife. A time of peril. A time of change.
Jacob, heir to the kingdom of his grandfather, the indomi-
table leader Abraham, is clothed in the robes of a shepherd,
having fled in mortal danger from his brother. While exiled in
the city of Haran, a city in great peril, he meets Hadad, a
young artist, a Child of the Lion. Hadad is poor and broken in
body, but mighty in spirit. Together, strengthened by the deep
love of two remarkable women, they forge a legendary friendship and begin their ascent to the greatness that is their destiny.

(Read CHILDREN OF THE LION and
THE SHEPHERD KINGS
wherever Bantam Books are sold.)

DON'T MISS
THESE CURRENT
Bantam Bestsellers

LOUIS L'AMOUR

BANTAM'S #1
ALL-TIME BESTSELLING AUTHOR
AMERICA'S FAVORITE WESTERN WRITER

THE SACKETTS

Meet the Sacketts—from the Tennessee mountains they headed west to ride the trails, pan the gold, work the ranches and make the laws. Here in these action-packed stories is the incredible saga of the Sacketts —who stood together in the face of trouble as one unbeatable fighting family.

☐	14868	SACKETT'S LAND	$2.25
☐	12730	THE DAY BREAKERS	$1.95
☐	14196	SACKETT	$1.95
☐	14118	LANDO	$1.95
☐	14193	MOJAVE CROSSING	$1.95
☐	14973	THE SACKETT BRAND	$2.25
☐	20074	THE LONELY MEN	$2.25
☐	14785	TREASURE MOUNTAIN	$2.25
☐	20258	MUSTANG MAN	$2.25
☐	14322	GALLOWAY	$1.95
☐	20073	THE SKY-LINERS	$2.25
☐	14218	TO THE FAR BLUE MOUNTAINS	$1.95
☐	14194	THE MAN FROM THE BROKEN HILLS	$1.95
☐	20088	RIDE THE DARK TRAIL	$2.25
☐	14207	WARRIOR'S PATH	$1.95
☐	14174	LONELY ON THE MOUNTAIN	$2.25

Buy them at your local bookstore or use this handy coupon for ordering:

Bantam Book Catalog

Here's your up-to-the-minute listing of over 1,400 titles by your favorite authors.

This illustrated, large format catalog gives a description of each title. For your convenience, it is divided into categories in fiction and non-fiction—gothics, science fiction, westerns, mysteries, cookbooks, mysticism and occult, biographies, history, family living, health, psychology, art.

So don't delay—take advantage of this special opportunity to increase your reading pleasure.

Just send us your name and address and 50¢ (to help defray postage and handling costs).